MW01108223

Reviews of the author's fictional works:

"Palpable Passions delivers a compelling story arc infused with historical fact that should appeal to readers…"

Blue Ink Reviews

The book…feels like a screenplay; its dialogue is abundant and punchy, its landscapes well defined, and its characters have significant bonds. Palpable Passions uses bright, earnest characters to show that a microcosm can be as complicated as the big picture."

Foreword Book Review

"Corbett has created a captivating novel. The book title perfectly describes the fragile thread that spirals around each individual… to create an enthralling story that anyone will love to read."

U.S. Review of Books

"This is … a fully rendered tale. Those interested in the complexity of relationships …will find some rewards here."

Blue Ink Reviews

"…Tenuous Tendrils, by Tom Corbett, is a compelling journey from exile to redemption. Like its characters, the book is quite clever and features an abundance of humor. Many heavy scenes are punctuated by conversations about the futility of war and the humanitarian failings of government also feature omniscient narrative wit that keeps the text from being bogged down by sentiment and also allows the characters' personalities to shine."

Clarion Review

"Corbett obviously loves to tell stories. Tenuous Tendrils, by Tom Corbett, is a captivating read with engaging vignettes which paint a picture of a retired professor, his life, and the connections which bind everything together."

Pacific Review of Books

**Amazon Readers' Reviews of
Tenuous Tendrils and Palpable Passions.**

"I loved how the author told each family's story back and forth chapter by chapter. The characters are so well-formed, and the accurate descriptions of life in Afghanistan really drew me in. Finished book in one day. I didn't want to put it down."

"This is truly a great read that will leave you feeling empowered and determined to make a difference in your own way HIGHLY RECOMMEND that everyone pick this up."

"It's easy to understand why this book comes so highly recommended. Palpable Passions is a powerful book. I highly recommend it to anyone who loves literary fiction."

"A penetrating look into the human soul and the fragility of relationships."

"Tenuous Tendrils is a conversational and meditative look back on a man's life. I really like the depth of detail that the author brought to these characters."

"This book was incredibly personal on so many levels. Overall, I found this to be an extremely touching and educational read."

"I personally loved this book. It was refreshing and thoughtful."

"The overall story is incredibly genuine, realistic to the time limits it covers and thoughtful. Each time I put down the book I found it moderately difficult since I wanted to know what would happen next."

"Excellent characterization and historical facts make this a compelling story as hope overcomes despair."

"Tom Corbett's "Palpable Passions" is the perfect combination of fact and fiction as it educates its readers about current events in our world today."

"In the end, we learn that no matter what this world throws in our way, our passion is what drives us to live our lives to the fullest potential. This book fascinates me because of how the author uniquely ties everything together at the end."

"This is an utterly compelling narrative of two disparate families separated by culture and experiences who come together by circumstances and serendipity."

"…throughout the memoir, Corbett's prose remains engaging, consistently mixing insight with the familiar jokes that one would from a close friend. A thoughtful memoir about life and politics told in a (n} … endearing style."

—Kirkus Review

"…the emergence of Corbett's humanistic world view…gives Ouch, Now I Remember intellectual gravitas. Corbett imparts an enormous amount of wisdom and humanity."

—Clarion Review

"If you truly want to understand how public policy works, read this book. Corbett's descriptions about how laws and programs are developed gives readers a real take away—genuine insight into the discipline of public policy."

—Mary Fairchild, Senior Fellow
National Conference of State Legislatures

"Corbett's stories from the front lines of policymaking, like All Quiet on the Western Front or The Things They Carried, provide great insight into the way the world actually works, not what the generals or policy planners think is happening."

—Matt Stagner, Ph.D. Policy Fellow
Mathematica Policy Research, Inc.

"The Boat Captain's Conundrum is a winning performance."

—Forward Clarion Book Review

"Corbett takes a topic often shrouded in numbers and dense writing and turns it into an intellectual, yet conversational memoir."

—U.S. Review of Books

"Corbett's reflections, woven together with great insight and humor, transform public policy from a class that is boring and mundane to a career that can be engaging and germane."

—Karen Bogenschneider Ph.D., U. of Wisconsin

"I enjoy his writing style, it was comfortable yet candid, like listening to a respected relative recount their own life with unabashed honesty."

—Pacific Book Review

ORDINARY
OBSESSIONS

by:TOM CORBETT

To order additional copies of this book:
www.amazon.com
www.barnesandnoble.com

Published in the United States of America

ISBN *hardcover: 9781948000345*
ISBN *softcover: 9781948000352*

DEDICATION

I dedicate this work to my spouse, Mary Rider. She now is enduring difficult times. Still, we have enjoyed almost five decades of remarkable moments and wonderful memories

ACKNOWLEDGMENTS

I want to give special thanks to Christine Tighe and Hilla Zerbst for reading and commenting on early versions of this manuscript. I also want to thank Ben Harris and Zoe Ryan of Papertown Publishing for seeing this project through to completion.

Other Books by the Author

Confessions of an Accidental Scholar (Hancock Press, 2018)

Confessions of a Clueless Rebel (Hancock Press, 2018)

Confessions of a Wayward Academic (Hancock Press, 2018)

Palpable Passions (Papertown Press, 2017)

Tenuous Tendrils (Xlibris Press, 2017)

The Boat Captain's Conundrum (Xlibris Press, 2016)

Ouch, Now I Remember (Xlibris Press, 2015)

Browsing through My Candy Store (Xlibris Press, 2014)

Return to the Other Side of the World with Mary Jo Clark, Michael Simmonds, Katherine Sohn, and Hayward Turrentine (Strategic Press, 2013)

The Other Side of the World with Mary Jo Cark, Michael Simonds, and Hayward Turrentine (Strategic Press, 2011)

Evidence-Based Policymaking with Karen Bogenschneider (Taylor and Francis Publishing, 2010)

Policy into Action with Mary Clare Lennon (Urban Institute Press, 2003)

"You can't go back and change the beginning, but you can start where you are and change the ending."

—C. S. Lewis

"I think hell is something you carry around with you, not somewhere you go."

—Neil Gaiman

"Men never do evil so completely and cheerfully as when they do it from religious conviction."

—Blaise Pascal

"What good fortune for governments that men do not think."

—Adolf Hitler

"Kindness is the language that the deaf can hear and the blind can see."

—Mark Twain

CONTENTS

PREFACE

Ordinary Obsessions is the sequel to Palpable Passions, which introduces the reader to the Masoud and the Crawford families. The patriarch of the Masoud family, Pamir, is a physician who trained in England. Pamir returns to Afghanistan to aid his homeland and raise his children. Pamir's wife, Madeena, is a mathematician who taught at university level in the pre-Taliban era. We tend to forget that this beleaguered country once had a substantial secular population.

The Masouds have three children: a son, Majeed, and two daughters, Deena and Azita. The youngest, Azita, is passionate about following in her father's footsteps despite the obstacles imposed by a totalitarian religious regime. In the first volume, we picked up the Masoud's story during the height of Taliban rule, but prior to Osama Bin Laden's 9-11 attack on the United States. The Masouds were determined to escape Kabul and the oppressive rule under which they felt captive. The family's goal was to flee to the area still held by the Northern Alliance, a group of tribal clans who bravely fought the Soviet invaders in the 1980s, and who are now fiercely opposed to Taliban rule. This northern area in Afghanistan is where Pamir was born and raised. It is home to him, a place where he hopes to find comfort and safety in troubled times, and where his children might pursue their dreams.

The Crawford clan is headed by Charles Crawford, Sr., who was born in Poland just as World War II erupted. He was spirited to the United States by his father who was a leader in the anti-communist, exiled Polish government. Charles Crawford grew up determined to accrue personal power and great wealth, part of which he obtained through a calculated marriage to Mary Kelly, a rich Catholic socialite from Philadelphia. Charles and Mary have four children: Charles Junior (Chuck), the oldest (and married to Beverly), followed by twins, Christopher (Chris) and Kristen (Kay), and their youngest daughter, Katerina (Kat). The Crawford family members know extraordinary comfort and privilege in Chicago but are gripped by serious internal divisions that eventually mushroomed into outright rebellion.

Other prominent characters include Abdul Zubair, an old family friend who helps the Masouds escape from the control of the Taliban, and Abdul's son, Ahmad. Richard (Ricky) and his sister Juliana (Jules) Jackson are unlikely childhood friends of Chris. Ricky and Jules are black and from very modest means, growing up in a tough Chicago neighborhood. Chris and Ricky bonded at a high school summer basketball camp and remained the best of friends throughout adulthood. Chris and Jules enjoyed a long on and off romantic relationship over the years. Karen Fisher is Chris's lesbian assistant in his international service organization. From a working-class British family, Karen is a tough, yet perceptive, professional partner. Amar Singh is an Indian-born doctor whose struggle to become a physician was made more difficult by her conservative family who wished little more than a good marriage for her.

Chris's twin sister, Kay, is a talented trauma surgeon who earned her medical expertise by attaching herself to the emergency room of a Chicago public hospital, partly out of dedication and partly to spite her father by working for the public good, something she knew her father would never understand. Kay married James (Jamie) Whitehead, a British Military doctor whom she met in Afghanistan.

The narrative of Palpable Passions traces challenges and struggles in both the Masoud and Crawford families. With the help of her parents, Azita continues to violate the strict rules governing the proper behavior of Muslim girls. She stubbornly insists on being educated at home by her mother and on helping her father with his medical work, sins that will no longer be tolerated by the Taliban as she approaches puberty. Azita will then be expected to become a servile and obedient woman as Taliban orthodoxy dictates. After Azita is almost killed by the religious police while she is under Majeed's protection, Majeed is determined to fight these oppressors. The Masouds decide to escape Kabul and the Taliban when Majeeb is about to be forced into military service for a system he abhors. Under false pretenses, the Masoud family makes a very dangerous escape to the Northern Alliance.

Following the sudden and tragic suicide of Chuck Crawford, who had been the forced heir- apparent to the Crawford dynasty, much reflection takes place among the remaining Crawford offspring who come to reject their father's obsession with right-wing causes. Christopher, a Rhodes scholar with a doctorate from Oxford, uses his wealth and connections to develop an international service organization. Chris is devoted to helping the world's most vulnerable people and is most gratified that his father dismisses these ambitions as soft and ridiculous. Chris makes his home in London and Oxford, England. Kay has also rejected her father's ideals by her choice of medical specialties. She decides to escape the family in Chicago by joining Chris's international organization and manipulates her initial assignment in Pakistan to relocate to Afghanistan, a very dangerous site at that time. There, she becomes friends with Dr. Amar Singh and the two risk all to help those desperately holding out against the Taliban. Chris is outraged when he discovers that his sister defied him and joined Amar Singh in the conflict torn and dangerous country. Frantic, he travels to Afghanistan to remove Kay from harm's way.

The Masoud and Crawford families connect in this desperate and conflicted part of the world. Representing radically different backgrounds, they find much in common. However, fate, as it so often does, intrudes in the most disturbing ways. Majeeb Masoud dies fighting for the Northern Alliance. Pamir and Madeena Masoud are murdered by the Taliban in the tumultuous days following 9-11. Kay stays in Afghanistan with Jamie Whitehead, and Chris finally loses his heart to Amar Singh.

Moved by the intelligence and drive of young Azita, Chris and Amar bring her to England where she can receive the education about which she has always dreamed but did not think possible. After some time, Deena and Karen, now in a relationship, join Azita, Chris and Amar in London. Palpable Passions ends with Azita Masoud finishing her pre-medicine studies at Oxford University and giving a University-wide talk about the obstacles she overcame to pursue her passion. That, however, is not the end of the journey. Rather, it is just a beginning.

PART I CHOICES

CHAPTER 1

OXFORD UNIVERSITY-2015: THE CALL

Chris Crawford settled into his university office. He looked about him with much satisfaction. The walls were lined with books while his desk and a couple of tables were piled to overflowing with academic papers and government reports. Yet, he had a rather amazing ability to retrieve what he needed. The detritus of his fecund intellectual life was not unlike an archeological site where layers of invaluable treasures were accessible only to the expert who knew where and how to look. His gaze briefly settled on the world beyond his personal academic cocoon. Outside of his dome-like windows, which were reminiscent of cathedral portals, lay the college green that served as the epicenter of academic life in the insular world of his Oxford college. He loved everything about this place, even the smells of ancient thoughts embedded on printed pages.

He found it remarkable that he had been so easily accepted into this world-class university. That made him smile since he had been such an undisciplined student early on, the very opposite of his twin sister who had always applied herself diligently to her academic studies. He had always rationalized his desultory performance as a student on the examples of Einstein and Hawking, the two physics geniuses of their respective eras. Einstein had been an indifferent student. Albert's original dissertation was turned down by his doctoral committee and he was the only member of his small physics class not to secure an academic appointment upon graduation. He made his significant early intellectual breakthroughs while sitting in a patent office, a position arranged for him by concerned friends. Similarly, Hawking always admitted to hardly studying during his undergraduate days at Oxford and with not much greater diligence early in his doctoral studies at Cambridge. He fully embraced his intellect only when his body started to give out on him. Both geniuses proved most creative when they permitted their imaginations to run free and when, for different reasons, they functioned outside of the normal expectations of the academic culture. Chris fancied that he did as well though absent, he concluded, the clear advantage of their native genius.

His private reflections were cut short by the ringing of his cell phone. He should have turned it off. Glancing at it, he saw a very familiar name, one that took him a bit by surprise. For such a public man, Christopher Crawford had the instincts of a hermit. He would prefer to unplug his phone and stay within his own thoughts. After all, there were many great thinkers who argued that reality was little more than an extension of our own consciousness. Perhaps he could shape what was out there into something that better met his expectations. But alas, he could never quite make the break, not when his younger sibling was calling.

"Kat?" Chris uttered with a slightly concerned tone.

"Yes, you got it right. It is your second favorite sister calling. Did I catch you at a bad time?"

Chris glanced at his watch and did a quick calculation. Why was the new titular head of the sprawling Crawford financial empire calling at this hour? It must have been the middle of the night in Chicago, or maybe terribly early in the morning. Still, nothing surprised him any longer about this sibling. As they grew up, she was the quiet one, almost invisible. He would tease her but very carefully for a guy whose wit rarely failed to take prisoners. In her case, though, he always feared that he might wound her vulnerable psyche. Yes, that was it, she seemed fragile as a young girl, with the most tenuous grasp on her own identity.

Time would prove that they all had miscalculated her. Unknown to him, and the others, she had been watching, absorbing, learning as the patriarch of the Crawford family, Charles Senior, appointed the eldest son as heir apparent to the family throne. She agonized as this ill-considered decision ended in tragedy and the rather predictable suicide of her eldest brother. All knew that Charles Junior, or Chuck, would break under the weight of this familial obligation. He was a poet, not a ruthless businessman. Kat remained closest to the eldest sibling while the twins in the middle had fled the family tensions in one way or the other, Chris to England and Kristen (or Kay) to a brutal medical career as an ER doctor in Chicago's busiest public hospital. Kat remained physically close to the family and thus could see the Greek tragedy play out to its inevitable denouement. Inside, she seethed at the man she felt bore the true responsibility of Chuck's suicide. Even the normal aspect of her father's demeanor, his easy arrogance, grated her sensibilities, often repelling her outright. To her mind, it was as if Charles Senior had put a gun to her sweet brother's head and blown his own son's brains against the wall. The shock of Chuck's passing did something to what had early on been a shy, retiring girl...the one whom seldom left a footprint in the family drama. After her eldest brother's demise, Katerina 'Kat' Crawford emerged from her cocoon, rallied the remainder of her family around her and then seized control of the family enterprise. Chris had watched in amazement. He knew his younger sister much better these days. Her accomplishments no longer surprised him. One thing was certain: he knew that this would not be a casual call. Of that, Chris was sure.

"No," Chris responded, "not a bad time at all. Just pursuing truth as usual, you know, unraveling the secrets of the universe to expose the face of God." He chuckled inside at his clever turn of words which, he admitted to himself, he had stolen from his favorite television show: The Big Bang Theory. "There never is a bad time for you, I can always wait until this afternoon to solve the world's most perplexing conundrums." Chris's weak witticism evoked a laugh on the other end of the line, which relaxed him. Still, he wanted to confirm his quick assessment. "So, I take it that nothing is wrong."

Her tone remained light. "If it were something awful, I would have an underling call. I delegate all crap to my lackeys these days."

"Bullshit," he chuckled, knowing she would get serious in her own time. "I just find it fascinating that you are still up at this hour. I thought you were an early-to-bed gal?"

"Not so much when Ricky is gone, nothing to go to bed for. By the way, fair warning: I got a text from him that he is headed your way, might already be there."

"Too much information." Chris joked, "no need to fill me in on your sex life or to ruin my day with news that I may soon have to endure my brother-in-law's attempts at humor, always at my expense I might add."

"On the topic of sex," her tone remained playful, "has Amar dumped you yet?"

"Hah, my devoted spouse worships the very ground I walk on. Her fawning adoration sometimes embarrasses me."

Kat laughed aloud. "Dear brother, if you are embarrassed, it is because you finally understand that she settled for a loser with delusional thoughts about himself."

"What?" He feigned shock. "She's fallen for someone else?"

"Oh, sweet Chris, you've always made me laugh. I miss that. You're not much good for anything, but you do make me laugh."

"That is me, all the gals say I am one big joke. By the way, where exactly is my favorite brother-in-law? Is he really coming to merry old England?"

"That is what he told me. He has been traveling abroad for a bit to make the Crawford empire even more money. Heading back now but has time for a short visit with you." She paused. "Maybe that was supposed to be a surprise. In any case, you do know that he's very talented, and not just in bed. Why in heaven's name did he befriend a loser like you, a mystery for sure?" Kat decided to switch topics before they descended into another round of good-natured insults. "And Azita, how is my favorite niece?"

"All I can say," he now sounded rather serious, "is that if anyone told me being a parent could be so rewarding, I would have tried it earlier."

"Hmm, and all I can say is that if a loser like you can do it so well, maybe I should give it a try." Kat then cut off what she knew would come, his encouragement in that direction. "However, there are things to do before we go there, things to do."

Chris sensed the change in her voice. "Ah, to the question, finally."

"Soon. First, tell me where Azita is thinking of continuing her medical studies?"

"I assume here, in Oxford or London. She loves it, we all love it. You don't have to worry about being gunned down in the streets by some whacko, you know like what happens all the time in Kabul or Chicago."

Kat paused, Chris braced himself just a bit. "And speaking about Chicago, or America at least, has she considered coming here for her future studies? It would be an internship next, right?"

"Why in God's good name would she go over there?" Chris waited for a response but heard none. He could not quite believe his sister was struggling. "Shit Kat, you have an agenda, don't you? Come on, spit it out."

"Damn, can't fool you. Guess that is why you are the Rhodes scholar."

"And you can forget the flattery. I already know I am perfect. What is it, Kat?"

He heard a heavy breath. "Jules was here, she just left in fact. Before you ask, just let me get this out. First the bad news and then, depending on your view, the worse news. The bad news is that she and her husband are splitting, taking time off as she says. It is supposed to be temporary but my instinct as a woman…"

Chris cut her off. "Why the fuck didn't she call me if there were problems? I knew nothing. Fuck, I would…"

Sensing a small tirade coming, Kat broke in to stop him. "Rule number one, stop with the fucks. Your talking to a lady here. Okay, forget that lady thing. Listen, she just didn't want to bother you, she feels you have your own life now, blah, blah, blah."

"Oh fu…fiddlesticks. She's been my best friend, like since forever."

"Time to pull the ego in, kiddo, she hasn't even told Ricky yet and he's her goddamn brother. And don't you go blabbing to him when he gets there, she wants to break it to him when he returns from across the pond. These things happen, there is no great drama as far as I can see. Frankly, I doubt the spark was ever there, not like you and her." Kat stopped, realizing her error. "Erase that. It has been a long day."

"It's okay. After all, she is the one that turned me down, more than once. Goddamn it to hell. And don't say a goddamn word about my expletive, it made me feel better. Okay, there is worse news you say? Mother is still okay, isn't she?" Chris momentarily panicked.

"Mother is fine, never been happier. This is a big picture issue. Remember when we fought the proxy fight and wrested control from Father?"

"How could I forget? Your finest hour."

"Perhaps. Anyways, we thought he would fight like mad to get control back. And he did, for a while. There were law suits and we knew he was contacting major stock holders. But then he seemed to back off. That bothered me for a long time. Why? Why would this man who always went for the jugular seem to give up, apparently just walk away?"

"And the answer is…?"

"Simple really. He was still making tons of money after I took over, maybe even more because I took over. Then he realized something, I think. Why waste time fighting us when he could spend his time doing what he really wants to do?"

"Like abuse his children - has he tried to rape you again?"

"I suppose but in a different way, a way he can hurt us all, and by that I really mean all of us…everyone. He is all in on his right-wing crap, not just as an old man's hobby but in a very, very dangerous way. And that is where Jules comes in again. You probably know that she continued to climb the ladder in the fascinating world of communications and what passes as journalism these days, from just being a smart and pretty thing reading the news to someone doing hard-hitting investigatory stories. I suppose I am somewhat at fault here, but I put a bug in her ear about Father, his causes and some leads into his money and connections to all these right-wing nut cases. She started running with it from there. Tonight, she came back with some feedback…and the separation thing."

"I am almost afraid to ask."

"It is still early, but she's focusing on this Trump phenomenon. I know what you are going to say, that clown doesn't have a chance. Sure, I know where all the smart money is but let me tell you, never underestimate just how moronic the typical American voter is. You know this better than anyone, the angst among the working class, stagnating wages and fewer opportunities, fears about rising competition from minorities and immigrants, automation and globalization demons everywhere. Bits and pieces are drifting in that some big money is going to his cause, or at least in support of his case. Not surprisingly, they are dropping big bucks on the usual Hillary is a serial killer crap. But they are also throwing money to 3rd party candidates like Jill and the insurgency of Bernie. If he sneaks in as the Dems' candidate, they will bury his ass so deep that the average voter will think he is Lenin's grandson. They see final victory here. And there is a lot of cyberspace chatter, misinformation and trolls working to sow discontent among the center and left. We think they are beginning to try out cyber-tactics for the upcoming general election."

"Wait, who is *they*?" he asked.

"Not sure yet but there is a lot of foreign traffic, much from Russia. Jules mentioned the FSB and GRU."

"Shit," Chris whispered aloud, "FSB is the new KGB and GRU is their military intelligence."

"See, you know this stuff." Kat responded, "This is very serious, very professional hackers, but why and for whom? This is all very sketchy now, but I sent you an email with an attachment. It has some more details. Money, vicious attack tactics, control of voting protocols like voter suppression and gerrymandering. They have been at this for several decades now and they can taste it. This is bigger than Father, but I never would have paid as much attention if it were not from him."

"All this from Jules?"

"Well, I don't want to say much now but Beverly is snooping around."

"Chuck's widow? What?"

"Yup, do you know any others? Hmm, with your past, you might, but hookers are never named Beverly I bet."

"Hah, hah!" he managed.

She cut him off. "More on all the details about the snooping later. For now, I think your native land, and you must admit that America is still your native land, is facing a huge crisis. The right is poised to take over."

"I have never been a conspiracy-theory type but even I can see that. Still, why go with a buffoon like Trump? Why not someone with a brain?"

"You nailed it without realizing it, in part at least. Many of the true believers behind the scenes, not the ignorant base, but the big players, want him precisely because he is dumber than a bag of rocks. It will be just like Cheney with Bush the younger, that kid wasn't smart enough to see where he was being led. The movers behind the scenes think they can lead Trump wherever they want and some of these characters are frightening. Check out Miller and Bannon, their pedigree will curl your pubic hair. And Putin would love Trump to advance his agenda. If the rumors are true, they own his family jewels. There are backroom loans, money laundering, sex tapes, and God knows what that they can use to get leverage over his silly ass."

"My God, you're right. Trump is the perfect unwitting Russian asset, too stupid to know that he is being played. Still, that is a dangerous game," Chris insisted. "I mean, sometimes an asshole you think you have in your pocket gets to the top and suddenly starts thinking about what is best for the country or, in this case, himself. Damn, if this guy is as deranged as he seems, why worry? I mean, why worry just because he is a stone-cold sociopath who only adores money and his own penis? Want to know my greatest fear? He doesn't know how dumb he is, which is very dangerous. That shit-for-brains could do crazy shit thinking he knows more than anyone else. I have heard business people I respect talk about him, not pretty at all. I am positive you have heard the same stories."

Kat emitted a very tiny chuckle. "Of course. You would think that would be a problem with most, but many on the right believe they will have his balls totally in a vice. He will have no wiggle room. That asshole has more skeletons in his closet than an anatomy professor in a medical school. The real danger, as I see it, is that you are spot-on right."

"Really, and you are admitting it?"

"Yes, about him being an idiot. He is so dumb and yet he doesn't realize it. My God, he believes himself to be a genius; how could anyone be so blind? Like you, I have chatted with quite a few business peers who know him well. Besides being your basic conman, he endorses some economic ideas that would get him flunked out of econ 101."

"Oooh, cleverly put but never forget that Von Papen and Hindenburg underestimated Hitler. They thought he was a clown that could be controlled." Chris wasn't sure he wanted to get deep into this but sensed there was no escape. Still, he tried a weak deflection. "And when did you start talking like a longshoreman?"

"My vocabulary improved when I started butting heads with sharks in the business world. Remember how you always said they were a sorry-ass bunch? Well, you were right, more correct than even you knew. Just listen now, okay? Forget his women and his bankruptcies and his stiffing of creditors and workers, he probably will lie and bully his way past that stuff. However, there's another concern festering just out of sight. This guy is toxic to American banks. He now shops overseas for capital, like Deutsche Bank, but really is keeping afloat with help from the

Russians in particular. These Red oligarchs know he is a terrible business risk, so why back such a loser? Again, not a great mystery. They are making a big bet that he can win the brass ring. Think how great for Putin to have his man in the White House. And don't say no way. If Americans could figure out their self-interest, we would not see today's Republican party in charge of Congress or running most states. Look at the worst states economically, they are all deep red. Kansas went big for right-wing orthodoxy and have wrecked their economy. They need to close schools early and eviscerate the most basic of services. It is a total mess. But people don't get it. They will probably reelect the same assholes."

Chris interjected as if struck by a thought. "I am beginning to get one thing. As you were talking, I struggled with the notion of Father working in concert with Russia. How would that be possible? He so hated the Reds. But, of course, they are no longer communists but an oligarchy of the uber-wealthy. They don't have democracy but that is not what he wants either. He is in love with control. And that is what Putin is about most of all: an authoritarian with the state and corporate interests intertwined…the very definition of a fascist state."

Kat chuckled again. "You do realize you answered your own question?"

"Of course, who better? Anyways, I always teach that the far right and left have much more in common than the extremes have with the center. The extremes are different sides of the same coin. It is a little like magnetic poles flipping left and right - or is it up and down? Okay, I'm now convinced of my own brilliance."

Kat responded drily. "And I always said you were slow, I apologize. The thing is that we cannot, or Jules cannot, quite get at the money flow behind all this. International finance is a swamp, more a cesspool, as you can imagine but she is working hard on it and I assigned some of my finance people to help her."

There was a pause. Then Chris asked in a more subdued voice: "Is this dangerous for Jules, for you?"

"You think Father could lash out?"

"Well?"

"I did worry for myself after we ousted him. Kept looking over my shoulder. He is a son-of-a-bitch but…"

"Just a concern. I still love both of you, though you can be trying at times."

"I know you do," she said in a serious tone. "And you are right that I am…quite trying at times that is. By the way, I have come to love her as well…Jules that is. You, not so much. But she is amazing… now that I know her. In the old days, she struck me as just another pretty face with a great body. Now I can see what lies underneath - amazing. Guess I am repeating myself."

"Same with her brother, Ricky?"

"No, he is just a gorgeous hunk with a great body." When Kat paused, Chris thought to himself that she had arrived at a conclusion. "Okay, here it is. What is the chance you can come back home?"

"For a visit, no problem."

"Yes and no," Kat said slowly. "I do want you back this summer, so we can talk more at length. But I am thinking of getting you back here on a more permanent basis, with the whole family. Maybe not forever but what we are talking about could be a long struggle. Chris, it is the future of the country, the world. The right today controls the Republican party and they are, how should I put it…?"

"Bat-shit crazy?" As Chris finished her thought, he wondered for a moment if he had heard her correctly. When her bottom line had come, it had still surprised him even as he realized that was exactly where her narrative had been heading from the start. "Kat, I have been here in England forever, I am becoming a British citizen. I have set down roots, finally."

"I know all that, Chris. I stared at the phone for half an hour before calling. Hell, I started and stopped more than once. I damn well know what I'm asking. I wouldn't have if I did not think it was so important. I need you, Jules needs you. For Christ's sake, the damn country needs you. Whatever you are doing for the world will be negated if these people get total control. Just think of the damage the far right could do to the economy, the international order, the environment, global warming, the safety net, inequality and opportunity - the list of potential disasters is endless. Have you ever heard Trump on protectionism? He could plunge the world into another depression that would make the Great Depression look like a mild dip into economic insanity."

"I know," Chris breathed weakly.

"Do you?" Kate barked. "Make no mistake, the nativists see where we are going if they don't seize total control: white America will lose control in a generation or so and they just cannot permit that to happen. They are going all in. Their venality knows no bounds. Their paranoia is palpable. This is not politics as usual, this could be a fascist takeover and an end to the world as we know it. If you think I exaggerate, listen to some of Trump's speeches, straight out of the early 1930s Nazi playbook."

"Kat, you are beginning to sound like me back in college, even the foul language."

"Goddamn it, don't patronize me. I am fucking serious here." Then, as if she had heard herself. "Maybe you're right on the language thing."

Chris toyed just for a moment about another comment on her use of colorful language before deciding that would not be wise. "Kat, I am not going to say no out of hand. I have worried about these very things myself. But it will take some time for me to think things through. Things are getting so settled for me. This…this will require time. Besides, it involves more than just me. No promises but I am listening, I am hearing you."

"Thank you. That is all I can ask for now. Chris, I know what I'm asking. You once told me that the best thing about doing what you did, or your people did, is that they provided helpless people with everything. There is no better feeling than that, you told me. I am not sure I can take them, Father and his allies that is, on by myself. There are other business types who share this apocalyptic vision, but we need someone to keep the oppositional glue together, not a known political operative but someone like… you. I hate to say this, but you have credibility. Many of them know you, have given you money. Best of all, you make them laugh as well. You are just so…disarming. I hate admitting this, but I need you, we need you. I suppose I am asking for at least as much as you provide to others, I am begging you for everything."

Chris winced at her subtle cut. "I get it, Kat. I do. Let me noodle all this, whatever can be worked out, if anything, will take a while."

"That I understand. And Chris?"

"Yeah?"

"Keep this close for a while, alright, just family? Well, I better get some sleep. I reenter the corporate war in the morning."

"Kat, before you go…I do love when you beg."

"You are such a shit." But he could hear a small chuckle. "Goodbye."

"Wait!" he cried out.

"Yeah?"

Chris took a big breath. "You never cease to amaze me."

"Ah." Now he clearly heard a tiny chuckle from his sister. "Be still my beating heart, my life is now complete."

He smiled momentarily as the connection was lost but that did not last long. He flipped on his email, and there indeed was a message from Kat with an attachment, likely written by Jules but unsigned. He glanced through the material just to get a general feel for it before settling back in his chair. He would read it more carefully later but the sense of it had already moved him.

"Shit!" he said to no one in particular.

Standing, he looked out over the quadrangle below. He was just high enough to glimpse the far countryside. He loved this place, the university and the town and even the country. From his mother, he had learned that he was not supposed to like the British. Since the days of Cromwell, if not before, they had done unspeakable things to his Irish ancestors. The English overlords had done everything they could to root out and destroy Catholicism and what they saw as the evil residue of the Celtic culture. Even amid the Great Famine of the late 1840s, the absentee landlords shipped off food stuffs to foreign markets for profit as three to four million natives died or emigrated. They offered soup and bread to those that would convert to the Church of England. Few did, the faithful embraced their religion and their culture with ever greater fervor. The Irish were driven even deeper into their cultural obsession.

Apparently, he had forgiven the English for all their ancient sins. He loved the life that he had discovered here, his family, his eclectic but rewarding career that included academic, literary, and consulting components. He was comfortable yet stimulated. It was a perfect world. Then a scene from a movie crowded in on him, from the Godfather trilogy. Was it Pacino or De Niro? Why couldn't he keep those two actors straight? In any case, by the third film the protagonist thought he had finally escaped his gangster legacy and gone legit when he was dragged back into the family business of murder and mayhem. Chris had escaped Chicago, his culture, his family, all the hate and now…they would drag him back in.

Then it hit him: that was why Kat started with where Azita might do her internship and residency. His sister was no fool. She knew that Chris would resist coming back if his adopted daughter were staying in England. She knew how attached he had become, how much of a protector of her he remained. That was true. Memories flooded back to him, landing for the first time in the Panjshir Valley medical and refugee site where Kay had, without permission, moved to join Amar Singh, who then was only a fine doctor who worked in his program but whom he had never met in person. He did not think that his sister could put herself in a more dangerous spot than a Chicago public hospital ER. But she somehow managed it. Was she trying to find a way out of the pain, like their older sibling had? He could still recall how furious and frightened he had been as he and Karen Fisher, his assistant, had travelled to the site. You just never knew when your life was about to take a different trajectory.

Chris leaned back in his chair and forgot about the writing he intended to do that morning. Rather, he saw and smelled that day in 2001 when the helicopter landed, blowing up dust from the desolate and scorched land. Normally agreeable, he was bright with anger when no one greeted him, when he and Karen were pointed to a non-descript building. Upon entering, all that greeted him was a fetching young Afghan girl whose wide, expressive eyes melted his hostility a bit and whose excellent English, though accented, rendered him momentarily mute. The girl told him that his sister was off treating wounded children from a shelling in a nearby village with this very girl's father. Amar, likewise, was busy dealing with victims of the same shelling at their facility. So, the girl took him on a tour. Her innocent charm and enthusiasm reached him. He could feel his resolve ebbing away. The need was so great here, the people so brave and thankful. For the first time, in truth, he knew with intimate understanding what his work was all about.

A while later, he was directed to Amar Singh, the woman he put in charge of directing the medical team but whom had, to this moment, merely been an image on his computer screen. Walking out the back of a temporary medical facility, there she stood holding a dying baby, providing comfort in the last moments of its life. He froze in place, first not wanting to trammel upon such a personal scene, then immobilized by his own feelings. He could not take his eyes off her, the one tear that coursed slowly down her cheek. What was that hollow ache suddenly inside him? He had never felt anything so intense before. Now, with time and distance, it all made so much sense. He had experienced two fundamental epiphanies in one day. He first had fallen in love with his work and then, inexplicably, he had fallen in love with a woman.

He was still sitting back in his chair, smiling, when his phone rang. He didn't answer. He did not want to give up his reverie. After some time, he did not know how long, he finally checked the number and recognized it immediately. It was his adopted daughter, the very same wide-eyed Afghan girl who greeted him that day during the height of the last frontier holding out against the Taliban. He kicked himself for his selfishness. He always answered for her, no matter what. After all, she had led him to a deeper love of his work and to the woman who would become his wife. He listened to her voice mail and quickly exited his office.

CHAPTER 2

RADCLIFFE SQUARE

Azita Masoud was troubled. It was odd that she should feel so discomforted, one might say out of sorts. She had just finished another successful semester of medical school, once again ranking among the very best students in her class at Oxford University. It was now spring in the smallish, quaint city she had come to adore, a lovely time of year in a place that typically offered such a dreary winter climate. Moreover, she lived with her adopted family, Christopher Crawford and Amar Singh, whom she had fully embraced with great affection. More than affection, she concluded, but with as much love as she had for Pamir and Madeena, her biological parents who had been murdered by the Taliban. Even the nightmares that had visited her since her remarkable escape from war-ravaged Afghanistan had become less frequent, diminishing from nightly intrusions to periodic harassments.

Her traditional nocturnal visitations had been largely the same. She would rush through the narrow streets of a prototypical Afghan village searching for something unnamed and unnamable. The identity of the terror she simultaneously sought and yet feared could not be denied for long.

It was her parents, Pamir and Madeena, whom she had adored with a kind of unreasoned desperation. Still, her connection to her father was endless and unique. A physician, he was her role model, her deity in human form, the source of her obsession to follow in his footsteps. Like him, she would be a healer. Nothing would stop her.

But dear Pamir now was lost to her forever. She drifted back to the ancestral village in the Panjshir Valley, mourning the death of her older brother Majeeb, who had been lost in a battle with the Taliban while fighting for the Northern Alliance. As she and Deena, her sister, were out before daybreak collecting eggs for breakfast, her known world had ended abruptly. The family had escaped the Taliban and were working with total devotion against all the oppression these fanatics labored so hard to impose. Thus, the family members were targets of their rage in the days after Osama bin Laden had struck America on September 11, 2001. Being a target of these fanatics was never a good thing but became particularly dangerous after the Western powers were stirred to drive them from power for harboring bin Laden. As the Taliban's control was threatened, the religious extremists came after the family for revenge one day. They harbored a special animosity against the Pamir clan after they had escaped their control. Important people had been humiliated.

Those moments crowded into Azita's mind as she walked down High Street toward Radcliffe Square. She was no longer the Muslim girl who had entered Britain, an emigre from Afghanistan, at the end of 2001. Then, every sound and sight were both a delight to, and an assault on, her senses. She desperately sought the blessings of a world-class education, which was possible through Chris and Amar, and which her biological father Pamir had desperately, if wistfully, hoped to somehow provide. Yet she feared the sudden changes and wondered if she could succeed in this strange land. For a moment, her mind's eye returned to the room at Heathrow where the immigration bureaucracy had challenged her right to enter the country. How could they think of her as a threat? But, of course, she looked exactly like any one of so many girls who had dressed as innocent children before blowing themselves up, and others, in the name of Allah. Besides, she had not possessed the proper papers.

She no longer looked like that young girl. She was a woman now, stylishly dressed in form-revealing jeans and a loose blouse that hung down below her waist and yet still managed to suggest a desirable female form underneath. Her only sartorial concession to her roots was a head covering, usually draped around her neck when in private and often, but not always, covering her head in public. Funny, she never could decide what to do. For years she would loop it over her head in public, even after she had converted mostly to Western dress to fit in. At some point, almost unconsciously, she would fail to cover herself if it were especially warm, which did not occur all that often in Britain.

Now, she felt a decided tug to return to traditional costume as an expression of Islamic modesty. She thought hard, but she could not recall the rules she had used for determining which culture to embrace: the old or the new. She thought harder but could not understand this tug toward the old ways. Today, that confusion bothered her greatly. She emphatically draped the cloth over her head in the traditional manner.

Passing by St. Mary the Virgin's chapel, she entered one of the many enclosed green areas that marked the university landscape. She particularly loved this one. It was like many others. However, in the middle of this green space was a circular structure of ancient origin, though not so old by British standards. She loved staring at this building, thinking back to the people who, so long ago, had erected such monuments in the pursuit of knowledge, or perhaps to honor long-forgotten institutional affinities. This structure embodied that encrusted ambiance of solidity and tradition. She could never forget that great minds had wandered over these grounds for centuries and now she was one of them. Then, she silently chided herself for such arrogance. She belonged, but did she? Doubt yet nipped at the corners of her confidence even after years of academic success.

Where was the man she needed most, her adored biological father Pamir? He had raised her during her years as a young girl. He had planted in her the dream of being a healer. He had nourished her desire for learning and her curiosity about the wider world. He had broadened her perspective beyond the narrow strictures that surrounded her, gently nurturing an appreciation of all people and the wisdom in most philosophies. He had even introduced her to Shakespeare and planted the possibility of studying at the same university where he had been trained as a physician. And now she was here. And he was not. How cruel is God! Immediately, she recoiled at her blasphemous thought, but her regret did not stay long. Larger doubts about her world view, the foundations of her culture, were more common these days

Her world as a young girl was in that house at the end of her frantic nightmare, the abode from where the screams emerged as she approached. She knew it but hated confirming that knowledge. She would never quite make it to the inside of that humble home in her fantastical journey. Fear and guilt kept her away in those tortured dreams. Still, she had to accept what awaited inside the structure. The Taliban had, in truth, crept toward the house that early morning when Deena, her sister, went about her normal morning chores. The family had prayed over the loss of Majeed the day before with members of Pamir's extended family. This morning, Azita could not sleep from grief and memory. Restless, she joined her sister just as only the most astute observer might catch the initial retreat of the night's blackness. She had never accompanied her sister before, rising early most mornings only to study her books. For some reason, one she never could quite recover later, she went with her sibling that morning. It proved an unscripted decision that saved her life. As Deena and she made a desperate escape into the pre-dawn darkness, they heard the door of their home being battered down and the screams of Madeena, their mother.

If Azita ever made it to her horror-filled destination in her nightmare, what would she have found? Would she have witnessed her parents being tortured? If Allah were merciful, their demise would have been swift. Her guilt, though, remained palpable. These fanatics were after her as well. Perhaps she was the prime target of their wrath as the girl who presumed to act like a man, who helped her father heal the wounded, who defied the new cultural and religious mandates by embracing the world of the mind. She could touch the source of both her anxiety and her crushing guilt. What if her parents had endured a slow, painful death as they were repeatedly asked about the whereabouts of their daughters? That was not likely the case. The assassins probably wanted to carry out their murderous intent and disappear before the village awoke. But she could not have known that in the moment. Deena and she had no idea of their numbers or their plan, other than to slaughter the entire Masoud family.

Azita could never have known the truth. Later, after her rescue, the villagers said that their parents had passed to the other world quickly, absent suffering. But she could never shake the sense that they had lied to her and her sister from kindness. Perhaps her parents had died quickly, no questions asked, their ultimate thoughts embracing the horror that their children were also being slaughtered. If true, their final moments were agony beyond physical pain. On the other hand, if their end were prolonged, with questions about where their children could be found, they might have realized that their offspring had escaped. Then, they would have paid an agonizing physical price for their silence but received much spiritual comfort. Neither possibility had ever brought the young woman anything but nauseating guilt. Thinking on those moments never brought her peace. She knew they would have wanted her and Deena to flee and save themselves. In her heart, though, she never forgave herself for not doing something, anything, to try to save them. Reason, what she did best, eluded her in this instance. Her superb logic proved utterly useless.

Azita shook her head. Her ennui on this fine, sunny day had not been brought on by the events from a dozen or so years ago. In fact, her nightmares from those days were less frequent, often being replaced by the more traditional angst-ridden nocturnal journeys common to those in academia. In the most frequent, she would be looking for the room where her final exam would be administered. As she wandered the halls, much like her trek through the byways of the unknown village of earlier dreams, she realized she had never attended a single class all semester. In fact, she had never bought any of the texts. Frantically, she wondered if there was time to study. But that was hopeless. She would have to tell her father she had failed, let him down. But which one, her biological father Pamir who was now long deceased, or her adoptive father Christopher? There was no way to choose between them. Perhaps she could hide this awful truth from both?

No, her present listlessness had nothing to do with any academic failure. It emerged from her breakfast with Benjamin, her fiancé, that had ended perhaps twenty-minutes earlier. It was three years, a bit more, since they had become engaged. They had pledged to one another as Azita was finishing her undergraduate studies. But now all this time had passed. They remained in a limbo. It had started as an improbable promise, a Jew and a Muslim slowly falling in love, or what she had presumed might be love. They met when a gang of youthful British nativists found this Muslim girl despoiling their pure heritage merely by walking down the street. A mindless terrorist attack had struck London the day before. Benjamin Kaplan, or Benji as he preferred, saved Azita by getting himself knocked out with one blow and feigning death until the miscreants fled in fear that they had just committed a homicide.

After this awkward start, Azita and Ben bonded with glacial slowness. Conversations turned to interest, which in turn led to affection and finally to them becoming lovers. Azita had been reluctant. This surely was not proper for a good Muslim girl, and with a Jewish boy no less. But she felt a comfort, even affection, for this young man. They would someday get married. That was a certainty, not only to her but to all those who knew them. So, there could hardly be any sin in discovering each other at a deeper, physical level. But now three years had passed since they announced their commitment to one another. Nothing had happened, no real commitment had followed. She knew the issue. It was clear: his parents liked her, perhaps loved her in a way, but they could not see beyond her Islamic background. They must be under incredible pressure from their community. And Benji could not break with them. He never said as much but now she was accepting this reality. The pull of culture, in this case, was stronger than the bonds of affection.

Nothing different was said at their breakfast. And that was the problem. Somewhere, deep inside, she knew things were the same, and they were not the same. When she looked into his eyes, she saw anguish. He was caught betwixt obsessions: his culture and his heart. She could see a hopelessness in his face. There was no need for words, for explanations, for excuses. As they parted, he asked if anything were wrong. *"Of course not,"* she had responded. He looked at her but said nothing. He knew what he might say and that was a place he did not want to go.

She felt tears drift down her cheeks and she pulled her scarf more fully over her head in the traditional Muslim manner. Her thoughts drifted back to the beginning. His parents, Abe and Rebecca, had been formal but cordial. Who was this girl? What did she mean to their son? Now, in hindsight, she could fill in the story. Don't force their son to push her away. That might backfire, bring them closer together. No, play a waiting game. Be polite but distant. Drop subtle hints, mere suggestions but with undeniable purpose. Never be direct. Their boy was bright enough. He would arrive at the correct decision on his own. This relationship was doomed from the start. You cannot join the diametrically opposed together. Particles that repel one another merely follow immutable physical laws. That was God's law and nature's way.

However, opposites did attract in this case. Their connection lasted and deepened, or so it seemed. After Azita and Ben committed to one another, she kept asking when he would tell his parents. The response was always soon, tomorrow, next week, when the time was right. His parents were not open-minded like hers. They were old fashioned. And there was the matter of personal loss. One of his Israeli relatives had died in some Palestinian raid, another in one of the several border conflicts between Israel and her neighbors. Islam was the enemy in an eternal struggle for the ancestral home going back centuries. Now, just last month, a cousin had been seriously wounded in one of those chronic uprisings near the Gaza strip. She seemed like a nice girl, but she was, at the end of the day, a Muslim. He had to take things slowly, he would know when the time was right. Just give him time, he would know when.

She pushed and pushed some more, but the futility became clear. She had given herself to him, the full measure of her womanhood. There was no turning back now. One day, she arrived at his home. Rebecca was cold, hardly said a word. Abe had made some excuse to be gone. Nothing was said, Ben looked as if he were experiencing a mortal pain. Azita looked for the first excuse to leave. He had told them, and it did not go well. Still, Ben assured her it was only a matter of time. But time, in this instance, solved nothing. Frostiness slowly turned into the bitterness of an endless cold war.

At breakfast, the topic remained the 900-pound gorilla in the room. It was like a periodic back pain, even when the nerves were not throbbing you simply waited for the inevitable agony to strike. She saw the pain and confusion on his face. He was such an adorable young man, but weak. He would never stand up to his parents, his people, his culture. Some norms simply ran too deep, they were preconscious. They were like pernicious toxins that surrounded and destroyed good tissue wherever found. She hardly touched her food, making some excuse to get away as soon as possible.

She felt better as soon as she was out in the street, away from his mooning expressions of concern infused with uncertainty. How could this continue? she wondered. But how could she break it off? She had committed herself to him. She called her adoptive father, Christopher, and left a message informing him where she was headed when he did not answer. She need not say more, he would immediately know she needed him. She would have preferred her adoptive mother, Doctor Amar Singh, but she was on duty at the hospital. Women were better when a heart was about to break. However, Christopher was on the Oxford faculty and was on campus today. When he did not respond immediately, she considered that he was unavailable. No problem. She would wait for a while, sitting in the sun, decompressing. Perhaps she would wander toward his office after her head had cleared. Now, though, she let her mind wander and thought about things that she had pushed aside during another phrenetic semester of medical studies.

A grim smile crossed over her lips. She recalled the trip her family had made north out of Kabul, the first leg of their hegira away from the Taliban and, in her optimistic mind, eventually to Britain and medical school someday. She had sat next to her biological father. She worshipped Pamir and grasped at any opportunity to be alone with him, to tap into his humor and wisdom. The rest of the family was in another vehicle, driven by Majeeb, along with many of their household goods. Pamir had convinced the authorities to permit him to relocate near the fighting between the Taliban and the Northern Alliance, the tribes that had held out as they had against the Soviets during the

1980s. They acceded to her father's wishes even though she had brought shame on the family by her thoughtlessness in a public square. She violated the new rulers by reading a poster when girls were not permitted to read. For that sin, she was beaten mercilessly by the morality police. She might have perished had her brother not rescued her.

She shook her head, don't go there she told herself. Next to her father, on that trip, she recalled saying that she would become a doctor like him no matter what. Yes, it was impossible. No girl in Afghanistan could do that then. Perhaps her mother could have been a university mathematics teacher in the old days but all that was forbidden now. Still, she insisted that she would do it. No one would stop her. When he gently suggested she might think of other things someday, perhaps even of a boy, she would have none of it. He would suppress a smile as she pontificated about the evils and faults of the opposite sex without hesitation or reservation. They were all smelly, obnoxious, dirty and stupid and those were the best things she could think about them. He humored her in the moment, and she knew it, gently reminding her that he, himself, was one of those dastardly boys. But he wasn't, of course. In her mind, he was a God.

On this day, so many years later, she could see her innocence plainly. Still, she had not been wrong. Boys were clearly more pain than they were worth, but she better understood why a woman might put up with one of them. In her head, she concluded that it was a very good thing she never abandoned her passion to be a doctor to chase after one of those worthless creatures.

She looked around. Christopher wasn't in sight. Perhaps she should seek him out. No, they might miss each other in passing. For once, she was not pressed for time. She would wait a while longer. Her thoughts went back to that special day, in the early summer of 2001, to the medical and refugee camp that served as a command center for the Northern Alliance. That was where her family had settled and where her father had worked after they had finally escaped the clutches of the Taliban. Instead of repairing the broken bodies of the Taliban he now treated those fighting them, among the very Pashtun people he had grown up with as a boy. Now she could once again work with him as he treated patients and he could teach her his trade.

Better still, there were two female doctors who renewed her hope about her own dream. She had known female physicians existed but never had met one before. She knew women could be doctors, could be anything. Women could heal as good as any man, even be as competent as her sainted father. But that knowledge was abstract, an exercise in logic. Seeing female physicians in the flesh made her belief substantive. It helped so much to see them every day, to work with them. Yes, her dream was not a fantasy. It was possible.

Doctor Amar Singh was from India. She headed an international team that was part of a service organization based in England. In Azita's young eyes, Amar had some things in common with her since India's culture was a little like her own. Perhaps that was a stretch, but this woman had realized her dream of becoming a doctor despite reservations within her family. Azita knew Amar had faced challenges. And there was Kristen Crawford, universally known as Kay, the sister of this man for whom she now waited. Christopher had not been happy that his twin sister had defied him and joined a medical team in perhaps the most dangerous site he supported at that time. Funny, Amar thought, the brother and sister were so unalike one another in many respects but, she strongly suspected, loved each other fiercely even if each was reluctant to admit it.

Azita smiled to herself in the spring sunlight as her thoughts continued to drift back to the Panjshir Valley. The timing of the arrival of Christopher Crawford to take his sister Kristen, or Kay, away that day could not have been worse. There had been fierce fighting. Kay, along with Azita's father, were off tending to the wounded including several children from a nearby village that had been shelled. Amar could not be spared from the hospital. Somewhat frantic, Amar told her to greet this man and his assistant, Karen Fisher, who would arrive shortly by helicopter.

On one level, Azita was pleased. Amar, who headed the local medical team, had asked her to greet this man who funded much of the medical operations. It was an honor to be given such a responsibility. Then she panicked, suddenly viewing this task with great dread. What if this man really did drag his sister away, as they all had speculated that he might? That would spell disaster since she admired Kay desperately.

Maybe he would also fire Amar who had encouraged Kay to leave her post in Pakistan and join the undermanned Afghanistan site. That was also unthinkable to her. Still, they were so near the fighting. This indeed was an extremely dangerous place, especially for women. This Christopher was right to be beside himself with worry for his sibling. Blaming Amar, if a bit silly, was not totally irrational. She could understand that, even sympathize. Still, she asked Allah to permit her new friends to stay. Listening to Amar and Kay talk, they had earlier chosen not to ask permission for Kay to move from Pakistan to this site but to do it and then see where the chips would fall.

Now, the chips were about to fall. She had come to love those female doctors. Kay was strong and unflappable. Amar was gentler, more sensitive, but with an iron will underneath. More importantly, they were so good at what they did, much like her sainted father. They treated her like a much younger sister, adding to her education as she sopped up all the medical knowledge they could share. By the time she had heard the helicopter, she had worked herself into such a state of both anxiety and conviction. She would stand up to this ogre. He was not going to take these women away.

She heard the helicopter land that day so many years ago but froze inside the medical office. Could she confront this symbol of authority? Then, Christopher Crawford appeared at the door. All her pent-up fears evaporated. She could tell, just by looking into his eyes, that he was not the ogre she had anticipated. He was much like her father in all the ways that counted. And now, he was her father, a substitute but so much more. Allah does work in mysterious ways.

She came out of her reverie and looked up. Across the rectangle, she saw his familiar figure appear, quickly look around and then head in her direction. He did cut such a figure. She remembered so well what Kay shared with Amar in anticipation of her brother's arrival at the medical site. "Don't fall for his charms," she had warned. "Women fall all over him and he just moves from one to the next." Apparently, Kay's warning had fallen on deaf ears and Amar quickly succumbed to his charms. The renowned playboy, surprisingly, did not move on. Chris and Amar were married just before they spirited Azita off to her new life in England. Maybe there was something to this love thing. Perhaps if she could find a man as kind and good as her new father, she would reconsider her dark assessment of the worth of the male species....

"Hey kiddo," Chris said and sat down next to her. "What's up? I was just about to make another stunning academic breakthrough when you texted. My legions of fans are waiting for my next breathtaking discovery."

She smiled, he could always make her smile. "Well, they have been waiting all these years, another day won't hurt."

He loved her wit, it was so much like his own. Did she get it from him or her biological father? He wished he had gotten to know Pamir at a deeper level. He knew, however, that this was not to be an afternoon of light banter. Searching her eyes, looking for clues as to why he had been summoned, one could notice a touch of bemusement in them but a wider pool of uncertainty. *Where did this grown woman come from? She seemed like a bright, earnest little girl just the other day,* he wondered to himself. That first day, so long ago in the Panjshir valley, she had struck him as little more than an impish, if precocious, child. Then, she had not lost all her childish baby fat and was fetching but not as beautiful as her older sister. It was her personality, large and prepossessing, that drew you in.

Over these past dozen years, she had sprung into adulthood. Taller, with fine facial features and a now well-proportioned female body, Chris had long noticed that young men stared at her as she passed them in the streets. Her copper skin and long, dark brown hair had immediate effect, but it was the eyes that captivated one. They were large and doe-like. No matter how often he looked he could never decide on their color. There retained a chameleon quality driven by the nature of the light that struck them. Sometimes they were a light blue and other times a light green. At some distant time in the past, her ancestors had drifted down from the north to now possess such light-colored portals to her soul. And that was exactly what they were, openings to her magnificent heart and mind.

"I suspect," Chris said softly, "that you didn't text me just to drop a few insults on my academic shortcomings, nonexistent as they are. By that I mean the faults are few, not…never mind."

"No," Azita sighed, "I can do that anytime." She paused, wondering why she was being such a little girl at this moment, running to her father rather than just dealing with this herself. But the hurt and doubt were real. "I am confused…lost."

"Well," Chris uttered slowly. "since we are located in one of your favorite haunts on campus, I'm thinking your issue is more existential than geographical."

"No shit, Sherlock." That came out harsh, she caught herself. She wasn't angry at him. "Sorry, you really are such a bad influence on me." She put her head on his shoulder and wept softly.

Neither one spoke for a while. Chris really didn't know what to say, emotions were not his strong suit. He swung his arm around her and rubbed the side of her head around her temple. Finally, she managed a short utterance. "All boys are awful. I figured that out as a young girl, how could I have forgotten?"

"I'm a boy, well a male at least. So, I guess that makes me awful too."

Azita raised her head to look at him. "Papa used that same line on me, probably won't work anymore." She always referred to Pamir as Papa and to Chris as Dad or Father.

"But it worked when he used it?"

"I was younger then, and I think he must have said it better." She let a small smile escape.

"Okay, kiddo, I am not going to compete with Papa. Tell me what is going on."

Azita looked at him and then sighed. "It is too much suddenly. Part of it is Benji. Remember the day of my 'Profile in Courage' talk and the family gathering after? We announced that we had committed to one another. I believed him. I believed in each other. I gave him…everything."

"Wait, has he broken it off?" Chris looked a bit angry.

"No," she responded sharply, "that would take courage on his part. But I know. I can see it in his eyes."

"Zita," Chris called her by his familiar name for her, "how can he be so stupid? You are the best thing any guy could hope for. I can't believe he has lost interest."

"It's not him… not him." Another tear made its way down her cheek.

"His parents?"

She nodded and then buried her head into his chest. "He doesn't talk about it. I mean he does but not really. Do you understand?"

"Sure," he murmured, though he was totally lost.

The girl continued anyway. "I mean, I've tried to get him to open up, really, to say what he is feeling…boys are hopeless."

"You won't get any argument from me. There are probably dozens of women out there that use my name as a swear word."

"I heard it was hundreds." She wondered what her words conveyed to him. She hoped her comment was light enough.

"Yes, my name is likely the eponym for male bastard." Chris remained silent for a moment, kicking himself for using a word she probably did not recognize. Perhaps she did, though. She always amazed him with her prodigious intellect, from the moment he rescued her some dozen years earlier after the death of her biological parents. She had stolen his heart then and continued to do so as she managed some humor despite her pain. He could feel her tears on his shirt. "Hmmm, methinks you listened to my evil sister. She had me pegged as the playboy of the Western world."

"Was she wrong?" With her face pressed against him, her voice was muffled.

"No…she probably did not know the half of it. I was a shit with women. I admit it."

"But why?" she managed to get out. "You are one of the kindest people I know, after your wife of course, and your sister, and Karen, and my sister. Okay, but you make it into the top dozen." Suddenly, the ache inside her subsided a bit.

"I was beginning to worry there," he smiled. "Well, kiddo, I can say that I never lied, and I surely never intended any harm."

"But you did, cause harm that is. You must have, and you probably knew you were doing it, somewhere inside at least." She pulled her head back to look at him. "You cannot love, or not love, and not know you are hurting someone. I have given him so much, trusted him so."

"C'mon let's walk." They got up and started to ramble around the perimeter of the rectangle. In truth, he wanted a few moments to collect his thoughts. He was out of his league and knew it. "All the rumors about me are true. Before Amar, I was a shit with women. I went through one after another. But like I said, I never promised anything to anyone. In fact, I was brutally honest."

"And you feel no guilt?"

"Some, but not as much as I probably should. I comforted myself that we usually were on the same page. Neither of us were ever serious, or so I convinced myself. But there were times when I knew the girl felt too much, maybe was falling for me. My heart told me to back off, but I didn't always. I was selfish. For that I feel like shit."

"But you aren't like that. You really are so very kind."

"Well, I blame it on the hormones, too much testosterone. But that is mostly BS. I have thought about my life before Amar, how I was. All of this might be a post-rationalization, but I felt so alone. Yes, I had siblings and friends and colleagues. Sure, I was always the man with a quip, the guy who could keep them laughing or inspire and even console. But inside, I was empty. I hated my father, my mother was a distant drunk back then, my older brother Chuck was on his way out, for good. Kay had drifted away from me, while Kat was too young and, back then, invisible. There was no one. Well, Ricky was my best friend, but he was an ocean away after college and, besides, he was a guy. You can't really be open with a guy, that is suicide. I kind of grabbed on to Karen as an anchor of sorts. She was a lesbian, so safe. And she didn't put up with my BS, which was good. But she could never fill the gap. And then…" He stopped.

"Then what?"

"I met you, and Deena, and Amar. Suddenly, I had a family. One day I had nothing, the next an entire family. Suddenly, I was…connected. Zita, you have no idea! People looked at me and thought my life was gifted, perhaps blessed. I had money, a trust fund, went to the best schools, had gained some respect as a college athlete, apparently had looks and charm and wit. Then, finishing my advanced studies at this university, I was able to look around and create whatever I wanted. I hated my father, his venality and his obsequious, grasping greed. So, I could create something I knew would drive him a bit nuts, how great was that. Women, however, came easy. Money and a few jokes will do wonders. Well, the money is magical."

"Except it cannot bring you happiness." she added, then murmured, "So sorry, didn't mean to interrupt."

To her relief, he went on as if she had remained silent. "I still have not figured out why I started my international service organization. Sure, I had this niche theory I felt strongly about, the program bridge-building and integrated-service theory. But mostly I wanted the challenge of building something myself. I would show Father that I could do something on my own, something he hated and could not understand. And the best thing, the very best thing, was that a good chunk of the early money came from his business associates, both those that admired him and many that loathed him. He could not dismiss that. No, he for certain could not ignore that. Maybe that is why I still raise money for the program from these sources, even if I am no longer involved full time and we are on a more stable footing money-wise. I love rubbing it in his face. In the end, I am not sure I did anything unique, but it has made me feel good. Wow, as I say the words, I sound pathetic."

"No… what you were doing, creating, was so good. No need for explanations nor doubts. There is no need to rationalize it as anger or revenge. It is a good thing."

"Zita, thank you. I needed to hear that. Frankly, I didn't know what to think about my creation until I met you and Amar and your family. I used to visit sites, just in and out, simply making sure that things were okay. I don't believe I connected with what was going on. When I came to pull my sister out of harm's way that might have been the first time that I really looked at what I was doing. Almost from the moment I landed I knew I was not taking Kay away. You did that to me. But it took me a while longer to figure the bigger things out. That first day, walking with you through the refugee camp opened my eyes, my heart. Seeing you with the girls in that school you started. Meeting your father, your family, those moments were a revelation. I remember saying to Kay later that we all have opportunities to help others just a little, at least from time to time, but few of us ever mean everything to another person. That is what you all were doing there, and my sister and Amar, you were giving people everything. Simple lesson, right there before me, a lesson that someone reminded me of just this morning. But sometimes I can be such a dolt."

"True," she murmured, "no argument from me." She grabbed his arm and leaned into him. She needed his touch. "Despite you being a total dolt, I still love you."

"That's it," he said too loudly, looking around to see if others were hearing them. Only a young man, probably a student, lurked in the vicinity and he seemed very disinterested. "I felt love for the first time. Oh, I was very close to Jules. She meant so much to me though I rather pushed her away emotionally after she rejected me. Self-protection, I guess. But love, deep love, you and Amar brought that into my life. Then, everything started to make sense. I wasn't driven so much by anger anymore."

Azita stopped walking and turned to him. "When did you know that you loved her?"

"Amar?"

"No, Angelina Jolie."

They both smiled. They both knew how to keep from getting too deep. From opposite sides of the world, yet so much alike. "You know, I can still take a switch to your backside, kiddo."

"Too late to start that," she responded. "Besides, I doubt you can match the morality police of Kabul. Face it, you're slowing up, old man. I can outrun you, but before I take off at a dead run, when did you know you loved her?"

He walked a few more steps without a word. "The first moment I saw her in person, not as an employee on a Skype screen. My response was overwhelming, undeniable. Isn't that something. People say that men can't commit. Well, some say that. But it has been my experience that men fall in love at first sight. Women take their time. Amar says that she knew early on I was the one because Kay had said all these nice things about me. I have never bought that. Kay and I hardly knew each other as adults until we connected again at the medical station."

Azita laughed. "Wrong again."

"Kiddo, after all this time, you still don't get it. I am omniscient and prescient."

"And an idiot." She smiled slyly.

"Better start running." He gave her his most obviously disingenuous scowl.

Azita was feeling better. She was glad she had texted him. Amar could commiserate but Chris could make her laugh. "Seriously, I can remember what Kay said about you before you arrived. Yes, we were all concerned that you would try to take your sister away and maybe fire Amar, but then Kay would talk about you. She loved you, she really did. She would talk about your kindness and your commitment and how smart you were... all those times you huddled together as youngsters, trying to figure stuff out. They were priceless moments for her, she held on to them tightly. She really held you in awe and that rubbed off on Amar. Her words even affected me...until I met you."

"Hmm, Amar once told me that, about what Kay had said about me, but I thought she made it up. Damn, I really do have a helluva time accepting compliments. But listen, back to the main topic. Tell me, do you love Benjamin?"

Azita was silent. Chris waited, and waited, and finally she spoke. "I'm not sure. I thought I did. I have great affection for him. I admire him. Intellectually, we are alike and have such common interests. I saw us working together, as partners, over the course of our lives."

"My God, girl, that is like talking about a colleague." Chris grabbed her shoulders and turned her so that she faced him. "When you see him, what do you feel?"

"Comfort, I think, when I am not angry with him." She offered nothing more. "We have shared so much. We do have common interests, similar aspirations. We talked about Omnism the very first time we met."

"Funny what works with women. I remember seducing a woman or two by noting how much I loved the philosophy of Pierre Teilhard de Chardin."

Azita laughed out loud despite herself. "You really are shameless, but I can see how that might work, though not with the women you were with before mother, at least based on what I was told."

"No doubt. But listen, kiddo, I am not going to tell you what to feel or believe. To this day, in the morning, when I look over at Amar sleeping next to me, my heart still flutters. I cannot believe I am so fortunate. When we are alone, doing nothing, I will look across the room at her…when she isn't aware of my stare. There is no pose in such moments, merely truth. It is not just her beauty, the sweet expression of her eyes or the way her hair frames her face. I know I am looking at a person capable of such enormous love. I have no idea how I was found deserving of her."

"None of us do." She hugged him, as if she thought he might need a clue that she was kidding. "And don't kid yourself, we women always know when the man we love is looking."

"Promise me one thing," Chris said seriously. "Never settle for anything less than you deserve. You are so much like Amar, so full of love."

She shuddered just a bit. "One thing, one more thing. Chris, I have been with him, you know, as a woman I mean. I could never admit this to you, silly I suppose but I never wanted you to be disappointed in me. Amar knows but…"

"I knew."

"Did Amar tell you?" she asked.

"No, if she promised to keep your secret, she would never betray you."

Chris smiled at her. "I could just tell. Besides, just how many virgins of your advanced age do you think there are in the world? Tell me, what is gnawing at you. Spit it out, kiddo. What's bothering you?"

"Dad, I need to know that are you not disappointed in me. It is so hard for a Muslim girl. I feel so ashamed at times. I know I am in a different culture but still…I cannot help but believe that no good boy will ever want me now. You have no idea how suffocating my culture is. Are you ashamed of me at all?"

He embraced her. "Zita, my love for you is complete, unshakable. I cannot imagine what you can do to be a better person though we might work on dialing back that so-called wit of yours. Of course, I would disown you if you voted against the Labor candidate. But my pathetic attempts at wit aside, have you ever thought about why I decided to adopt you? I was the guy who was never going to get married and certainly not have any children of my own. This was a harsh world and raising children seemed like a responsibility that was beyond me. You changed me, forever. Well, you and Amar, and Deena helped. You taught me love, how to feel hope. I doubt you can even begin to understand how much I owe you. Me be disappointed in you? Unless you are a secret serial murderer, that is never going to happen."

"My head tells me that this is what you would say. My gut is somewhere else. How I was raised permitted no compromise on some things. There were girls who were killed by their parents, or who disappeared, for doing what Benjamin and I have done. They are called honor killings. The Taliban encouraged such things, but they are found throughout the Mideast."

They stopped walking. "You cannot believe Pamir and Madeena would have rejected you. I met them. I saw their love. It never could have happened."

"Perhaps not, but my own shame would be worse than death. How could I disappoint such people? You know as well as I. It is not the reality of things that matter. It is the way we see it, feel it. Hell is not a place that we go to, it is a torture we carry around inside of us."

Chris pulled her to him once again and held her tightly. He wished to squeeze the anguish out of her. "Listen, kiddo, I have to run. I have a meeting with Karen and others about this trip through the Mideast she is putting together. We need to pick this up later. For now, here's the thing. You need to figure out how you feel about Ben. I don't give a damn that you slept with him. That takes nothing away from what makes you special, and certainly is no reason to stay with him. You are, though, facing a big life choice. If you decide that Ben is not the one, let him go. If he is what you want, need, then fight for him. Just don't hold on to him for the wrong reasons, that would disappoint me. That would really, really disappoint me. One last thing, if you do let him go, I guarantee the boys will flock to you. Your problem will be me, beating all those horny bastards off with a stick." He displayed his crooked smile and she relaxed. "Will you be okay? We will chat more later. I promise."

"Wait," she yelled as he started to walk away. "One more thing." He looked back, but she looked away as if deciding whether to continue. "Okay, listen, this trip of Karen's must include Afghanistan. I want to go. I need to go."

"But I thought you were going to help Doctor Aronson with his research?"

Suddenly, Azita looked directly at him, as if her decision was final. "He can always get another assistant, there are students lining up who are dying to work with him. I think one of them tried to poison me last week just to get my spot." She smiled but that did not detract from her resolution.

"But your future as a research doctor. I have talked to some of your professors. They rave about your prospects…your potential as a teacher and researcher."

"But that's it," she yelled. "I don't know what I want. Sometimes, I feel that I am blessed. How could I not pursue a career as a teacher and seeker of knowledge? Is there any higher calling? But then, like you, I remember those moments in the villages, the refugee camps, the front-line medical clinics, the schools for girls. You realize that you do mean everything to these people. They have nothing, nothing but violence and despair, nothing but your caring, and your skills. Such moments are irreplaceable."

"I understand," he said out loud but thought to himself that he should be more careful about what he said. Somehow talking her into a return to her homeland, where war still raged, was the last thing he wanted. Yet, he knew at some level that he could not stand in her way. So, this also was a part of parenting: pure terror. There should have been a warning label that this was part of the deal.

Azita pushed on. "I…I feel like I'm getting lost. When I came here, I worried each night that I would not be good enough. Sometimes I would half dream that they discovered I was a fraud and were sending me back to Kabul. And then, they started praising me, asking me to assist in their research, I was flattered. But…"

"But what, Zita?"

"I think I started losing track of me, who I am or should be. I was being what others expected of me. Does that make sense? What you keep saying, about meaning everything to someone. I cannot shake that very feeling I once had. You are right, it is special." Before he could respond, she went on. "When I came here, to this magical place, I wanted to be a healer. I wanted to go back to my country and heal that broken place. But all that is slipping away. The magic here is strong and, because of that, my culture is slipping away. When was I in a mosque last? I have not been back home since starting medical studies. Look how I dress. I have committed many sins. I…I am not sure who I am anymore…who I want to be. I must go back. I need to feel the warmth of my country, see the mountains again, hear the call to prayer. Most of all, I must do some real healing for a change."

"You know I will die a thousand deaths sending you back into harm's way."

"Hey," she said and smiled at last. "Afghanistan is safer than Chicago and we go there a lot."

He sighed. She had a point. "I will see what I can do. I am not sure what Karen and the others are up to."

She nodded. As he walked away, she called out, "Dad, I love you."

"Hah," he yelled without looking back, "that's what all the girls say."

✂ ✄

Azita walked slowly toward St. Mary's Chapel and the exit back to High Street, lost in her own thoughts. But something intruded at the corner of her awareness. This sense had been there for a while, an irritation, but one that could not quite be identified. With suddenness, she spun around to find a young man standing there.

He stopped, startled. "Sorry," he mumbled.

"Why are you following me? Who are you?"

"I...I..."

"Go away!"

But he moved even closer. "Wait, let me explain."

"I can take care of myself. I survived the Taliban."

"As did I."

That stopped her. She looked more closely at this threat. No, he was not a threat, of that she was sure. She had suffered harassment on the streets, many a time, typically from nativists who resented the influx of Muslims into Britain. But that seldom happened in liberal Oxford. Besides, this young man looked scared to death and the color of his skin suggested something familiar to her.

"You did what, did you say the Taliban? Who are you?"

"I am Ahmad Zubair."

"That means nothing to me." With that she turned to walk away.

"Wait, please. Do you remember Abdul, the man who helped your father escape Kabul?"

At that, she stopped cold. Slowly, she turned back to look at him again. "Yes…of course. Sweet Abdul. He was my father's best friend back then. He would visit the clinic often at the end of the day. And he would sometimes bring his obnoxious son, a boy I could not stand. But that boy was fat, an irritating boy who bothered me no end. That could not be you."

"Guilty. I am the obnoxious, irritating boy he would bring to your father's clinic. And yes, I was fat then." With that he held his arms wide and said, "Ta, da."

"Oh my God," she exclaimed. "I do remember you. I would never have recognized you. Yes, you were this pudgy, smelly boy who would follow me around with this silly look on his face. You were always offering me sweets which you would eat yourself when I turned them down."

"So silly of me, I now shudder at the memories. That was the face of desperate love and, alas, unbridled gluttony." He laughed nervously as he said that.

Azita could not take her eyes off him. "I will say one thing. You confirmed every nasty thought I had about boys back then."

"Yes, true enough, I was one of those smelly, obnoxious things. And you were very free with your opinions back then, at least with what you thought of me. Most Afghan girls were retiring, polite. You, however, never held back. Maybe that is why I had a crush on you."

"You did?"

"Why do you think I was so irritating? I was trying to get you to notice me."

"Not such a great strategy." Now she smiled.

"You should be kinder, like a good Muslim girl." And he smiled back. It melted her even more. "Hell, I was a kid, only a year or two older than you. I had just hit puberty."

She looked at him hard now. He was lean and muscular, nothing like she recalled. His longish, curly brown hair fell over his ears and down the back of his neck. His face had well cut features that framed a set of kind eyes. His voice was deep. It was not the same one she recalled, which she remembered as shrill and annoying. Beyond being generally irritating, the sounds he usually made were on the precipice of breaking as the boy teetered on the cusp of manhood. "Yes, I have seen you, I think. I cannot recall where or when, but you do look familiar. I think I considered registering you as a threat that women should watch out for. By the way, have you been stalking me?"

"No, of course not…well, maybe, just a little." Now he was uncertain, not knowing what to say next. "Actually, I had this whole speech I had prepared for you but now I cannot think of a single word. Listen, in truth I have searched for you several times, and tried to get up the courage to talk to you. I knew you were here in Oxford, my father kept track of your family, told me about your parents and brother. I am so sorry."

"And Abdul?" she asked and began to relax slightly.

"He is fine. We also left Afghanistan when you fled north. My father knew the Taliban would eventually blame him for helping Pamir escape their clutches."

"Oh, I never thought about that. I am so selfish."

"No, please don't! We had to get out no matter what. Helping your family just pushed our timetable along. My father hated the regime. He was sabotaging them whenever and wherever he could. It could not go on forever, he would have been caught soon enough. We eventually made it back to Saudi Arabia and then to Qatar, Abdul had made his first fortune there as a young man. He is now quite rich and happy, though mother has passed."

"Sorry, I did not know her." Suddenly, Azita felt a rush of emotion she could not quite place. She drew near and threw her arms around him as he backed up slightly. "Sorry, again. Too forward for a nice Muslim girl, forgive me."

"No, thank you, perhaps I still have that crush." He was not sure how to finish that thought. "Anyway, I looked you up some time ago when father told me you were also at Oxford. But I am a coward. I think my self-image is still that of a pudgy boy that no girl could like."

"But now you are now not so awfully irritating. In fact, you are…"

"Sexy?" He smiled, just like Chris would, and she felt that frisson of unidentifiable emotion again.

"Different." She smiled back.

"At some point I decided that going through life on a diet of sweets was not in my best interests. When we got to Riyadh, I got into football, or soccer if you prefer, and even some cricket. I like athletics. But I am more than an athlete. I graduated from the London School of Economics and am now doing advanced studies here. So, I know I am well rounded and…"

Azita laughed. "So full of yourself. I think you should just give me your vita."

He looked down at the ground. "Sorry, I am very nervous I guess."

"Please," she said and reached out once again to touch his arm. This time, he did not pull back. "Please tell me why you wanted to connect again. I will be nice, I promise."

It took him a moment to resume. "Hard to say, really. Even if you were such a terrible Muslim girl back then, I liked that, your spirit. Part of it was wanting to tell you directly how deeply I was touched by the loss of your parents, and brother. I did not know Madeena or Majeeb, but Pamir was a saint. I knew how much you adored him. I had this fantasy when I heard what had

happened that I could look you up and somehow comfort you…"
He wanted to say more about his feelings, but his courage failed.

"Thank you, Ahmad. That is sweet, it means so much to me."

"When I finally got around to seeking you out, I was stunned."

"What? Why?"

"You are so different, so beautiful. I…but then I kept seeing you with this boy. I was too late."

"Too late for what?" She asked and then regretted the silly question. "Never mind."

"Every once in a while, I would check back. Then, today, I saw you with him at that restaurant, it was just by accident. Really! You looked so unhappy. My heart sank for you but beat faster for me. This time I followed, trying to get up the courage to say hello. I was walking toward you when that man approached, your new father I figured out. I had heard about the adoption, my father kept track of your family as well. I hate to admit it, but I hung around close by. I heard much of it though I wanted to ask you to talk louder." He tried a small chuckle.

"Sad story, no?" She did not smile.

"Not sad, familiar. I have been where you are, am where you are. I mean, not so much with your fiancé, I have no one. But not knowing where I should be. Sometimes, I feel like I am trapped between two worlds. Where do I belong? I remember the first time I used alcohol, here in England. I threw up after one drink, not from too much poison but from guilt."

"And what happened the first time you seduced a girl?" She asked without expression.

He paused, sensing she was leading him into sensitive territory. "Well, I had nightmares after."

"I think not," she broke into a smile. "I suspect the girl had the nightmares."

"Hah," Ahmad laughed, "that is why I love you, you always had that wicked tongue." He realized he had used the word love. Had she heard it? To his relief, her expression did not change.

"Ahmad, that was mean of me. I guess I am not ready to go there…yet. Humor is a great defense. I learned it from Papa, and especially from Chris. His humor is a bit wicked, but perhaps so am I." She wondered for a moment what he made of her last words. They looked at one another, not sure what to say next. Azita broke the silence. "You really understand, don't you?"

"Being caught between worlds, not really knowing where you belong or what you are meant to do? Yes, I understand that. Where have I been raised? In Afghanistan, Qatar, and England. My father is secular, my mother was pious, my siblings are all over the place. The thing is that I am a man of reason. I gravitate toward rational arguments and evidence. Still, it is as if something primitive inside keeps pulling me back toward some past understanding of life. I can't quite embrace the Western world, not fully. I don't know if the girls I have dated had nightmares or not, but they have all been Western. I kept thinking, go after the Western girls, they are easier to seduce. Why put up with all that old-world garbage? But with them, something was missing. I cannot connect with them, not in the way I want. Okay, I am beginning to ramble now. I am sorry. Perhaps I should let you go."

"Don't you dare," she said. The words slipped out of her. She did not intend them to be so strong. Again, they looked at one another uncertainly. "Ahmad, if you heard my conversation with my Dad, you know I want to visit home this summer. Like I think you were suggesting, I need to connect again, get back to my roots I suppose. I am not even sure why. It is as if I don't want to slide into things without thinking about them. Back when you knew me, it was all so simple. I would become like my Papa, despite the Taliban. I would spend my life doing good works. He never seemed to have any doubts, never second guessed anything, at least in front of me. He came to study here and returned to Afghanistan without further thought. Too late, I wished I had asked him more about that decision, if he had doubts. In any case, I am getting close to the time when I will need to decide on where to intern and what to focus on for my residency. I am blessed with options, which is also a curse. Those decisions determine the arc of your professional life. Some things I can discuss with Amar, my new mother, and Chris, but there are things they cannot possibly know."

"Azita," the boy said softly. "We both escaped hell on earth. We should be ecstatic. But it is never that easy, is it? There are things inside, things that are imprinted deep inside. It doesn't make sense. I want to ask you something."

"Of course, anything." Again, she kicked herself internally for not being more guarded.

"I am wondering. Well, I have things inside… I mean maybe we…" Finally, he took control of his churning emotions. "Azita, let me tell you what I think. You should go back home, to Afghanistan, and think things through. You should figure out how you feel about this boy, Ben. Then, if you want, call me. I will wait. Even of it is only to talk, to sort things out, call me." He found a piece of paper and wrote out his cell number.

"Ahmad, I can't explain this but your voice… you are so comforting. I never…" She stopped herself. She felt like a schoolgirl, as lost as he was. Why couldn't she even express herself?

"One question now. Am I too late?" He looked pathetic.

"Too late?" But she knew what he meant.

"Did I find you too late?"

Azita looked stricken. "I don't know."

Ahmad leaned closer and kissed her on the cheek. "Whenever you are ready, if you are ever ready." With that he turned and walked in the other direction.

He was a distance away when she let out a small cry. "No, no! You are not too late." He seemed to turn slightly but kept walking. She could not be certain he had heard her words nor certain that she wanted him to have heard.

CHAPTER 3

THE HAIRY HARE

Chris walked toward the small office he kept in Oxford for what had come to be known as the International Services Organization or ISO, this program he developed almost by accident as he finished up his Oxford studies many years ago. It started as a concept that he had nurtured in one of his academic papers. Too many service agencies focused on specific issues. He could never shake the image of several silos standing next to one another yet never touching. Each silo contained a different grain. While each silo's contents were tasty and nutritious, what people really needed was a medley of grains, the combination of which exceeded the benefits that each grain could provide on its own.

When his Oxford professors acknowledged the merits of his arguments but raised numerous doubts about their feasibility, he was spurred to action. They were so smug in a hubris supported by the isolation of the ivory tower, sitting comfortably in their insulated world. He first took some time to travel to the hot spots in the world at that time, observing and thinking. Satisfied he was on to something he swung into action. A few other academics shared his perspective, particularly two researchers at the University of Wisconsin, though none had his depth of knowledge and insight. He would show that it could be done.

His trust fund and the business contacts he had cultivated from his father's world gave him the means to pursue his vision. He had focused on international affairs in his studies, so he managed to speak with potential funders with authority.

The people he recruited became good at what they did. The early experiences eased his initial doubts about viability. The needs of vulnerable families were multidimensional, particularly in areas bereft of any safety net. They often needed several kinds of assistance simultaneously that were situationally relevant and holistically delivered. He began visiting sites in various international hot spots, diagnosing what was wrong with the current efforts, and then working with existing aid systems to put together comprehensive plans. Soon, he was forging more systemic alliances across systems and raising money to grease these relationships. He did not have to create a new wheel, merely get the existing wheels moving in the right direction. His staff grew with time as did the reach of his ambitions and his efforts.

All these years later, he was proud of his institutional offspring. Still, it was not something that would maintain his interest forever. Now, Karen Fisher, who grew from a questionable and impulsive hire to be his right hand, was the CEO who ran the overall operations. She did not possess his smoothness and charm. In fact, she retained just a bit of her working-class rough edge. She was, however, considerably more organized and focused than he would ever be. She was perfect for an organization moving toward maturity. In the meantime, Chris had periodically taught courses at Oxford but that had evolved into a part-time faculty member role. He had proved a popular instructor: intelligent, humorous, with a seemingly unlimited supply of relevant vignettes. In addition, he cranked out several books on various topics of interest to him, and writing proved a bit of an addiction after a while. Despite a frantic schedule, he remained involved as a consultant and money raiser for his programmatic offspring while devoting more time to pursue long-deferred literary interests.

Through his uber-wealthy father, he had many business contacts on both sides of the Atlantic and was an accomplished schmoozer. Further, his touch with Foundations was legendary, particularly when the project officers were female. Males, the business-types, were tougher but the reputation of his famous father helped in that testosterone-dominated world, some believing that helping the son might bring favor with the patriarch while others concluded that helping the son would irritate a despised business foe. In any case, he was damn good at it. As Karen often joked, he could persuade a starving man to part with half of his last meal, a drunk to share his last drink, a prostitute to give away the goodies for free.

Today, he would be meeting with Karen, who was coupled with her domestic partner and Azita's older sister, Deena. He had heard a rumor that Kay, his sister, might come down from

London where she worked part time with the National Health Service and increasingly helped Karen oversee the medical services which that IPO provided. She also taught a course at the London School of Economics on comparative healthcare systems, which gave her a platform to rant about the failings of America's healthcare system. She had always exhausted Chris with her boundless energy.

Chris was so glad that he had reconnected with his twin Kay after years where their relationship had struggled. She really was his complement, as if God had perfected the whole from their separate parts. When she married medical officer James Whitehead of her majesty's military services, Chris had had his doubts. He could not imagine any man getting her to settle down. However, they seemed happy or at least not unhappy. Chris merely dismissed his initial doubts to an inherent inability to understand human relationships. With her husband's imminent departure from his army medical career, they had options to consider. His retirement was a move that would open new possibilities for them, though they had yet to decide on their future. Chris could never shake the sense that, despite obvious differences, his twin sibling was much like himself. She had a short attention span and would keep seeking the perfect niche in life, if such a thing existed.

One or two other staff members were likely to be there, though he was not yet sure which ones. They would have come down from the main offices in London, the size of which had grown over the years. In recent months, he would look around in wonder at the faces he did not recognize. What had started out as a challenge to prove his professors wrong was now an internationally recognized service organization. He smiled at a private recollection. There was a story he ran across once about the founder of Federal Express who had gotten a low grade on a paper that proposed the concept of what became a multi-billion-dollar operation. He was told by his business-school professor that his concept lacked feasibility. That drove him to prove them wrong and he did. In any case, the topic today would be an upcoming trip to the Middle East. It was time to take stock in several programs, particularly one close to Chris's heart: Afghanistan. It had been there that he had met Azita and Deena and, of course, his wife Amar. That was where he had discovered his life.

He always smiled at the thought of those early days as things came to a head with the Taliban and he frantically flew into the Panjshir valley to set things right. He would drag Kay out of harm's way. Kay had bridled at the thought that her twin brother was being protective of her, as if she were a child. After all, she was fourteen minutes older than he was.

Kay had her choice of medical careers. She had chosen a position where, night after night, she would face the detritus of society as they poured through the doors of Chicago's biggest public hospital, victims of a broken society's carnage. He certainly knew why she had defied their Father, that bastard had raped her repeatedly when she was a young teenager. He even knew why Kay eventually fled the States to work for Chris's operation in Pakistan. Then, she had defied him and joined Amar in the Panjshir Valley. Who was Chris to tell her what to do? After all, he had fled to England, ostensibly for a Rhodes scholarship, but then had never returned. She well knew the reason for his personal exile: he was running away from his tyrant of a Father and a family falling apart. She eventually would do the same, by running away to a place even further away. The home of the Northern Alliance was just about as far away as anyone could run.

Chris came out of his daydream, retrieving his ringing phone. Glancing at the screen, he saw it was Amar, calling him back. He seldom got to her on his first call when she was on duty at the hospital. Surgery was a morning routine, but her afternoons were also very busy.

"Hi, glad you called back."

"No problem, I have saved enough lives today already. Did you know we have a quota on that, how many lives we can save in a day? In any case, you are my favorite husband today but, then again, the day is yet young." Over time, she had fallen seamlessly into his incessant dry wit and loving banter.

"Yeah, that is what all the girls say, you have no idea how burdensome it is to be a sex object." Then Chris thought about a fact that always concerned him. Men must come on to his wife all the time, she was a beauty. Funny, it used to be the women in his life worrying about his roving eye. Now, the roles were reversed though women were still attracted to him. He was not blind.

Amar let out an involuntary chuckle. "The burdens of being a sex object…you would not have a clue, of that I am sure. What's on your mind, stud?"

"Here's the thing. I had a serious chat with our oldest and dearest."

"Something wrong?" There was concern in her voice.

"Well, yes, and it is something that needs a woman's touch, not that I don't have a well- developed feminine side."

"Go on while I search for a barf bag," she joked but her voice betrayed her concern.

"There is a semi-serious and a serious issue." Chris remained on point. "Which do you want first?"

"Start with the less serious."

"She is having problems with Ben," he said simply.

"Only a man would not consider that serious…developed feminine side my ass. What's the problem?"

"It is something we have wondered about before. She thinks he is having trouble with his parents, they apparently have never come around on this love affair. Remember when we thought they would set a date after she got her last degree? Well, I suspect the parents had first waited things out, assuming it would never last. I am sure they applied soft pressure on him, trying to convince him that this Muslim-Jewish partnership could never work without confronting him directly. You know kids, saying no might drive them to do the opposite. I give the boy credit, he hung in there, but I suspect they are upping the pressure and he is buckling. Of course, he might just be taking time to finally find his balls. At least, that is how I see it."

"Quite astute for a guy, but then you do have that feminine side." Her sarcasm was obvious. "Yes, it is time for a mother-daughter talk. I have never had *the* talk with her."

"Sex."

"No silly, about the fact that all men are total jerks and complete idiots."

"I thought all women knew that instinctively, it was something they inherited through their mothers. Anyways, now to the bigger one: I think she is going through a 'meaning of life' crisis."

"We all do that from time to time, I question my marriage choice all the time." She sounded light, concluding that his bigger issue was not that big.

"Yeah, well, joke if you will but here is the thing: she wants to go with Karen and the group on the Mideast tour, and especially back to her home. She said she needs to reconnect with her culture, her roots I guess."

"Shit," he heard over the phone. She seldom used even the most innocent of foul language, and this caught his attention. "I don't want her going without me, us, me."

"Well, she is technically an adult. We can't stop her, and she would be helpful to the team. I could tell Karen to simply refuse to take her, but she would be furious with me. I mean Zita would be furious. Though Karen might also be pissed that I was interfering." Chris had used his pet name for his adopted daughter. "The problem is that Karen would be delighted to have her along, as would Deena."

There was a momentary silence as Amar processed the choices. "We cannot forbid her to go."

"Damn," Chris clearly was exasperated. "I don't think I can go with her. Something came up this morning that will take me back to the States. On the other hand, I agree. I don't think we can say no if she is serious."

"At the same time," Chris could hear anguish in his wife's voice, "I don't care if she is the next Albert Schweitzer and wants to save the world, that place is still dangerous. The war there has been going on forever."

"Just since 2001, the current American one that is, and before that the civil war and before that the Soviets. Not so long, really. Europe once had a one-hundred-year war, which in truth went on longer than that. Of course, we don't know if this one will ever end. Maybe when America runs out of money."

"Don't." She obviously was concerned and beyond his attempts at levity. "Okay, this is all boy trouble. That is all it is. I can handle this. By the way, what commitments back in the States? I don't recall you mentioning anything."

Chris didn't want to go there, he should not have mentioned it. "Not now, later."

"Okay, later for sure. Right now, I am getting a medical page. One last thing, if she goes, I am going with her."

She was gone. On the one hand, he was glad not to have to get into the issues Azita raised that morning about her deeper conflicts over cultural identification. On the other hand, he wanted to tell her that this was more than Azita's feelings for Ben. His daughter felt torn in two fundamentally opposed directions. Amar should know that from her own background. Sometimes she had confessed missing India, the beautiful but conflicted area of Kashmir, over which India and Pakistan contested for control. Then it hit him: both his daughter and wife might be going into harm's way. Damn, everything had been so good.

Chris walked on. He was debating whether to call her back when he noticed Karen and Deena standing outside his local ISO office. Obviously, they were waiting for him. With them were Carlotta, a long-time staff member who also had doctorate in nursing, and a young man that Chris did not recognize. After perfunctory greetings, Karen announced: "To the Hairy Hare, your favorite watering hole. Ricky and Kay are waiting for us there."

"Ricky? I had heard rumors that he would make it but thought my luck might hold out."

"He called to say he desperately needed to once again make your life a living misery, those were his exact words I believe," Karen chirped. "Came in from Brussels this morning on his way back home. He could not miss out on our torture session of you. Very kind of him, no?"

A few minutes later they entered the darkened interior with its faux 16th-century English pub ambiance. Chris suddenly exclaimed excitedly: "Oh look, Karen, the barmaid still has it. Her rack looks just great after all these years. Good thing you never left me for a job here, you just wouldn't make the grade with this competition."

"Bite me, you idiot, that is the original barmaid's daughter. Hell, she might not even be old enough to work here and she is certainly too smart to give you the time of day. You are way too long in the tooth my friend. By the way, her mother now owns the place."

"Really, why didn't I notice that?" Chris squinted to get a closer look. "Hell, the tips here must be great if her mom could buy this place."

"They are if you have a great rack, like the one I have. Besides, she probably robbed the former owners blind."

"Deena," Chris yelled. "You would know. How good is Karen's rack?"

"You are terrible." Karen's domestic partner mumbled, hitting him lightly on the arm, though with a smile. Unlike her sister Azita, it had taken Deena a longer time to become accustomed to Chris's irreverence. He often wondered how the attraction between Karen and Deena had begun. On the surface, they were so different. Then again, Azita's sister was a real looker, a fantasy or two had nibbled at his own conscience at first before being pushed away. He often laughed at the men who almost tripped over their own feet to get a better look at this dark-haired beauty. Then he realized that he would have been one of those foolish men were she not a part of his life.

"No, Deena. Like I taught you. Like this." With that, Karen gave Chris a good whack.

"Ok, I give," he said, wincing with some real pain. Now the answer about how these two opposites connected was clear. They were co-conspirators in a plot to inflict great pain on him.

They joined a table where Ricky was already was seated with Kay, Chris's sister. He hugged Ricky, whom he had not seen in a while, and exchanged warm greetings with his sister. Odd, Chris thought, he and his twin sister seldom hugged despite their growing affection for one another, a connection that had fallen on hard times for a while.

"Well," Ricky intoned. "I see nothing has changed, Karen is yet beating the shit out of you. I wasn't sure if I would need to call the EMTs or the local constabulary. It was worth the effort to bust my ass getting here."

"And to think," Chris intoned without expression, "when she came to me begging for a job, she was hanging around street corners, plying the most ancient of all trades."

"Careful, Chris," said Deena. "You will have to deal with the two of us now, maybe four with Ricky and your sister. And never forget that now I am well trained by Karen."

"Okay, I surrender. I am an idiot but not a total idiot." He knew a witty comeback was coming his way, so he preempted it by continuing. "So, Ricky, been doing the Lord's work around the world. Nice of you to stop by on your way back to the windy city."

Ricky smiled with the confidence of someone who had come far from a ghetto on the west side of Chicago. "If you mean your sister Kat's work, yes. I have been visiting the money makers in Asia and Europe to firm up the far-flung enterprises of the Crawford Empire. You can thank me personally when your share prices increase even further. Also raised a little money for your international efforts; my heart is still with this program."

Karen reached over and grabbed his hand. "And we thank you, you are the best of all the men associated with the Crawford clan."

Ricky smiled. "You always were the discerning one in this crowd. I will say one thing, for a black kid from the ghetto I have gone far in this world. While in Asia, I visited this coastal city that was little more than a tiny fishing village in the late 1970s. The government selected it for development and now it is an ultra-modern metropolis of over 12 million. Unbelievable accomplishment and the investment opportunities there are amazing. What the Chinese are doing with renewable energy sources...but we are not here to hear my adventures as a contemporary Marco Polo."

Chris decided to follow up with Ricky later regarding what he was seeing. Rather, he looked at his sister. "Say Kay, what will you and your far better half be doing once Jamie is no longer healing her majesty's finest?"

"We will take some time to look at our options, I have a teaching commitment this fall. But, then, maybe we might look overseas again. We still feel the pull to be where the need is greatest. Helping Karen run the medical program has its rewards, but I miss getting my hands bloody."

"Oh, I do know of this international organization that used to do good work. However, I hear that they have fallen on bad times, poor leadership." Chris deadpanned as Deena threw a pretzel at him. "Or you can attend to me after the daily beatings. *Et tu*, Deena?"

"The young woman smiled. "I have learned from the best."

Karen took over the initiative. "Before we get serious, though nothing is more serious than torturing this poor excuse of a man." She nodded toward Chris. "Let me introduce Atle Bergstrom. Not all of you know him since this is his first trip to Oxford. For some reason, he wanted to meet the great founder of our enterprise. Despite this deplorable lack of judgment, he has been a great addition to the staff. He has done some work with UNICEF and Oxfam, but he likes us the best. Go figure. Anyways, he is a computer whizz and hales from one of those Scandinavian countries. I forget which one, they are all pretty much the same."

Atle laughed. "Don't say that when you have a Swede and a Norwegian in the same room. Professor Crawford, you will be happy to know that I read a paper of yours when I was an undergraduate, the one on better organizational strategies for delivering humanitarian services. That is probably why I am here."

"If I had known that," Karen smiled, "I never would have hired you."

"Atle, I can see you are a man of considerable acumen and an exemplary judge of people and ideas. Welcome aboard and call me anytime if Karen gives you trouble."

"Barf bag, barf bag," Karen called out, making the universal hand gesture suggesting she was throwing up her lunch.

Chris missed this banter. The academy was too stuffy, too formal. Academics tended to take things, and themselves, way too seriously. People who worked directly with the underside of society needed a release through dark and unforgiving humor. "Okay," he said. "let's do a little bit of work before we get too drunk or I am stoned to death by some angry females."

Karen started: "Nothing terribly unusual. On our proposed tour, we are mostly going to our sites in Pakistan, Jordan, Gaza, and Afghanistan, then over to the Horn of Africa. We will do the usual site reviews, but just in the more problematic sites. Deena will evaluate our educational programs. Carlotta will assess the service needs. Jamie, as I think all of you know by now is mustering out of her majesty's service, but not in time to join us, so your dear sister here will evaluate the medical services if he is unavailable. More likely, he will stay with the children. One big issue is ISIS and how we might respond to the damage they are doing. Osama is gone only to be replaced by Abu Bakr al-Baghdadi. There is an endless supply of assholes ready to make mischief, so we will give Syria a hard look. Of course, we will look at opportunities to insert medical teams into some new sites there, the medical teams remain the heart of what we do. Perhaps we can lend a hand if we can get some of our top people to go."

"We are still talking about Jamie, right, for the sites near the fighting? Not…" Chris did not finish but looked at Kay, his sister.

Karen smiled at Chris and said: "Still the protector, I see. You can relax. If we nail Jamie to help with the overseas start-ups, your sister here will stay behind to care for the kids. She thinks they are still a bit young to be left behind."

"Wait," Chris needed to regroup. "I am not protecting my sister. Hey, she is a big girl, she can take care of the young ones all by herself. I'm not worried. After all, she raised me all those years."

"Girl?" This came from Carlotta. "Is that what I heard?"

"*Oy vey*, for such a highly educated guy, I really am a dumb shit. Most people don't know this but, until I was twenty-seven, I thought my legal name was dumbass."

Ricky just smiled. "This makes the trip worth it, to watch the master screw-up try to wiggle his way out of all the trouble he gets in with his big mouth."

"This from the man that would yet be a gang-banger in Chicago had I not discovered him during his misspent youth."

"Karen, you finished with the barf bag yet." Ricky smiled. "I need it next."

Chris suddenly turned serious, the others noticed and paused to see where he might go next. "Listen, here is an unexpected twist you might have to deal with. Azita wants to go, I think."

Deena let out a muffled shout: "Really? How brilliant!" She was obviously ecstatic. The sisters had grown close but had trouble finding time to be together. Then it struck her that Chris might not share her excitement.

"Listen, I am not totally clear regarding what is going on. There may be boy problems, you did not hear that from me, or she may be undergoing a more existential turmoil."

"What the hell do you mean by that?" Kay asked.

Chris knew enough not to go into detail about her love issues with Ben. Still, he had to say something. "She may be sorting out her identity and what she wants to do in life…the big questions. Is she Eastern or Western, a researcher or a practitioner at heart? She is such a prodigy that her professors are pushing her along to a medical research career. On one level, she knows that few are gifted enough to reach for that kind of career. On the other hand, she wants so much to follow in her father's footsteps. That is just so important to her. For those who have never met him, he was quite a man, makes me feel like a slug."

Karen was poised with a comeback but held her tongue. They had some unwritten rules about when to be frivolous and when to get serious. Rather, Deena spoke up. "I know what she is going through. She and I don't need to talk about this to understand one another. I hope she goes, I want to spend time with her."

Very softly and seriously, Chris encouraged her. "Deena, tell us whatever you can about her cultural struggle. You would know best."

"Well, it is not such a dark secret." The young beauty looked distressed for a moment. "You know, you come here to this land and it seems like a dream. One day you are surrounded by conflict, death, poverty, sickness, and oppression. The next you are walking amongst those who have plenty and go about their lives without fear. For a woman, the change is sudden and shocking, you cannot prepare for it. One day, you were a prisoner of your culture and even your clothes. Everything is dictated to you and for you, first by the males in your family and then by a husband and others in his family. Then, without preparation, you are told you are free with a blink of an eye. All the old gender rules are suspended. Can you imagine that, how liberating that is, and how terrifying?" She looked around the table. "I think not. We are all like fish in the water. We are not aware of the water until we are taken out. But then, we either adjust or desperately want to go back, even if that means remaining in a small world that the fish bowl represents. If you are from the outside, it is impossible to see what we might miss about Afghanistan. But when you have spent so many years in such a bowl…"

Carlotta seemed puzzled. "I know my question will sound insensitive but what can you possibly miss about Afghanistan?"

"No," the young beauty replied, "it is not an insensitive question at all, it makes total sense. In truth, it is a tortured land. Most of what I miss are small things, the warmth of the dry breezes, the rugged mountains, the loyalty and bravery of many of our people. Some things are very small indeed. I loved walking through the markets. You could smell the charcoal that was used to prepare the ears of corn or brew the teas. You could breathe in the various sweets being prepared and nuts being roasted. I have never forgotten those smells, or the everyday chatter of those about me. Here, you have so much. So, nothing means anything. There, finding something a little different in the marketplace can bring great pleasure. Most of all, you really learn how to love… your family and friends. It is special." Then she stopped.

"I think I get it." Ricky filled in the slight pause. "I have gone back to my old Chicago neighborhood."

"Voluntarily?" Chris was incredulous.

"See, that is Deena's point." Ricky enthused. "You were never a part of that fish bowl. No matter what, your early life stays with you. Sometimes, even the bad stuff takes on a familiar, even a seductive feel. When I return, I listen to the, what shall I say, patois of the streets. The accents are still Delta, the laughs, the topics being bantered on the building stoops. Even the lengths to which kids go to maintain their creds. There is a singular rhythm to it all. It is yet enticing, for a few hours that is. Then I thank the Gods for permitting me an escape."

Chris looked at Ricky as if he'd lost his mind. "I dare you to find one banger from your old hood who knows what the word patois means, never mind use it in a sentence. In fact, try finding a banger who can construct a sentence."

"Point taken, my racist friend, though some of those brothers from the hood were a lot smarter than you would imagine. They never got the breaks I did." Ricky smiled and nodded toward Chris. "But even you must have feelings about your roots that tug at you. You know, the caviar for breakfast, the weekends at Vail, the gold-plated crapper. You know, I am still pissed, no pun intended, that you never let me use the gold platted crapper, you made me use the carved ivory one reserved for unwelcome guests."

"Hilarious, my former friend." Chris put on his offended look. "If you fail as a robber baron, maybe a gig as a stand-up comedian. Besides, you never paid us back for all the silverware you purloined when you visited."

"That was Jules, not me," Ricky protested.

Chris had a faraway look. "Sure, I remember the good old days. Early on, we would get our report cards. Of course, Kay's was always perfect. I found school, even the high priced and selective one we attended, easy but, as you might guess, I floated a bit. Okay, I downright coasted. Too many distractions, particularly sports which, I might add, helped greatly to get

me into Princeton when my grades showed a certain lack of...
diligence."

"You mean you were not perfect." Karen feigned surprise. "I
am shocked, shocked."

"Carlotta," Chris said with his familiar tone of sarcasm, "you
must be ready to take over control of this organization. It is clear
poor Karen is long past her prime. I don't know what she will do
after I fire her. She has no shot at a barmaid job here any longer."

Carlotta laughed gently, then spoke with her sweet,
Mediterranean lilt. Chris found her attractive though she was
not a classic beauty. Her nose was a bit large but black hair
framed a pleasing face dominated by expressive eyes. "No one
can replace Karen. She is the only one willing to put up with you.
And besides, you are no longer in charge."

"Perhaps, Carlotta, but I have always been impressed that
you could ignore me with such style and, even better, that you
can tell me off in so many tongues. Just how many languages can
you speak?" Chris was enjoying himself.

Carlotta ignored him. "Still, it is true about what you say. I
miss things about the Costa Del Sol every day, like the sun. But
that is the obvious thing. The English seem to think that food is
for consumption. How ordinary. It is for socializing, connecting.
You drink beer. We can spend hours over a good meal, and wine,
of course. It is a bonding experience. I miss that, among other

things. But I sense you were about to tell us more about your misspent youth." Carlotta looked directly at Chris.

"Oh, nothing really." But everyone kept looking at him. "Okay, okay, I would bring my school grades to my mother who would praise me and overlook the fact that Kay beat me one more time. Eventually, mom would make me show it to my father. I can still feel those moments…my stomach still churns. He would look at the card, and then at me. For an eternity, he would not say anything. What I recalled was the first time I disappointed him. Maybe it was the second grade. I forget what distracted me then, it was too early for my fascination with the fairer sex. But I had a couple of B's and a written comment that I was not living up to my potential. How the hell would they know my potential in the fucking second grade? I suspect what really pissed off Father was that Kay was doing better. Females were never supposed to outdo males in his perfect, hierarchical world." He paused, taking a long drink of his Guinness and regretting his language. "I never saw his hand until it struck. I flew across the room. I think it was more shock than pain, though I was bleeding from the nose. Why is it always my nose? I lay there trying not to whimper. I would not give him that satisfaction. He walked over and kicked me in the chest, broke a rib."

"Someone surely did something?" Karen seemed genuinely touched.

Chris laughed. "Right, make a complaint against one of the most powerful men in America. Friendly medical help was brought in, they do house calls if you are wealthy enough. It was always the same. I had 'fallen' down the stairs. I fell down a lot of stairs. For some reason these mandated reporters never said a damn thing about the obvious abuse. The pain was nothing. It was him standing there, sneering at me. 'You are such a disappointment,' he would say. 'You have been given much and I just know you will throw it away'. Then he would kick me one more time and walk away. It was the way he dismissed me that got to me."

Ricky seemed very taken. He had never heard this before. With all these two had been through together, Chris had never shared this part of his life. "But you must have responded to him. I mean…when we connected, you were rather an academic star. At least I thought you were. You kind of sucked at basketball but you were a winner in the classroom." He turned to Kay. "I can see Mr. Tough guy here holding this in but why didn't you ever mention this to me or Jules?"

Kay never took her eyes off her brother. "I knew but didn't know. Chris, you never said a word to me. I…never…figured it out. Yes, the bruising, a broken bone on occasion. You kept saying they were sports accidents. I just remember thinking that those street games were rougher than I thought. But somewhere

I knew. We were broken kids, and we kept secrets, even from one another. Damn, how pathetic."

Chris laughed grimly. "Ricky, I may have looked like an academic star to you, but never to the patriarch; Kay always did better." Then, he looked directly at his sister. "In truth, I didn't want to bother you with my troubles. Maybe I was reluctant to admit that I could not stand up to him. I was not man enough. That was embarrassing."

Kay exploded, half rising out of her chair. "For Christ's sake, you were a fucking boy at the time." She then realized people in the area were looking in their direction. She controlled herself.

Chris rescued her. "We are a pair, aren't we? We did keep our secrets, we were a family of secrets, and it almost destroyed us, almost." His voice became a whisper. "Perhaps Father did help me. Eventually I started to excel but I suspect the beatings had little to do with it. I wanted to do well so that one day I could tell him to fuck off. He had me becoming part of his twisted world and I fantasized about telling him to stuff it. That is what got me interested in the Rhodes scholarship. It was a way out, not the free ride at a top university but the excuse to flee the country."

"Wait," Karen asked. "Did you imply that there were many of these so-called encouragements from your father? This went on for a long time?"

"Oh yeah, early on, I think I would make sure I did not ace all my courses. I would not give him the satisfaction of winning.

I recall just not answering the last few questions on an exam, even when I easily could. And guess what? I had many more so-called accidents on the stairs, or the playgrounds. There is this T-shirt that says, '*The beatings will continue until morale improves*', and shows a pirate ship with the poor crew been abused by the captain. That one always resonated with me, I think I bought a dozen of them. He treated Chuck, the eldest, differently. I think he knew that Chuck was not as talented, that bullying him would never work. I gave father a target to release his rage, which probably kept Chuck safe. At least, I had hoped to keep Chuck safe. But no, he would torture Chuck in a different way, until the poor boy killed himself to escape. Funny, I still refer to him as a boy though he was the eldest. He was so sweet." Chris brushed at his eye, there had been a tear he hoped no one saw. Chris looked around, suddenly realizing how open he had become. "Well, no need to belabor this. At some point, I realized that I really liked school. I loved learning, became a voracious reader. Books were an escape for sure, but I also wanted to absorb all around me. Kay was the quantitative one, the math and science whizz. I was the eclectic sponge. What poor Father did not realize was that my academic renaissance doomed his hopes of turning me into him, a little Hitler. The more I learned about the world, the more I rejected his world view."

"Any good memories from those days?" It was Ricky.

"Yeah, as I have said before, many times, I loved your family. You didn't have money. You had something infinitely better… love. I would have traded with you on a dime."

"And I would have taken that trade on a dime." Ricky said too quickly.

"No, you wouldn't," Chris whispered.

"No,' Ricky murmured, "I suspect not."

"And maybe my nights with you, Kay, when we were young," Chris continued. "As we started to learn about the world beyond what Father drilled into us, we would hide at night, sometimes under the covers, and talk about what the patriarch was shoving down our throats. Remember, we would whisper though there was no chance of anyone hearing. It felt like we were disobeying God. I loved those moments of sharing. I can yet recall us reading passages from *Atlas Shrugged* and laughing at Ayn Rand's view of the world, though we never would admit that when Father quizzed us on that damn book." There was a silence before Chris seemed to shift his attention. "Back to the topic at hand. Azita and your trip. Karen, what do you think?"

There was a long pause before Karen spoke up. The shift was too abrupt, but she recovered quickly enough. "We can always use her, right now we are light on senior medical folk. She is better than most of the doctors we have. After all, she has been doing medical procedures since she was what? Ten years old? And she can communicate in that part of the world, what a plus.

You do realize, though, that Amar might want to go if Azita goes. She has a strong mother instinct. And you would be a single dad for a while."

Chris expelled a deep sigh. "I thought of that and yes, she will go if you take my daughter. Afghanistan is still at war. No one thinks about it anymore since it is yesterday's news, but it goes on and on as we know. It will be the longest war in America's history, if you don't count Korea, which never officially ended after they quit shooting at one another. I know she wants to go back, just been looking for an excuse. Regular medicine does not do it for her."

Karen beamed, looking directly at Kay. "Now, if we can just get Kay, we will be in business."

"You got me, without question," she said without hesitation. "I have plenty of vacation time accumulated. Besides, I can take this as an opportunity to figure out our future." She smiled. "That's right, we all know who makes the big decisions in every married couple. I am thinking about getting out of the NHS entirely, just do ISO work and teach."

"Whoa," Chris said. He did not like where this is going. "That's it. I am drawing a line in the sand. It just occurred to me that if both Kay and Amar go, and Jamie gets tied up before leaving Her Majesty's service, I will have four kids to care for. And I am committed to spending part of the summer in Chicago. How will I handle that?"

Ricky laughed aloud. "That would be a sight. Chris, the man who would never be tied down, the playboy of the Western world, caring for four kids on a transatlantic trip and all on his own. Now that would be worth the price of admission."

"Wait," Chris suddenly looked more concerned as he looked toward Karen and Deena. "Who is taking care of your girls when you are gone?"

Karen never cracked a smile. "I am sorry. Didn't Amar tell you? She and I arranged for the two of you to care for them. But now if Amar joins us…you will have them all. Chris, they love you so."

He stared, not sure whether she was kidding. "I…I…"

Deena seamlessly picked up the narrative. "We considered other possibilities. At the end of the day, however, I insisted on you. I figured, once you have two, it is not such a big deal to go to six. The ages are roughly the same, easy-peasy."

Chris momentarily considered how much of the local vernacular Deena had mastered but mostly continued to stare in horror. Karen would bullshit him, of that he was sure. But he was always surprised when Deena was not polite and nice. Azita always had that mischievous streak he had noticed in Pamir, but Deena was more like her mother, somewhat on the serious side and just as beautiful. "No way," he finally exclaimed. "No way you would risk your precious children with me."

Karen smiled. "Got that right, buster. My parents are coming down from Birmingham. Amazing, no? We are finally getting along. It was the girls that did it, these two adorable, orphaned girls from Afghanistan. If that is not enough to melt your heart, you are made of stone. Besides, they have warmed to Deena. What is not to love? It also helps that my sister is a single mom and one of my brothers is on the dole, when he is not in the pokey that is. I now look like a raging success in their eyes."

"You are a success," Ricky said emphatically. "You took over a failing program from this pathetic guy and turned things around."

"Once again, hilarious." Chris breathed again. "I think I will know about Azita and Amar tonight."

Kay then added. "By the way, if I go Jamie will surely find some way to take care of our children. This will give him a chance to enjoy a little free time and play at being Mr. Mom."

There was a silence as they all realized that a shift in the conversation was upon them. It was Atle who spoke up. "This is perhaps not my place but the discussion about your father intrigues me. I vaguely know about him by reputation, very right wing. I am very curious about American politics. You have some strange things going on, don't you?"

"Strange, or pathetic?" Chris asked.

"Well," Atle seemed quite anxious to get to this topic though he was concerned he might offend if he were too careless. "We

Scandinavians are perplexed. Obama is so popular around the world. You Americans punished him by allowing the Republicans to control your Congress after Obama tried to improve your healthcare system. I mean, really, you have the most expensive system in the world and it doesn't work very well. In fact, your sister here has written a wonderful paper on this very topic. All Obama was trying to do was bring you into line with the other civilized nations. We just do not understand."

Karen rolled her eyes. "Oh, no, Atle, you know not what you do. The rest of us have heard the Crawford screed on what is wrong with America once too often."

"Then once more won't hurt, will it? I am delighted to have a new audience." Chris gave his broadest smile. "But first, let us have an intelligence report directly from the States. Ricky, what is going on in the backwater of the free world? And you cannot bullshit me since Kat called this morning though we didn't have much time to chat. She had to get back to her boyfriend."

"Hah, hah, in fact Kat pushed me to stop here to see you guys, this is my opening to pile on." Ricky looked directly at Chris, there was no ambiguity regarding his target. "Well, on the surface, things looked okay when Obama was reelected. Underneath, though, it now looks bad. The Republicans have a stranglehold on Congress and hold most of the gubernatorial seats. The Supreme Court teeters between the two competing ideologies but leans to the right. All the hard- right needs is one more seat. Lose the White House in the next election and the country, if not the world, faces a holocaust."

Karen scoffed and said, "That will never happen, Americans are not that stupid."

"Don't be so sure," Ricky responded. "Underneath the surface, a festering ugliness simmers. The number of active hate groups has skyrocketed since Obama gained the White House. Not only is a black man at the pinnacle of power but he is competent, eloquent, and scandal-free. This grates the racists to no end. And believe me, probably 30 to 40 percent of Americans are avowed racists. You team them up with the oligarchy that operates out of self-interest and you have a recipe for a right-wing takeover. The economic elite that benefits most from the Republican agenda is like two or three percent of the pyramid, but you add in the gun nuts and abortion wackos and you might just have a core majority given that so many don't give a damn. It all depends on how many people vote."

"What do you hear below the surface?" Chris asked. This was a conversation he wanted to have with Ricky after his conversation with Kat in any case. He now wondered if all this was a well-rehearsed plot to reel him in. No matter, he was interested.

"Both Kat and I will be very happy if you visit this summer. We are worried. Your Father, now that he has been pushed aside in the family business, is focusing even more on his right-wing political agenda. I guess you can say this was an unintended consequence of your coup."

"Not mine," Chris protested, "it was your dear wife's coup, but I will admit to the role of a more than willing co-conspirator. I never thought it through, I guess. We never thought it through. Kat is more than worried. Father is, as I mentioned, still as wealthy as Croesus. Unfortunately, now I am being told that now he has time for his favorite hobby, destroying what remains of the American democracy and installing an economic oligarchy in its place, a kleptocracy if you will. He was always a firm believer that a select few are ordained to rule over the masses, a distorted dystopia based on Plato's theme of philosopher kings. The problem is that their philosophy sucks and they tend to be brutal czars and not benevolent overlords."

Ricky picked up the theme. "Your father is working tirelessly behind the scenes. His cabal of wealthy co-conspirators are relentlessly nipping at the underbelly of democratic institutions. Rebekah Mercer is a frequent visitor, the daughter of Bob Mercer, the hedge fund guru. Talk about looney tunes. They are very confident that they will take the White House this time around. Hillary is likely to be the Democratic nominee and they have been using their well-funded propaganda machine to turn her into Satan's daughter. They have been at it for a quarter century but watch what they do over the next year plus. They will hit her with so much mud, all spurious, that even Democratic women will reject her. She probably could not be elected dog catcher."

"But surely Americans will see through all this?" The protest came from Atle.

"No," said Ricky emphatically, "you cannot imagine how naïve and simple minded the typical American is. And then there are some disturbing rumors, not even sure if I should mention them."

Chris pushed him. "Go ahead, you are among friends. I heard some of this earlier, but this is something we all need to know about."

"We are getting information that the Russians are getting involved, that they want to help the Republicans…one economic oligarchy supporting another. Something called the Russian Federation Internet Research Association is being formed, or perhaps has been formed and is being expanded. By the 2016 election they hope to have thousands of operatives spreading misinformation to millions of Americans. And it may go beyond that."

Atle looked unconvinced. "America is an old democracy. It will never permit its democratic institutions to be compromised."

Ricky laughed derisively. "You would think so. I suspect that this is my cue to let Chris take over. People, time for the lecture. Take good notes, this material will be on the exam."

"In fact, my younger sister, and Ricky's long-suffering wife, called me this very morning. I cannot say much more than all of our paranoia is justified." Chris seemed reluctant to go further, looking at Ricky whose countenance remained impassive. "Back to my lecture, I will try not to become too pedantic."

"That will be the day." Karen smiled.

"Okay, then, the long version. America, despite the rhetoric, has never been a democracy. One of my favorite quotes is from John Adams: *'Property is surely a right of mankind as real as Liberty.'* Few realize that our iconic phrase of pursuing: *'life, liberty, and happiness'* was almost *'life, liberty, and the pursuit of property,'* which he stole from John Lock who originally penned *'life liberty, and estate'* as the core verities of the good society. Think about what they provided for in the original constitution. Women could not vote, nor slaves, nor even most men without property. They instituted an electoral college under the assumption that only propertied men would be electors and that they would overturn any foolish vote by the rabble. As another protection against the will of the people, senators were not elected but appointed by state legislators. America was to be a country of the propertied class, by the propertied class, and for the propertied class. Sure, they wanted democracy but only if it was controlled by people just like themselves. What pushed the colonists toward breaking free from England? It was taxes, even though the mother country spent untold treasure defending them from France and the original inhabitants in the French and Indian War. Let's face it, the colonists were a bunch of selfish ingrates. The Boston Tea Party had less to do with political protest than to sustain the lucrative smuggling operations of John Hancock and others of his ilk. More to the point, they did not trust the electorate. Not much has changed."

"But as democracy matured, things changed, no?" Atle protested, but rather meekly.

"Nominally, yes. In the early 1900s, the constitutional amendments that were introduced extended suffrage to women and ended appointed senators. Most Native Americans were not franchised until World War II, and it was the 1965 Voting Rights Act that nominally extended access to the voting booth to most African-Americans in the South. Never forget that the long history of America has been a battle between competing ideologies, first a rural agrarian feudal system against the industrial revolution and then capital versus labor."

"Here we go," Karen intoned while Kay issued a small chuckle.

Chris ignored them. "The civil war was a conflict of cultures - big agricultural estates versus big industrial corporations. But what is most fascinating is that the poor on both sides bore the brunt of the conflict. Less than five percent of southerners owned slaves to any extent, at least enough to have a commercial impact, yet thousands of poor whites suffered and died for a social and economic system that oppressed their own economic hopes. Think about that. The North was just about to enter the industrial revolution in a big way, and crushing the agrarian South pushed that along and helped them gain regional hegemony. While some of the wealthy put it on the line, affluent northerners could buy their way out of the war for $300 dollars, a small fortune then for an average worker."

"Remember, the robber barons needed a cheap labor supply. They focused on ensuring a steady stream of immigrants and crushing any signs of labor organization. The state came to their aid whenever their prerogatives and advantages were threatened. With no taxes and few regulations, it was Katy, bar the door. The gilded age saw enormous accumulations of wealth. Of course, even academia came to support the existing inequalities. Herbert Spencer twisted Darwin's biological Theory of Evolution into a social context. Those who won the titanic battles of that age were the fittest, the smartest, and the strongest. Success was a sign of worth. It was the natural order of things. And religion played its role. Calvinistic thought developed the notion of predestination. God knew everything including who would be in heaven with him. Success in life was a sign that you were among the select. Thus, biology and theology supported the belief system underlining the new economic order. My father is the perfect expression of this new economic man, destined to win and to rule."

"A little cynical, aren't we?" This was a weak protest from Carlotta.

"I think not. The basic alignment of capital versus labor began as the 1900s arrived. I think the economic elite saw dangers on the horizon. There were obvious inequalities where great suffering existed alongside conspicuous wealth. Monopolies controlled many economic factors such as rail prices, thus systemically hurting desperate farmers who needed to get their goods to market. The capitalists and bankers wanted a gold system to keep the worth of their wealth strong while the populists wanted a money supply backed by silver. History recalls the words of the first national populist, William Jennings Bryan who railed against being: 'crucified on a cross of gold.' He desperately sought cheap credit to free up over-extended farmers and smaller business people."

Chris sighed and continued. "Probably for the first time, corporate leaders tried to buy a national election. J.P. Morgan stuffed cash in a duffle bag and delivered it to McKinley's campaign. Except for Teddy Roosevelt and maybe Ike, the GOP would become the water carriers for the elite after this. Oddly enough, workers in the North tended to side with the industrialists. Their bargain seemed to be they would take a job no matter how low paying rather than depend upon utopian dreams spun by revolutionaries. In any case, the Republicans went from the liberal, anti-slavery and pro-infrastructure, party to the conservative party while the Democrats struggled to sew together northern urban immigrants with southern racists. The Republicans might have remained unchallenged except for the Great Depression. It turns out that conservative economic orthodoxy doesn't work, except for those at the top."

"I'm getting lost." It was Deena. "What does all this ancient history have to do with today?"

"The short story is this: The Great Depression of the 1930s shattered conventional thought and brought us great ruin that was international in scope. The Weimar Republic was getting the economic ship righted in the late 1920s with American help. Remember that Hitler was considered a marginal buffoon by many until Germany's recovery was aborted after America called in the loans it had provided them. The U.S. did this right after the market collapse of 1929. America sneezed, and Europe got a bad case of the flu, and a huge price was to be paid. Still, economic collapse prompted a change in the old ways of thinking. Perhaps a government could be a force for good? Let us not forget that the original catastrophe might have been deep but short-term except that there was only one tool in the government's bag early on: you protected national interests with tariffs and a balanced budget. This was the economic orthodoxy embraced by virtually all, even Roosevelt in his weaker moments. That made things worse. Eventually, the thinking of that famous Brit, John Maynard Keynes, percolated into the national consciousness.

The government had to step in to stimulate demand when normal markets failed. That was anathema to the traditionalists, but World War II intervened to prove his point. This was the pump-priming strategy of all pump-priming strategies and even the conservatives loved it. If there is one thing that they love more than money, it is killing people and making tons of money off the weapons that do the killing."

"That is a little harsh," someone interjected.

"Not at all. It is all too true. But my point is that the economic elite saw things slipping away from them. With the drubbing of the hard-right candidate Goldwater in 1964, it looked as if we had a new economic orthodoxy firmly in place. Even Republican Richard Nixon said that *we are all Keynesians now.* That could not be allowed to stand. The elite saw their stranglehold on wealth steadily fall since the end of the 1920s, when it stood at almost 24 percent of the total. By the 70s, it would drop just below 10 percent. They wanted their advantages, their dominance, their preeminent social status back. There were always advocates for right-wing orthodoxy: Hayek, Kirk, Buckley, Rand, and others. But they had been fringe-players after the depression and the war. As early as the 1950s, a new school of economic thought was being pushed by James Buchanan, the so-called Virginia School. Simply put, economic outcomes of the market, unfettered by government intervention, were the just allocation of resources. Anything else impeded the market and, more to their point, was morally indefensible. It was social Darwinism and Calvinism on steroids. Slowly, particularly after the Goldwater debacle, the hard right finally got serious. For some time, they were viewed as fringe-type nuts seeing communists everywhere. Now, they banded together, fueled by great wealth, to systemically turn things around. They needed to purge moderates from their ranks and hijack the party. A way to do just that was right in front of them. De jure segregation may have died but racism was alive and well and those deep hatreds could be exploited for their own purposes. In the 1930s, the first black scholar to get a Ph.D. from Harvard, W.E.B. Dubois, wrote about a psychological wage that poor whites accepted in preference to substantive compensation. If the elite permitted them to feel superior to others who did not look like them, were of a darker color, white laborers would gladly forego collective action to maintain an imagined superiority. It was a classic Faustian bargain and a hollow pyrrhic victory. We give you the right to hate, you give us your obedience and cheap labor."

"Okay," Karen offered. "Now you are descending into bitterness."

Chris did not seem to hear her. "They first needed to realign the parties. Obviously, the Democrats had become the party of labor and minorities. Truman integrated the military in the late 1940s and liberal stalwarts like Hubert Humphrey were pushing the party leftward. The realignment would have taken place in the 1950s, but Eisenhower enforced the Brown versus Board of Education decision, bringing in federal troops to help end segregation in some schools. But that just delayed things. After the civil rights legislation of the 1960s, realignment was a guaranteed outcome. The South became solid red while liberal Republicans slowly disappeared. With the parties polarized, confrontation became the norm. Now, the elite had a party they could control and that would willingly carry a hard-right agenda. This country would finally get the redistribution of wealth that liberals always wanted. Unfortunately for them, it would go in the wrong direction, from the bottom 90 percent to the top one percent. But how to get their people elected? Therein lay their challenge. Their natural economic base, by definition, is a minority of voters. You need to be creative to get the multitude to vote against their self-interests."

"I may regret this," Atle said, "but what did they do?" Suddenly, he let out a howl as everyone realized that Karen kicked him under the table. "Now I know what Chris suffers," he whimpered.

Even Chris laughed at this. "Well, if you want the whole story, perhaps take my course in American political institutions. Sign up early though, it is a popular course. You must remember that, just prior to Goldwater getting clobbered, Americans basically liked and trusted the government. This, of course, was before Vietnam, Watergate, and school bussing. Some 80 percent said they trusted the government to do the right thing most of the time. Now, it might be in the range of 20 percent. That was their challenge. They had to chip away at the foundations of political thought in the country, transform the underlying precepts that shaped the average guy's perceptions.

Through a massive educational campaign, they convinced many that the government made things worse, not better. Free markets were sacrosanct. Personal liberty trumped economic security. They launched a multi-dimensional strategy for transforming how Americans thought about things. Fox news is just the tip of the iceberg. I could go on about the think tanks, the Leadership Council, the Club for Growth, the Federalists Society, and so many other tentacles formed to strangle the life out of progressive thought, but I fear we would be here all night. They also knew that demographic trends worked against them, the share of native whites would decline as a proportion of the population pie while immigrants and minorities see their share grow. Time was running out, they felt. They had to work hard to destroy the protocols of democracy, and soon. Through gerrymandering, voter suppression, massive misinformation and other tinkering, they could slowly extend their control."

"Sounds apocalyptic," Atle said and then instinctively moved away from Karen.

"They are almost there. Consider this: in 2007, the elite now held the same share of the nation's wealth that they did just before the great economic collapse of 1929. Starting with Reagan, they have gathered all, almost all at least, of the newly generated goodies for themselves. But they wanted more. They lost some ground with the 2008 crash, but their greed is insatiable. They want it all. Worse, they have virtually unlimited resources to pour into the political process. Wealth, coupled with a total lack of scruples, is a deadly mix. Of course, they see themselves as engaged in a holy war. They see this as a battle of good versus evil. They have developed a philosophy that rationalizes the practice of unbridled greed. My father has enthusiastically embraced such a belief system." Then Chris stopped. He seemed to be considering something.

"Lecture over?" Karen offered hopefully.

"Yeah, sorry. But I am thinking. Maybe Kay has been right all these years." He looked directly at his sister who said nothing.

After a pause, Karen had to ask: "About what?"

"Perhaps I have been a coward, running away to England. Perhaps you are right, perhaps Kat is right. Maybe it is time for me to fight back." Everyone looked at him, but nothing was said.

CHAPTER 4

CHRIST CHURCH MEADOW

Amar and Azita walked along Christ Church Meadow walkway that meandered adjacent to the river that flowed through the ancient university town to London and the sea beyond. Azita broke their silent meditation. "Spring is so beautiful here. Look at this green space. Sometimes, during this month, the color is so vivid it hurts my eyes, or so it seems. My country is so brown except for the white of the winter snows and the brief existence of some brightly colored flowers after the snow melts and before the heat arrives. I should be so happy amid such beauty."

"That is why I am here," Amar said with a hint of concern. "You should be happy, but you are not. That is for all to see."

"I'm fine, really. You should not have torn yourself away from the hospital just for a pouting daughter. How did you get away?" It was as if Azita had just realized what time it was. Suddenly, she was embarrassed by her own self-absorption.

"It wasn't hard. I merely said that my eldest daughter needed me. Everyone knows about you, your promise. You are my biggest priority."

"I am fine, it should be your husband. You should focus on him, he needs help."

Amar smiled. "That clown can take care of himself."

"Are you sure?" Azita emitted a sound that was almost a laugh. "Sometimes he looks a bit hopeless to me."

"Good point, he is, as you say, hopeless." Amar agreed as she slipped her arm through Azita's. After a small expression of mirth at Chris's expense, they ambled in silence for a while.

Azita once again broke their quiet contemplation. "Look at the river. It is lovely, gentle at this point. But you cannot know where it is going, what it will become. Might it turn into raging rapids, or a broad lake of water, or perhaps a waterfall that cascades into a churning froth? Of course, we know the truth, it widens and meanders through London and southeast England to the sea. Once there, the end of the journey, it loses its identity. It is no more. With your own life, all you can see is the patch of water before you." Azita paused. She said no more.

"When did you become such a poet?"

Azita thought about Amar's question. "I suspect when my Papa introduced me to Shakespeare."

"Pamir was a saint. But what are you trying to tell me, sweetheart?" Amar asked.

"I sometimes feel that our lives are like this patch of river. We know what we can see, and we know the end game because that is universal. We all die. But what happens around the next bend and all the way to where it is swallowed up into a seemingly infinite ocean? That is unknowable from where we are now. I am not even sure what I would want the river to become.

Should it continue to wind a gentle path, or maybe it should create angry currents or sometimes crash over its banks to waken the surrounding areas? As I look at what I can see, the rest is unknowable. And I cannot even decide what I would want even if it were in my control."

'I take it you feel you are drifting." Amar's words were gentle. She thought back to those moments when she sat with this barely twelve-year-old girl as they were trying to bluff their way past British immigration without the proper paperwork. At that moment Azita was so close to her goal but frozen in fear that it now would be denied. Amar had both distracted and supported the hopeful, yet frightened young girl at that point as they all awaited the decision. Now the task was infinitely more difficult. Azita no longer depended on her to make things right. All she now could do was ask the right questions and help this young woman understand herself and her world.

"Yes, drifting…" Even Azita's words seemed to flow away with the gentle river.

"Okay, let's start with the obvious. Something is very wrong with you and Ben, right?"

Azita stopped and turned toward her companion. "Tell me, have you ever doubted Chris's love for you?"

"Are you asking if he has ever cheated on me?"

"Oh my God, I never thought of that. He wouldn't, would he?" Azita seemed flummoxed at the thought.

"Well, I must admit, I had grave doubts about the man as husband material. When everyone said that he would, as the phrase went, 'mount a coat rack' if he could, I wondered what I was getting into." Amar considered what she had just said. "Hmm, just how did that disgusting phrase become so universal? He probably started it, thinking it a compliment."

Azita looked at her puzzled, and then surprised Amar by breaking into a laugh. "Mount a coat rack? Oh, I get it, just like all men. All they think about is sex. I had heard that one before, but never quite understood it until now even as I repeated it. How innocent I was. Yes, I have heard the stories of his younger days. How did you get past all that? Haven't you worried about him, with his traveling and women clearly finding him attractive?"

"More than attractive, you can just tell women find him sexy. My sisters do have such poor taste." Amar grinned at her own witticism.

"Why did you marry him then?" Azita looked at her quizzically. "You could have any man? Why choose one with so many…difficulties?"

Amar paused to consider her response. "I think, like the river, I had no choice. The river cannot stop, change direction, can it?" She noticed Azita's confused expression, so she rushed on. "Listen, Kay had warned me about him when we thought he might be coming to drag her away from the Panjshir Valley site.

She warned me that he was what women called a 'player'. Do you know what that means?"

"I can guess. I have grown up a lot in the past few years." She wondered internally why she pretended ignorance. She knew what a player was. Still, she didn't want her mother to realize how sophisticated she had become. *How silly*, she thought.

"Wow, we should have talked about men more," Amar mused aloud. "No matter, she also told me her inner thoughts about him, his passions and commitment, his intelligence and kindness. I had primed myself to ignore all that good stuff. I convinced myself that I would dislike him. He had come to take Kay away from us and I was going to fight him tooth and nail."

"Guess you failed. I mean, he caved on taking Kay away immediately, but you failed on disliking him."

"Miserably. I remember that moment. I was comforting a baby we could not save, just holding it and singing a sweet song until the end, a Hindu lullaby from my childhood. The child passed. I turned. He was standing there, watching me. I was startled. There was such a look on his face. I had expected a tyrant and this man before me looked so open, vulnerable. I felt this tremor course through my body, something rather new to me. To tell you the truth, my knees weakened. I almost buckled."

Azita squeezed her arm. "That is so…"

"Pathetic? I never thought of myself as some love-sick teenager. I have a confession to make. You don't know this, you were still rather young at the time, unless someone blabbed which I hope no one did. In any case, I seduced him that very night. At first, he said no. For a moment, I thought I must be so ugly, the man who would mount a coat rack turned me down."

"Wow. I remember those early days. I thought you hated him. I never would have believed…" Azita did not know how to conclude her thought. "Still, you seemed like a perfect couple in my innocent head, after a while at least."

"Well, my dear, when you realize you love someone, that is terribly scary, a bit like a painful affliction." Amar looked deeply into Azita's eyes. Silence hung in the moment. "I have to ask. Do you love Ben?"

"Before I answer, tell me one thing: when did you first know you loved Chris? Wait, that is not my question. How did you know?"

Amar's response came without consideration. "The moment I touched him, when he shook my hand. It was just a touch, but it was everything."

Azita gasped. "I…I have something to confess." Then nothing.

"Sweet Azita. I know very little about men. Like you, I was raised in a protective household, shielded from the manipulations of the evil sex. But life has provided me with one lesson, maybe two. I think we are meant to do something in life. We can wander across various paths but once we realize what we are meant to be, that is what we must do."

"And the second lesson?"

"When we stumble across our soulmate, we must grab onto them, no matter the risks or the doubts. Azita, what do you have to tell me?"

Azita looked at her new mother for a few moments, absorbing the lessons. Then she shook her head ever so slightly, signifying that she was about to reveal a secret. "Ben cannot face up to his parents. They like me but never have gotten past the Jewish-Muslim thing. He can't quite accept this reality. He keeps stalling, hoping that something will change."

"And you, what do you feel?"

"That is the problem, I am not sure. I was, am, very comfortable with him. As I told dad, Ben is a scientist and I am on track for a medical research career, if I want it. We would be a perfect team, so compatible. It could be a good arrangement."

"Azita, dear, do you hear yourself? You sound like you are hiring a personal assistant."

The young girl looked stricken but said nothing. Finally, she spoke: "I have a small confession as well. I met a boy, well a young man. I guess that is not such a sin."

"When? Chris didn't mention this."

"It was right after he left me."

"You mean today?" Amar was flummoxed.

"This young man, he approached me. It turns out he had been following me for several weeks, he heard me say I was hoping to join the trip home. So, he made his move."

Amar stopped walking abruptly. "Wait, you talked to this stranger, a stalker? Azita, what in heaven's name were you thinking? I am kicking myself for not warning you about men."

"No, not really a stranger. I knew him from Kabul. Not well, mind you, but he is the son of Papa's best friend, from the old days, the man who helped us escape to the north. He…I guess… has liked me all these years."

Amar said nothing for a few moments as they restarted their aimless rambling. Then her expression softened in understanding. "Let me ask. Did you touch him, like shake hands?"

"Yes."

"And?" Amar pushed her.

"I am not sure how to explain it. There was a, what shall I say, a shock."

Amar laughed gently and hugged her adoptive daughter. "I am so sorry and, I suppose, so excited for you. I am sure you are totally confused but God never promised us an easy path."

"No shit." Azita seemed stricken at her uncensored words while Amar chuckled. "Don't be disappointed in me. I will wash my own mouth out with soap. I have been around Chris for too long."

"No shit," Amar repeated, and both women laughed out loud. The tension eased. "Okay, tell me what is in your heart."

Azita looked at her new mother. For a moment, in her head and heart, she saw Madeena. There was the same love and concern and wisdom. "I will try. In truth, I cannot say many sensible things about Ben. I have given my all to him, as you know. That was not easily done. Worse, it cannot be retrieved. I feel affection for him, respect, and trust. Those are important things, are they not?"

"They are important indeed. But let me ask you this; when you look at him, do you feel excitement? When you are not with him, are those moments heavy with regret? When you brush against one another, even by accident, do you ever tremor with expectation?" Azita looked at Amar rather blankly. "One more question. When you are intimate with Ben, what do you experience? Do you…I mean, have you…what am I trying to say?"

"Have an orgasm?"

"Wow," Amar said and smiled. "I must still be a good Indian girl, having trouble with the concept of my girl having an orgasm."

Azita laughed again. It was becoming easier. "I seriously doubt you were ever that good of an Indian daughter, seducing a man on first meeting him. Not much a role model for me, I must say."

"Young lady, I can still put you over my knee. Oh, I now see that I never should have told you about that first night."

Azita's smile dissolved slowly as she thought on the question presented to her. "When I am with Ben, physically, I feel good things, usually. Most times, it is pleasant. All right, on occasion, maybe I am merely being nice to him. But he is nice to me. Damn it, I am not sure what the rules are or what to expect. Madeena and I never talked and …"

"Neither have we. My bad. You know, no one had the talk with me. I thought I knew love with a young man who ran away when I was with child by him. I had thought…oh never mind about that. The important part of the story is that, much to my regret, I aborted the fetus to please my parents. They wanted me home. I resisted, and they forced me into a marriage as a condition of continuing my medical studies in Canada. I felt nothing for this man to whom I was joined in an arranged marriage, he virtually raped me every night. Talk about hell. There were a couple of other men after that, but it was not until Chris that I realized what lovemaking was all about. It was not about serving a man, doing your duty, making a sacrifice for a relationship. It was about completion, realizing what it is to be a female, a sexual being. It happened that first night with him. You want to know how I reacted?"

"Yes," Azita said quickly, afraid Amar was going to stop.

"I panicked. I tried to push the poor man away, confusing him no end. It was all too frightening. Besides, he was the guy who Kay and Karen said would mount a coat rack."

"Did you ever answer my question, whether you worry that he will cheat?"

"He is a man. Of course, that is a concern. But I am comforted by the fact that Kay would break his kneecaps, among other things."

"So, would I." They both laughed again. "Seriously, mother, I know what you are saying. Love is more than like, much more. But there is a problem."

"You don't know what love is."

"I know what some love is. I loved Papa and Mama. I love Deena and you and that man who would mount a coat rack. But a boy, a young man, that remains a mystery."

"Azita, just don't rush things. Be sure, okay, be sure."

"Mother, here is the thing."

"Ah," Amar said with gravity, "the thing."

"When I talked with this boy from my past, I saw something very clearly, something that has been bothering me more and more of late. I do feel like this river. When I came here, to England and then Oxford, I knew what I wanted. All was clear, totally. I would study hard, like my father did at this same place. Then I would return home as he did. I would work with the people who so needed help, especially women and children.

Most have so little. I can still recall Chris saying that it was not until he saw us working with the girls at the new school, most who were refugees from the Taliban, that he knew what it meant to offer someone everything. You give someone who has enough a little more and they are appreciative and that is nice. You give someone who has nothing hope and it is everything. I can remember working beside my father with villagers suffering from so much. Too often we could do little. But there were those moments when death became life, despair hope. You know the feeling, few do. You can get it here as well, but the moments are never as dramatic."

"Yes," Amar affirmed softly, "I know."

"The thing is, those memories are getting vague, lost in the rush of events and my studies and my confusion about Ben. I have mentioned my original aspirations - maybe I should call them obsessions? - to my professors. They look at me as if I have lost my mind. They say things like I am so gifted, too gifted to be a mere practitioner, as if that were being a failure. They keep telling me that I can be a great teacher, a remarkable researcher. Madeena and Pamir both talked about the glory of teaching and discovery. I just don't know. I simply cannot decide what to do."

"Azita, dear, you don't have to make up your mind today. You probably have heard this in medical school, I did. We were told there were three groups of students. The top students became researchers and teachers. The middle group became the best clinicians. The bottom group made the most money. I never cared about money, but I did wonder where I fit between the top two groups. My decision was easier, I think. I was a very good student but not at the very, very top. At some point, I knew my comparative advantage would lie in being a good clinician, a practitioner. You, my dear, are cursed with being too talented. But, before seeking a shrink to deal with your depression, remember this: many others have no choices at all."

Azita looked directly at Amar. "I'm being a selfish shit, am I not?"

"No, sweetheart, you are the most amazing girl I know."

"I am not so sure about that," Azita protested quietly before turning in another direction. "The thing is, time is running out. I must decide on an internship, residency, a future. I cannot meander forever. I am not like this lazy river. No, I must go back this summer. Deena has been back from time to time, but my summers have been so busy. Even this year, I was supposed to help with some research. No, I need to feel my country again, smell and taste my culture, look my people in their eyes. I cannot make such decisions in the abstract. Do you understand?"

"More than you know."

"Who knows. Maybe then I can make sense of Ben and Ahmad."

"Who?" Amar asked but knew.

"The boy I met today, his name is Ahmad Zubair." The girl was not aware of this, but her face lit up as she uttered his name. It was an autonomic response that Amar noticed. "He used to be an obnoxious fat boy when I knew him in Kabul."

"And now?"

"He thinks he is sexy."

"And?"

"He is, very." Azita felt her face flush. "Wow, I am glad I am not trying to have this conversation with dad."

Mother and daughter looked at one another a moment before breaking out in laughter. "Chris would have bolted by now and handed you off to me. In fact, that is what he did earlier. Ran off to some appointment I bet. I am glad he did. I always want to be there for you. And you know what, I love it when you call me mother."

"And I have a confession to make." Azita smiled at Amar. "I love calling you mother."

"Listen Azita, you must go back home. But here is my condition. I will go with you. Don't even try to argue. The girls are old enough to be without me for a bit. Besides, maybe we can fit in a visit to my home in Kashmir. I have a family you have not met." Azita made one attempt to respond. "Don't even try to talk me out of this. Besides, then we will have a lot of time to talk about boys and love and life."

"I would like that," Azita murmured.

"So would I," Amar responded. "Besides, I am sure there is so much you still can teach me about boys. Okay, time to go home and torture Chris for a bit. That always relaxes me."

"Me too," Her daughter responded.

They both laughed again and continued walking along the path, arm in arm, lost in their separate thoughts. Unbeknown to the other, each reflected on the river of their individual lives up to this point. But when they did speak again, both returned to a safe topic, making fun of Chris.

CHAPTER 5

CHICAGO

Chris leaned back in his seat for the flight to Chicago. He sat with one of his daughters while Beverly, the wife of his late elder brother, sat with his other offspring. He leaned over to speak across the aisle to his sister-in-law. "I do thank you for coming over, but I could have handled this on my own."

"Nonsense," she responded. "The women in the family all agree that you are hopeless."

"As long as it is unanimous." He looked at her with genuine affection.

"What have you heard from your wife and daughter? I have gotten emails from Kay but have not heard directly from Amar and Azita. They are still in India, isn't that right?"

"Yes, but they soon will be in Kabul, the whole entourage will be together for a while. I am not a happy camper about this. I still have nightmares about searching the hills and caves for Azita and her sister after their parents were murdered. Then Karen goes and gets shot while trying to rescue me, almost dies. Just to save my sorry ass. That makes no sense, but she did also save the girls at the same time. I still owe her large for that. Anyways, that place makes me very nervous. Damn, life has become complicated. Used to be all I worried about was not getting STDs and not getting shot at by an irate husband."

Beverly guffawed involuntarily. "Sorry, you are now so domesticated that I almost forgot you were once the playboy of the Western world. I understand your concerns, but they will be fine, I am sure. It is not so bad there now."

Chris still looked glum. "The damn Taliban doesn't run the place, but they are a huge presence in the countryside and just as nuts as ever. I can't help but worry about their safety, I always will. But I will let you in on a secret." He leaned closer to her across the aisle. "What I really worry about is my wife and daughter and my evil twin sister are plotting evil things to do to me. They are spending a lot of time by themselves and that cannot be good for me. Few realize the horror I live every day."

"Kay is right, she always said you were full of shit. Oops, that was brave." She cupped her mouth for a moment. "But really, you are such a typical man, you think women are talking about you all the time."

"What, they are not scheming nefarious plots against my sanity and well-being? Really? You think I have nothing to worry about?"

Beverly patted his arm. "Not at all, I think you are screwed royally. I cannot wait to hear what tortures they have cooked up for you."

She had surprised him. He looked closely at her as she smiled broadly. She was not the young, uncertain girl that his brother had brought home as he finished up college. Then, he could not warm up to her. Neither could Kay, his sister. In those days, she seemed sculptured into some preformed mold, looking upon the world about her absent of any emotion and speaking as if through a prepared script. Her hair was perfect, her make-up just a little on the excessive side, her demeanor crafted not to offend. But it was the smile that struck Chris as being off. It was always there but never suggested real mirth. Nothing about her suggested authenticity in the beginning. It was as if she were after a prize and the way to get it was never to make a mistake nor offend any on the family members.

Chris and Kay could ever figure out why Chuck, Charles Junior, had been attracted to her. He was an artist by temperament while she seemed socially rigid and consumed by materialism. Where was the connection? What could they possibly talk about after sex was finished? Even there, Chris was puzzled. Beverly was very attractive in a brittle sense but displayed no sensuality. He had a difficult time believing that she did little more in bed than lay there while Chuck finished his business. Kay and Chris could only conclude that their elder brother was still seeking approval from the patriarch. Father only saw women as extensions of a man's will and needs. Beverly would not challenge that view.

It was only after Chuck's suicide that Chris noticed something different in her. She evinced real emotion, affection for the man she had married. She even stood up to the Patriarch as the family decided whether to take Chuck off life support as he lay in a coma. As Chris looked at her across the aisle, he could not help but notice the physical differences. Her hair now had a natural style, more auburn and not the bleached blond look of her youth. Her make-up was subdued and suggestive, not the harsh caricature of a woman on the make that it once had been. But her smile was the big change in his mind. It now reflected an inner joy. No longer was it merely painted on the outside, revealing absolutely nothing about her inner state. This was the longest time Chris had ever spent with his sister-in-law and he liked what he was discovering.

Suddenly, Chris realized she was talking to his daughter seated next to her, the young girl was restless, and Beverly was quietly working to keep her calm, perhaps even persuade her to take a nap. The girl wanted to be next to her sister but that would invite squabbling which was not exactly what you wanted on an extended flight. Chris was impressed by her innate parenting skills. It made him wonder about things that had never entered his mind before.

"Beverly," Chris whispered as his daughter quieted down, "you are a natural."

"Thanks, they really are so sweet, I could love them to death."

"Well, you will get a chance when we get to Chicago. You will have charge of the little dears as I jet around to various foundations and such. I am so grateful, I might have left them with mother, but she is getting frail I think." Chris hesitated and then decided to plunge ahead. "Okay, I am going to be obnoxious here, not so much obnoxious as intrusive."

"We expect nothing less," she smiled, "but I can guess where you are going: why didn't Chuck and I have kids of our own?"

"Okay, that is one of them. There are others." Chris paused. "Funny, I don't know you very well."

"You never tried," she said the words quickly and regretted them immediately. "Sorry, I think we are both at fault there. I must have seemed so inconsequential to you. I was this blond bimbo while you were out changing the world. And before you deny anything, just let me get this out. You and Kay awed me, while your father scared the bejesus out of me. I would almost upchuck whenever I was in his presence. It sure wasn't easy at first. I still hate admitting how terrified I was of him, of all of you." She paused, her eyes closed as if she was looking deep into the past.

"Bev..." he started but she silenced him with a gesture.

Then she started out with slow words, as if each were ripped out from a recess of her psyche. "Everything bad you thought about me was probably true. I saw a rich family and a weak man. I wanted the name, the money, the status. Chuck was so innocent, so easy to manipulate. He had so much going for him but never figured that out. I don't think I appreciated how special he was until it was too late. I did not think I was as manipulative as the other barracudas out there, but in truth I was. I went after weakness, or what I saw as his weakness. To nail him, all I had to do was pay some attention to him, feed his shattered ego, and he was mine. He was so insecure that he never figured out he was a catch. I could see these other girls, just sharks like me, circling around him. For the life of him, he could not see he was a catch, thank God. Oh, he didn't quite have your looks and certainly not your bad-boy charms, but he was so sweet and kind and gentle and, of course, so wealthy."

"Really, Bev..."

Again, she silenced him with a gesture and continued. "I thought I had a chance to get by the other female barracudas who were after his money, but the family, the infamous Crawford clan, worried me. The rest of you, and for sure the patriarch, were different altogether. I knew I couldn't fool people like you or Kay; maybe your mother and Kat but I wasn't sure of that - Kat I mean. Your mother had some sweetness to her when she wasn't miserable and drunk, which was seldom. I never kidded myself. I know what you saw at first a sphinx. I just smiled at everyone, but I never revealed anything. I feared you would not like what you saw. Hell, I did not like what I saw looking in a mirror. I was little more than a grasping bitch."

"Don't be..." He was going to say *don't be hard on yourself, that is my job.* It was one of his favorite lines, but he held it in. In any case, she cut him short with a look.

"My dime now, so you listen. Understand? I kept smiling in the beginning while revealing nothing and guess what? I got the prize. He asked me to marry him. Then, I had to ask the real question: is that what I wanted? I didn't know. But this is what I was raised for." Her lips trembled slightly. "We were a family in economic decline, good name and pedigree but fortune and hope waning, desperately hanging on to our former social status as more money went out to keep up pretenses than came in. You know what I am talking about. This was like the plot from one of those Masterpiece PBS miniseries, the titled family with the big house and no money so they send the sons out to marry a rich American girl to give her status and, at the same time, shore up the dwindling bank account. That was me, I was to find a rich prince to bail us out. I was the best bet, the best hope. My sister had a weak chin and too many pounds, my brother was a dopehead. So, I got the ballet lessons and the fancy girl's school we could not afford. In fact, that was how I met your poor brother, I had been refined in the better things in life, to better trap some poor schlepp who didn't know better. I still recall mother telling me to go out and snag a guy with more money than brains. I did my hunting in two kinds of territory, upscale bars and artsy museums and concerts. That is how we met, in a museum. I was there nominally for a class project, but also because I was scouting out the talent. He was there because he loved this stuff, it was his secret Walter Mitty life. But even then, at the very beginning, I could see his passion for art, and his deep despair. Want to know something? I don't have much to do with my family anymore. I do send some money but mostly to keep them away. Greed does terrible things to people, terrible things. And money, whomever said it could buy happiness was an idiot." She leaned back into her seat, her eyes focused on something far away.

Chris wondered if she were finished. "Why bring this up now?"

She continued as if he had not said anything. "When I first got the prize, I rather panicked. Hell, I would now have to live with this guy. Worse, I would have to service him all the time. It was a life sentence. What had I done? Why had I done it? Was I just pleasing my folks? They cared not a whit for me. I was just a pawn, someone to use, maybe except for one brother who seemed rather genuine. In any case, there were moments early on when I came so close to bailing out. So damn close." A tear escaped her eye. "I even cheated on him, more than once. I hated myself, but even more I think, I hated being dishonest to Chuck. Want to know something funny? I…I think I even remember when it all turned around. I was about to leave the house to meet…someone. Then, Chuck came home early. I remember being upset, he was making this difficult for me. God, it really was all about me then. But he was distressed so I sat and listened. I think, maybe for the first time, he poured out the depths of his unhappiness. Oh, I knew the basic story. He had been tapped as the heir to the family dynasty, forced to study business when his heart lay elsewhere. He had this terrible need to please his father, it was a desperate need he could neither ignore nor dismiss, something none of his other siblings were afflicted with apparently. You all looked strong and independent to me, maybe except for Kat. She remained a cypher for a long time."

"I always felt that Chuck took after mother, more than the rest of us at least. Oops, sorry for interrupting."

"That's okay, your family jewels are safe this time, I am nicer than the other women around you, no violence. You really do get wacked a lot, not that you don't deserve it." She emitted a tiny smile. "That night, he poured out just how desperate he was. Let me be clear, he had complained often. But before that night, he never fully expressed his anguish, or I never had really listened. Odd, now that I think back on it, for a while, his catharsis sickened me, he seemed pathetic. I was still thinking about how to get out of the house to make it to this tryst with someone I can no longer even remember. Slowly, so slowly, I began to listen, to really pay attention. He was no longer just whining, complaining. His words were different. Maybe they had always been like that, but they seemed different to me that night. His words focused on his dreams, how he felt about art and beauty and life. Oh sure, he had touched on such things before, many times. Before, it always struck me as idle conversation, just a way to pass the time. Now, it struck me as communication, a sharing that was… intense and rather special. There was a depth that evening, as if he were reaching to a new place, some part of himself that he had never revealed before. I think…I think now that he had always been reluctant to open up. Perhaps he feared that I would not like to see his gentle soul, that I would find that man weak. God, what kind of monster had he thought he had married?" She paused a moment to regain control. "I can understand that reaction, but what happened that night was so different. For the first time, I rather fell in love with him. Funny, it really was just like that, so easy. I saw inside him, all the gentleness and sweetness and, above all, the sensitivity. And it swept over me, this was a man I wanted to be with. Better yet, he needed me… he needed me, goddamn it. I recall looking at him at that moment, just feeling this tragedy along with the part I must play. It was just like Greek tragedy, you know, with no escape and the awful ending having been scripted from the beginning. That end game had been determined by some malevolent God bent on satisfying their own sadistic wishes." Then she looked hard at Chris, betraying a small bit of anguish, before continuing. "The amazing thing was that he needed me. This man needed me. Just as important, I needed him. That is a mystery, is it not?"

When she paused, Chris wondered if she were waiting for him to say something. All that came to him was a question: "What mystery is that?"

"That you can be with someone for so long and not see them. They can be right there, in front of you. You can share a bed, make love to them, and see nothing. How can that be you ask? I am not sure, it was as if scales fell from my eyes and I could see for the first time. And what I saw was a revelation, a man that cared deeply about things." Her gaze shifted slightly. "Chris, he loved you. He saw in you everything he felt he was not. You do realize he regretted not escaping to England with you, but that would have been impossible for him. I am still destroyed by guilt that I was partly responsible for him not following you. In the end, he was such a people-pleaser. He tried so hard not to disappoint those around him, but he never quite figured out that you cannot please everyone. He was like one of those rats in an electrified maze with no possible escape. He ran around his maze, his personal prison, and it drove him to his death. In the end, his sense of doing the right thing was way too strong. Right thing, my ass, what was he thinking? How could listening to that monster be the right thing?" She saw him respond to her sharp words. "Yes, he is a monster. Didn't you know how I felt about the great Charles Senior?"

"No," Chris whispered. "Of all of us, you seemed close to him."

"An act, a fucking act." Beverly glanced at the child next to her. "Good thing she is asleep, she didn't hear. What else could I feel, watching every day as he mercilessly drove my poor husband to escape the only way he could? Couldn't he see what he was doing? Didn't he get it? Didn't he give a fu…?"

"I am not sure he ever did," Chris responded slowly. "You have to understand. Father is a stone-cold sociopath, like most of the uber-wealthy elite he hangs out with. They, he, don't see much beyond their own interests. Their world literally ends at the end of their nose, for some it is the tip of their penis. They are somehow insulated from the pain and suffering of others. That seems incredible to normal people, but something is lacking in them. I guess it is what gives many of them an edge. Obviously, we cannot get inside their heads, but I have watched him and his associates for a long time. They are different, believe me, they are hard-wired in some perverse way.

Once, when I was 10 or so, father and I were walking, and he was lecturing me about politics and life according to neo-Nazis philosophy that he had embraced so fully. Then, of course, I still clung desperately to the hope that he might be a dad to me, not the imperious Father that he was, and I yet listened even if there were doubts on the edges of my residual respect for this larger than life icon. We came across an injured dog, not sure what the problem was but it was whimpering and in pain. I instinctively responded, wanting to help the poor thing. I reached out before

Father yanked me back and kicked the poor animal to the curb. He walked on as if this was no more than a minor inconvenience to him. At that moment I thought the animal may have been diseased, rabid and therefore a danger to me, and that prompted his response. But no, not really, he was unaware the pup was suffering and belonged to someone. It had a collar. But it was outside his world, he cared not a whit. I paid more attention after that. I saw that he was just as vicious to other people. The evidence had always been there. Still, that was the moment when the epiphany about Father hit me. Our relationship was never the same."

"Meaning?" she asked, though knew the answer.

"I started to detach from him at that moment. It took a great while before the break was complete, but that image stayed with me." Chris was aware she was looking at him with great intensity. "You know my favorite saying."

"Ah, you have so many pearls."

"Oh, the one about how you cannot throw away what God puts inside…well, He gave me a conscience, much to Father's disgust." Chris shifted in his seat, signaling a new topic. "Bev, I need to ask, and this is difficult. So, just tell me if I am getting too personal."

"Yes," she said simply.

"Okay, then, I will let it alone."

"No, you don't understand. I am saying yes, he did what you were about to ask. You were wondering if he abused me sexually, right?" Chris just nodded, wondering how she knew where he was going. "It started even before the marriage. At first, I was appalled and shocked. He said he wanted to get to know me better but then trapped me in a room. He simply took what he wanted as if I had no say in the matter. After, he dismissed me as if I were a piece of garbage but made sure I realized the price of mentioning this to anyone. No cooperation, no access to the family resources. Hell, I assumed it was simply part of the package, part of the price to get my reward. Want to hear something funny? Sad, really, sad beyond tears. I was positive that you would rape me as well. At first, I just assumed this, what shall we call it? – a tradition that just ran in the family. You were rich, entitled males who simply took what you wanted, and I would soon be added to your list of…conquests. That smile you saw painted on me in the beginning. A lot of it was merely a grim anticipation of the horrors that for sure would come from you as well. After all, Kay and Kat were always going on about you being the great womanizer."

"But you must…"

"No, no, I figured things out after a bit. It quickly became apparent that you were safe, especially when you ignored me totally. Of course, then I went into a funk about not being attractive enough to get raped by the very same guy who, by wide reputation, would mount a coat rack. Now, I laugh when your sisters make that crack, then it was not so funny. Who first used that phrase? Everyone now describes you that way, at least the way you were before Amar. In the beginning, though, you made me very nervous, in fact."

"My God," Chris managed to utter.

Beverly continued. "After a while, I realized you were not so bad. All that playboy stuff was a façade, playacting. In fact, the more I saw of you, the more I came to admire who you were and what you represented. You were a bastard toward women but not a mean bastard by any means. I guess you were more of a casual and humorous bastard."

"There is a difference?" Chris asked.

"There is a big difference, all the difference in the world. But listen, I now know the family skeletons. Your sisters and I have talked a lot recently, at least after they first opened up to you about the peculiar tastes of the family head. They approached me recently, I suppose expecting the worst. I don't know what we were all thinking when it was happening. It must have been our fault, we couldn't embarrass the family, and the 'no one would believe us' if we did open up. After all, he was a great man, courted by politicians and king-makers, seen on the media all the time. Who was I? Just a gold-digging blond bimbo out to score big through marriage. I was totally sure no one would have believed my story, that it would merely look like another effort to shake the family down for money. What kind of crap was that?"

"Bev, you could have come to me, to Kay." He realized how stupid he sounded when she gave him a withering look. "Okay, that was way too dumb even by my low standards."

"I never even told Chuck. I couldn't. He was so fragile, had such a big heart. I remember, as things got worse between his father and he, I would plead for him to step away, to escape. We could run away, to Europe, where he could spend his time in the great museums and even find his own muse. I begged him to call you. We didn't need more money or status. That was crap. All the things I had wanted, had schemed for, were just crap. I just wanted him and for him to be happy. I literally begged him to just turn his back on the family, the business at least. I didn't need any of that any longer. Shit, by that time, I loved him so much I would have slept on a straw mattress in a cold water flat if he were next to me. I did, you know, love him."

Chris reached over and took her hand. He thought she might pull it away, but she grasped it tightly. "I know that now, Bev."

"That is what this trip was all about, by the way. Oh, I wanted to help, of course, and maybe see a few sights and thank you for the London tour by the way. Always nice when a native, and you are one by now, shows you around. But really, I wanted to share this. Funny, though, I had trouble getting started, this is not easy stuff. Then I realized we would be back in the States and I would have shared nothing. How ridiculous would that have been? But I had you on a pedestal. I could not escape the feeling that more whining from me would prove, at long last, that I was the brainless bimbo you thought I was. When we got on this plane, I realized it was now or never."

"Beverly, there is one thing I have been meaning to say to you. This goes back to Chuck's passing I think."

"What?"

"Welcome to the family. I mean really welcome to this crazy family. Of course, being part of this clan proves the old saying about being careful of what you wish for. I am often reminded of the Oscar Wilde saying, '*When the Gods wish to punish us, they grant our wishes*'."

"Clever boy, as always, you I mean, not Oscar. Your family is not so bad, I have finally gotten to know your sisters and you did not turn out to be a monster." She smiled.

"Good point. You know, you are as much a sister to me now as Kay and Kat and, better still, you don't beat me up like they do."

She squeezed his hand. "Thank you. You have no idea what that means to me. One thing though, please treat me better than you treat them." Then she smiled. "By the way, your sisters promised me lessons on where to hit you for maximum effect."

Chris, however, didn't absorb her final bit of wit. He suddenly wanted to scream but stuffed it in. "I feel like such a shit for not going back and dragging him across the pond, both of you."

"For God's sake, don't beat yourself up," she admonished him. "He would never have gone with you and physically kidnapping such a public man would have hardly worked. There was no way he was going to give up on pleasing your father, trying to that is."

"Speaking of that bastard, you have stayed in touch with him, haven't you? What is with that, after what he did to you?"

She did not respond right away. Rather, she segued in a slightly different direction. "What have you decided about seeing the patriarch while in the States?"

There was something about the sardonic tone in which she used his father's honorific that drew his attention. "I was waiting to chat with Kat and Ricky before deciding on that."

"Wise, I suspect." She looked directly at him with level eyes. "I am going to recommend that you do so. Chris, I have not stayed in touch with your father out of any sense of affection or loyalty. No, indeed. I have a story to tell. Maybe you should get a drink before I start?"

Chris called an exceptionally attractive stewardess who smiled fetchingly at him until she concluded he was married and with his family. Chris ignored the brief drama and ordered drinks for both himself and Bev. After they arrived, he looked at his sister-in-law with increasing attention as she launched into her narrative.

∽ ∾

Chris looked about as he arrived at the center of power for the Crawford business empire. It had been a while, but the feel was different. His sister had stamped her own style on the place. Instead of luxurious furniture and expensive paintings on the walls, she had imported functional pieces and wall hangings with a more socially conscious message. Chris examined one wall. The hangings were pictures from various sites around the world where his people were working, blown-up and carefully framed. Most often, the shots were of children, sometimes whole families, either suffering from one atrocity or another. Interspersed were shots that communicated various emotions reflecting renewed hope in life and the future. In many were shots of Amar, Kay, Azita, Deena, other on-site staff and a couple with Karen and himself. He was touched.

"Has everyone gathered? I hope I am not late," he asked an efficient looking receptionist.

"No, Doctor Crawford. You are the first. Ms. Crawford wants to speak to you privately before the meeting starts." She then pushed a button and a door opened.

As Chris walked to the inner sanctum, he turned back to the receptionist. "And it is just Chris, by the way. Unfortunately, I am not the kind of doctor that can prescribe drugs, a disappointment to all of my friends." The receptionist looked at him blankly.

"Chris," Kat called out to him as he entered her inner sanctum. A middle-aged woman in a power suit who had been chatting with Chris's younger sibling rose immediately and discretely exited through a side door.

"I didn't mean to interrupt."

"No, no. Everyone knew that my favorite brother was expected. They also were aware that the world would stop immediately upon the arrival of the prodigal sibling."

"Well, I certainly would hope so."

Kat suppressed a chuckle as she circled her desk and threw her arms about him, hugging him deeply. "You don't know how good it is to see you."

"Hell, I say the same thing to myself every morning."

At this, she laughed out loud. "Oh, I keep hoping for some change but, as you have drummed into me so often, you cannot take out what God has put in."

"No, you can't, but I must come up with some new material, the usual stuff is getting stale. Everyone says they want me to change but I know they love me as I am. By the way, I tried my wit on the receptionist and got nothing."

"They are my palace guard, there to protect me. They have seen all kinds of wiles and tricks from better than you. They are especially trained to ignore the common rabble and all forms of disingenuous charm and flattery. Besides, you are not that funny."

Chris feigned being insulted. "Disingenuous, me? Just look at this honest face - and this crap about me not being funny?"

"Ah yes," Kat tried unsuccessfully to look disapproving, "the face that seduced a thousand naïve and now suffering females."

"Hey, they were not all naïve and only a few hundred were left suffering. That is my story and I am sticking with it."

"Good that you keep deluding yourself." Kat pulled herself away and walked to a pair of easy chairs that were used for informal one-on-one chats. "You won't believe this, but you have no idea how hard I have practiced not to respond to your so-called wit. One of my few failures in life, I keep instinctively reacting to your pathetic attempts at humor, a genetic deficiency I presume. But you look good, Amar must be taking good care of you."

"Yes, she is. And you and Ricky?"

"Well, it is not what I imagined marriage to be," Kat deadpanned. When she saw the hoped-for expression of concern from her brother, she continued. "It is much better. As you might imagine, my role models as a girl were not the best. There was the disaster of a mother and a father, the less than inspiring example set by Chuck in the beginning, and two siblings who, for the longest time, seemed set on avoiding being ensnared within the web of marital bliss. Let's just say I did not run out to order a subscription to Bride magazine."

"But now you are happy, right?" He looked at her intently to seek out any subtle signs of deception or reservation.

"Depends of the day, but he is pretty much trained now."

"Don't joke on that, he knows I would take him on if he treated you poorly." Chris assumed a pugilistic stance.

Kat laughed. "Now there is a fight I would pay to see. My money is on the black guy. But listen, how are your girls?"

"Good, growing like weeds. It is amazing to see them develop. I keep thinking no other child ever did such amazing things as these two."

Kat continued to smile. "Oh my, you are a besotted parent. I have to see them."

"You know they are with Beverly, go over anytime. After this, I will be running around to the East Coast foundations, using my famous charms on all those female program officers. There is a world of need out there and we always could use more money. Besides, I love flirting with women who hand out money."

"Amazing you get a dime." Then she shifted her body language, it was subtle, but Chris noticed. "Your schedule is good, I think. Here is your itinerary, all the arrangements have been made."

"Thanks," he said, looking at the papers she handed him. "I take back some of those nasty rumors I've been spreading about you."

Kat ignored him. "I have greased the way with some new marks that even you cannot screw up. But, to the business at hand. I want to brief you first, the big picture, then get a couple of my team to brief you in more depth. Then you can mull over things on the road and we can chat further on your return."

Chris evidenced a look of a man who had just experienced a minor epiphany. "Damn, now I get it. You sent Bev over to Oxford, so she could fill me in on Father and what she was doing with him. Interesting, she never got around to that topic until we were on the plane."

Kat cocked her head but decided to let his last aside go. "See, you are not as dumb as you look. I plead guilty though she was wildly ecstatic about getting to play babysitter. But yeah, I wanted her to fill you in. She never visits here. She and I sometimes talk on burner phones or meet in dark alleys. Times are tense, Chris. We must be careful. That's why I wanted to chat privately first. Some things are very sensitive."

"Sounds a little paranoid." Chris was torn between wanting to accept what he suspected was coming and not wanting to hear it at all. "Before you go any further, let me say something. I am here to listen and maybe to help where I can. And yes, Beverly told me an amazing story about…well, about spying on

Father when she could. Some of the things she told me about him appall me and I know what a bastard he is. But what is new? He is an asshole. We all know that."

"Oh, grow up!" Kat spit the words out and then relaxed. "He is not just bad. If he had merely cheated on mother, that would have been bad. What we are talking about here is way beyond bad. This monster is pure evil. Besides, there is far more at stake here than a family feud. We are talking the fate of the country, perhaps democracy as we know it, perhaps even the world order as we have come to know it. Not to get overly dramatic, but Western civilization might be at stake."

"Glad you decided not to get dramatic." Chris then realized humor would not work. That threw him off and he was not certain how to respond. For the first time, he saw the raw strength and passion that drove his younger sibling from family wallflower to a titan of capitalism. She really was tough as nails. "Alright, I know you are a serious person and I will listen carefully. But I will be brutally honest with you. I am finally happy with my life. Hell, I have a family I adore, am surrounded by interesting colleagues, function in a stimulating professional environment, and live in a country that, while quite imperfect, remains far ahead of this hellhole. At least English children are not gunned down simply for going to school. You are asking me to give all that up for some hopeless cause."

"Yes, and without a smidgeon of reservation," she responded coldly.

"Why, for God's sake? Political battles and conflict in this country have been going on since the creation of organized parties in 1800. Things get better and then worse and then better again. The normative pendulum swings back and forth."

"Absolutely correct." Then Kat seemed to settle into a new mood, one of grim determination. "There are times in the past when we have had greater conflict in the streets and the same concentration of power among an economic elite. And we also had great inequality and suffering. But one thing was different back then. America was not such a world player nor was the globe so interdependent. My business world involves intimate connections with the far corners of the globe. And they, my business peers, are worried about what will happen in a post-Obama America, and many of these are traditional conservatives on economic matters at least. Here is what my associates see. The Republicans have been trying to hang on to their sanity but now are losing ground rapidly. They tried McCain in 2008 and Romney in 2012. The base didn't like either and both lost. So, that battle is over. This time around, it is feared they will go with some loose cannon and certified nut case."

"Cruz maybe, but it increasingly looks like Trump, God forbid."

"Yup, and what if it is Trump? He is a moron who has the most primitive understanding of world economics. The problem is that he has no freaking idea of just how dumb he is. He would start a trade war that would make the Smoot-Hawley fiasco look like a walk in the park. Ready for a worldwide meltdown, the fracture of the Western alliance? Fortunately, not even I, in my darker moments, believe that we are dumb enough to hand the country over to that total idiot. Increasingly, however, I have been experiencing even blacker moments in recent days." She raised her eyes skyward as if in brief prayer. "In a few minutes, a couple of my top experts will fill you in on the global money laundering, particularly from Russian oligarchs through Deutsche Bank, Cyprus, and Geneva. Money, narcissism, greed, nepotism, and stupidity are a lethal combination. Perhaps more importantly, they are putting together a profile of the country's mood, not necessarily overall but among those who would embrace a dictator in a heartbeat."

"Wait Kat. Yes, you say Trump has little chance, but clearly you have doubts about that. The Republican base is just stupid enough to go with this class clown. Being half Irish, I tend to walk on the dark side of pessimism. I can easily see that asshat being elected."

Kat appraised her brother with a cool detachment and decided not to pursue Trump's possibilities any further. "You have been away a long time. Nevertheless, I know you are aware of the well-financed right-wing campaign to shift the foundations of the political debate in this country since the 1970s at least. I have heard you discuss these things much better than I ever could. In fact, it is because of you that I became aware of the world about me. And all that time you thought I was not listening."

Chris assumed a bemused look. "We all underestimated you."

"No matter. What you may not be fully aware of is how successful the right has been in undermining the democratic process through gerrymandering and voter suppression and widespread misinformation campaigns and, when all else fails, outright fraud. Each success leads them to update and extend their game plan. You can tell when they are upping their game, their hysterics about the Dems cheating cranks up another notch. Have you ever seen a site called Prager U?"

"No."

"It is a full-blown social media effort to flood the youth of this country with right-wing misinformation. It is one of several. This entire campaign has seemingly unlimited resources. Most of us know that the Leadership Institute has been attacking higher education, along with Republican-inspired budget cuts to some of our world-class public universities. Whole segments of the population think that Fox News is truth and that Hillary Clinton is a serial killer and that she and John Podesta run a child sex trafficking ring out of a pizza parlor."

"Sure, there are nut jobs out there but…"

"More than you would ever imagine, dear brother, more than even your darkest side can envision. You have said for years that the American electorate is dumb beyond measure. I scoffed. I only hung with educated people. Now, I agree with you. But listen, my people have been educating me, no easy task I admit." She caught herself. "My God, why do I throw these softballs in your direction? In any case, I know the business world, but politics and psychology are a bit out of my league. What I am learning is that there is a vast reservoir of people out there afflicted with a debilitating set of pathologies. They are like putty in the hands of would-be authoritarians: easy to manipulate. We are running out of time, so let me run down their set of afflictions for you. First, this group yearns for an unquestioned authoritarian leader, someone they can literally follow without question. Second, they see the world as a structured hierarchy with everyone in an assigned place as ordained by some divine presence. Third, they have a strong sense of tribalism or an identification with a group that, surprisingly enough, looks and believes just like them. Fourth, they are isolated culturally, only associating with like-minded people and listening to their preferred information outlets. Finally, they are in deadly fear that other groups, the ones that they despise, are gaining on them. These people are paranoid, it is a biological panic, programmed right into how they see the world. There are clinical names for all these syndromes; I have something for you to read."

"Now Kat?"

"Not yet. You are going to protest that this is the fringe. Perhaps. But remember this, dear brother, half of the electorate don't even bother to vote. They are too busy watching the Kardashians. With voter manipulation and those who would never vote anything other than Republican, even if the candidate were Satan's brother, only 20, maybe 25 percent of the entire population needs to be sick to elect a true Nazi to power. After all, there will still be those who will vote for Lucifer himself if he promised to support their narcissistic self-interest and cater to their personal hates. Republican policies only help a sliver of those at the top but many of the near wealthy can be easily bought with the promise of another tax cut and the elimination of a few more inconvenient regulations. A larger slice is driven by abject fear and vitriolic hate. They really don't have to get much more than a quarter of the adult population. Once that happens, once they get all the power, who knows? We may never see democracy again."

Chris looked deeply at his sister. "Yeah, I keep telling everyone that Von Papen and Hindenburg thought they could control that clown Hitler. After all, he was little more than a bombastic buffoon. That has to be one of my favorite historical vignettes."

"Exactly," Kat agreed as she tried to recall who Von Papen was but refused to admit to her brother that she had no idea.

"Now, let's go next door to the small conference room. I have a couple of key staffers ready to run through some drills. I want you to get to know them. Chris, these are people I trust. Everyone worries about industrial espionage. Well, I worry about political espionage, trolls planted to keep tabs on what I am up to and bugs in phones and walls. Life has become…complicated. I even have this place swept every month."

"Did you find electronic bugs?" Chris seemed shocked.

"What do you think?"

Chris opened his mouth but did not get a chance to speak. His sister grabbed his arm, guiding him through a door into a moderately sized, windowless room. Two people were already seated, waiting: a petite Asian female sporting a stylishly cut crown of jet-black hair and a male with a round, pleasant face and a receding hairline. Both looked up expectantly. Chris could not escape the impression that they were students waiting to defend their theses.

Kat spoke first. "This is my much older brother, as you know. Chris, this is April Song and Josef Spiglanin. They both have intriguing backgrounds. Let's start there. I hope you will get to know them well so a little background from them should be useful. They already know yours."

"Wait, I don't get to give my side?" Chris smiled.

Kat ignored him. It was business time. "April, you begin."

The young woman seemed to start, as if surprised. Then she spoke with a distinct oriental accent but in precise English. "It is good to meet you, Doctor Crawford, your excellent reputation is known to all of us and…"

Chris stopped her mid-sentence with a quick laugh. "I am sorry April but let's agree to a few ground rules. First, it is Chris, not Doctor or Professor or His Eminence. I only demand that Kat refer to me as His Eminence. And I hope Kat sends out a general message to that effect. Second, I want equal time to dispute whatever you heard about me from my sister. Wait, you haven't heard anything about a coat rack, have you?" Chris could see the puzzled look on the girl's face and quickly moved on. "Never mind. Finally, let's all relax here. I haven't bitten anyone since…Tuesday. April, April Song, that is a lovely name, lyrical even."

The girl smiled, and then visibly relaxed. "Thank you. My mother birthed three girls over five years, all in the spring. So, she named them April, May, and June. My two brothers were spared such by being born in the fall. I think, this is just my speculation, that the lyrical names, as you say, were chosen to counter the dreary early years my parents endured. We were born in North Korea. My father had technical training and was working on nuclear military projects, don't ask me the details. He was considered a desirable asset by the West and very careful contacts were made through his academic colleagues. Of course, he would not consider leaving without his family, we would all have been killed, after being tortured. But plans were made, which I cannot discuss…national security."

"Fascinating," Chris murmured.

"Anyways, after a short time in South Korea, we all moved to the United States where father took up an academic appointment, among other things. We were too vulnerable in any part of Korea. The rulers of the North are not very forgiving, or I should say, the ruler. There is only the one."

"I imagine not," Chris whispered and kicked himself for interrupting.

When April was certain Chris would say no more, she continued: "I eventually studied mathematics and computer sciences at MIT. I did some work on Wall Street, for the quants who make big money mathematically anticipating small shifts in market fluctuations. But that proved dissatisfying. I was never into the money. Then one day, an operative of Ms. Crawford, someone I knew from college, approached me. We talked for some time about where this country is going, the dangers we faced. You must understand, Doctor…I mean Chris, I love this country. I love democracy as only someone who has lived in an authoritarian regime can. There is nothing so oppressive as a regime based on terror, on blind obedience and total control."

"And you think that is where we are headed?"

"I think you should listen to what I, I mean we, have to say and decide for yourself." April leaned back, now seemingly self-assured. "Josef has an interesting background as well," She added, confirming to all that she was finished.

Josef cleared his throat when he realized he was up. "I was also raised in an authoritarian regime, communist Poland. You see, I was a believer when I was young. I was chosen for a bright future, sent to Moscow to study economics at university. Unfortunately, I was too rational, the inconsistencies and failures of the regime were too obvious, hard to ignore. You cannot plan everything from the center. I left Moscow to continue my studies in Warsaw just as the Solidarity Movement gained traction. I nibbled at it in the beginning before getting caught up in the exhilaration of simply the promise of basic freedoms, like speech and association. It was remarkable, it really was. Years of indoctrination melted away in weeks. I am sure I experienced something akin to what your evangelicals do when they are 'born again'. So, I joined the union of economists, each profession had a union back then, we mimicked the workers in the Gdansk shipyards. I am not sure they were so much unions as they were political or protest clubs. I was suspended from university as many of our more outspoken members were, but we persisted. Then, the day arrived." He stopped as if reliving an old experience.

"Go on, please," Chris encouraged him.

"Sorry, some of the memories are still raw. I still hung around the university. One day I was alone and printing off flyers for distribution. I knew I was on their list. After all, I had been among the chosen but betrayed them. This day, I heard the front door bang open, some shouting, and then heavy footsteps. I may even have said a prayer at that moment, not that I knew any. In a moment, heavily armed police barged in pointing guns at me. It hit me that this might be my final moment on earth. Instead, I was hit in the head with the butt of a rifle and then dragged off to the police station where I was interrogated, if that is what you want to call it. To put it bluntly, they beat me rather badly. I assumed these were my final days…hours."

"Yet, you are here."

"Yes, the best part of the story. It turns out that news of my arrest spread like wildfire. They would have been better to come for me at night, when there were no witnesses. They were not a smart lot. In any case, the lawyers also had a union and the economists worked closely with them. Some figured that both lawyers and economists were professions spawned in Satan's evil mind, so it made sense that they were close allies. Anyways, they organized a mass rally in front of the police station. By this time, they could legitimately threaten to bring what passed as a legal system to its knees. Besides, they had contact with the outside world. I had already published economic and political articles which had been published abroad, so I had a small following in the West. They brought so much pressure on the government that the officials in charge soon released me and basically let me leave the country. Not so much leave as strongly suggested that I do so. I had academic contacts here and was able to pick up my studies at the University of Chicago. It is a little conservative there, but I was able to study under Heckman. One day, as I was debating my future, Ms. Crawford gave a talk, largely on the intersection of business and politics. My future was decided in that moment."

For the first time, Kat spoke up: "Chris, as you can see, I have the brightest and most committed working with me. The commitment comes from personal experience, the best kind. They now have a little show-and-tell presentation to make, some of which will be new to me I am sure."

April and Josef began their presentation, aided by numbers and graphics that were flashed on a large wall surface that could serve multiple functions. It was a masterful tour through summaries of many data sets along with surprisingly deft interpretations of what the kaleidoscope of numbers meant or might mean at least. There were two main themes. One focused on money flows in support of numerous organizations dedicated to entrenching right-wing thought in the American political dialogue. The second was an illuminating exploration of the belief sets embedded in a large portion of the American electorate.

Chris was amazed at how adroitly they had integrated several surveys and related data sets to paint a coherent picture of how so many people saw the world about them. He could see the bottom line coming. Unlimited money targeted on those evidencing preexisting personality pathologies could result in a permanent authoritarian rule in what once had been the world's finest example of a free people, or so the conventional story long presented went. What amazed Chris the most was the detail that was available at the individual level. He was discomforted by the thought that unknown computer whizzes out there knew his food preferences, his reading habits, and his favorite sexual positions. It was not only creepy from a privacy perspective but a potentially devastating tool in the hands of those out to manipulate political divisions. This invasion of his inner world was the work of Cambridge Analytica. It struck Chris that there were so many of these entities out there, plying their dark arts in cyberspace. He was getting lost, but the name Cozy Bear kept coming up which turned out to be a main source of mischief aimed at the American election...a plot straight out of the Kremlin and run by the FSB or the new KGB loyal to Vladimir Putin.

Chris was rather relieved when their presentation turned to domestic issues. Still, he mostly listened but occasionally weighed in on something that caught his attention. He did not know all that much about the intimate connection between

Washington lobbyists, congressional committee assignments, and partisan leadership. "So, let me get this straight. There are levels of committee assignments, A and B and C, based on how much a given seat will generate in political contributions to your reelection. But to get a choice assignment, an A-level committee assignment, you must cough up so much money to the party leadership to help them keep control. An A-level committee, as you say, enables the congressperson to shake down lobbyists for more money, which keeps them both in office and on the lucrative committees. It sounds as if Congress is like the Mafia: all about the foot soldiers raising money for the dons. Doesn't anyone spend time governing, thinking about the public good?"

Josef smiled. "Sure, some of the Democrats do but they have little influence and zero power. And, of course, the president does, or did, but Obama is very limited in what he can do with a Republican Congress and so little time remaining in power. Whatever you see coming out of Congress now, or many statehouses, are prepackaged bills that have been spawned and drafted by right-wing enablers like ALEC. Policy debates and thinking are a lost art form. It is government by predesigned script."

Chris remained totally absorbed when he noticed Kat glance at her watch. That seemed a cue for April and Josef to wrap things up. As they shifted gears, Chris stopped them. "I get what you are trying to tell me. Bottom line is this: a targeted campaign to shift public perception and undermine our institutions, embedded cognitive and behavioral pathologies among 30 to 35 percent of the whole population, widespread political indifference, and a concerted effort to suppress and distort democratic protocols can result in a permanent authoritarian government in America. Is that pretty much it?"

"Yes, more or less a permanent fascist government with only nominal gestures to democratic forms," Kat responded, then smiled. "I remember you saying that Stalin often noted that people could vote anyway they wanted, as long as he got to count the votes. See, I did listen to you. The hard right in this country are not there yet but are getting quite close."

"Let me add a quick historical note," Chris mused as if thinking to himself. "This has been a long time coming but I must admit that I am alarmed at their progress and the international reach of the operations. It strikes us as amusing now but the Republican Party once had a conscience. Even the icons of the conservative wing like Goldwater and Reagan had principles. They would be outcasts today. You could see the drift over time. In the most recent elections, Romney and McCain managed to hold off the inevitable, but I agree that the red tide has swept away what remains of reason within one of our two major parties. This time, the base will not permit a centrist, by Republican standards, to run. And while I cannot imagine that anyone as damaged as Trump or Cruz could win the general election…you never know, you just never know."

Kat arose. "But, as my wonderful people here have shown, they can and might. However, I am afraid we must wrap this up. I am needed elsewhere. Great job." She nodded to her two staffers.

Chris also arose and walked around to first shake Josef's and then April's hand. The latter said softly: "I read your book on international needs. I was inspired." She held his gaze and Chris felt a frisson of emotion stir somewhere. Then both staffers exited.

Kat remained standing. "I am running a bit late so two quick points. First, I see that April has a crush on you. You touch her, and I will break both your kneecaps."

"Wait, I can't help if I am still adorable."

"Oh, barf, you have been warned. And second, I need you. This is a personal plea. Ricky is a great business partner, and I have a great management staff, but I can't handle everything on my own. I want an idea person who can write persuasively and schmooze with other like-minded rich people and political savants. That person, by the way, is you. I don't want you confused on that point. By the way, it is as close to a compliment as you will get from me."

"I see that Kat, not that I agree that I am the only schmuck for this job. But even if you were right on that, this is not easy for me. It is such a sacrifice, a big change, and not just for me. I have a family now. Wow, listen to me, talking about family!"

"Dear Chris, I get that. Believe me, I get that. Maybe, just maybe, I am not as tough as I seem. I am quite tough, don't get me wrong. I talk with Bill, Warren, George, Nick Hanauer, Tom Steyer, and other kindred souls. They worry about the same things and clearly are willing to help. There is something different between the liberal and the ultra-conservative elites, we are not as desperate for power and control. And surely, we are not as Machiavellian. I was chatting with one of the Disney heirs just yesterday. Lovely woman. She was beside herself at being approached by her rich friends to support the Republican agenda. They promised another tax break. Her response was one of incredulity, she kept repeating how insane that was, what would she do with more money when we have so many common needs to be addressed? She is in totally. However, my political compatriots are likely not as obsessed with this as I am, probably since some cannot believe it will happen in the end. Good people see others as they want them to be, not as they are. Besides, perhaps they did not grow up with a father as evil as ours."

"And you think I am that obsessed with this or, even more humorous, that I am a good person?"

Kat permitted herself a tiny smile. "YES…and yes! You did have passion, I remember it. Once there, inside, I don't believe you lose it. The fire, the caring is inside you, it is never extinguished.

With one hand, she hit her breast in the area of her heart. With the other, she reached out to grab his hand. "Here is the thing, though. In the end, I feel so alone. I simply need someone at my side, someone I would trust with my life. I know you cannot be here immediately, I am looking at this in the longer term. Listen carefully, there are many private moments when I feel overwhelmed, straight out frightened. I have these moments when I believe Father would…remove me."

"He can't fire you." Chris looked puzzled.

"No, remove me in a more permanent way, for betraying him."

Chris thought for a moment about dismissing her concern. Then he looked very carefully into her eyes. He pulled her nearer to him, embracing her as she grabbed on to him with a hint of desperation. "We will talk again when I return from my money-raising trip. We will chat at length then, okay?"

"You bet your ass we will." Kat yet held on to him, reluctant to let go.

CHAPTER 6

KASHMIR, INDIA

After dinner, Azita wandered outside Amar's family retreat in a remote area of Kashmir. The past few days in India had been a whirl of sensory overload. While the others on their entourage did site visits to their medical and refugee camps throughout the Mideast, Amar took her adopted daughter on a tour of northwest India. There was a quick stop at Mumbai, which impressed the young girl with its cosmopolitan beat and sharp contrasts, the glitz and drive of a modern, westernized city which sharply abutted shanty towns of almost Dickensian poverty and hopelessness. Though prepared by her own past, Azita was yet moved by impoverished mothers pimping deformed children for a few rupees. For a bit of refuge, she even took time for a Bollywood movie with its fairy-tale storyline and lavish production numbers. She was a bit surprised by how sensual the boy-girl relationships were.

Then it was on to Rajasthan where they first flew to Udaipur, one of those fabled Rajput cities. Azita devoured works on the history and culture of the region. It was there that India's fabled warriors often stood against invaders from the northwest, tribes and nations that swooped down out of what is now Eastern Europe and Central Asia, circumventing the Himalayas that protected the sub-continent's northern flank. She was taken by one story, whose authenticity she doubted but which still moved her. A local prince, from the town of Salumbar to the south, was called for military service by the Udaipur Rajput. He had just married a beautiful woman and had difficulty leaving. He did, several times, but kept returning to ask for one more remembrance from her. She became desperate, fearing dishonor if he did not meet his commitment. When he returned one more time, she fell into despair. She had her servant bring her severed head out to him. So, like her native home she thought, honor was above all.

In Udaipur, they stayed at the Lake Palace, a renowned hotel situated in the middle of Lake Pichola. Azita marveled at the luxury. Nothing quite like this could be found in Afghanistan. It was a fairy-tale place she once had seen as a location used in an old James Bond movie. In lighter moments, she imagined being a character in a cloak-and-dagger spy plot. In truth, she was more taken with the ancient Raj palaces and the local historic temples with their intricately carved friezes and decorative pictorials. The nuances of the complex Hindu belief system were played out before them.

On a boat trip around the lake, Azita found herself musing about what she had seen and felt. "I am very confused about Hinduism. There are so many Gods."

"Don't feel bad." Amar laughed. "I am supposed to know this stuff but gave up long ago. There are literally millions of deities of one sort or another. It is like all those Catholic saints. Each saint serves some individual need, much like the panoply of pagan Gods. If there is a need, wish, desire, or fear, there is a God, or saint, to satisfy your desire. It is all rather convenient to be able to pick and choose some larger presence whatever your malady or concern might be."

"Did you ever believe, in anything?"

"Sure, in Chris."

"Hah," Azita blurted out, "that is settling for sure."

"Hey there, young lady. That is your dear father, and my sexy husband, that you are insulting, but, alas, your point is well taken."

"No need to worry, even I thought he was so handsome when I first met him." Azita giggled.

"And now you don't think is so handsome." Amar laughed gently but then turned serious before Azita could respond. "I will be very honest with you. Even as a child, Hinduism was too passive for me. The world was a given, not to be changed or altered. Too much was about acceptance of what existed, even the evils of the caste system. That too, was much like the early Catholic view of the world with a perfect hierarchical universe with a place for everything and everything in its place."

"Sounds almost Newtonian in its precision, all things related to one another in a fixed, ordered, and mathematical fashion."

Amar looked at her daughter with admiration. "You make the most marvelous connections. Anyways, there was this demand for personal perfection, or the consequences of karmic justice would befall you."

"Your dear husband would surely be in trouble if karmic justice were real. He would probably be reborn as a slug."

"That is a terrible thing to say about your father, but…" Amar broke into a broad smile, "quite accurate, I fear. I…I drifted toward Buddhism quite early, another disappointment for my parents. I have never gotten over all the guilt, so many ways in which I disappointed them. I suppose a child never does."

"I am curious…you don't believe in any form of deity now?" It was a question not an assertion.

Amar looked thoughtful before answering very slowly. "No, I don't but you have long known that. What I have found is that we don't need to embrace a religious tradition fully to get something out of it. Buddhism can also stress personal enlightenment, but there is much in the teachings that can help us be better people. Besides, I have a crush on the Dalai Lama, such a wise man. And I like some of the rituals, the chants, the mantras, the meditations above all. I practice some private techniques that keep me centered, which is very important when you have an inquisitive, obnoxious daughter to raise."

"Aha," Azita blurted, "for that you will join your husband as a slug in the next life."

"At least he and I will be together. But seriously, dear, in the end we all must find our own definition of God. People like us, who think deeply, are burdened. We have to figure it all out on our own."

Azita was about to respond when the boat guide pointed to an outcropping of a small island that was crowned with trees. At first, she noticed a quivering array of color that she could not place. What was that? As the girl looked closely as they approached, the reality of it came to her. The island was covered with parrots. Azita had never seen such a sight and marveled at the scene before her. The brightly ordained birds in the hundreds, perhaps thousands, flitted about their perches as the boat approached. It took her breath away. *This is an amazing country*, she concluded. Then, she decided to put her remaining questions away for another moment.

Next, they journeyed by car to Jaipur, the pink city. Along the way, they stopped at small villages so that Azita could get a feel for the other side of this vast and complex country. Some of the smaller ones reminded her of home, the narrow, dusty streets lined with tea shops and small enterprises selling an amazing variety of goods. The heat of the day seemed to embrace and enhance every sensory input. Vendors also offered sweets, nuts, and ears of corn roasted over coal-fed flames. Oh my God, she felt, this is home. The sights and smells reached deep into her, arousing familiar emotions that tugged at her heart. She missed this, even the daily heat and a sun that permitted no escape.

The palaces and temples of Jaipur, the provincial capital, were even more spectacular than Udaipur. It was known as the pink city since the buildings embraced a pink hue as the sun set in the west. These Rajasthani cities looked more like the traditional India she expected, which conformed closely to her image of the subcontinent. This was the very heart of that land of warriors, the defenders of India, before it was India, from invaders who periodically emerged to seek plunder and territory in this fascinating land. Even Genghis Khan arrived at the gates of India during his conquest of much of the known world. There, however, he was to be thwarted, not by any military defenses but by the humid weather that sickened his warriors and their horses. Beyond the history, there was the enchantment of the place, especially at sunset when the palatial structures transitioned to their pinkish blush. Azita thought it would be nice if Ahmad were there to share this, but then immediately banished the thought. Why had she thought of him and not Ben? Then she knew, Ben could not understand as she and this new boy could.

From there, they drove north toward Punjab and Chandigarh. Now the land changed. The dusty, desert-type terrain mutated into lush fields brimming with crops, which were fueled by advanced irrigation techniques. This was a prosperous land where the Sikhs dominated. Historically an ambitious, even aggressive, people, they had long ago transformed this region into a breadbasket for the county, not the only one but one with a more abundant agricultural output. Yet, many of their sons and daughters excelled in academics with a disproportionate number of young men serving in the military as officers, a career consistent with their tribal traditions. In Chandigarh, mother and daughter joined Amar's family where the two had an opportunity to work with Doctor Vijay Singh, Amar's father, as he met with his patients. Azita saw this as an opportunity to show off her medical knowledge and skills, an opportunity she did not pass up. On more than one occasion, Amar noticed her father's eyes raise in wonderment as her daughter diagnosed a situation or performed a procedure which he permitted her to undertake. *Yes, dear father*, Amar said silently, *she is that talented, much more talented than I was at that age.*

Next, they travelled to a place high in the mountains of Kashmir, a sanctuary used by the Amar clan to escape the summer's heat. Perhaps, there, under the emerging stars, she might have begun to process it all...what she had been seeing and feeling There was just enough light remaining to capture and frame the towering peaks about her, some still crowned with snow, or so it appeared. She felt at home, her original home. She missed the mountains of Afghanistan but, she had to admit, these peaks in the northernmost province of India were far more majestic. She realized she was not far, at that very moment, from what was considered the top of the world: the place where the Asian and subcontinent's tectonic plates had collided in some distant past and thrust rock skyward to the heavens. Such violence, she mused, and yet a clash that resulted in such beauty. God worked in strange ways.

As darkness surrounded her, she gazed away from the mountains and toward a field of stars that was coming into sharp relief. If she were not dead set on becoming a doctor, she surely would have studied astrophysics. The vastness of the universe and the mysteries of the origins of the cosmos fascinated her. *It all makes God so insignificant,* she pondered and then pushed the thought aside. It was always a struggle; her reason had long ago crowded out any simple faith in a deity but her emotional roots held firm. It had become an ever more difficult trick to integrate the two sides of her: reason and emotion.

She decided to push this conundrum aside and focus on the mundane. Had Amar's family accepted her? She was not sure. They were polite enough, but a subtle reserve remained. Perhaps that was just their habit, or perhaps it revealed a deeper, more sinister set of feelings. Maybe they were just trying to make it through a social obligation for Amar's sake, simply gritting their way through the niceties with a young woman they secretly despised. That thought struck Azita deeply. It would have been awful if her adoptive mother were enduring yet another strain with her family because of her. The mere possibility of this caused the girl to shudder. She knew that Amar had had moments of great tension with her parents when she was a younger, unsettled woman. They kept pulling her back just as she was fiercely defending her chosen path in life. Such family struggles are ubiquitous but that never makes them any easier. On occasion, Azita regretted the freedom that Chris and Amar afforded her. They kept telling her that she was free to choose. Such choices, it struck her, can be the worst of prisons - a curse. It really was easier to be told what to do, wasn't it?

Seeing a little bit of India helped her to understand how Amar was like her and the many ways that she was not. Yes, older cultural ties persisted but in an uneasy compromise across generations and geography. Elders held on to traditions as did many of those who resided in rural areas. In so many ways, this was a country being propelled into the modern era, one that was brash and cosmopolitan. Yet, progress was not easily done nor linear in trajectory. Many conflicts and doubts and even points of resistance remained. And yet, this was so much better than her native land. She found it jarring when she recalled seeing photos of women wearing Western dress, dating while attending university, and entering the business world in 1960s Kabul. Since then, her country has slid backward into a medieval period. Was the slide hopeless, irreversible? Should she really care? Were her feelings for that troubled land misplaced? She hated such doubts but could not rid herself of them.

"There you are. I wondered where you had disappeared to." Amar's father appeared out of the enveloping gloom and sat next to her.

Azita looked at the elderly gentleman. Amar was the youngest of the children and Dr. Singh was now well into his 70s. He wore the traditional Sikh turban and closely cropped beard, which had turned mostly white. She thought him distinguished looking, not like the Taliban with their scraggly facial hair and wild looks. There were moments when he reminded Azita of Pamir, brief moments. The good doctor had that same quiet voice, a similar avuncular air about him. The young woman scrambled inside her head to find something appropriate to say. "Yes, I had been admiring the mountains, and now the stars. I forget just how magnificent the sky is when you can escape the city. It is awesome. I think…I think the stars keep you humble."

"That is why we bought this place, to escape everything for at least a few weeks in the summer. Of course, this beautiful land periodically is contested between India and Pakistan, it is not difficult to see why. At times, the peace has been threatened but that seems to have passed for the moment. Now I can treasure this silent refuge. Even as a younger man I was attracted to the Rangdum Gompa Monastery, which we passed on our way. My dear daughter, I owe your mother a debt for acquainting me with the Buddhist rituals and philosophy." Azita experienced surprise at his words but kept her counsel as he continued. "The devotees at the monastery also fled from what they found to be a frantic and irrational world. They always struck me as sincere, so simple and peaceful inside. Besides, they do wonderful things with the mind, amazing things. They have shown even sceptics like me that the brain can be so elastic, even physically changing through focus and meditation. Working with monks attached to the Dalai Lama, a professor in America has shown this scientifically…a Richard Davis or Davidson. I know that your mother, Amar, was also attracted to their ways even as a young girl. I was not happy at the time but came to understand why."

Azita looked at him sharply, he referred to Amar as her mother, more than once. Perhaps he did accept her. Should she ask? No, she did not know how to frame the question. Instead, she lamely offered a query: "But it is so remote here. There are no people except for the monks and a few others escaping the world. Don't you miss civilization?"

He smiled but paused as if considering her question. "Escaping the world. I suspect that is not so bad. For me, I am refreshed after a few weeks here. This space and the vastness are much like a medicine for me. Look to the sky. What do you see?"

She paused, knowing there was depth to his question. "Blackness, and a field of stars."

"Then, my dear, think upon this. You are only seeing our own Milky Way Galaxy. They now believe there are 300 billion stars in our galaxy alone, more stars than Hindu deities." He chuckled very lightly. "There are billions upon billions of galaxies in the universe. And there may be many more than what we have discovered so far. Just think, it was not that long ago that we thought everything revolved around us, the earth. Then we pushed the center of all to our sun, and then the likely black hole at the center of our galaxy, and now we see whole clusters of galaxies probably moving about something we can barely imagine. I think of such things as I sit here many nights."

"I…" Azita said but could not figure out where to go next.

"I know what you are thinking. This doddering old fool has lost his mind."

Azita quickly protested. "No, no…my father, my biological father, would have had the same thoughts. He was also a very wise man."

"High praise, indeed, to be compared to your own father. I am flattered but Amar has talked to me about Doctor Pamir. I doubt very much that I am as wise as he was. I simply parrot what I learned from my offspring. My eldest son is a cosmologist, at university in Canada. This sky has affected many including my children. The son now teaches the father, it is the way of things."

They sat in silence for a while, both looking at the heavens. Then Azita suddenly turned to him. "I try to be a good Muslim girl, but I am not, I fear. I no longer feel I measure up…"

"To what?" the older man asked when she stumbled on her words.

Azita knew she had no answer, so she segued to what really was on her mind. "I must ask…do you dislike me? Are you bothered that your daughter adopted me or that she married a Westerner? I must tell you the truth, I feared meeting you. I did not know what to expect."

"And now?"

"No fear, surely, but I still wish to hear what is in your heart." She looked at him intently.

"My, you are a brave girl. Sometimes, that kind of question is very difficult to answer." Then he looked back at her intently. "I am not evading what you ask, if I understand it correctly. But let me answer in my own way. You have heard of the praying mantis, have you not?"

"Of course." She was annoyed inside, thinking he might, in fact, be doing exactly what he said he was not doing: evading her question.

"Yes, most people know that the female devours the male after mating. This is the subject of many jokes, particularly among women who rather favor the practice." He smiled. "But it is rather a matter of evolutionary necessity. The male provides the female with rich nutrients as she initiates the process of producing the next generation. He is sacrificed so that the offspring are stronger. Think of the male penguin that marches to the sea for food and brings it back to the infant. It is an arduous journey, some die in the effort. The point is this - all is sacrificed for the next generation. Various species have evolved creative ways to create stronger offspring. In so many, males vie for the right to mate with females with the losers often sacrificing their lives. Human males also compete with one another though the losers typically suffer only a bruised ego, not much of a sacrifice when you think on it."

Azita's expression hung between a smile and a hint of exasperation. "I can see that but…"

"Patience, my child. The young are so impetuous." He smiled again. "I think we humans have developed our own mechanisms for producing strong offspring. They are less biological and more cultural. Like our more primitive living creatures, nothing is more important to us than the next generation. Many species have developed amazing strategies for protecting their young. The elephants in a group will encircle a new mother and baby to give protection and security to the new offspring. I saw this as a young man. Such behaviors are imprinted within them, it is instinctive. The behavioral rules for us, however, are not built in. We look to our traditions to give us guidance. Rightly or wrongly, we look to rules that have guided us for generations. In my time, that meant arranged marriages, staying within our own tribe, if you will, and remaining chaste until one is safely married. In hindsight, perhaps some things look dated, rather ridiculous. But never forget what drives culture in the first place: survival and strength and love."

Azita looked far away. "Your own daughter has broken these rules. I know about some of the troubles she had when she was younger. Did you reject her - me?"

"Hah," he cried out with some passion and Azita jumped a bit. "Now we get to it. We all need to remember that, as humans, we don't have built-in rules for doing the right thing. We are not like the animals whose mating rituals are part of their biology. The female leatherback sea turtle finds her way back to the same spot on a beach where she was hatched to lay her eggs. This occurs years after her own birth, no matter how far she has roamed. We do not enjoy the same kind of behavioral imprinting. Yet, we still have that same biological imperative - to raise our children as best we can, and according to the rules bequeathed to us. And then, often when it is far too late, we find that the rules don't always fit. The mantis and the penguin don't need to worry about such things. It will be as such generation after generation. We do. When Amar was away from us, we worried all the time, my wife was beside herself. She and I are in an arranged marriage. We are therefore different in many ways but still managed to love one another. But she had much trouble with Amar being out in the world. Then there was the pregnancy and the divorce, and the fetus lost in a way we never discuss. These were great challenges for any Indian family. But remember this: the pain was always there because we loved her so deeply. That never changed, not for a moment. She is my brightest jewel."

"Sometimes," Azita said tentatively, almost a whisper as she fought the moisture forming in her eyes, "we show our love by letting that which we love so dearly fly away, even if they fall to the ground."

"My God, you are both very young, yet have the wisdom of an elder. You are blessed to have such an insight and yet too young to realize the pain involved." He smiled again and Azita continued to warm to this man.

"Doctor Singh…"

"No, Vijay, please."

"Now," Azita laughed, "that will take some time. About me being so young. Sometimes, I feel old inside. It is as if I lived through so much as a child that I skipped that part of life when I should be young and carefree. I don't regret much but that maybe, not being allowed a childhood, I am incomplete. Still, from my earliest memories my life was consumed with accomplishing a great goal, fighting every obstacle in my way."

"And this goal?"

"To be my father, what he was?"

"My child," Vijay said softly, "you can never be what he was, only what you are meant to be."

"I am not sure I understand the difference," Azita responded, wondering if he would be disappointed that she did not understand. Perhaps he would realize she was not so wise after all.

"No matter, you think upon it. And what is this obstacle of which you speak?"

"My world...my culture." Azita thought no additional explanation was needed.

He looked away again as if peering into a mystery. "Yes, my earliest memories are covered in images of death and conflict. India and Pakistan were born in great strife. Our poor Mahatma tried so hard to make men see but hate is such a stubborn disease. My mother was dragged from a train carriage and beaten to death. My favorite uncle was cut down with a machete. The land flowed with blood, hundreds of thousands were killed, millions displaced. There were rivers of people winding their way in opposite directions looking for safety, for any refuge just to get out of harm's way. I, my family at least, was part of the human flotsam flowing to God knows where, a fate that was unknowable. The fear, even the hate, stays with you for a long time."

"So, it must have been Muslims that struck down your family members. Why wouldn't you hate me as a Muslim girl?"

"Ach, I doubt you were old enough to wield a machete all those decades ago." The sound and words came out in a rush and she jumped a bit. "You can be very dense for someone so smart. I am merely painting the background for you. Yes, when Amar told us about adopting you, who you were, there were some doubts. But listen to me. The more we learned about you, the more we came to know you, and the more you have found a way into our hearts. You have taught us something. No, wait, it is more like you have reminded us of something."

"And what is that?"

"That love, decency and promise come in all kinds of packages. I sensed that when Amar described you, the joy and pride in her voice, that you were a very special girl. When we finally met, I could see that for myself right away. My wife is not someone who shows emotions well. She also suffered as a girl. But we have been married sixty years, our marriage is almost as old as those twinkling stars up there."

Azita now laughed. "You are not millions of years old. You might look it." Then she froze. This was not Chris in front of her, nor Pamir. Had she gone too far?

The good doctor laughed heartedly. "I should spank you as I promised Amar that I would do to her, but never did. Rest assured, my dear, you are loved in this household. And now a secret that we must keep. Can you keep a secret? You must promise me that you can."

"Yes, of course."

"Hmmm, I will trust you. Women are not so good with secrets, but you strike me as exceptional. Here it is, I am so proud of my daughter for not backing down when we pressured her to end her studies and return home. We would have dragged her back here. Then, we put her through hell with that arranged marriage only because we could not stand for her to be alone outside our control, not after her issues. There is not a day that goes by that I do not regret my stupidity. I do love her so much."

"So do I," the girl whispered.

"And never forget this, my child. The world can do many things to you, some very cruel things. At the end of the day, they cannot take what is in your heart unless you permit it. Figure out where you belong and stay true to it. That is what my daughter taught me."

Azita felt her own eyes watering, she could no longer hold the tears back. She was not sure she wanted the world to see her emotions, so she threw her arms around her elderly companion. Thank you so much Dr…Vijay, thank you."

They heard a voice approaching them. "Azita, I think my father is too old for you. Besides, he is married to my mother who can be quite violent when crossed."

"Ah, we were just taking about you," Azita responded and then fell back on Chris's trick of using humor. "Yes, your father was telling me how bad you were as a little girl, how you never listened to his wise counsel."

"Oh, Amar," the old man chuckled, "I think you are stuck with a mischievous one here. She will cause your hair to turn grey, much like you caused mine to turn."

Amar smiled broadly. "Such a way to treat your favorite daughter, the girl who has always been so docile and obedient to all your wishes. Old man, I am thinking that your karma in the next life will be very bad. Yes, I am certain of it."

"Actually, my daughter, I believe I have already suffered sufficiently in this life, my final issue was such a disappointment."

At this, Azita burst out with a laugh. "Now, I feel I am home, with everyone insulting one another."

Dr. Singh arose, "Hah, if that is all it took, we could have started much earlier. But I will take my leave now. I am an old man and I like to read before sleep. Even an old man like me can still learn something. Besides, I am sure you two have much to talk about."

After Doctor Vijay Singh had made his way back toward the house, Amar sat next to her daughter. "What were you two chatting about? No doubt you were filling his head with lies about what a terrible mother I am."

"Though I was tempted, I didn't. No, we were simply discussing what a disappointment his daughter turned out to be." Azita had her mischievous smile.

"You know, young lady, this is very rough terrain. I doubt they would ever find your body, that is if anyone bothered to look."

Azita let out a small chuckle despite trying to hold it in. "And we also talked about the stars. You never told me that one of your brothers was a cosmologist."

"I suspect you never asked. But yes, at McGill University in Canada. When we were younger, we were often here at the same time though he was quite a few years older so not as often as I would have liked. Early on, he would spend so much time out here, memorizing constellations and the names of individual heavenly bodies. Poor father wanted him to follow him into medicine, but it turned out that none of my brothers were so inclined. Sanjay, though, had real scholarly promise. The others were smart, but not quite as gifted. One studied business and is a successful entrepreneur while the other studied agriculture and manages the family's estate. On the other hand, Sanjay spent his time out here, his gaze fixed on the heavens. I was the pest who followed father around, much to his general disgust. Unlike Pamir, who recognized and nurtured your talents early, my father was rather conservative."

"But he did accept you, eventually."

"Well, I wore him down."

"Funny," Azita mused. "You never told me about your family before. You don't talk about them."

"You are right. Guilt? But I do like talking about Sanjay because, I suppose, he is most like me. As he studied more, he went from memorizing the heavenly bodies to telling me what we were looking at, all the amazing mysteries that exist out there. Our universe is breathtaking. I doubt you will find many places on earth where the view is better. Just look at than canvass of stars up there. It really puts it all into perspective, at least for me. The moon will rise shortly, over there." She pointed in a general direction. "When it gets high enough, you can see it so clearly, and the mountains and valleys because it reflects the sun's light so. It is as if you can reach out and touch it."

Azita had a faraway look in her eyes. "This is mesmerizing, I can see why your family escapes to this place, why the monks erected a monastery here. I remember from a philosophy course once, we read some thoughts of the great thinker Pascal. He was also struck with awe by what he saw up there, the immensity and, by comparison, his insignificance. You feel so near to God and yet…"

Amar waited but nothing more came. "I would listen to my brother and wonder at the vastness and complexity of it all. I thought I was very clever, but he would lose me as he got into the details of his world, it all seemed so fantastic."

"What do you mean? You are almost as smart as Chris." It was an old joke that Azita loved to play on Amar, that she might not be as smart as her husband.

"Like I said, they never would find your body. I know places." Amar put on her fake cross look. "But seriously, he would go on about the possibilities of what all this means." Amar's arm swept in a wide upward arc from side to side. "At the smallest level, they do not really know if reality is composed of miniscule particles or tiny strings of energy. Think what that means. If the latter, nothing is solid, just undulating movement or potential. Did you know that there are as many atoms in one DNA molecule as there are stars in our galaxy? How are such things possible? And then he would talk about the Big Bang, that maybe it was all a fluctuation in a tiny, incredibly compact mass of this undulating energy which expands from something we could hold in our palm to all that we know lies out there. It is all beyond belief. But maybe there were many such fluctuations and therefore multiple expansions, multiple worlds - what he called the multiverse, I think? No matter, that would mean there are an untold number of parallel universes in which all kinds of realities can coexist. I would look at him cross-eyed and he would insist that the math, which even I cannot understand, of string theory leads not to one set of equations that explain all things but to untold solutions, one for each distinct universe. While the number of such equations is limitless, they are all internally consistent, and each is as internally consistent as the next. What if all that is true? What are we then, our small lives, our insignificant selves?"

Azita was looking at her intently. "But what if it turns out that we are the only universe. What if, among all the billions of galaxies and trillions of stars and millions of planets like earth that exist out there, we are the only place with intelligent life? What if that were true? And what if we cannot identify which among the billions of humans that might be born will be the special one to take us to a new level of understanding of all this mystery about us? What if, for some shortsighted and stupid reason, we end the life of this human who might save us before that individual can lead us forward? What if everything depends on what we do right here, depends on our stewardship of this planet and our people, and our nurturing of those special lives that move destiny? Or what if that special life is not ended early but she takes the wrong path? What then? Do we get a dead universe overtaken by entropy as our ultimate destiny unless this fragile life form - we stupid and weak humans - can evolve into something that can reverse what science says is inevitable? What if it is all up to us, each of us - and we fail God?"

"Tell me this," Amar said dreamily as she gazed to the heavens. "Do you think that there are some humans who are more advanced, who are better able to please God and lead us to a greater evolutionary destiny?"

Azita looked up at the stars for a rather long time, long enough for Amar to conclude she would not answer. Then, however, she spoke. "Yes, I think there may be some humans that see things differently and can pave the way to the future. Life is not a constant, existence really is a flowing river, and some are better at figuring out where it should go. At the same time, I cannot presume to guess who those people might be. I know from evolutionary history that we had huge dinosaurs living alongside small, insignificant shrews. You would have bet all your money on the dinosaurs being the future. But it was that silly creature scurrying around the ground and up in trees that proved to be the winner, our ancestors."

Amar looked at Azita for some moments. Finally, she spoke. "You amaze me."

"What?" Azita mumbled.

"Sometimes you still strike me as that little girl who scampered around after her father, and then later dogged Kay and I in the medical camp. Your eyes were always wide and curious, everything was a learning moment for you, especially the technology and methods you were seeing for the first time. You were the kid in the candy store absorbing everything that came within your reach. So excited back then, and yet so confident in what you wanted to be and do. And then I turn and look and suddenly see a woman whose grasp of many things exceeds mine. And yet, and yet…"

"She is more lost than the little girl you remember," Azita inserted quickly.

"That is certainly part of it, but that part I understand, at least I think I do. When you were 11 or 12 years old, the full canvas of life had not been made available to you. You knew so little of what the world might offer you. It was easy back then. You could look around and see the person you loved the most in the world. Your father indeed was a special man. To be him, to be like him, made all the sense in the world. And now, this world of ours is so much more complicated. Even though, to you,

I probably look as old as some of those stars up there, I can see what you are dealing with."

Azita started to interrupt, "I doubt if anyone…"

"Shush girl, listen to your elders," Amar said gently, "you will have plenty of time later to tell me what an idiot I am." She paused to see if her daughter would continue but the girl remained silent. "Azita, you are burdened with what most would die for, something I have mentioned to you before. You have these choices, too many perhaps, but you are burdened with deciding which to follow. You are attractive and so you have boys with which to contend. But that doesn't worry me all that much. I really feel you will sort out your heart in that regard. Just, for God's sake, don't get yourself pregnant." When she saw Azita about to respond, she hurried on. "The bigger thing is taking your time on some things, no need to rush."

Azita looked puzzled. "Do you mean Benjie?"

Amar said nothing at first. "Just don't be like me, I threw myself at Chris an hour after I met him. Of course, I thought he would just use me and throw me back. Some judge of character I am."

"But that turned out to be a great decision, no?"

"Okay, bad example." Amar regrouped in her own head and started again. "Here is my lesson in love and, in fact, all the tough decisions we are required to make. More than anyone, you know how complex the human body is. I have thought from time to time about the core parts of our brain. To make this simple, I focus on three essential parts. We have the midbrain and spinal cord, which is where we feel stimuli and sensation. Some of those stimuli are pleasant, some not. Then, we have the cerebral cortex where deep memories lie along with autonomic and instinctual responses. Finally, we have the prefrontal lobe where the intellect and judgment operate. This is a highly stylized set of distinctions but these parts of the brain and nervous system that some refer to as the 'me, myself and I'. Think of them as the dimensions of identity."

Azita's slightly confused look brightened. "Perhaps they are analogous to the id, ego, and superego of Freud's understanding of human behavior? Are you suggesting that I get mental help, some therapy?"

Amar grimaced but more in frustration than anything else. "Yikes, they should take my parenting merit badge away. I am doing terrible at this."

"In truth," Azita responded with a tiny smile, "it is quite difficult to decide how you are doing, I have no idea what you are trying to say. But that is okay, you have only been at the mother thing for a dozen or so years."

"Yes," Amar said and gestured toward where the distant mountains had been when some light remained, "I know exactly where I will dump your body. Now listen, you naughty girl, I am trying to tell you something important."

"Yes ma'am." The young girl looked on with feigned seriousness.

Amar ignored her daughter's bemused look. "Despite my labored explanation, my dear, I do have a point and you need to hear it. My point is that women like us, lucky enough to be highly educated at the best universities believe we are different. We think we can approach everything with our highly developed pre-frontal lobes. Everything is an equation to be solved, a mystery that can be unraveled with the correct data or analysis. Just apply the same methods that work in the lab to our life and all will become clear."

"Mother, are you talking about boys?"

"Azita, my dear, I am talking about everything: boys, your career, your cultural confusion - where the hell you feel you belong. I would bet everything that your heart tells you that your confusion is unique to you. No one else in your circle is struggling for answers like you are. But you know what, we all are. I did, that is for sure. And if you pushed your peers hard enough, you'd find most of them are similarly afflicted."

"I…I thought you and Kay the two most wonderful women I ever met, maybe except for Madeena. The two of you are equal to her. Maybe I should throw Deena in as well, I will think on that."

"Well, I am taking myself off that pedestal for the moment, we can put me back up there later. At your age, I was beset with doubt and confusion. I cried myself to sleep most nights. Who was I? What was I? Where did I belong? What were the rules I was to follow? I was so confused I found myself swept along by the expectations of others. What happened? I ended up pregnant, getting an abortion, and then agreeing to a loveless marriage to a man who treated me like a piece of furniture. No, that is not true. He loved his La-Z-Boy chair much more."

"I…"

"Just listen, now. That is why I brought you here, to my home. I am not so different than you. Hindu and Muslim, India and Afghanistan, yes there are differences for sure, but we're so much alike in important ways. I feel everything you feel, maybe worse. I will tell you a secret: being a mother has more joys than I ever imagined. But it also has pain that cannot be anticipated. You can see your child confused and hurt and you cannot just take all that away. That is the definition of agony. You want to suck all the bad they experience out of them, make it your own and you simply can't do it. That is the private despair of every parent."

"Amar, mother, is that how you feel toward me?"

"What?"

"About taking all my pain as yours. I mean, I am not even your real daughter."

Amar sprung to her feet and walked a few feet away as Azita was struck dumb with surprise. Then, the woman spun around and faced the now mute young woman before her. "Don't you ever say anything like that again, ever. You are my daughter…

MY daughter. In fact, you are even more special. You were not some accident of birth or lust or some bio-genetic lottery wheel. I chose you. I wanted you. I love you more dearly than anything. I would give my life for you in a second. Do you understand? Never doubt…" Then she caught herself and stopped.

The two women looked at one another in silence. They only had the light from the moon that had creeped over the horizon by which to see but that was enough. They knew that the other had tears that were finding a way down their respective cheeks. Neither bothered to hide the evidence of their emotions. Amar slowly walked back and sat next to her daughter, wrapping an arm around the young woman who slowly buried her face in the neck of her mother. "I am sorry."

"No," Amar quickly intruded. "I am sorry. Do you remember those early days in the camp? I remember meeting your father, dear Pamir. I was so happy he had escaped the Taliban to join us, we needed his medical skills and his knowledge of the language and the people and the land so badly. But he came with this package, you. My first impression was: how cute. Then I thought, I hope this girl does not become such a bother, I am too busy to babysit her. And then I remember the very first day working with him, we both were needed to save a young girl about your age at the time, she had been struck with shrapnel from an IED. When we had her stable, Pamir said we should move on to the next patient, there were so many that day, and that you would suture her up. I was shocked. I wanted to protest but he said this in such a matter of fact way. How could we let this girl do that, I argued to myself, but we were so busy? I kept glancing over from the next table and watched your fingers move with such skill. You were…a natural. Later, in the refugee camp, you were such a comfort to the children. You were the same age as many but had such a presence, such love and compassion. I will tell you a secret: I thought that I would talk to your parents about letting me take you back to England with me. I would tell them it was to give you a good education, and that was true, but also you would be like a daughter to me. I thought I would never have any of my own. When your parents were murdered, I never doubted that I would take you away, not for a moment. If Chris didn't agree to you being a part of the deal, there would not have been a marriage. You were a deal-breaker for me."

"Really?" the younger woman said.

"Yes, about this I would not lie." Then Amar felt a need to lighten the conversation. "I would have just used him as a sex object and thrown him away when finished." Amar could sense a slight response to her small joke from her daughter. She remained grateful that she could make her daughter laugh, like Chris. "Remember how we feared his arrival? I think I promised to separate his family jewels from his body, if he tried what I thought he might try."

Azita now giggled at her own memory. "I thought for sure he would have horns, like the devil."

Amar continued as if her daughter had not said anything. "His sister told me so much about him before he arrived. I did not know what to expect other than the horrendous possibility he would try to take her away. I mean, I had seen his face on Skype but that is not the same. But he was her brother and she was the best woman I had ever met, like the sister I never had. I concluded that he must have some redeeming qualities. I think she had somehow made me love him before he arrived. What else could explain that I seduced him that first night?"

Azita pulled her head away from her mother's neck and wiped the moisture from her cheeks. "Yes, you were a wanton woman, not a good role model for a young girl like me."

"You really didn't suspect that back then, did you?"

"Oh no, you were still on a pedestal for me. But please forgive me for what I said before. I sometimes pinch myself at my good fortune. You and Chris seem too good to be true. How has God blessed me so? It does not seem possible."

"He has blessed us both. But Azita, you know I don't believe in any traditional understanding of God. Still, I admit to embracing Buddhism in some half-assed way."

"Such language from a believer." Azita now could smile.

"Well, sainthood might be a stretch for me. But I have learned much from the monks, from the writings. You have always talked about omnism, finding and using the good in whatever spiritual tradition it can be found. That has always struck me as very wise. I can recall talking with some monks at the monastery here once. It was some time ago, way before you and Chris, and I talked about my loneliness, the pain that brought me. One of them told me that no other person could ever take my loneliness away. That was not love, that was giving into one's craving and looking for a false remedy."

"Did the monks share the secret of love or, better yet, the secrets of life?"

Amar considered this. "Well, one of them talked at length about finding a balance within where all the human properties were in sync with one another. I call it allostasis, a way of maintaining some semblance of homeostasis where all is proportional, and a sense of symmetry prevails. Each of us must find a way to sustain homeostasis in ourselves, he told me, but sometimes another person can help. This other doesn't satisfy our cravings for sex or any other need. If they complement you, help you find that inner peace and balance, then you have found love. It sounded profound at the time. I think he explained it better."

"And you have discovered allostasis, this secret formula?"

"Most days, except when I am not thinking of ways to dispose of my inquisitive daughter." Then Amar turned serious. "I suspect it is not like finishing a race, crossing the finishing line or reaching the top of one of those peaks out there. For me, it is always remembering what is important."

"What is important? I mean, how will I know I am approaching this…state?"

"The trick, my dear Azita, is not to deny what you are becoming, an intellectual and a scientist and a Westerner and a complete woman. Never forget that Islam was creating algebra and advanced mathematics and astronomy when the Celtic tribes were worshiping trees and rocks. You have to bring all this together and, I think when you do, all these conflicts inside you will dissolve away."

"I desperately hope you are right. There are moments when my mind shuts down in conflict. Sometimes it is silly things like should I put a scarf over my head or not in public. Sometimes it is things I try to think of as silly but are not, like how do I really feel about Ben and…Ahmad. I get emails from both, but the ones from Ahmad are so…special."

Amar spoke up. "You know, when it comes to understanding boys, I sometimes think we should bring in Chris for a consult."

Azita looked at her mother and then broke into a real laugh. "Seriously, talk with dad about boys?"

"Okay, okay, I sometimes say stupid things." Amar was also laughing.

"There are questions on which Chris can help. There are the big questions - am I a scientist or a healer? Which path should

I follow, where exactly is my heart? With all my conflict inside, I am drawn to the certitude of science. Physicists can predict phenomena with one one-billionth of a degree of uncertainty. It is so clean." Then the girl fell silent, not knowing where to go next. "But healing, that power is breathtaking, total, even if you can only help one at a time. Through science, you can affect many. As a clinician, you can reach few but in such a dramatic way. I have felt that on occasion. There is nothing else like it."

"Oh, my dear Azita." Amar pulled her daughter even closer to her. "You are the only woman I know who would not consider a conflict of the heart the most important thing in her life."

"Mother, do you know what helps me? The same heavens that bewitch you. I look up at those stars. Yes, I am humbled by the immensity of the universe and how much we still cannot see and know. But there is another thing. I know, as both a scientist and as a spiritual person, that I am connected to those stars even if what I see at this moment is something that existed before human history. What I am as a physical being is composed of heavy elements such as carbon. Those elements were forged in the fiery core of some star that died eons ago and whose death throes flung what was created inside it out through the universe in gas clouds that became our solar system and this planet. I am one with those stars. Think about that."

"My dear, I think about that every time I come here. This is my temple, my church. I saw a picture what represented what cosmologists think our universe looks like, at least the one universe we know about. It is a funny shape, with great spirals of clustered galaxies. And there we are, out at the tip of a spiral in the Milky Way. It is like we are on an outpost in the far reaches of the known world, a backwater place. But I keep worrying that maybe we are the only ones."

"The only ones what?" Azita asked.

"As you said before, the only ones conscious of the universe and of their place in it. That is a scary thought for sure. But it is also a glorious thought, and don't you ever forget it. You might be one of the few beings that can comprehend where we are in existence, one of the very few." After a pause, Amar said, "You know what?"

"Probably" Azita responded with her mischievous smile.

"After you achieve some humility, if you ever do, you are going to find that balance you are seeking. Then, love will follow, and contentment, and the balance we all need. I have never been more certain of that than tonight."

Azita sighed. "Tonight, it has been so special."

"How so?"

"Well, when I get pregnant by some bloke I meet in the pub, I can blame your example."

Amar did not respond as Azita giggled. Then, she did so quietly as her daughter leaned closer to hear the words. "Yup, they will never find your body out here."

Mother and daughter resumed looking at the sky, now in silence.

"Thank you for bringing me here, this is like a mosque, a church, a temple." The daughter said at long last. The two of them continued to wonder at the sky above them without needing to utter another word.

CHAPTER 7

AFGHANISTAN

Azita was tired as she sat down to catch up with her emails. She and the others had spent another long day visiting medical facilities, hospitals, schools and social service centers. They had been meeting with seemingly countless government officials, international humanitarians, local service providers. Karen and Deena had arranged the tour to assess how far the Afghan government had come in repairing the human services infrastructure after decades of conflict. Of course, the conflict was far from over, but it was seemingly contained most of the time, at least in parts of the country. Kabul, during their visit so far, seemed much changed from when they lived there as children. The purpose of the review was to assess whether existing program efforts were well considered and targeted or were new tactics required. For Azita and her sister, though, an additional and more personal agenda dominated their minds - an opportunity to revisit their past.

Before she would huddle with her sister to debrief on the day's events, Azita would catch up on her personal world. There were emails from classmates and friends back in Oxford. The notes were chatty but a couple that brought her up to date on the research she would have been doing had she not decided to

join Karen's expedition to the Mideast. There was a little bit of
gossip and an update of the doings at the university. She found
herself longing for the weather back in England as they endured
the summer Kabul heat. She relished her brief note from Chris
talking about the visit from Beverly and his trip to Chicago.
She so missed her new step-sisters, the girls whom she found
delightful as she watched them grow. The process of becoming
a fully human being was endlessly fascinating to watch, she had
concluded. She looked up from the screen for a moment. She
had never felt a strong maternal urge but her up-close experience
of shaping young lives had made an impression. Her reverie was
short-lived, however.

She had saved the notes from Ben and Ahmad for last. Which
to read first? She chose Ben's. It proved newsy but not terribly
personal. He went on about his work and what was keeping him
busy but did end with how much he missed her. Then she turned
to Ahmad's email:

> *Hi,*
>
> *I hope your trip is going well. Wow, that is a dull
> beginning. Perhaps I should just end with 'I wish I
> were there'.*
>
> *So, let me start again. The truth is that I think of
> you every day, every hour, every moment. The fact is,
> I am obsessed with you. I have wanted to admit that
> ever since that day back in Radcliffe Square. I was*

just too scared to expose my feelings, afraid to scare you off. There, I said it and don't take it back.

Funny, you should be in Kabul now. Perhaps that is what brings back so many memories. When I would tease you when we were hardly more than children, I can well imagine I did nothing more than affirm your opinion of boys as smelly, obnoxious creatures not worth the time of day. But how is a young man experiencing his first full-blown infatuation to act? I merely wanted you to notice me. Silly, I suppose, but I was just a kid feeling his raging hormones for the first time.

When we were ripped apart to different parts of the world, you to the north and me to Qatar, your presence to me was never extinguished. I was nothing to you, this fat kid who could think of no better approach than to act like an obnoxious fool. But you remained this ideal to me. Now, I try to recall what the attraction was, how it could be so complete. It was not a physical attraction. You were sort of cute but that was not it. Even then, absent any conversation longer than a few sentences, I knew in my heart you were special. No, not special, you were unique. How does a child know such things? I do not know other

*than the heart wants what the heart wants. OMG...
sorry for such a cliché.*

*I never stopped thinking about you. When
circumstances suggested that our paths might never
cross, my feelings never diminished. Other girls were
distractions, but none could replace you in my heart.
At some point, I recognized that such a release from
my torment would never happen. By the time I made
it to England and finding you was a possibility,
I embraced a new hope out of desperation – that
you would be disgusting and ugly and that all my
memories had been the creation of an overactive
boy's mind. However, my worst fears were realized.
You turned out to be more beautiful than I recalled,
more special than I had imagined. Now, it is a clear
that you will remain foremost in my heart. That is a
certainty.*

*By the way, I have not had any alcohol before
writing this. I will admit that some courage emanates
from typing these words into a keyboard and not
expressing them while looking into your eyes. And if
my words force you to flee from me, so be it. I cannot
refuse what is in my heart. Okay, I am going to hit
send before I chicken out...*

Damn it, I love you Azita.

She stared at the screen for a long time as she reread his message several times. She was not sure if, upon rereading, she wished the words and sentiments were different or that they remained the same. Eventually, she realized that her cheeks were wet. As she was about to brush the salty moisture aside, she recognized the voice of her sister.

"Tears? What is wrong? Did the medical school realize that you are really an idiot and kick you out?"

Azita quickly brushed the tears away while struggling for a good comeback. Her wit failed her on this occasion. Rather, she came back with a question. "How did you decide what you wanted in a relationship?"

This was not what Deena was expecting and looked uncertain for a moment. "Are you talking about me deciding I preferred women or choosing Karen as a partner?"

"Both? No wait, Karen. Hold on, how did you fool everyone so completely when we were young girls?"

Deena laughed and held up her hand. "Hold on. First, we are still young women. Second, tell me what is going on, what was on that screen? It really has been a long day and I am too tired for riddles."

"Nothing of importance," Azita responded without conviction.

"Listen, I just popped in to mention that we are free in the morning and to suggest we visit our old home and neighborhood near the hospital. But come on, open up. I can spare some time to indulge my favorite sister's neuroses."

"The visit, yes, we must do that. It would be brilliant." Azita's eyes did brighten a bit.

"And the tears?"

"Foolish girl stuff…just boys."

"Brilliant! I knew it. This really is delicious. Everyone thought I would be the hopeless romantic. Fess up. You have been somewhat distracted, that I can see, but Amar won't spill on what's bothering you. Yes, my theory was that it was a boy."

Azita was happy for her sibling's interest and, for the first time, laid out what was going on with Ben and her reconnecting with Ahmad just before the trip materialized. "But I want you to realize that my so-called distraction goes beyond mere boys, there are bigger issues as well. But you might as well read this message from Ahmad."

"Sure," Deena said with a skeptical voice as she bent over the screen. "Oh my God," she exclaimed as she read. "This poor fool is besotted. Is he having trouble with his eyesight?" Then she plopped back on the side of the bed opposite Azita. "He needs to be put out of his misery." But Deena saw the expression in her sister's face and changed her tone. "Sorry, so this is more than some crank admirer in your head? You like this boy."

Azita looked at her sister. "I am so confused I don't even know the right question to ask. I understand chemistry, but this hormonal affliction is beyond my understanding. What…how did you sort out your feelings about Karen? I can see Amar and Chris but the two of you…"

"I am guessing that you are talking about how different we are…not my love for another woman?" Deena waited as Azita nodded affirmatively, then continued. "I wish I had the magic words, but my feelings are a bit of a mystery even to me. You know what I went through as a lesbian in this country, my faking an interest in boys to keep a secret even from those I loved the most. I so feared you would reject me. Believe me, your disapproval would have killed me."

"I would never…"

"Oh Azita, I know that now but not then. Everything was so raw when I met Karen. I was getting to the point where I could admit my needs were not some disease when I looked closely at this woman. At first, you know, there was not much attraction. I was rather put off by her fling with Kay. But slowly, slowly, I saw how comfortable she was with herself. And she was funny and smart, not like Chris smart or you smart but very smart indeed, more like quick witted. She made me laugh." Deena seemed to concentrate hard on her thoughts. "Beneath that tough exterior of hers, I found a person who does care, rather deeply. She knew people, how limited they were, yet still had this deep pool of compassion for all around her. I was initially appalled at the way she treated this man who was supposed to be her boss, our poor

Chris, until I realized how much she loved him as a brother, that she would die for him in an instant, which she almost did in fact. Yes, Karen made me laugh, helped me understand who I was and accepted me as is."

"That is lovely."

"One more thing, and I will say this only once since I don't know what to do with it. I...I don't feel much passion with Karen. Funny, those romance novels I devoured as a teen seem ridiculous to me now. Those romance novels are fiction, right? No one experiences those things I suspect. In any case, I've got something deeper than that." Then Amar paused with a quizzical look. "Still, there are times...so many times when I wonder..."

Azita waited for the rest but then knew nothing more would come. "Thank you, sister. This has helped, and yes, I am much looking forward to tomorrow."

"Good." Deena quickly arose, came over to kiss her sister on the cheek and headed toward the door. "One thing," she said as she paused at the exit, 'listen to your heart."

Everyone says that but what does it mean? she said inside her head. Then she looked at her computer. Slowly she brought up Ahmad's message and hit the reply key. She typed in the letters to three words, pausing between each: *I love you.*

She then examined the screen forever as if she did not understand the words she had just typed before hitting the send key.

～ ～

"Come, my love-struck sister, before the sun gets too high in the sky." Deena prodded Azita out of the door.

"You are right, we have become too much like those mad dogs and Englishmen that Kipling wrote about or was it those Gilbert and Sullivan fellows?"

"Both, I think," Deena laughed, "you really are like Papa, such an anglophile."

It was not long before they stood outside their old childhood home. It was different and the same. It had been larger, more ornate than most homes and now served as a medical facility that dealt with a host of health and physical issues for residents in the area. The two young women entered cautiously, and several patients were awaiting help and there was a general bustle of activity about them. Each girl scoured the walls and walked around peering into the rooms that were open to them, assuming the closed doors were treatment and examination rooms. They said not a word to one another. It was as if their minds were a private palimpsest on which faint, older memories were being redone with the aid of the scene before them. They were still lost in their reveries when someone approached and said in the dialect often used among the non-elite of the city.

"Excuse me, if you are in need of medical help, you must register over here." An attractive woman pointed toward a desk in the corner.

"Oh no, I am so sorry," Deena said quickly in English before catching herself and switching to the local language, "we just wanted to see what was here."

"Ah," the woman responded cautiously, herself switching to English. "We don't get many tourists, and everyone is yet cautious of people they do not recognize, those who seem out of place."

Azita scowled slightly. "There is still danger about, then."

The woman remained cautious. "The government does its best, but we treat women and children here, including counseling those who wish to limit their family size. There are those…" Then she stopped. "I am sorry, what is your interest here?"

Azita now smiled. "My sister and I apologize. Allah will not be pleased with our impoliteness. We used to live here, a number of years ago."

The woman's eyes narrowed for an instant before opening wide. "Allah be praised, you are Deena and Azita?" Before the girls could respond, she called out: "Bahiri, come here quick, quickly."

A tallish man, probably in his 30s with a brown complexion indicating a Mideast origin, emerged from one of the rooms. He wore the white coat of a physician and sported a stethoscope around his neck. "What is wrong, Ferhana?"

"These are the Masoud girls, Pamir's children. They simply walked in."

"This is true?" When the girls nodded, he went on with excitement. "There are small miracles every day. My wife and I, we manage this facility. I am Doctor Bahiri Gupta and this is Doctor Ferhana Gupta, my wife, but then you have already met. We must have tea. There is nothing pressing, and one of the nurses can handle the patients for a half hour or so."

Once the tea arrived and the formal introductions were completed, Bahiri explained how the Masoud home remained a medical clinic while his wife went off to check on a patient. "You see, Ferhana grew up in this neighborhood. She knew your parents very well, your father inspired her to become a physician. She talked about you girls, though you were probably too young to recall her. She had come of age before the wicked Taliban crushed the hopes of young girls and managed to be sent to India for her studies, that is where we met. You were still children then, most likely."

"Wait," Deena said, looking at Ferhana as she returned. "I think I do remember you. You were the kind neighborhood young woman who would give Azita and me sweets."

"Aha, yes, that would be my wife, though I think her generosity was intended to impress your father, whom she rather worshipped. I met my wife, Ferhana, in medical school. She was fortunate, her family escaped to Pakistan before it was too late and are quite wealthy. She could have had one of many suitors but chose a relatively poor boy like me." Bahiri smiled broadly.

"Ferhana? A lovely name. Does it not mean one born to a comfortable life?" Deena asked.

"Yes, indeed. My parents thought I would lead a life of ease and luxury, they had worked hard to build a fortune. But I chose love instead and a devotion to good works." She looked at her husband with obvious affection.

Azita and her sister glanced at each other but Bahiri broke the brief silence. "After the Taliban was driven out and we finished our studies, she convinced me to come here to start a practice. This is where her heart remained. Her parents were not happy with that, and neither were mine. Fortunately, for me, love really is blind." He patted his wife's hand.

Ferhana spoke softly. "I personally was crushed to hear about Pamir and Madeena, I am sure they both are with Allah now. On the spot, that very moment, I turned to Bahiri and said that we are building this clinic back up. We shall not let Pamir's dream die. Partly, all this was in honor of your father, and your mother who treated me as their own daughter. I knew this is what I must do, and Bahiri was good enough to agree."

"I thought her crazy, but what was I to do? I loved this woman. As I am sure you girls know, this love thing is the death of many a man's dream of happiness. It almost makes me favor arranged marriages." He laughed as he expressed this opinion. "But now, I see she was right. We do so much good here."

Azita spoke up. "I think…I think that I speak for my sister as well when I say that you have done much honor to our parents and to us. We wish to thank you so much. I myself am studying medicine…at Oxford University." She could see that both were impressed. "My sister now has a degree and has devoted herself to the education of Afghan girls, both in England and here. Even without the Taliban, so much must be done to bring women from this country forward."

Bahiri and Ferhana glanced at each other. "We will talk more, but I will ask one thing of you. So many leave this tortured land never to return. The seductions of other, less troubled, lands are many, especially in the West. What I want to ask of you is that you should never forget your home, your culture. In the end, it is who we are, what we are. Someday, I fervently hope Allah guides you back here. We…we need you."

Bahiri went back to the patients but Ferhana showed them around the clinic and then the three women went out into the neighborhood. Azita struggled in her head about what Bahiri meant by 'here' - was it Afghanistan or his clinic? And by 'we', did he mean the country as an abstraction or merely he and his spouse? For the moment, she decided not to ask.

"Does the market look familiar?" Ferhana asked.

"Yes and no," Deena replied. "Of course, Azita would not know. She never had to go to the market since she was permitted to study all day, being Papa's favorite."

"You shush, Deena, I…"

Ferhana cut them off with a hearty laugh. "Ah yes, I so remember that you girls squabbled all the time, even at such a young age. You two were such a distraction to your dear mother. She would tell me that it would have been better to have all boys, much less trouble. I guess some things never change. But look, you can see many of the stores are the same, but they offer more items and, most of all, people smile more. Fear remains but things are better. Bahiri is right. We can yet save this country. It is possible."

They reached a kiosk where Azita stopped suddenly. "This is the place where…"

"What?" her two companions said almost simultaneously. "I did go to the market one day to do the shopping, I felt so guilty. But Deena and Majeeb, my brother, were right. I was clueless and stopped to read the posters here. I just did it, never thinking. But that small act enraged the morality police and they beat me mercilessly. They might have killed me, but my brother intervened." Then she drifted off into her own memories.

"Your brother must be a brave man, is he with you?"

Deena spoke as her sister remained lost in memory. "Yes, Ferhana, he was very brave and very foolish. He was killed fighting against the Taliban."

"So sorry, I think I knew that now that it is mentioned. Would you like to see more?"

Deena looked at her watch "Oh, look at the time. We must join the others. Come Azita. And Ferhana, thank your husband. We will visit again, and we surely will stay in touch."

Suddenly, Azita seemed to have returned to the present. "Yes, tell Bahiri that we definitely will be in touch and I will think on what he said very, very seriously."

The two sisters walked in silence for some time. Then Deena spoke softly: "You know, after all these years, I am still guilty about that day you went to the market instead of me. For certain, I goaded you into going, knowing full well how foolish you were."

"Good that you feel guilty for your terrible sin," Azita responded before laughing gently and taking her sister's hand. "But it is all balanced out now."

"I am not sure I follow…"

"You almost got me killed that day, that is true. Then, that terrible morning in our family village, I joined you to select the eggs also because I once again felt guilty that you did all the chores. Had I not, I would have been killed like our sweet parents."

Deena only squeezed her sister's hand more firmly. "I will admit to one thing. I did not like you very much when we were young. There were moments when I despised you. Oh, it was jealousy, you know that, we have talked before. But let me now admit to one thing: I could never…never quite imagine that we would be friends as adults. We seemed so different, like not from the same family. I saw us going our different ways as adults, me with a husband and family and you with fame and a career. Now, I cannot imagine my life without you."

Azita stopped so abruptly that Deena was startled. "And you listen to me. You stay in my life, do you hear. If you go and get yourself killed, I will follow you and drag you back into this world. Promise me to be safe."

"Of course, silly sister, why do you worry about such things?"

Azita remained very serious. "Because you have become the famous one. You are known as a champion of girl's education in the Panjshir Valley and other rural areas. Things have changed in this country and they have not. Many yet wish to drag us back and strike out at those pulling us forward. Just…just be careful."

All Deena said was: "I love you dear sister." The two continued on their way.

Back at the hotel, Azita ran to her room to check her emails. She skipped over the rest and found one from Ahmad. It was short:

Do you mean what you said?

She stared at the screen. Did she? Time was short. The others would soon knock on her door to begin the afternoon events and meetings. But she felt compelled to respond and not wait for her thoughts to clear. That might take forever.

Yes…I do.

But you must understand, things are complicated.

Life is complicated, my life at least.

Sometimes, I wish I were just a simple girl but then I realize that you would probably not like me. I am not beautiful like my sister. The reality is that I am very complicated, and I have hard decisions about what to do with my life and the gifts that have been bestowed on me.

I cannot say more now, I must go. One thing for now, though: I have always felt this great passion within me, something I inherited from my father, from both my parents. But figuring out what to do with it is much more complicated than I ever imagined. That is becoming something different…more like an obsession. That is a terrible burden.

Then a knock came at the door. It was time to go. She stared at the screen for another moment and hit the send button.

The group flew in two helicopters from Kabul to the north. As they flew over the hard, sunbaked earth below, Azita reflected on her last journey north. They were little more than refugees sneaking away from a terrorist regime through deceit and trickery. Every mile was fraught with uncertainty, each roadblock an exercise in terror at various levels of intensity. Now, the land below flowed past them with ease. She knew the war yet raged but it seemed out of sight to her. Perhaps a new day had dawned, the worst was over. She permitted herself a small hope.

They landed in the old camp where her father first practiced after the family's escape. It was here that she met Amar and Kay and Chris and Karen. It was here that the trajectory of Azita's life shot off in an entirely different direction. As they descended from the aircraft, she looked around. Deena had been here on several occasions to look after the schools and education programs. But this was Azita's first return in many years, her medical studies had been rather absorbing. It looked both different and the same. The buildings were in the same location, performed similar services. Yet, they struck her as smaller, with less bustle. Was that accurate or merely because she had been smaller and younger back then and perhaps had attached so much significance to the place? Perhaps that reaction was a natural response to a location which had meant so much to her early in life.

As Azita glanced about, she saw some evidence of foreign troops but mostly she noticed numerous Afghan soldiers in their military uniforms. There was no presence of the fierce looking Northern Alliance warriors who bravely fought the Taliban in her youth. Were they still around? These soldiers looked more professional. Yet, they did not strike her as likely to prevail against fanatical terrorists. Then again, who could protect you against someone willing to die just so you would no longer live?

"Welcome," she heard. The accent was not quite British, Australian she concluded. Doctor Archibald Singleton, trained as a physician in Melbourne she would soon learn, was in his fifties and sported a decidedly avuncular air. He greeted them with a warm and genuine smile. This was the head of Karen's team here. He started off with a small joke he had obviously used many times about hating his name Archibald and that he never forgave his parents for this unforgivable sin. It was Archie, and nothing else. Azita immediately liked him. As they toured the medical operations, Azita noticed that a good many of the patients were children. She inquired about it.

"Yes," Archie said, "there is fighting, and we do have wounded combatants to treat, but we see many more children now. Of course, this country has a disproportionate number of children. So many adults died young through conflict and poor conditions. I also have a couple of personal theories about our abundance of young patients. I suspect that parents used to accept the death of the young as God's will but no longer. They may now see a future for themselves and their families and they know full well that their offspring are the key to that future. That's an intriguing thought if correct."

"What is your second hypothesis?" Azita asked.

"Oh yes. It is the school. The work that Deena has done to build up girl's education here and in some of the villages that draws both the young and their parents to our services. It is more than a school. We teach public health and pregnancy prevention and so many other things. The older generation have come to trust us through their children." Then Archie looked at Azita. "You are the younger sister, the one studying medicine at Oxford?"

"Yes." For some reason, Azita felt a bit embarrassed.

"My advice is to focus on pediatrics in your post-grad work. This is a young country as I mentioned. So many of the adults were killed off in decades of war and civil conflict. Ridiculous the way we slaughter one another. Young lady, you learn to work with children and come back here, do you understand me? We will keep you busy."

Then he moved on to the next topic without waiting for her response. Then, it hit her - perhaps he simply expected her to return. By late afternoon, Archie mentioned heading over to the educational facilities. Deena demurred: "I am not sure that there is anything to see. This is summer, no school will be in session, they will be at home."

"True enough," Archie said, "but we have made a few structural changes to the buildings that I want you to see. Besides, we have other ideas that cost money and as long as Karen is here…" With that, they headed over to the school area. As they approached the buildings, sounds could be heard, muffled sounds and rustling sounds that suggested the building was not empty.

"Wait," Deena said, stopping. "what is going on?"

Archie yelled something out and soon dozens and then several hundred children and parents and teachers emerged. They surrounded Deena, trying to touch her, and calling out her name repeatedly. A chair was brought out and she was asked to sit. Deena looked at Karen and her sister with a perplexed, somewhat helpless, expression on her face. *What's happening?* she mouthed silently.

With a few shouted instructions, the girls scrambled to order themselves into rows. A woman in her early 20s, obviously a teacher, stood before Deena and explained how the students insisted on coming here to honor the woman they saw as responsible for the education they were now getting. Deena tried to protest that the new government encouraged girls to learn, that schools were open throughout the country where the Taliban was not strong. The teacher dismissed her comments, emphasizing that no other rural area had the resources they had. They were able to tutor girls individually, work with the reluctant parents, and use education as an overall modernizing strategy. What Deena and the others were doing was far more than teaching reading and writing. They were bringing hope and a future to this area. A small girl brought Deena some flowers while the assembly broke into several native songs of joy and thanks.

Archie moved closer to Karen and Azita who stood as spectators nearby. "Touching, is it not? When they heard that Deena was coming, they insisted on doing something. I thought a few dozen would come but look."

"I am…speechless," Karen murmured, "and no wisecracks from anyone." She quickly looked at Kay and members of her staff to make sure all were behaving.

Azita stood silently, but Archie noticed a tear working down her cheek. "You know," Archie said, "this is for the entire Masoud family. They revere all of you, your parents are saints and martyrs in their eyes. They yet speak of you as the girl healer. That young teacher who spoke earlier began as a student in the school you and your sister started in her village. And you, and your dear father, healed her wounds suffered in one of those cursed roadside explosions. She will thank you later."

"I don't recall her," Deena whispered softly.

"No matter," Archie responded, "she remembers you. You never forget those that give you everything."

Azita whirled and looked directly at the man. "That is what dad, I mean Professor Crawford, has said often to me."

"I know. I had the good fortune to meet him once, in England, not all that long ago. I was traveling, restless. My children were gone on to their own lives, my medical practice had been very successful, and my wife and I had all the creature comforts we could want. And I kept saying, this is it? This is all? Funny, I don't even recall how Christopher and I intersected, it was not planned. It changed my life, though. Here I am, with my lovely wife, who is a nurse. She thought the idea crazy at first. I am sure she had no idea what a dreamer she had been stuck with. But now… you never get this kind of affection working with people who have everything to begin with. In a short while, at dinner, the staff here will lay out how we are working in all areas - community development, entrepreneurship, family planning and strengthening, public health. Sometimes, we help the government, sometimes we are the only game in town. The one thing we do, most of all, is that we keep it all glued together."

Azita spoke with a distant look on her face. "What you are doing in this, of all places, is amazing. Back when I was here…I remember so much tragedy and despair. I think there is more hope now. I feel it. You should be proud."

"My dear, it is not about me. I am here because, in some way, I was meant to be here. But listen, over the next couple of days, I want you to work with me. I will be treating many children who will be here from all over the area. You will see all manner of infections and problems endemic to a poor country with primitive conditions. Then, I believe it has been arranged for you and your sister to go to your home village with your aunt Kristen, Kay I believe she prefers. She wants to visit the place.

In any case, are you willing to help a poor country doctor who wants to see the skills he has heard so much about?"

"I would be most pleased, and I suspect I can learn much from this country doctor. I am yet young in years, but I have learned one lesson; those who protest they have little to teach others have the most to share."

"And wise also," Archie smiled, "and one more thing you might do for me."

"Of course," Azita replied, "if I can."

"Tell Chris that his vision works."

That night, Azita snuck away as dinner ended. Deena was yet glowing from the attention she had received while Karen expressed her opinion several times about how impressed she was with this site. Karen mentioned to her team that she could not wait to email Chris, who by now was in the States, about the reception here and how well things were going. She might even spare him her usual wicked wit and be nice. Then she thought, no way. If she were nice, he would worry that something was amiss, perhaps go into cardiac arrest. He was, after all, getting older and the shock might be too much for him.

Despite the good feelings all round, Azita was restless. Was she jealous of her sister? They had fought all the time as young girls, but she must have grown out of such childishness, or had she? After all, she had been the gifted one in everyone's eyes back then, the prodigy and academic star, the healer who would assume the mantle of her Papa's life work. That had been her passion and her destiny. Now, Deena was being fawned over while she continued to labor in school with her endless studies. What was she doing with her life? An unease had settled deep in the pit of her stomach. It had been there, gnawing at her, ever since running into Bahiri and Ferhana. She was improving herself but contributing so little.

She wandered the camp rather aimlessly that evening until she noticed a bench. It brought forth a memory. Yes, she recalled sitting there with Amar so many years ago when they had first met, also a time when she had been much troubled. Azita finally permitted herself an ironic smile. She was older now, more mature. Yet, Amar's counsel still reached her. She wondered for a moment if she could possibly be as wise and as understanding if she were to be blessed with children. She pondered that question as she looked up at the evening sky. There was yet a dim, burnt orange light to the west since the coming canopy of night was not yet in full relief. Still, many stars were visible. Were the patterns the same as that which looked down over Kashmir? She could not be certain, at least not as certain as she was that no way could she ever rival Amar as a mother.

"Counting stars, are we?"

Azita jumped at the sound. "Damn you, Deena, you frightened me. How did you find me?" But she smiled slightly. "Now I will have to start anew."

Her sister sat next to her. "It wasn't difficult. I merely asked people in the camp if they had noticed a morose and pouting young woman. They all knew exactly who I meant."

"I was not pouting."

"Morose, then?"

"Oh shush…" Azita realized her sister would not go away. "You are wrong if you think I am jealous that everyone is paying attention to you. It matters not to me."

"I never said…"

"All right, it matters a little but not for the reason you think."

Deena shifted her body somewhat to look directly at her sibling. She started to stroke Azita's long dark-brown hair, hoping that her hand would not be swatted away. It was not. "I will admit to something," the older one said in a confessional tone, "after a lifetime of being the one ignored and invisible, this does feel good."

"Oh Deena, I hate myself."

"Please, sweet sister, no need for such self-loathing. I can loathe you enough for the two of us."

It took Azita a moment to catch the jest. Then she let out an involuntary laugh. "Oh, praise Allah, I needed that. Just as if dad, Chris, were here."

"I know who dad is by the way. We both may have learned much of Chris's terrible wit, but I have learned some equally evil talents from Karen," Deena said.

"And we were both such good Muslim girls who always respected one another." They both laughed at this shared joke. Then Azita turned serious. "I will admit to a moment of jealousy and I am ashamed. Don't say anything. You know, I came on this trip because I feared I was losing my roots. What is my faith, my culture, my purpose? Can I relate to my homeland any longer? You have been back many times, well several times. I have buried my nose in books, and Shakespeare, and a Jewish boy who probably will reject me in the end because his parents cannot accept who I am. I walk the streets of Oxford and I cannot decide whether to throw a scarf over my head or not; the last remaining vestige of my culture. When is the last time I attended mosque for prayers? Everything is a choice and I cannot choose. What is wrong with me?" She looked at her sister but continued. "No, I was not jealous of the attention you were getting. I was jealous that you know who you are. You have a life partner, a vocation, a mission. I cannot figure out what to wear, whether to be a clinician or an academic doctor, whether to focus on healing people or solving medical mysteries and, worst of all, I cannot decide whom to love."

The last item caught Deena a bit by surprise. "Ah, boy trouble. Who would have thought, ten or twelve years ago, that you would be afflicted with boy problems? Now, you and I disagree on much, but we surely can agree on this one thing - they really are stupid, smelly, obnoxious creatures." But this time her attempt to lighten the mood fell flat, so she left her attempt at lightness aside. "You are still hearing from the Ahmad boy?"

"Yes…" the word came from Azita so weakly that Deena barely comprehended it.

"And he professed his love?"

Azita nodded but could not form any words.

"Well, isn't it simple? Tell him you are not available until you settle things with Benjamin. I am sure that boy will come around. You are the best he can do. Besides, he loves you. I realize that there is no accounting for taste in matters of the heart, but he does love you dearly." When Azita said nothing in return, something hit her sister. "Wait, you love this other boy, this boy you spoke to once and who was a fat obnoxious kid from our childhood. He really was so irritating. I recall wondering how such a nice man like Abdul could have such a bratty, spoiled offspring. Have you lost your senses?" The words were out, and she could not take them back.

Azita, however, did not argue. "When he professed his love in a message to me," she said slowly, "I told him I loved him also."

Deena tried not to betray her feelings. How could her sensible and rational sister be such an idiot, such an emotional mess? All that came out was: "I see."

Azita, though, had more to say. "I am not sure you do. It is all bound up together. I came here thinking that I would find this backward country that was hopeless. That would decide things for me. I would put all those romantic notions from my childhood aside and focus on a career in academic medicine. That is where my professors say I belong, that I am one of the talented ones, a special one. But that is not what is happening to me. Yes, there is still corruption and poverty and violence and religious intolerance but there is so much more as well. What we saw at our Kabul home, what Bahiri and Ferhana are doing. Look what you are doing here, what Doctor Singleton is accomplishing."

"Archie…he would yell at you if you did not call him that."

"Yes, Archie. It is the old puzzle all over again. What if you can give someone everything? Can anything be better than that? I always knew I had passion for knowledge and for medicine. That never wavered. But what if there is something beyond passion?"

"What can possibly be beyond passion?"

"Obsession," Azita said solemnly.

Deena paused before saying. "That sounds…evil."

"Well, perhaps there are extreme obsessions that can be evil, like being a serial murderer. But maybe there are more ordinary obsessions: passions that are strong enough that you know they are what you are meant to be, what you were born to be. That is what I need to figure out, that I thought this trip would help me figure out but…" She lapsed into silence.

"And then there is this boy."

"Yes, damn it. Amar told me how she reacted to meeting Chris, what she felt inside as a woman."

"Oh God," was all Deena could say.

"But Ahmad is fully Westernized." Azita frowned. "He would not want a girl who might drag him back to the old country."

"And you know this for a fact?" Deena prodded.

Azita just looked at her and burst into tears. The two sisters embraced under the now dark skies that covered the Panjshir Valley.

⨳

Kay looked around. "I've been here before but not since…" She stopped suddenly.

"That is alright, Aunt Kay," Azita said and smiled. "We know very well what happened in this place."

Azita, Deena, Kay, and Agnes Singleton, a nurse and the spouse of Archie, had just alighted from a helicopter near the original family home of the Masoud clan. They were accompanied by four Afghan soldiers, something on which Karen and Amar insisted. This visit was part business. The team would screen the local women and children for signs of disease or medical issues that would later become problematic. When possible, teams from the home base would make visits to the larger villages to inoculate the children and do preventative work. Early on, these trips could be difficult. Suspicions remained high and outsiders were distrusted. The connection to the Masoud family eased the way in this area and word soon filtered through the various valleys in the low-mountain terrain that this was a good thing.

In this instance, the medical mission was something of an excuse. Deena and Azita wanted to visit their old village even if they had not spent much time there as children. It was family, roots, and the soil from which their revered father had emerged. Besides, the elders had insisted. They wanted to personally honor the offspring of their favorite son. After some greetings and introductions, they would get to work. The formal ceremony was scheduled for later, but they did spend some time looking over a small village park that had been developed near the school in honor of Pamir, Madeena, and Majeeb Masoud. It was on an elevated area, as was the school. The girls stood under some trees and looked down over the village. They stared at what had been the family residence here, which now served as a community center of sorts. Someone had decided that the school would be used for medical services, not as a community meeting place, which it had been used as in the past. Perhaps the Masoud children would be more comfortable at the school.

Deena was handling the administrative chores, Agnes was doing the inoculations, while Kay and Azita did the medical screenings. Kay decided to take advantage of her time alone with Azita since the work was rather routine. "So, how does it feel to be back here?"

"The country or my village?"

"Good question, I'm not totally sure." Kay looked pensive.

Azita paused as they moved to the next patient and briefly discussed the last one. "I will answer your question with a question."

"Oh no!"

"Something wrong?" Azita looked more closely at the patient before them.

Kay tried to look serious. "I believe this patient is fine, but you have been infected with a disease. Responding to a question with a question, that is my brother's trick. You have spent too much time with him. I think surgery is called for, a Chris-ectomy. I know just how serious this affliction can be."

Azita smiled, and then broke into a giggle. "Nevertheless, here it is. Are you satisfied with the choices you have made? I mean about your career, becoming a trauma specialist and not an academic like your twin? Chris has told me you had options there. And marriage, and children, what about those decisions? These are wonderful things but once made you cannot easily undo them and the paths in life become…narrower."

Kay's eyes narrowed a bit. "Good thing we are really not talking about anything heavy here. Okay, let's take a break. One thing about these village women, they are very patient." When they reached the shade of the small memorial park, they paused, and Kay picked up the conversation. "Look about you. This is a harsh land, unforgiving. It is also a land of beauty and even kindness. The same people who can fight each other so fiercely also love one another without reservation. It would be very easy for me to spend my life in places like this, working with such people. You know Chris's saying about having that special opportunity to be everything for someone. But maybe that misses the point a bit. Working here, with such need, is a gift that is given to you. You don't give them everything, they provide you with this special opportunity to be a complete physician, a complete person even."

"But that is my...agony right now. You are in England, with a husband and children and doing work that would get done anyways." Azita abruptly stopped. "I am so sorry, it is not my place to ask such personal questions, nor presume on the choices you have made. I..."

"Hah," Kay interrupted. "this is what aunts are for, to be asked embarrassing questions. Just don't expect any good answers. Listen, life is an endless string of choices. We'd drive ourselves crazy if we kept reliving each one. What I have learned so far is not to expect perfection. I remember taking an economics course in college, I had to take some stuff outside of my major for breadth of knowledge. Aside from all those supply-demand curves, I do recall this discussion of decision-making. Basically, we cannot make perfect decisions, we make satisficing decisions always based on imperfect knowledge in the face of competing ends and pressures. Perfection, it turns out, is the enemy of the perfectly fine."

"Hmm." Azita looked unconvinced. "It sounds as if you have settled."

"My, my, you are an impudent girl, I am glad Amar got stuck with you." Kay now laughed. "Do you know that Amar and I drew straws to see who would get to adopt you?"

"No, I did not know that, and Amar won I suppose."

"No, she lost. In fact, she has never forgiven me for getting stuck with you."

Azita had a moment of uncertainty before breaking into an involuntary guffaw. "I am so glad to have you in my life."

"You know, I may have gotten that satisficing thing from an organizational behavior course, I really cannot remember. They forced me to take these social science courses to broaden my outlook. Science my foot, my butcher has better insights into the world. That satisficing thing was a good insight though, I remembered that one. But I will say one thing: I can imagine a life different from what I have, in some respects. But I am very happy. You are going to be confronted with choices. Just do the best you can and keep moving. And speaking of that, we have patients awaiting us, patiently. Hey, that was a clever segue."

"Is that the best you got?"

"Yup, way too impudent. Poor Amar. However, my brother gets no pity, he deserves to suffer. But I will leave you with one more pearl."

"Don't you mean the first pearl…sorry." Azita chuckled lightly.

Kay stroked Azita's head affectionately. "I will still share this with you. Remember, quantum physics tells us that nothing that is observed is unaffected by the observer. That statement, from a real science, holds an enormous and powerful insight. It means that everyone sees a different truth, because everyone is creating what they see, at least to some extent. An observed phenomenon is shaped by the observer. Most people look to religion or philosophy for inspiration. I look to science. For me, that insight suggests that we alone are responsible for our world. Whichever road you take, or is forced upon you, make the most of it. Or, as I read on a bumper sticker once - happiness is a choice."

Later in the day, they all gathered for a ceremony honoring the visit by the girls and the memory of the Masoud family. Azita and Deena decided to spend a few moments back in their old home by themselves. It was very different now, but many memories spilled forth, particularly in their parents' bedroom. This was the place of their death. Azita looked about her. Everything was different and yet she looked at the past. Over there was her parents' bed. That was where they lay that monstrous morning, unaware of what was ahead. She could imagine their confusion, then shock, then horror as reality came into focus. It was all too painful for her. She shook her head to erase the images that crowded in on her.

"We had better join the others," Deena quietly suggested.

"In a moment," Azita responded. She was looking through a set of drawers in a chest pushed into a corner. There, she found a few pieces of clothing she knew had been her mother's. She rubbed each piece across her face, smelled them to detect something from the past. She thought there was something there, but she could not be sure. It may have been pure wish, a fantasy. She brushed a tear away. At the last moment, she noticed a book buried deep under a pile of clothes. No, it was a journal. As Deena wandered toward the door, Azita opened it and knew immediately it was in her mother's handwriting. She almost called out. Instead, she slid the volume into her blouse.

Deena called to her. "They are waiting. We should go."

"Yes, let us go."

They exited into the strong daylight. A young man was standing nearby. Deena had noticed him on their way into their old residence since, in her mind, he had such an odd look on his face. Now Deena noticed a different look, grim and determined. She considered saying something to her sister when the teenager spoke. "Miss Masoud?" It was a question and not an exclamation.

As Deena said: "Yes, what do…" she was distracted by the quick movement of his arm. Something in his hand glinted in the sun as she instinctively ducked low and tried to turn away. Instantaneously, a pain pierced Deena's head followed by blackness.

Azita froze for what seemed an eternity as a blow to her chest knocked her backward.

CHAPTER 8

THE PATRIARCH

Chris emerged from the O'Hare terminal after completing his money-raising trip. It had also been an opportunity to do some political intelligence gathering on the political mood in America. To his delight, he could see Beverly and his two girls waiting. This would be a moment to repress the negativity that he had heard so often at his various stops. It bothered him that so many otherwise savvy, intelligent men and women harbored such hostile views of Hillary Clinton. A quarter-century of attacks had taken their toll. Goebbels had been right: tell lies loud and long enough and people embrace them, even those that should know better.

His little girls squealed and ran to him. *I have become such a boring, middle-class family man,* he said to himself. *I like my life just as it is.* That was the debate that had raged inside him as he traveled to several East Coast cities. During the day, he remained his jocular, smooth self as he charmed, or tried to, one program officer or foundation executive after another. It had gone well. It usually did. Once again, he raised a great deal of money for a cause he cared for. He read a report that 400,000 had lost their lives in the ongoing Syrian conflict. That was more lives lost than American soldiers in combat in World War II. Worse, children were dying horrible deaths from gas attacks. They had to do more there. Such realities - no challenges really - kept him going.

Night was a different matter. After exchanging emails with Amar and Azita and various folk back in London and Oxford, he would lie back in bed and let his mind wander. It always came back to Kat's pleas, her warnings, her fears, and her needs. He was drawn in three directions - his sense of duty to some larger good in a cruel world, his family drama and all the conflicts that his father's perverted obsessions brought out in him, and the love he felt for his new life as a husband and father. It was, he knew, one of those unsolvable conundrums. No matter how he approached the choices laid before him, or what techniques he applied to arrive at a solution, the result was predictable. He simply could not make a clear choice.

At one point, he made a classic pro-con list on whether he should return to America in support of his sister. He had to admit, the points in favor of heading back to take on the dark side were numerous and persuasive. Yes, he could do no other. Then, however, a single memory that he could not shake would haunt him.

It was a pristine fall day not that long ago in his past, though the date was irrelevant. This was a special day, a perfect tableau. It was a Sunday. The whole family went for a picnic on an expanse of green along the river as it lazily meandered through Oxford. The sky was azure, the air still warm yet refreshed by a crisp dryness and a gentle breeze. The trees swayed in a languid dance while the weekend punters pushed their boats along the water that flowed with a desultory resistance as if it never wished to reach the end of its journey. It was perfect.

He recalled sitting on a blanket, having just eaten some of the brunch Amar and Azita had prepared. His youngest daughter had insisted on helping, making the point that she was more than a mere bookworm. It was a residual guilt from an early life script when her mother, Madeena, had permitted her to escape the usual female chores if she applied herself to her studies. She dove diligently into her studies, much to her older sister's disgust, which in turn had led to numerous sibling squabbles. Though the bad feelings were past, the guilt that she had been selfish was not.

Chris had managed to get under her skin earlier that morning by threatening to email Deena with a picture of her doing a domestic task. Azita chased him around their kitchen waving a spatula in his general direction. Even at that point, he could not resist one last jest, asking Azita which delicacy she had prepared. Then he consumed a bit of her contribution before feigning the symptoms of acute poisoning and an agonizing death. His antics, to his disappointment, were ignored. Now, with the repast being mostly consumed, he made a mental note to praise her culinary efforts. Chris had paid enough attention in his psychology class at Princeton to know the benefits of positive reinforcement.

Azita was lying next to him in his memory, her head propped up on his thigh while reading a Shakespearian play, one of his comedies. He tried to remember when she last read something other than science or historical biographies, which she also loved, and for which she would lavish praise on her deceased brother for stimulating this interest. Majeeb had a fondness for stories of his country's past. Still, she had never lost her fascination with Shakespeare, something her Papa had implanted in her when she was a child. The Bard, for her, represented this enchanted land where she could fulfill dreams that had seemed so impossible in Kabul when the Taliban ruled with a fierce and rigid will. Now, she was here, her dream closer than ever, living with a family she adored in a country that she loved while studying at a university that seemed like paradise to her. That, at least, is what Chris felt was in her head and heart as he looked down upon her. He gently patted the top of her head. How much he loved her, how deeply she had become part of his life. She instinctively brushed his hand away, murmuring something about not being the family dog. Chris responded with a quip that a dog would at least love him unconditionally. With that, he could see Azita stretch her neck to catch his eyes. *No dog could love you more than I.* He thought his heart would burst in that moment.

Then Chris recalled looking up, seeing Amar a few feet away playing with their two biological daughters. They were now at an age where scampering about the expanse of greenery as their mother pretended to chase them was just about more fun than anything. *Here I come,* she would cry out. They would respond with unrestrained glee and frantically run in circles, the last thing they wished was to escape this woman about whom their world circled. As he looked upon them, he marveled at how deeply he had immersed himself in their development. He once had looked down upon fawning parents who bragged about each of their child's accomplishments, like uttering a sensible word was the equivalent of winning a Nobel prize. Here he was, no different, amazed at the process where a red, squiggling mass of wrinkles slowly evolved into a human being with such obvious potential. Was he this amazing at a similar age? No, that was not possible.

All efforts to apply prefrontal lobe logic to his decision seemed about how to respond to Kat's plea were hopeless. Reason battled desire. Conscience confronted selfishness. Duty squared off against pleasure. Why all this guilt? Was it his mother's Catholicism, some lingering detritus of internalized sin and innate failure - the inescapable consequences of original sin? He remembered some of those early religious lessons, when he was quite young, and his mother remained involved in her children's lives, before despair and depression and the Irish curse overtook her. Man was inherently sinful. There was an old catechism his mother had kept from her childhood. The soul was depicted as a milk bottle. When you were born, your personal bottle was empty, black. You had to earn your milk, your grace, through devotion and especially through good deeds. If you were not good enough, or slid back, your bottle might be half full or splotchy. No eternal reward for you, you faced a future of regret and suffering. He thought on such lessons. It really was a form of child abuse.

On that day, his always active mind had reflected on insights that seemed relevant to his present dilemma. He and his late brother were more alike than he ever would have admitted, and quite different from his two sisters. Chuck and he were the sensitive ones, the artists, the dreamers. They were the ones that had embraced the early Celtic mythological sentiments and emotions with greater fervor, the guilt and sense of omniscient failure that had to be overcome but never could be. The girls were different. Kat, he sensed, would never have children. He was sure of that. Kay had two offspring, but Chris was sure that was mostly for Jamie's sake. She loved her children but not with the singular passion that many true parents possessed.

His two female siblings were disciplined and focused and had clear vocational and life ambitions. Kay was a dedicated healer and hands-on humanitarian while Kat loved the creative challenges that the business world provided but in a socially conscious way. All four children had rejected their father's vision and philosophy, but the girls had inherited more of his traits. Much is hard-wired, he mused. It does not dictate who we become but the way we become who we are meant to be. It bothered Chris just a tad that he might have more of his older brother in his makeup than he liked to admit. Did he also possess his darker demons?

Still, he mused that the milk bottle reflective of his soul must be mostly full. After all, he had gone off to save the world. He could have led a life of leisure and indulgence, continuing the chase of compliant women. Had not he done more than most to make the world a slightly better place? Why now confront windmills against which he had no chance of prevailing? He did not possess that kind of hubris, such arrogance or inflated sense of importance, to believe for one moment that he might stem powerful political interests or the tide of history. If America was doomed by its own selfishness and stupidity, let it go. Empires rose and fell all the time. Assign it to the ash heap of history, who cared? It was not his responsibility to save a people so selfish, narcissistic, and moronic that they could not figure out their own best interests. In the end, he was not his brother's keeper. They must take responsibility for their own destinies. He merely was the keeper of this family that played on the Oxford green that fine morning.

When that did not work, he tried a different tack. He could contribute to the greater good through his writings. He had just published an acclaimed book that blended his academic understanding of international challenges in vulnerable parts of the world with accounts from his foundation's on-site experiences, both obtained first-hand and through his staff. It was a rare work that appealed to both scholars and educated laypeople. He had hoped for some cross-over success - a book with substance and readability. This was his gift he had concluded, something special bestowed by the Celtic muses. He could pull this kind of thing off. Most chose either a scholarly or a popular audience. The academy had a rigid culture, he had decided. It forced you to choose between having a broader impact or appeasing the whims of the intellectual elite. He loved being around smart people but found their myopia off-putting. But he just might be able to pull it off, perhaps reach many to inform and inspire them while not alienating his colleagues by seeming too concerned with the real world. It was the book that April Song had praised. Yes, this was a noble endeavor to keep his milk bottle white and yet permit him to remain in Oxford.

A decision was right in front of him, ready to be plucked and embraced, when he became aware of two small bodies hurtling toward him. He was back in the O'Hare terminal as his daughters grabbed onto him. He dropped his bag and deftly lifted both up into his arms. All he could hear were the words "Daddy", "Daddy", as he smothered them in kisses. "How are my two favorite girls? Were you good to aunt Beverly?"

"We were very good," the older one shouted and the younger sibling nodded.

"Well, should I check with auntie Beverly?"

The older child became a bit uncertain. "Noooo, no need to."

Chris laughed as Beverly reached him and managed a kiss on his cheek. She smelled good, he thought. Yes, he could see how his brother had fallen for her. In his head, he calculated how long until he might be reunited with his wife. His thoughts wandered to an image of Jules, but he fought off the sense of raw need that elicited. "Were these urchins good? I have my doubts." He tried to sound gruff.

"They were perfect angels."

"See, I told you daddy." His daughter beamed.

"When they were asleep," Beverly added.

Then Chris laughed even louder as they walked to find Beverly's car. "That is okay, girls, I have some gifts for you in my bag, which you can have when we get back to the apartment." The apartment was a luxury suite on the Gold Coast of Chicago with a view of Lake Michigan. Chris loved the location. Then he added for Beverly's sake: "I could have easily arranged for my own transportation. Schlepping out to this hell hole of an airport was not necessary."

"Are you kidding? The girls were half crazed to see you. They insisted we come. Besides, they think O'Hare is a great adventure."

"Hah, I knew I wasn't the main attraction."

"No, they still love you to death, but I am sure they will grow out of that soon enough. Besides, your father returned to town yesterday and wanted me to accompany him to some fancy event today. I am like a public companion for him, now that your mother has nothing to do with him. I used your return as an excuse. By the way, he will be coming over one of these days to see the girls. He is trying to sound like the concerned grandfather."

"Fine," Chris barked, "but don't let him alone with them. I believe they are still too young for him but…" Then he switched directions. "I have to ask. I wanted to on the plane over from England."

Beverly cut him off, anticipating his question. "No, I don't let him touch me. I doubt he has grown out of his various perversions, but he now knows I am no longer a vulnerable kid. Besides, he thinks he is using me to get information about what Kat is up to, and you. Mostly Kat, though. He may have finally concluded that you are a frivolous child that never grew up. Rather exciting, playing the part of a mole. Kat thinks it is dangerous but…"

"Don't underestimate him Beverly."

She looked at him sharply as they reached the car. "Like I said, I am a big girl now. And listen, I have this feeling he wants to come over when you are around. I thought he asked about your schedule so that he could visit when you were not around. I told him you had one more trip, up to Madison, right?"

"Yup, I'm seeing people at the university there, they have an acclaimed poverty research center, a good international affairs program and a wonderful children's hospital where Azita might intern. Honestly, I have been thinking about things, the Kat request, and I am not totally sure this Madison trip is necessary any longer."

Bev said nothing until they were all in the car. "We won't talk about that now. I will beat the living crap out of you later, when the girls are asleep." Looking to the girls in the back seat, she said excitedly. "Okay, back to my place where daddy will give you your presents." The squealing resumed.

"Jules," Chris said as he slid into her car, "how nice of you to drive me up to Madison. This must be terribly inconvenient."

"So good to see you, and no inconvenience at all. I have some contacts up in Mad city I want to touch base with in any case. Besides, I owe you something for getting my brother to settle down into blissful married life. One of the Jackson kids has to meet our parents' expectations."

Chris smiled and replied, "I really have to see your mother soon. She should know that one of their kids, her white son that is, has turned out well. She always told me her biological offspring were such a disappointment to her."

"Tell me again, just how did you seduce all those women? I just cannot see it," she retorted.

"Hmmm, I will skip that one. I know a trap when I see one, all possible responses are bad. I didn't fall off the turnip truck yesterday."

"Really? You believe you are such a clever boy. How delusional." Jules broke out into a fetching smile.

Chris looked at her. She was as beautiful as ever, ebony skin, perfect features, and eyes that would not permit you to look away. No wonder the network loved her. Even better, she was smart as a whip, not just a pretty face. Now, apparently, she brought more to the news scene. She had access to information that Kat's team was digging up, political doings that took place out of public view. She had to be careful. She didn't want to reveal her sources, which would embarrass Kat and inflict great harm on the Crawford empire. Looking at her now, it seemed impossible that he knew her as a slightly awkward teenager, before her full beauty and sophistication blossomed. In fact, they never would have gotten together had he not met her brother on the basketball court. She and Ricky were from a poor, black area on the near west side of Chicago while he was from a privileged white enclave of the super wealthy residing on the Gold Coast. They had reached across a cultural chasm to connect. Chris decided to cut through the easy banter. "Listen Jules. I'm not exactly a clueless cretin. Kat put you up to this. She told you to drive me up to Wisconsin and work on me, right?"

"Boy, you are not a Rhodes scholar for nothing. But you are wrong, smarty pants. She did not order me, she asked me. And by the way, I only agreed to do this since I love listening to you talk. Really, who else uses the word cretin in everyday conversation?"

"All I am saying, gorgeous, is no games. Let's be straight with one another."

"Okay," Jules responded. "I must admit, you were always a straight-up guy. I suspect that is how you managed to survive all those women without getting your balls shot off. You never played games. You told them straight-up that you were a bastard, even when they didn't ask."

"Damn straight," Chris seemed reluctant to finish his sentence but then did, "but it also helped that I only dated women with terrible eyesight, and shaky aims…the ones that drank a lot. They were such poor shots, thank God. The sober ones that could see clearly wanted nothing to do with me. However, in the spirit of openness and transparency, let me be clear: I'm still not at all sure I want to move back to the States, despite all the compelling reasons. I left for good reasons. I now have even better reasons to stay away. Besides, what in God's name makes me so critical? There are hordes of smart folk out there, people who have been paying attention to American politics. I can't believe that Kat needs me to hold her hand."

Jules was silent for some time. Chris wondered if she would remain mute for the remainder of the trip. "I hate this," She finally said, then more silence.

"Hate what, being stuck with me for a day?" Chris asked.

"No, you idiot. I hate giving you compliments. But here's the thing: you are brilliant, have an encyclopedic knowledge of most of the issues, and are a writer of compelling talent. Even better, you can schmooze effortlessly with virtually any crowd and have an uncanny ability to BS with anyone. You could chat with Bill Gates and Warren Buffett in the morning and street organizers in the afternoon. You grew up in one world and learned the other world the hard way. What makes you unique is that you are not in any fixed orbit, neither by discipline nor technical skill nor social class. You are everyman and good at everything. And that is what she needs, we need. People look at your face and, once they get past the BS, they trust you. God knows why?"

"Oh, Jules, that's what all the girls trying to get into my pants say." Almost immediately, her right arm flashed out in the direction of his rib cage but missed. The car swerved nearly clipping a Lexus to their right. "Jesus," he exhaled. "no need to kill us to make a point. This is the interstate for Christ's sake."

"Sorry," she murmured, and then continued with more conviction. "You are going to have to come up with something better than *I am not good enough*. You are good enough. You want to hear something funny? There is not a day goes by that I don't regret not saying yes when you asked. Trying marriage myself drove home the point of how godawful stupid I was back then. You are special, and don't you ever forget it, you - cretin."

After a long while during which they both stared straight ahead, Chris said quietly: "You are damn special yourself. Really, I don't know many women who would use the word cretin in a casual conversation." After a pause, they both broke out laughing. As they recovered, Chris asked. "What did happen in your marriage, if you want to talk about it? I don't know if Kat told you, but I was furious that you never called me. I hated hearing a *fait accompli,* and no comment on my fancy language."

"Sorry, I should have called. I just…just didn't want to bother you with some typical whiny female crap."

"Jules, I am surrounded by women every day. All I hear are whiny female problems. Think about that. I am surrounded by women, all the time. It's a living hell." He broke into his crooked smile. "Christ, just what god-awful thing did I do in my past life?"

"Oh, I cannot wait to tell Amar that one." Chris was relieved when she chuckled before turning serious again. "I think, and I am being honest here, that there was nothing specifically wrong. In the end, there just was no spark. We didn't laugh together. We didn't stimulate each other, or at least he did not do it for me. And I don't mean sexually, I mean intellectually, emotionally. He was fine in the sack but that does not do it over the long haul.

Let's face it. You and I could talk for hours. Sometimes, we would laugh ourselves silly. Hell, after a few months, my husband and I had little to talk about. It just was not there. He had already drifted on to other women and I, frankly, was at least looking around. We both decided that it was better to split than live out a life sentence."

They rode in silence for a while, each alone in their private thoughts. Occasionally, Chris would glance in her direction. Such beauty, he mused silently. They were heading west through what was now countryside toward Rockford where they would swing north toward the swelling rural landscape of southern Wisconsin. It was Chris who shattered the personal reveries. "The children, how are they dealing with this?"

Jules seemed reluctant to talk about them but resigned herself that they must be acknowledged. "We have agreed that he will take primary custody. I do love them but hey, I travel a lot. It is not easy being a network star." Her attempt at humor floated away in the ensuing silence. Then she continued: "I have thought about this whole 'kid thing', and how it has played out within our circle. Just consider this: Ricky and Kat are not likely to have any. They are too immersed, might I say obsessed, in what they are doing. Kay and Jamie both love their boys. But you know what? I am not sure Kay would have had kids were it not for Jamie. Truth is, I'm told, he is the primary caregiver. She loves to be around them but not quite as much as saving people and the world. She will never admit to this, of course, and she will be a decent mother. But she does not embrace the role, not all women do. I know her, and I know myself. She and I are more alike than you might imagine."

"I'm not sure I agree, and I really am losing your point." Chris seemed to focus on the countryside.

"Don't play dumb, handsome, it is unbecoming of you. My point is that those of us who should have been the wonderful parents are not and those of us who were damaged as children are. You loved my parents, our home. That always puzzled me when we were young. What the hell was with that? My folks had love, but we struggled while you had everything. It took me a long time to get it. Wealth is nothing. Affection and support are everything. And yet…" She then paused as if to think about what she was going to say next.

"Yet?"

"Sorry, I just realized my hypothesis is flawed." She wrinkled her face slightly.

"I expected no less than flawed logic, considering the source that is." Chris tried to lighten things a bit.

"Careful kiddo, we are in open country here. No witnesses. Anyways, Ricky and I should have taken to parenthood. You should not have been a parent, at least if your childhood determined one's aptitude." She seemed to be thinking out loud at this point.

Chris spoke up: "I suspect Chuck would have been a great parent, and Beverly. Yes, if Chuck had been allowed to be who he was, he would have been great. He had so much love, more than the rest of us put together. Ever think about that?"

"Not until this very moment," Jules responded. "Anyways, my theory almost works. Those who should have been the natural parents given their own childhoods are not. Losers, like you, turn out to be great at the job. Go figure. It is as if growing up in loving households makes the challenge too difficult, how can you match what you saw as a child? But Kay and Kat ruin my neat theory."

Chris quickly responded: "No, they don't, well maybe just a little. Despite how much they hate the patriarch, they did inherit a lot from him. They are the tough ones. Chuck and I take more after mother, the Irish dreamers. Life is funny, biology rather a total crap shoot, or mere nurturing."

They rode in silence again, lost in thought and memories. "Shit," Jules suddenly said, "Wisconsin already. I promised Kat I would give you my pitch on what I am finding out."

Chris leaned back and pretended to listen.

At the end of the day, after many meetings and discussions with officials and potential colleagues for Chris, the two of them met up again at the apex of Observatory Drive on the university campus. Behind them remained the shell of a celestial observatory that had fallen into disuse decades ago as the lights of an expanding city encroached on this idyllic spot. Before them, the land fell away to Lake Mendota, one of five bodies of water that had been ground out by glacial actions thousands of years ago during the last ice age. It was a magnificent vista.

"This is gorgeous," Jules offered with sincerity. "How could you not move here? I recall coming to Madison during my college years for a football game or two and for Halloween. The Halloween celebrations here were legendary but I don't recall getting to this spot. Then again, perhaps I did but I might have been blitzed at the time. But I repeat…how could you not move here? By the way, I just assume all went well."

"Piece of advice, my dear. Don't quit your day job to go into real estate. You are not a born sales person. I still love Oxford and my life. However, I do have options now, damn it. I rather wished they hadn't been so eager to get me, it would make life easier. Apparently, however, I could take a leave from university, come here as a visiting scholar. They have exchange precedents and protocols for such a move, all designed to make it as painless as possible. Damn them. They even have a scholar here who intends to spend next year at Oxford and we can even swap houses, if we wish. Then, to really screw me, Amar could get a position at the university hospital and Azita could intern at the children's hospital on campus. There would still be some hoops for them, but promises were made and, more importantly, the usual hurdles have been magically bypassed. I have a very strong feeling that someone has been pulling strings behind my back, no names need be mentioned. I would not be surprised if some judicious financial contributions to certain cash-starved academic programs were made, which covers the circumstances of most public universities at present. Nothing in academia ever, ever works this smoothly. If you really want an advanced glimpse of hell, survive a few faculty meetings."

"Fantastic, including your very astute observation about people needing to be bribed to want you." Jules beamed.

"Don't you dare gloat." He scowled at her. "I've not decided yet. And I haven't even broached the topic with Amar and Azita. They think I am just raising money for the international work. I rather hate going behind their backs."

"When they see this, they will forgive you."

"Truth is, the possibility of Madison is keeping this scheme alive. I don't think I would go back to Chicago and be that close to all the memories. But I have always liked this place, a university town, liberal and cosmopolitan, yet small enough to be livable. Reminds me just a little of Oxford. And close enough to work with Kat on her crazy schemes."

"And me," Jules added.

"You should focus only on the positives."

"Watch it buddy."

"And you. Time to go. We are having dinner with several of the people I met with today. You won't believe this, but they are excited to meet a real network star. But I told them I couldn't get one of those, just you. Surprisingly, they didn't cancel."

"You do know that the way you are sitting there gives me a direct shot to your mid-section. Speaking of pain more generally, however, did you decide to meet with your father?"

"Yes, when we get back. I called Beverly while walking back over here, just to fill her in. She is arranging it. I hate the thought, but I need to get it over with. It must be done. Well, I suppose it doesn't have to be done. I will admit to a form of morbid curiosity."

Jules looked pensive, torn between being happy that this was happening and concerned about what this would mean to this man that she yet loved in her own way. The chasm between father and son was something she could hardly appreciate, way beyond her capacity to comprehend. She looked away in case this sudden swell of emotion translated into some visible sign of intense caring. Tears at this moment would have been hard to joke away. Why had she turned his marriage proposals down? Had she assumed they would keep coming, and that she might accept one at a more convenient time? Had she worried about all his casual relations with women even though they had never entered an exclusive relationship? Was it her drive for a career and worry that a husband or children would deter the realization of her deep obsession to succeed, to show the world that a girl from the ghetto could make it? Then an irritating thought intruded, she was a girl from the ghetto. Had she felt unworthy, or maybe held some residual bitterness based on the inescapable racism of her childhood. You don't ever escape those scars, not entirely. She could not shake this insistent thought, she had rejected him because he was white. He was her brother's best friend, her most intimate male or female confidant and she might have spurned him because of the color of his skin. Did she believe that accepting him as a formal partner as a betrayal of - something? She tried very hard to focus on the pastoral visage of water and the distant green countryside before her but that proved futile. She needed to say something, anything. "By the way, I made a reservation at the Edgewater Hotel, that nice place on the lake you suggested." When Chris looked at her questioningly, she added: "Two rooms though - that killed me, to waste money that is."

"Jules, it won't be easy for me either, believe me. You were my 43rd favorite lover." Her fist shot out and caught him right in the tummy.

"Shit, that hurt," he wheezed.

"Good, now let's go meet your future colleagues and then a cold shower for me."

"On the way, you might drop me off at the goddamn emergency room," he managed to get out as he struggled to his feet.

"You have not changed, Father." The two men appraised each other from across the room of Beverly's luxurious suite of apartments. In fact, Chris was being sincere. In his mind, his father had swiftly transformed from an energetic young man of frenetic energy to a stately prince generating an aura of power and invincibility. It struck Chris that there were very few interim steps in this miraculous transformation. Once he had arrived at the status of the all-powerful patriarch, time appeared to stop. The aging process was nullified. He seemingly looked the same as he did in his late 70s as he did in his late 50s. Chris knew this not to be true, that one's perception could easily play tricks, and he was aware of all those visual tricks that Psych 101 textbooks covered. Still, he could well imagine that his father had entered into some pact with Satan himself: eternal life for his soul. "*I hope you negotiated a good contract with Lucifer*", he murmured, surprising himself that his private thought had almost escaped him.

"What?" His father seemed unsettled.

"Nothing, Father, just a private joke. I am always trying to keep myself amused. Did you enjoy a good visit with my children?"

"Why yes." The older man grinned in a way that made Chris's skin crawl. "They are delightful. You and …what is your wife's name again?"

"Amar…Amar Singh, as if you did not know."

"Don't be so harsh, my son. You must excuse an old man. After all, I was not invited to the wedding."

"Well, dear Father, it was short notice and officiated in a war zone in Afghanistan. It was, by necessity, an intimate affair, as you might imagine."

"Of course. I had assumed that the rushed affair involved an inconvenient pregnancy. Did she miscarry that one?" The forced grin seemed stuck in place.

Chris so wanted to lash out at this man, as he had done the last time they had met. Why the gratuitous insults when they were so unnecessary? Perhaps it was true that you couldn't take out what God puts in a person, even a deep pool of unnecessary evil. At their last meeting, Charles Senior had struck his mother in a fit of pique. Chris, in that moment and fresh off the news that his own father had raped his two sisters when they were young and defenseless, smashed his fist into his father's face. Every sensible instinct within him was needed to restrain himself. Now, similar urges erupted deep in his stomach and roiled upward throughout his body. He had prepared for this moment, though he now questioned whether any amount of preparation would be enough.

"Just the urgency of love, and the desire to take Azita to England with us." Chris fought to keep his composure. "Perhaps you are unfamiliar with the concept of love, that human sentiment being denied to you."

His father chose to ignore the obvious insult. "Ah, yes, that Afghan orphan, or young woman by now."

"Hardly merely an orphan, Father, top of her medical class at Oxford." Chris enjoyed throwing that in, even though his father must be aware of that fact since Beverly was the conduit to him for all things Crawford in her role as a secret mole.

The patriarch's smile spread a bit wider. "Of course. I expect no less of anyone raised as a Crawford, or by a Crawford I should say. Though I must admit to being just a bit surprised at her success absent the proper, what shall we say, genetic material?"

Chris's voice hardened. His words emerged sharp and uncompromising. "She is a Masoud, daughter of Pamir and Madeena Masoud. Her father fought his way from poverty in the Panjshir Valley of northern Afghanistan to graduate from England's premier medical school. He might have done anything, but he went back to help his people. He died in the effort. If anything, Azita reflects her parents, the very best of... genetic material, as you put it."

"Yes, yes, of course," Charles issued in a dismissive tone. "But I have given this much thought. It is my belief that the traits we often desire in our offspring often skip a generation, like colorblindness or hair loss or even common sense. That can be such a tragedy."

Beverly had been increasingly uneasy at the direction of the conversation. "Listen, why don't you both sit, and I will get us drinks after I'm sure the girls are settled." She left the room, silently saying a prayer that when she returned there would not be a prone body on the floor.

The two men appraised one another for a few moments in silence. Neither wanted to be the first to look away. Charles Senior first broke the silence. "Of course, Christopher, I do know that you detest me. And I don't mind admitting that this knowledge upsets me. What father does not wish for the admiration of his offspring, does not want his son to look up to him and follow in his footsteps? I thought I had a chance with Junior, I really did. I am aware the rest of you did not share my optimism, you have all made that sufficiently clear. Still, I had such hope for him. I suspect the father always believes the best of his first-born son. They have always been the natural heirs, by convention and tradition. But he was soft, so soft. I still think if the rest of you had not been so negative and had supported him…"

"Father just cut the bullshit. Yes, I have one regret about not supporting Chuck enough. Out there, on Navy Pier one day," Chris nodded in the general direction of Lake Michigan, "I begged him to come to England with me, begged him. But I guess I did not grovel nearly enough. What I should have done was drug him into a stupor and simply kidnapped him. I should have forced his silly ass on to the plane with me. But it was like he was imprisoned in a cult. Leaving him in your clutches was as good as putting a gun to his head and pulling the trigger."

"The boy simply was soft. I did try my best…"

"To do what, kill him?" Chris spit out. "Well congratulations, you did a fucking swell job of doing just that. You could have had the decency to make his death spiral quicker, just a bit less agonizing."

"Chris - always with the dramatics." The older man apparently decided to shift direction just slightly. His voice now sounded almost sincere. "Tell me, honestly, do you think of me as such a monster?"

Chris did not answer right away. He looked over the view of the lake out of a panoramic window. The sun, now in its western descent, had developed its daily burnt-orange glow that managed to cast its reach back over the waters to the east, touching the clouds that had formed just above the horizon. That scene always refreshed him, water always refreshed him. As a child, he would come down to Oak Beach when troubled, sit and look over the water. It truly was one of God's more special gifts to His ungrateful progeny. Then, he forced himself to snap back to the present. "Let us skip over your perversions, that would not lead to any productive dialogue." He saw his father open his mouth. Chris raised his hand to stop him. "I think, at least in your head, that you are a unique blend of an Ayn Rand character who worships selfishness along with a caricature of Nietzsche's notion of superman. Oh, and let us not forget that a healthy dose of Calvinistic predestination which must be thrown in, just to give a spiritual imprimatur on the master-race panache that so blinds your vision. After all, you need some way to identify the select, to satisfy yourself that you are among them."

His father betrayed no emotion whatsoever. "Very perceptive, son. I am gratified that all those years of schooling were not totally wasted. And all this time I had thought you majored in basketball with a minor in sex. But I have another question for you. Why are you here?"

Beverly appeared at that moment with the drinks, relieved at the seeming calm that prevailed. "Here," she said and handed the drinks over to the two. "I am going to check on the girls."

Chris toyed with being relatively honest, at least to the point of indicating that he might return to the States for an academic sabbatical at Wisconsin. But why be even that honest? Perhaps evasion might reveal what his father knew or thought he knew. "I am just here to raise money for my international work, see my sister and some friends. Amar and Kay and Azita are gone for several weeks. With no teaching commitment now, it seemed like a good time. Beverly was kind enough to help out."

"Yes, Beverly, she is…so helpful." His smile widened just a fraction for a moment. "And this trip to Madison? Surely, that was not fund raising? Perhaps a little sight-seeing, I seem to recall you running up there as a teenager. You would call it Mad City. Personally, I always thought that place infested with communists and juvenile revolutionaries, but that is where we differ."

Chris sensed that he was not directing the conversation, his father was in control. That, he concluded, needed to be changed. "Speaking of communists, what is left of them, are you celebrating their demise, or have you found a new outlet for your, shall we say, energies? Odd, is it not, how old enemies can so easily switch sides."

Now his father's smile turned from a grimace to a sneer. "Please don't be so disingenuous. You don't do coy well. You of all people should know of my unending work to save society from itself. Yes, you labor to save the world in your way and I in mine. You see, we are very similar people, not so very different."

Chris felt his face flush a bit. Had that shown? What did his father know about Kat's work, about his discussions with his younger sibling? Maybe his comments were innocent, merely referring to Chris's philanthropic and service initiatives. Yet, Kat had implied danger, mentioned using burner phones for some conversations. What might he have been getting into here? Was his father just guessing about why Chris was here? If not, how did he know anything about what was going on? Several possibilities flooded Chris's mind. "No, I have no idea what you are up to these days. Please enlighten me." Chris hoped his own smile was equally enigmatic.

Charles Senior paused while he brought his fingers together in front of him. He looked at his hands for several moments, obviously calculating what to reveal and what not to reveal. "I think, son, that you have always misunderstood me." Christopher made a note of the fact that his father referred to him as his son and not by his name. "You have always thought of me in the simplest of terms, that I am some greedy capitalist only concerned with acquiring great wealth. But that is just a tool, not an end." Chris momentarily thought of challenging that statement but held back. "I am a far different person. In truth, we are very much alike. I know, I know so very well that you do not see that, which pains me deeply. But we are, drawn from the same genetic material, the same historical roots. You are way too intelligent not to see that." He paused, apparently waiting for Chris to provide some affirmation or denial.

"Go on, I am listening."

"We are both idealists. True, I did not appreciate all your work in the hell holes of the globe but, eventually, I did understand. It was just your - how should I put this? -your early and perhaps immature way of finding meaning in life. And that, right there, is where we are alike. It took me some time to determine what is important for a man to pursue. And yes, yes, you were right about Chuck, I was mistaken about him all along, and I hate making mistakes. Fortunately, I do it so infrequently. But you, you are my true offspring. We both want one thing, the same thing: a better world and better future."

"However," Chris said and breathed slowly, "the devil, as they say, is in the details."

"True indeed. You want to bring everyone up by their bootstraps, save the unwashed masses and permit them to participate in some mass delusion about a global society and democracy. All that, I admit, is very well intended but, I am afraid, it is a hopeless fantasy. Not even the founding fathers of this great country believed in democracy. That is why they built in layers of protection against the will of the people like the electoral college and appointed senators and limited voting rights, but I am preaching to the choir now, am I not? After all, I have read many of your written works, perhaps all. Some of those wise protections were eroded but we are slowly putting them back in place."

"We…?" But Chris could not finish his thought, still puzzled that his father might have read his books and articles. What did that mean?

"Not important now. What is important is that we gather together those people born to lead. Plato, it turns out, was right. Society is best led by philosopher kings, those, who by breeding and training, can see the future clearly and identify what we need to do to get there. Let me anticipate your concern." Now

Charles Senior leaned forward, warming to his topic. Chris decided not to interfere. "There really is no safe word for what we have in mind. I hate the terms master race or the select or the predestined. Semantics aside, even you must admit that the messiness of democracy is no way to run things in a complex and interdependent world. Society needs guidance. I have even backed off from my unfettered free-market views. In fact, government, or perhaps we best call it leadership, can be a necessary tool, a useful partner."

Chris wanted to respond by saying his father was giving a classic definition of fascism but instead said, "Go on, I find this is interesting."

Charles was not always easy to read but his body language seemed more relaxed. "Son, you are the student of history. Even I know that both empires and ideas wax and wane over time. Yes, I am capable of larger thoughts not related to making money. Are you shocked?" Chris was but kept silent. "The thing is, I have been convinced we are on the threshold of big changes, this singularity that the computer nerds talk about." Now Chris was openly surprised, such a concept seemed way beyond his father's ordinary concerns. "The thing is, having my financial empire stolen from under me, and thank you for that by the way, has been a blessing in disguise. Now I have an opportunity to read and think about things. That would not have been possible before.

We all cannot while away the hours doing nothing productive in some ivory tower, living off our parents' largess."

"I thank you for that opportunity by the way, father. Your wealth, and mother's, gave me great opportunities." Chris hoped his sarcasm was evident.

"I am sure you are very grateful. But yes, I have indulged my curiosity about many things, about amazing possibilities for the future. I am convinced we are on the precipice of great advances, my son." The patriarch paused at this point. "I can see you are taken aback by all this."

"Just a bit. I can admit to falling short of total omniscience. Continue, though." Chris assumed his father used the term 'singularity' to signify man melding with machines one day to achieve a kind of immortality and not what happens inside a cosmic black hole where time stops.

"Let me get to the bottom line. I hope, someday, we might pick up on this again but, for now, let me just say this. Evolution is all about survival. That, we can agree on. The issue is who will survive. Species and peoples have been going extinct for thousands of years. We don't cry over the losers, it is simply a natural law. I won't sugar coat things. Life is struggle. Creative destruction is not evil but a necessary component of progress. Sympathy is for losers. I never want to be a loser. I saw, or was told at least, what happened to my native land when tougher and more purposeful men, the Russians and the Germans, simply came in and took over. I am never, never going to be on the losing side again. You can be damn sure that I am doing everything possible to be on the winning side. The thing is, most people hope to be on the winning side, they just have trouble deciding who that is. How shortsighted of them. I, and my associates, intend to be on the winning side because we will define what winning means. It is all so simple, really. And by the way, we also intend this country to be on the winning side, not the Chinese or the Japs or the damn Muslims. But to do that we must make sure our nation is… undiluted by weakness."

"Father, what the hell does that mean?"

"Let's not go there now. Just remember this: there is no point worrying about marginal people whose lives are about mere survival at best. You keep them alive for what purpose? Just to keep breathing, just to endure miserable and pointless lives, procreate and leave behind more useless beings. Now, before you get angry, I know you mean well but think about it, for what real purpose do you prolong their lives? Tell me, for what possible purpose?"

"Is that a rhetorical question?"

"Never mind. The point is that you should think about being on the winning side, being part of the future. We want the best and the brightest as we make the next leap. Just think about it. We have an opportunity that is unique, to move to the next stage in our evolution as a species. To do that, we need to guide people and we can do that now. Technology is an extraordinary opportunity. It gives us the means for leading the masses without them realizing it. We can now identify the weaknesses and fears and wants of the smallest groups while targeting appropriate messages to them."

"Brainwashing!"

"Call it what you will. It works with some at least, way more than you might imagine. One other point to remember: most people want to be led. They want to be told what to do. Only half the people vote in presidential elections, for Christ's sake. Americans want a strong figure to tell them what to do and run things with strength and a clear vision. Trust me on that. But I have talked too much. Your hero, Stalin, had a point…"

"Not my hero, for Christ's sake," Chris sputtered. "My God, you yet labor under the illusion that I am some goddamn communist."

"Oh, I apologize, I still confuse socialism and communism, as if they truly are distinct," the patriarch said in an unctuous tone. "Nevertheless, the so-called man of steel said it is better to listen than reveal what is inside. What do you think that I want, my associates want?"

Chris leaned back, considering the question. He had his thoughts, of course, but should he reveal them? His father was right about Stalin. Few know what lay behind those cold, evil eyes. After musing for a few moments, he decided to reply. "Fine,

I will play the game. I think you are after several things. First, you need to wrap up the mechanics of government in America. You need the presidency and one more seat on the Supreme Court. You are also within striking distance of controlling 36 states, a magic number for passing constitutional changes. With the Koch brothers and their allies bankrolling the effort, you should make that happen with relative ease. Second, you need to dismantle what remains of this country's democratic traditions and principles. You cannot win fair elections at the national level since your real agenda favors such a small slice of the population. No, you need a stranglehold, which will still be called democracy - an even more unfavorable electoral college that violates the one vote and one voter principle. Rather, the votes coming from conservative and easily manipulated rural America will count more. Then, with help from a solid Republican national government and thirty-six states, you can put in place the other vital provisions like appointed senators as we had up until the 17th Amendment and a much stronger presidency with unlimited veto power and the ability to govern through executive orders. Naturally, you will refine all the other strangleholds on voting such as gerrymandering, voter suppression, and outright tampering. As our mutual hero, Joseph Stalin was fond of saying, 'It is not how people vote but who counts the votes that really matters'. Should I continue?"

"Please do, I find this fascinating."

"With an unbreakable lock on government, abetted by the effective suppression of a free and independent press through monopolistic purchases and outright intimidation, you will institutionalize this, what shall we say, appropriation of democracy through what looks like legal means, through a constitutional convention that will be rigged and controlled. Just like Hitler first assumed power, and then total control after burning down the Reichstag, it will have the appearance of legality. But that is not the end game, oh no. The purpose of all this is to establish a kleptocracy, a few of the wealthiest will govern in perpetuity. I doubt that Plato would consider the men you have in mind to be philosopher kings but let us not quibble." Chris paused.

"Finished? Charles senior asked.

"Not quite. You gave away the next step in the plan, so just like the Soviets you suddenly admire to have a plan. You have some natural allies in the world, other totalitarian powers such as Russia and China and even some oil rich Middle-Eastern regimes. You just need to take care of the European Union and places like India and Japan, and world domination is yours. That should not be difficult, merely encourage widespread migration of refugees to Europe to destabilize these countries, encourage internal dissent, and a simple divide and conquer strategy should do the rest. There are neo-fascist parties cropping up all over Europe. Get a nutcase like Trump in the White House and you can quickly emasculate the Western alliance. Then, you can make the rules for the world. Who could challenge you then? You would have all the money, or virtually all, and money is power."

"That's it, just acquire more of the same?" The elder man's smile never wavered.

"No, there is more. Here, my crystal ball is a bit murky. But you mentioned evolution earlier…perhaps dreams of becoming supermen. Gene splicing, really creating a super race through advanced science, but just for the elect. That is very likely the end game. Then again, is that not the dream of all megalomaniacs?"

"Precisely." The patriarch's smile widened to an almost grotesque grin. He seemed to be about to continue when, at that moment, Beverly returned. Charles Senior for a moment appeared annoyed at the interruption and then relieved. He then rose to his feet, a signal that the visit was over. "Think about what I have said and, most of all, don't do anything that will make things worse. For once in your life, think hard before doing anything foolish."

"I will, of that you can be certain," Chris said with conviction.

The patriarch took one last hard look at his son before quickly thanking his daughter-in-law and exiting.

"So," Beverly asked. "How did it go?"

Chris looked at her without responding for a while. His words then emerged slowly. "I have no fucking idea. I think, I really think he was trying to recruit me. Can you believe that? I don't think he has a clue about who I am. You know, as a kid he scared me. Now, I am an adult, and guess what? He still scares the crap out of me. Listen, I am going to just sit here for a while, look at the traffic below…and think."

Beverly crossed the room and kissed her brother-in-law on the forehead. "Consider this, I put up with this all the time." She smiled and started toward her bedroom. "By the way, thank you, I am grateful."

"Grateful, for what?" Chris called out to her.

"That I am not cleaning up blood from my carpet. It is new and very expensive." She smiled to indicate she was kidding about her concern for a material thing, though the carpet was new and very, very expensive. "I tried to leave you two alone. I was not sure about that, but I wanted to give the two of you some space."

"Thank you, Bev." Chris seemed distracted. Then he picked up his phone and dialed. When no one answered, he murmured "damn" in a low voice. Then, in a louder voice, "Kat, Chris here. I am in, you got me, damn it…but only if I get the family to agree. That would be a deal-breaker. Talk later."

Beverly walked over and kissed him on the top of the head. "It will be nice to have you with us, even for a while. Kat needs you, I need you."

"Tell me one thing, Bev. Please." But then he said nothing.

"What, just ask?"

"How does he always get to me? Can you explain that to me? How does this piece of shit manage to squeeze my balls so hard that I am left screaming on the inside? It is like I am an eight-year-old all over again. All those years of education and experience evaporate and there I am, a fucking kid again. Does that make sense?"

"Chris, dear, that makes all the sense in the world. We never escape our parents." She looked at him with deep concern, even pity. But he was looking at the ceiling, deep in another world. She quietly rose and went to her bedroom.

Much later, he was still sitting there. His mind and emotions would not turn off. He wanted another drink but had always disciplined himself in that regard. He knew there was a genetic component to alcoholism and he remained attentive to any hint he might be so inflicted. The images of his mother falling into decline and despair were yet real to him. And after all, he was convinced that he had benefitted from a disproportionate amount of her genetic contributions, including the bad stuff. He, and perhaps even Chuck more than he, had dipped deeply into the mysteries and menaces of their Celtic heritage. He loved to write, to dream, to weave fanciful narratives and worlds in his imagination. Yes, he was a member of that tribe from *Erin*.

But they also were cursed with a dark cloud, susceptible to morose bouts of brooding and always sensing disaster everywhere. That was what he kept buried under cascades of irrepressible humor and wit. For many of this lost tribe, when wit failed, alcohol became the last refuge. He had this theory he shared with all who listened. Alcohol was first developed in the Mediterranean region. So, those people had long experience with this toxin. Those members of local tribes who were more susceptible to the ravages of this poison tended not to survive. They could not hunt when hammered nor fight off the dangers around them. Eventually, only those not chemically susceptible to the scourge of alcoholism remained. They could drink but not become addicted. Thus, you did not find many drunks in southern Europe. On the other hand, it took a long time for this technology to make its way to the northern tribes, a long time. The Celtic tribes never had an opportunity to weed out those biologically susceptible to this drug. Yes, he had always been careful. Early on, he fought any tendency to see himself as more witty or attractive after a few drinks. So far, his discipline had prevailed. He would not relax now.

That always happened to him. When alone, his mind would drift aimlessly. He forced himself back to the issue at hand. Yet, no matter how he looked at the question, the answer was the same. After some time, looking out over the lights and the darkness, he knew. There was no need to turn it over in his mind one more time. He had made the commitment. He would return, at least for a while. He had no choice.

Beverly emerged from her bedroom. Her face was ashen. "Chris, I guess you turned your phone off. I just got a message, from Afghanistan. Something is wrong, very wrong."

CHAPTER 9

OXFORD ENGLAND: A DECISION

"Stop fussing, you are like a mother hen."

"And you stop complaining. If I thought that all my future patients would be like you, I would become an accountant. I think I liked it better when you were in a coma." Azita finished checking her sister's blood pressure.

"And if I have you as my doctor in the future, I will jump out the hospital window."

Azita made a face at Deena. "Hah, you will probably be on the first floor, silly girl."

Deena scowled back. "I knew it. I should have stayed in London with Karen. How did I get stuck with you anyways?"

"I, dear sister," Azita articulated the words slowly, "am the only one who will put up with your crap. Besides, you were still out of it when the decision was made. Amar argued that we could give you better care at the university hospital in Oxford. She could look after your recovery and, at least until my classes started, I was assigned to give you tender, loving care, which I have at great cost to myself and, which, you obviously do not deserve. Karen is swamped with work and Kay is taking over a lot of your stuff at ISO. Unfortunately, I have time right now and Chris also has some spare time until the semester starts. He also looked after you when you were still helpless. That way, he could also get some writing done. Then you improved, and he could see very clearly what an obnoxious patient you would be. He is no dummy, he has fled to his office."

"Hmm, I think he is the one that should always be my doctor. At least he is kind, and funny, and smiles a lot. I hope your classes start this afternoon. Where is everyone who was here when I dozed off?"

"Well, they decided to head to the Hairy Hare. They are still discussing our move to the States next year."

Suddenly, Deena's expression changed. "Oh…I keep forgetting about that. When I first heard it, I did not think it was serious. Of course, I was still having a hard time thinking at all. Sit with me, sister."

Azita could now see uncertainty in her sibling's face and sat on the edge of her bed. "Of course."

Deena looked at her younger sibling through moist eyes. "The thought of you going to America, all of you going, hurts my heart. I feel so scared."

"No decision has been made. Chris wants to but the rest of us…well?" Azita said in a soft voice, "Try not to think about it."

"These days, I have too much time to think. I know I am getting better. Every day I feel stronger, remember more. They say a full recovery is likely, unless I murder my caregiver, which is a distinct possibility."

"Aach, if only that evil assassin had been a better shot." Azita held her sister's hand.

"Azita, I am grateful that this killer, a mere child, shot me and not you. But that scene remains so hazy to me. At first, I could recall nothing. Now, brief images pop into my memory, still rather confusing."

"Deena, I cannot get that day out of my head. We are not sure what was in his head. He was only sixteen or so. Some of the villagers believe that he may have been a child of one of the Taliban killed during our rescue."

"Oh my, perhaps he was the child of the man I killed that day at the caves, probably just a baby at the time."

"No one knows for sure. He may have been after me, for doing what they think of as man's work. Most likely, he intended to kill both of us. That is what I believe. You turned to him and responded when he called out. Don't forget, he used the family name, not Deena or Azita. My guess is that he shot at you first simply because you spoke up. But your movement saved you, the bullet hit a glancing blow which fractured your skull but did not penetrate deeply into your brain, which would have taken you away from me." Azita fought back a tear. "Then again, now that I think on it, a bullet rattling around an empty space would cause few problems."

Deena half scowled but it faded to a grin. She recognized what her sister was doing. "You are a shit."

Azita stroked her head. "You, we, are very lucky. It was still a very serious blow but not fatal, at least not immediately. It was the bleeding inside the brain that caused problems. Funny how things work out. Kay is a great trauma surgeon, most experienced at treating wounds. She is the one who could give you the best immediate care. And for some mysterious reason, she happened to come with us that day. Kay knew what to do immediately but, even more important, called ahead as we headed back to the base camp in our helicopter. She knew exactly what would be needed when we got back, timing was everything in this case. Another hour's delay, perhaps less, and we might not be having this conversation."

"Allah looks after us I think."

Azita smiled. "Perhaps, or perhaps it is another kind of protector."

Deena looked hard at her sister. "You have something to say. I can tell. What is it?"

In any case, I was staggered by that first shot, no one knows that since I stayed upright. It was as if I had been punched in the chest. Then, every instinct made me reach for you. His second shot missed my head by an inch, likely because I had moved toward you."

"Then I did save you, in a way at least." Deena tried to keep it light.

Azita did not smile. "Sister, that first bullet, the one that glanced off your skull. I think he was aiming at me. You ducked into it just as he fired, but it struck me in the chest."

Deena looked at her without understanding. "That cannot be. You were never wounded. At least I don't remember that. Did I forget? No, I would not. That I would not forget."

"No one knows," Azita repeated softly. "The bullet hit a book I had just put inside my blouse, something I found in the drawers we were looking through in our old home. I can yet see the hate in this boy's face as he levelled his gun at my head for another try. At that moment, praise Allah, one of the Afghan security men with us shot the boy. Allah was kind to give us such a quick guard to be with us at that moment."

"The boy said nothing before he died?" Deena asked.

"Just the usual, *God is great*. Think how pathetic that is, believers who hate one another invoke the same God. Same with Christians. I wonder if they ever think about how silly that is? You know I read history for relaxation. I came across this story about the Great War in Europe a century ago. They were in trenches in France charging one another and suffering horrific losses of life. Christmas came, and an unofficial truce settled over the battlefield. No one knows how it started but the German and Allied troops came out of their trenches and greeted one another in what they called 'no-man's land'. For several hours, they exchanged small gifts, like tobacco and wine, sang their seasonal songs, shared some food, and prayed to the same God. Then it was over, and they returned to the same trenches to start the slaughter all over again. What an odd species we are." Azita seemed lost in thought for a moment but then shook her head slightly. "In any case, our assassin died before anyone could ask why he hated us so or which of us he hated the most."

"A book? Finally, your love of books came in handy." Suddenly, Deena smiled and grabbed Azita's hand. "Enough of that. Since I am stuck with you right now, I want to talk about something funny. How is your love life? That always amuses me."

"Oh sister, you are the devil herself. Ever since we were children, you have been a torment to me." But Azita was happy for the change in topic. She had not meant to tell Azita about her mother's journal, not yet. For the moment, it could remain merely a random book that had saved her.

"That is my mission in life, my personal obsession. So, tell me, do I have any hope for nieces and nephews from you, with Benjamin or maybe this mysterious new boy? His name is Ahmad, right? Tell me all, everything."

"What I should do is give you an overdose of sedatives." Azita looked cross but that dissolved into a pensive pose. "I can hardly think of these things. I have not told anyone else this yet, you will be the first. The other day, I finally broke it off with Ben. We met, nothing had changed. He was saying the same words. Then I knew. So, I just spoke the words…*we are finished*. He was stunned. I could not believe he had no idea of my anguish. He then desperately tried to argue that we could elope, he would defy his parents. I would not hear of that, I did not believe him."

"Sister, I think you would have if you truly loved him."

Azita looked intently at her. "Perhaps you are right. Perhaps you are. In any case, it is over. I think he was relieved, hurt yes, but relieved. Then again, perhaps that is what I want to believe. I can still remember him walking away, in the rain, his shoulders slumped. It broke my heart but there was no other way. Tell me, why does it rain so much in this country?"

"And this Ahmad?"

"Oh, him! Well, I have some news about Ahmad which you will be the first to know. I am pregnant with his child."

Deena registered shock until she saw Azita laugh. "When I get better, you little shit, I will have my revenge. Now the truth or, sick bed or not, I shall beat you to within an inch of your miserable life."

"We have seen one another but only very briefly and not since I broke it off with Ben, though I am not sure that boy accepts that it is over. Truth is, I keep putting Ahmad off, using you as an excuse."

"Hmm," Deena said and grinned, "I must get his email address and tell him what a wicked girl you are."

"He should know that already, but it doesn't seem to matter to him. What should I do Deena? I am serious now. How did you decide about Karen?"

Deena thought about that. "I will be honest. I don't really know. I think Karen decided for me, but I am happy she did, I think. I am not sure my relationship is of much help to you. All those years, as a girl, I would talk about boys and read romance novels when I could find them. And yet, inside, my fantasies were different. I was hiding the real me from all of you. I felt so dishonest but what choice did I have, in that culture?"

"Oh, dear Deena, you must have been so lonely. Why didn't you talk to me?"

The elder sibling laughed. "Then, you were this spoiled little girl with whom I fought all the time. Back then, you must remember that we were not so close. So many times, though, I almost told Papa and Mama what was inside of me. Do you think they would have understood?"

Azita reflected for a moment. "They were such kind and wise people. I think they would have tried very hard though our culture was so unforgiving. Of one thing I am certain, they would always have loved you."

Deena nodded. "I know. I do know that. There are some Muslim countries where I might be beheaded for my love for Karen. We must be so careful when we are around the true believers. That pains me so much. And speaking of pain, I fear a headache coming on."

Azita stroked her sister's head. "I will give you something to help you sleep. Then, I am going to join the others for a bit. Perhaps I can convince them that this move would be silly. When you awake, Karen will be here to see you again before she heads back to London."

"I hate being an invalid. I hate imposing on you like this."

"Listen to me. It may not seem so, but you are getting better by the day. And put this nonsense about imposing yourself on me out of your mind. You are good training for me. How else will I learn how to deal with impossible patients?"

"Ha, ha. And when I do recover, just remember that you are in big trouble."

Azita leaned over and lifted her head so that she might swallow some pills. "This will relieve the pain and help you sleep. And believe me, nothing would make me happier than for you to be well enough to chase me around the room threatening me with a long, wooden cooking spoon."

"Oh my, I did that, when we were young. I had forgotten."

"I haven't." Azita laughed. "Good thing Mama came in to save me."

"Azita, before you leave. Do you love him, this mystery boy?"

The younger sibling looked out of the window before responding. "Sister, I have always been a woman who focused on the intellect, on knowledge. These matters of emotion and the heart, the things located deeper in our consciousness remain alien to me. All I can say is that I feel something when I see him, hear from him, that I have not felt before."

Deena smiled broadly. "Finally, my sister has found love. How delicious."

"Oh, you are a wicked sister, enjoying my torture. But remember this, I know of many ways to do you in that are virtually undetectable. It will look as if you had died from meanness, which everyone who knows you will believe." Azita leaned over and kissed her sister lightly on the lips. "Now, get some rest. But you are wrong, I found someone to love a long time ago, someone pathetic whom no one else could possibly love."

"And who might that be?"

"You, of course. You - my wicked sister."

As Azita headed for the door, Deena called out. "And you, silly sister, run to that boy and make love to him. Do you hear me?"

"Hah," Azita yelled back as she exited. "Even if they detect the poison that I used on you, no jury would ever convict me for ridding myself of such a wicked sister."

Deena smiled and realized how exhausted she was. She leaned back to seek the relief that sleep would bring.

Azita looked up at the sky. It was cloudy, she should have brought an umbrella. After all this time in England, she still had not gotten into the habit of expecting rain. It always seemed to be sunny in Afghanistan, at least that was her memory. Apparently, early lessons were hard to dismiss, they clung tenaciously to one. But she knew that already. One does not shed one's culture easily at all. She talked and acted like all the other Oxford students about her. Only her olive skin, perhaps her long and dark brown hair, and the occasional head scarf denoted her heritage from the outside. But inside was a different matter. She took her scarf and aggressively positioned it to cover her head. Let the world know who she was. Damn them.

"Azita," she heard, "wait."

She whirled about to see Ahmad moving quickly to catch up to her.

"Are you back to stalking me?" She said more gruffly than she had intended.

"No," he stammered. "Well, maybe. Yes dammit, I am."

"That covers all the possibilities." Her voice was slightly less aggressive though she yet sounded cross. "What do you want?"

"I...I..."

"For God's sake, spit it out." Azita saw his face dissolve in pain and then was distraught at her tone. Why was she being so mean? She was not angry at him but at herself, at her inability to make any decisions. "Listen, Ahmad, I am sorry. You deserve better. You should find a girl who can be there for you. What can I offer? I might be going off to America next year, then maybe someplace in the world…perhaps even home, to our native country. Would you really like that? You have spent your whole life escaping our culture, would you go back to it for a girl, especially for a girl as confused as I am? That would be foolish, beyond foolish."

"You really think so?" He interjected quickly.

"I know so. You probably have fantasies of wild sex with this female you hardly know. But that can never last long. And then what? You would resent me and the life I forced upon you. I would no longer be this exotic temptation but merely this boring wife who dragged you away from this world you worked so hard to find."

Ahmad held up his hand. "Just wait…wait. Is this why you have been avoiding me, telling me that you are too busy attending to your sister? I thought maybe you and Ben had made up, that I lost you to a better man. But it is all about you knowing what is best for me. If that is the problem…"

"No, it is about knowing how boys think. Besides, you are… nice looking. You could have any girl you wanted. Why torture me?"

"What! You know how boys think? Young lady, you may know many things, but I guarantee you know precious little about boys and love."

"Oh," she snapped back. "And now you presume to lecture me on what I know and don't know."

"In this case, yes." He did not back down while Azita, in fact, did take a step back. "Here is what I know. My father told me that your parents loved one another until their tragic deaths. He could have escaped to England with his family when he was younger and lived an easier life, but he stuck it out hoping to provide some comfort to his people and his country. Madeena lost her position at the university, she was forced to be an ordinary housewife, one of the invisible women. Did she stop loving him or he her? Not from what I was told. And my father, his marriage arranged for him as a young man. He took my mother to foreign lands where she sometimes knew no one, even had trouble with the language. And yet…" his voice was softening in a subtle way, "they never stopped loving one another. My father wept uncontrollably at her passing. That is where I learned about love." He stood there breathing hard. Suddenly, his face registered a new awareness. "Wait, did you say that I am nice looking?" His face broke into that crooked smile that Azita found endearing.

Azita looked up at the sky. It had begun to drizzle; harder rain was likely on the way given the darker clouds to the west. "Ahmad," she whispered. "There is no more Ben in my life."

"Really?" Ahmad seemed to be absorbing the news. "I think I am sorry for you."

Azita smiled faintly. "Wow, you really are a terrible liar."

"No…" Ahmad began to protest when she grabbed him by the arm and pulled him into a nearby alleyway. Once they had privacy, she flew into his arms and kissed him hungrily. Shocked, Ahmad stumbled back against the alley wall, but she followed him and pressed her body hard against his. Both instinctively began to grind against each other as Azita emitted a low, primal groan, almost a desperate wail. Ahmad by now had recovered from the initial shock, pulling her more fully into his stronger body as if he could absorb her body into his. His mouth sought out her neck and face and then they found each other's mouths and the frantic search began for deeper levels of sensation and connection.

Suddenly, Azita pushed him away. "Damn you."

"What?" Ahmad was confused as the rain increased.

"Damn you," she repeated.

"Why?"

She turned and started away. "I must go."

"Why?" he repeated as she reached the main street.

Before turning the corner and disappearing, she turned back and looked at him directly in the eyes. "Because you made me fall in love with you, that is why." Then she was gone, and the rain came harder.

"I am beginning to think that the Masoud family village is cursed. First, I got shot while rescuing the girls and this guy's worthless ass." Karen nodded in Chris's direction.

"And I yet appreciate the gesture, even if I were not your primary concern," Chris offered.

"Not even close." Karen smiled. "And then the love of my life gets shot in the head during a celebration of all things. I may never let her go back."

"But you would be fine if I did?" Chris asked, knowing the answer.

"Hell," Karen responded immediately, "I would pay your airfare. After all, you are going to run off to America and abandon me. You are not my bloody favorite right now."

"Nothing has been decided about America," Amar quickly added and then was silent.

"I am thinking," Kay added, "I doubt we could stop the girls from going back to their homeland, if they chose to. My poor brother here went apoplectic when I defied him and joined Amar at the Panjshir site without his permission. He straight away flew in to yank me out, lot good that did."

"You can say that again, my trip there was a disaster. I wound up with a wife."

Kay hurled a pretzel in the general direction of her brother. "What I am saying is that you cannot keep someone away from something that is their passion, and certainly not if it is an obsession. And this village in the middle of nowhere has some hold on them. I mean, they never spent much time there, but it represents something special to them, maybe symbolic. They will go back, I am sure."

"That will kill me," Amar said.

"And me," Karen added. "Kay, have I thanked you for what you did that day? Thank God you were there."

"Only about a dozen times." Kay rolled her eyes back in mock frustration.

"Well," Karen became a bit defensive, "probably not in front of this fine crowd. So, here is my thirteenth thanks. But to change the topic back to our roots, which is what I think we were discussing, I do understand the pull. My family, going back in time, worked the land."

"A farmer's daughter, I just knew it." Chris smiled broadly. "All this time, I wondered what fragrance you used. It is *Eau de la Swine Trough*."

"As I was saying before the rude interruption, I have visited aunts, uncles, cousins, grandparents who still live in that region, northern England near the Scottish border. Poor place, lots of small and hardscrabble farms with nothing much going on. Even though I never lived there, I still feel a tug when I have visited. It is like returning to the earth, your origins. This place, and these people, are where I came from. It is spiritual in a way." Karen looked at Chris suspiciously, waiting for a sharp retort.

He decided not to disappoint her. "I get it Karen, you are one with the common folk. That is why I have often said you should buy the Hairy Hare. You would be the perfect entrepreneur-owner. Everyone knows you are a people person."

"Here we go," Karen sighed.

"No, really, you could work the bar listening to the woes of the common folk and solve their common, everyday problems and issues."

"Oh, bite me, you sot." Karen threw another pretzel at him, which sailed over his head and glanced off the back of a nearby patron who seemed not to notice.

"See, right there," Chris said with satisfaction, "the common touch."

Karen affected an exasperated tone. "No matter how many times I tell him, Chris doesn't get it. This is a fake pub. There are no common folk here, just pseudo-sophisticates who think they are getting the common folk experience. But, as much as we are trying very hard to ignore this, let us at long last focus on the question at hand: are you going to America?"

Chris took a deep breath, looking at Amar as he did. "Well, it is doable, for the family I mean, if we relocate to Madison, which is in Wisconsin," he added for Karen's benefit. "That is close enough to Chicago but not right in Father's neighborhood. I could do what needs to be done quietly. Besides, they want me at the university, which has an internationally recognized poverty research center and a fine international program. They have assured me a position for Amar at the university hospital and a chance for her to teach a course in international health topics at the medical school. They believe that some students might be attracted to working overseas. Since Azita came back from Afghanistan, she has seemed to settle on children's health as a specialty; there is a great children's hospital on campus where she could do her internship. If we want, we get to swap homes with a professor who will be at Oxford for at least a year. His place is right on this gorgeous lake called Mendota, adjacent to the north side of the campus. And the girls can start elementary school in a place that teaches the children of a whole bunch of foreign graduate students who live in what is called Eagle Heights. The diversity there is amazing, like going to a United Nation's school."

"Sounds perfect," Kay offered. "Then again, I sense a but coming."

Again, Chris looked at Amar who remained silent. He ventured a response. "We are not all on board. After meeting with Father, I concluded that there is a reason to do this. It was not anything he specifically said, but rather his look. He had this look about him, as if he was privy to something very scary. I wish I could explain my feelings about him, what I saw that day. His smile, his look. It was like staring into the heart of evil. Amar is neutral and not enthused. Azita leans against but, of course, does not have to come with us necessarily, though it will kill me if she does not. And the girls, well they don't get a vote though they could benefit greatly from a cross-cultural experience."

Karen looked at Chris, then Amar, and then back at Chris. "Okay, one more time. Why is Kat so hot to get you back there? I mean, I have heard some of the stuff about your father but, frankly, that just sounds like an eccentric old fool playing politics. You have more than your share of political nut jobs in America, it must be something in the water. What makes him different?"

Ricky had been holding back. "Perhaps it is time for me to chime in. Kat sent me in to nail down this deal, and to give me an opportunity to check on my pet interests at ISO." He was about to continue when something in the distance caught his eye. "Ah, I see that the prodigal daughter has arrived."

Azita made her way to their table dripping wet. "Forgot my umbrella again. Some English woman I am, cannot remember a bloody umbrella."

"How is my love?" Karen asked.

"Good now. She is sleeping. Was getting another headache but they are not nearly as severe anymore. And as you might see for yourself, her cognitive abilities are much better now. I can tell because she is giving me much grief. You can still see some short-term cognitive lapses, but they also are getting rare. All good." She lapsed into silence as if her mind was elsewhere.

"Well Azita," Karen said with enthusiasm. "you have been an angel, a healing angel."

"Nothing special. She is my sister." Again, a lapse into silence. People looked at her, a bit perplexed but lacked any specific reason to ask what might have been wrong.

Ricky broke the ensuing vacuum. "Okay, I was about to give the spiel on why we need this miracle worker back home for a while. By home I mean America."

"Go for it," Karen urged him on. "I am not at all convinced."

"My wife, his good sister, and I have been hammering away on Chris about this for weeks now but here is a very abridged and selective version. You have all heard of boy wonder here," Ricky nodded in the direction of his old friend, "and his discourse at great length about the long decline of the American state. Hell, I recorded one of his monologues and still use it as a very effective sleeping aid…"

"Doing one helluva job of sealing the deal here," Chris said and smiled.

"My turn fella," Ricky responded, and plowed on. "We all should have listened carefully since, though I am loath to admit this, he has been right all along. In fact, his seemingly bottomless cynicism may not be deep enough. The election of Obama was, for a black man like me, a miracle. Growing up in a tough Chicago ghetto, I never in a million years thought an African-American would hold the highest public position in the world. And I knew him, from his days as a community organizer. Well, not as a friend but I met him on occasion when I was a mere lad. But here is the thing, millions of other Americans were as equally taken with his election, and not in a good way. This gentle and wise man stoked the worst possible fears and paranoia throughout the land but especially in the deep red states."

"This is common knowledge," Kay inserted. "What is the point?"

"Has anyone else noted that the Crawfords are an impatient lot? Freud says that is due to early, and unsuccessful, potty training. But I continue undeterred. Obama stirred up the seething rabble that have always been there. But it was also a signal that the time was right to strike the final blow for the slow but inexorable right-wing coup that has been decades in the making. And I hope neither of the idiot Crawford twins asks what a coup is? I will get there."

"Before my nap time, I hope." Chris made a snoring sound.

Ricky threw yet another pretzel at him and continued. "Several things raised the hopes of the far right. Obama inflamed ancient racial hatreds. Their long-term campaign to marginalize labor and redistribute wealth to the top of the pyramid was proving more successful than they had imagined. By 2007, the one-percent was getting as much of the economic pie as they were getting in 1928, just before the big crash. The financial crisis eroded that a bit but now they are determined to shift everything permanently in their favor. In a generation or two, they had been successful in building a political infrastructure across media, both social and conventional, and all the other institutions that count: education, the courts, mainstream religious groups, think tanks and lobbyists, you name it. They even had managed to replace the necessary 'ism' needed to keep the common folk afraid after the communists committed the unpardonable sin of imploding. How convenient that a small segment of the billion-plus Muslims chose to act like our evangelical Christian nutcases. I mean, don't you sit up at night worrying that sharia law will replace the constitution next week or that Obama will sweep in with the blue U.N. tanks to get everyone's guns? The conservative base obsesses about such fantasies even as toddlers kill more Americans every year through gun accidents than Islamic terrorists could dream of knocking off. And if the Islamic terrorists are not cooperating by attacking America again, don't worry. Look at this Trump character, beating the bushes about hordes of immigrants endangering our women and children. He may be a joke, but his fear tactics are not. Bottom line, the forces of the right sense that they are poised to make the final blow to democracy."

"Sounds like you have been reading too many political thrillers," Karen said and smirked. "Who are 'they' again?"

"It is not the America-first nativists nor your garden-variety racists. They are merely the dupes. It is the usual gang of economic plutocrats that have yearned for total control forever. Remember J.P. Morgan and his gang from the gilded age? Well, think of the current crowd as their ideological descendants but with more tools to exercise total control at their disposal. They absolutely hate democracy and are captured by the ancient notion of a group born to dominate and rule, though not so much in the classic Nazi Aryan sense. The new plutocracy is global and defined by wealth and power. They are yellow and brown though none of my tribe as far as we can tell. Some of the names are very public while others, like the Russian oligarchs, Asian tycoons, and European bankers are more invisible but together they have virtually unlimited resources and a common purpose. What is the common trope, a few dozen families have more wealth than half the world? Listen, they may have many differences among themselves, but they have one common vision - to undo the vestiges of the great, global experiment in Western democracy and replace it with an oligarchic control even if the appearance of some participation remains. While some of these men, and a few women, hate a good deal of science since it is based on evidence, they do see things emerging that they potentially love. They would love to harness the power of artificial intelligence to control the masses more effectively, ever hear of Michal Kosinski?

"Who?" Karen asked.

"No matter, a tangent. These men see what is called a window of opportunity. Putin and Dmitry Medvedev are in control of the Kremlin, Xi Jinping controls China, the European Union is under strain with Britain wanting out, and America is on the verge of becoming a permanent right-wing plutocracy. They can feel it. Now, the natural question is how can a small minority, tiny really, control electoral outcomes, no matter how much they spend? The answer to that would take the remainder of the afternoon but, believe me, the right is doing everything hey can to short-circuit what remains of American democracy. Think about this - ever wonder about the insides of voting machines, how easy it would be to manipulate them? My point is that they just need to tip the executive and they will have total control of what is still the most powerful nation on earth. Just think about what is at stake for them. Take one obvious example. How can the Koch brothers hold back those wanting to respond to global warming and the need to end our reliance on fossil fuels? The reason is clear: the worth of their financial empire is based largely, though certainly not totally, on the presumed value of oil and gas and other such reserves that have yet been tapped. What if we no longer need them? Hundreds of billions of dollars of assets become worthless since they have no intrinsic value without a demand for them. They are what we business types now call 'stranded assets.' These people do not like to lose. People kill over a pair of Nike shoes. These people are worse, they are stone cold sociopaths. I know some of them, at least I have met a few. You would never want to turn your back to them. You would spend the remainder of your day trying to extract the knife stuck between your shoulders."

"But what can you do about this, what could Chris do?" It was Amar who spoke, looking pained.

Ricky lost a bit of his animation, either by her question or her expression. "I am not sure. Neither is Kat. I will say one thing: there is something about the Crawford clan. They have passion. No, let me correct that, they can entertain some serious obsessions. Kat's interest was first piqued by what she heard through the shenanigans of her father. We all knew the public story, but she was further drawn in by what she heard from some investigative work by my sister, Jules, and tidbits from Beverly, who remained in touch with the patriarch, as we call Charles. Then she hired some whizzes who started plumbing the dark reaches of the internet and various data sources. They are uncovering more all the time, they briefed Chris earlier. By the way, why does Charles trust her?" Ricky looked at both Kay and Chris.

"Beats me," Kay offered, "I didn't think he trusted God."

Chris spoke uncertainly, as if his mind were elsewhere. "I can't be sure. Maybe he wants to hold on to one member of the family, even if she is only connected through marriage. Could be he is making amends for his treatment of Chuck. No, that would imply he has a soul. My best guess, and this makes more sense to me, he is using Beverly to spread misinformation to us, or believes he is. My guess is that he knows what we are up to, or at least what we are likely thinking about."

"Shit," Ricky interjected. "why hadn't that occurred to me? Could Bev really be working for him?"

"Oh, no, never," Chris interrupted. Then he paused for a moment as if collecting a thought. "I have been getting a lot of information about this in recent weeks. But something Ricky said gave me a thought." Karen opened her mouth but decided against her own witticism. "This potential oligarchy, if you will, is a bit like the old Mafia Commission. They are seemingly cooperative but really are deadly rivals. They will work together to defeat a common enemy, everyone who believes in social justice, opportunity for all, and full participation in society. After all, they are the elect, the realization of Ayn Rand's superior man, or Nietzsche's superhero. But, once that victory is theirs, they shall turn on one another. Something Father let slip stayed with me, that we cannot let the Chinese win. This is one titanic battle that he will lose, Father will be on the wrong side. In the end, I suspect the Asians will prevail which will come as a shock to the white supremacists in the cabal."

"And the reason?" Karen asked.

"Not hard to see. Look at the evidence right now. China is working on renewable energy. They are investing in the future, in science, and in infrastructure. They will be way ahead of us in technology and artificial intelligence within a decade. It so reminds me of the Japanese after they opened to the West in the late 1800s. They had been a feudal society, backward in technology. Suddenly, they changed course and flooded westward, absorbed all they could, and went on to modernize in a generation. The world was shocked when they defeated the Russian naval forces, in 1906 I believe it was. I ran across a European golf tournament on television recently, from China. It was being played in a city I had never heard of, but which Ricky had mentioned to me, so I paid attention. The commentator mentioned how this place had been a small fishing village in the late 1970s, just a few thousand people. The central government decided to make it a primary commercial area. They showed shots of the city skyline in the distance. It is a stunningly modern city of well over twelve million souls with gleaming buildings that would put any American counterpart to shame. Hell, America cannot even fix its goddamn bridges and roads and the Chinese built the equivalent of a New York in a generation or two."

Amar spoke again, softly. "But what can Chris do?"

"None of us are sure," Ricky offered. "I think our feeling is that, if we don't do something, we risk enormous guilting in the future. You know, if not us then who? Our kids and grandkids will look at us and ask, *what did you do when there was still a chance to resist?* Besides, it won't be just Chris, or Kat and me. There are other wealthy individuals who have not gone over to the dark side. We are talking among ourselves. Damn, I hate to say this in public, but we need someone like Chris."

"Why, for heaven's sake?" Karen's face was screwed up with incredulity.

"Why did you even ask? Isn't it obvious? He has charisma, and he is known among the liberal elite. They actually trust him."

"Bollocks!" Karen shouted a bit too loudly. "I thought the liberal elite would have some sense."

"I am afraid Ricky is right, Karen. There has never been any accounting for taste," Kay added. "One last question - which of the unsavory crowd of Republican candidates are the purveyors of evil embracing?"

Ricky smiled for the first time, but grimly. "They apparently are divided. Some want a known nutcase like Cruz. A few yet believe they need someone mainstream like Jeb, but that approach is not gaining much traction. In fact, I think the centrists, what remains of sanity among Republicans, are totally dead. Until that is finally determined, though, they are holding their fire other than the steady drumbeat of anti-Hillary BS. It is freaking amazing how gullible most Americans are. And backward - there is still a lot of misogyny around."

"It is amazing," added Chris. "We had Gandhi, Indira that is, in India, Bhutto in Pakistan, that one in Sri Lanka whose name I can never remember, not to mention Meir in Israel. Now we have Merkel in Germany and May right here. But America still asks whether a woman can lead. No wonder I left. That crowd is so provincial and backward."

"The real problem is that a quarter-century of vile attacks have the common folk believing she is evil incarnate. That success buoys the right that the big lie still works. It worked for Goebbels, no need to think the Americans are any smarter, they surely are not." Ricky shook his head as he finished.

"And Trump?" Kay asked.

"No one thinks anyone that damaged and obnoxious has a chance but…"

"Then again," Chris mused, "the political pros cannot completely control their own party. Once the passions of the base are inflamed, it could get away from them. Even the hard-right players behind the scenes are not in total control yet. If he does pull off this miracle by getting nominated, we will see. They probably assume they can control him. After all, he is dumber than dirt, the whole business community knows that. But that makes him dangerous. He is in the pocket of the Russians, he owes them large. And he is a malignant narcissist. I can see him being swept up by the rabid dogs of his base, pushing him ever further into bat-shit crazy land as he strives to sustain their adulation. And I certainly can see him believing his own delusions of grandeur. Even I don't believe I am as great as others say I am."

"Who in God's name has ever said you were great?" Kay tried to lighten things. "Those voices in your head?"

Chris ignored her. "Trump hungers for adoration and approval, he could never admit doubt or failure. He is the sort of megalomaniac that will never listen to wise counsel. He easily could go rogue if it keeps getting him attention. I can see it now. The more aggressive and bizarre he gets, the more rabidly devoted his base becomes. It will be a death spiral for what remains as reasoned governance back in the States."

At this point, silence reigned. Then, Amar spoke. "Azita, you have been very silent. Hope you are not obsessing about a forgotten umbrella."

"No," her daughter responded slowly, "I am suffering from an endorphin imbalance." Amar betrayed an understanding while the others looked at her with a hint of confusion. "It is true, I am thinking about something else. I ran into…a friend on the way over. But you are discussing important things, my thoughts are nothing."

"No," Karen half-shouted. "Save us from this political babble."

When everyone continued to look at her, Azita decided to go on. "He reminded me of something very important, this friend. Our families, his parents and my biological folks that is, both were much alike. Each had some very difficult decisions to make, decisions that involved great risk. But through it all they remained together, they loved one another unconditionally.

I love my family, this family. I also know what it means to be committed to ideals. You cannot live in an authoritarian regime and not come out of that experience without scars. In the end, people do count, and people should have the right to find their own destinies. I would never want any child of mine to ask what I did when all was on the line and have nothing to say in response."

Amar let out a tiny sound. All looked at her, but she said nothing. She merely reached out to take her daughter's hand. They looked at one another and arrived at an unspoken agreement between them. Amar softly broke what seemed like a long silence. "I suspect my daughter and I will be going to America next year."

"Well then, I am not the brightest bulb in this room, but I know when I have lost," Karen exclaimed with a kind of finality. "I had thought of all kinds of arguments I was going to throw out on the table. Hell, I was even going to say nice things about Chris, how indispensable he is to ISO and to me. You must know how much admitting that would kill me, or at least require a dash to the loo to barf. But I cannot argue with this young lady. So, let us order another round of drinks. This relocation won't happen for some time yet, but it is never too early to start planning how we are going to handle things from the two sides of the pond."

Chris looked at his wife and daughter. They had turned to gaze at him, their expressions set in a loving smile. *Are you sure,* he mouthed absent sound? Amar shrugged her shoulders but nodded her head. Azita mouthed her own silent response. *I am sure.* He thought his heart would burst through his chest.

PART II CHALLENGES

CHAPTER 10

MADTOWN: SUMMER 2016

"I am ecstatic that you could come over to America and spend a few days with me before my internship starts. It is good to have familiar faces at the start of any new adventure." Azita embraced her older sister. "I don't know why but I am nervous. It's like my first months in England again."

"Stop that."

"You mean my constant insecurity?" Azita asked.

"Not that, silly. Why worry about that? The Americans will undoubtedly discover that you are a total fraud and send you packing soon enough. I am talking about all this affection in public." Deena looked about to see if others were on the same path. A couple of joggers were approaching but they appeared totally indifferent. "If you keep hugging me like this, people will think we are lovers and not sisters."

Azita laughed aloud. "That would be so embarrassing for me. Surely, they will all say that I could do so much better."

"You think?" Deena scoffed. "You have only been here a few days and already your ego is swollen. Just like all Americans, your head is too big to fit through the door. I suppose I should let you hug me. When I was complaining about you, Kay did tell me recently how much you did to save me right after the shooting, about you not panicking and tending to me right away until she could arrive. But then you blew it by torturing me so during my recovery"

"Hah, you were a horrible patient, always whining."

"And don't worry about how you will do. You have fooled everyone so far, that will not change. And I promise not to tell people here that you are a total fraud." Deena had decided to ignore her sister's most recent attempt at an insult so that their sibling exchange would not go on endlessly. Instead, she looked about her. "I must admit, this is so lovely, what is this place?"

"Picnic Point," Azita responded. "As you can see, it juts out into the lake and you can look over to the state capitol and the skyline of Madison. I love it as a place to walk. If you are up to it, we can walk to the end and return to the entrance. Then we can walk all the way along the lake and the campus to Memorial Union where the students hang out, which is also on the lake and very lovely. If we have enough energy and time, we could then walk up State Street which connects the campus to the capitol, a most beautiful building with the second biggest dome after the U.S. Capitol or so I was told. Anyways, they do not permit cars on the street and there are many interesting stores and outdoor restaurants and so many fascinating people. And then we could walk down to the conference complex that was inspired by Frank Lloyd Wright - have you heard of him? He was a world-famous architect, and this is also on the shore of another local lake and..."

"Wait. How long is this walk?" Deena inquired.

"Just a few miles," Azita mentioned nonchalantly. "Have you become a lazy cow?"

"Sister," Deena guffawed, "just listen to yourself. Two weeks ago, you were pouting and groaning about agreeing to come to America. Now, you sound like a real estate agent."

"Well, a couple of weeks ago I was feeling sad that we would be separated by six or seven thousand kilometers but now I realize that is a blessing, with you being such a shit and all." Then Azita hugged her sister again as Deena let out a groan. "Get used to this, soon, you will be gone from me. I understand you will be heading back to the school sites again."

Deena beamed. "Yes, everyone has said I am totally cured, 100 percent."

"Except for your obvious personality flaws." Azita could not resist.

"Hah, hah, the doctors confirmed that my biggest medical threat was not the bullet to my skull but my obnoxious, bratty little sister who tortured me so during my recovery. They tell me it is a miracle that I survived her so well." Deena detected a small movement from her sibling. "Don't, no more hugs."

Azita pouted. "Sorry, it is just so good to see you and we both know the opportunities will be fewer after this. I will be in training, this endless training, and you will back in your world."

"It could have been much worse, you know that. Just think if that boy back home were a better shot, we both would have been killed. How would we share things then? How? I would be in heaven and you would be in that other place." Deena smiled at the cleverness of her own quip.

Azita hesitated for a step or two before registering the sarcasm. "Oh, you really have become such a shit. Where did my good sister go? I thought I had learned such bad things from Chris, but I believe Karen has been a worse mentor to you. Our dear mother would be so disappointed in you. She always thought you were the good girl. And you have me using this bad language all the time. Our dear mother would be disappointed in me as well."

Deena seemed to absorb her sister's words with care. "I will tell you one thing. When we were young, I never would have believed we would have hated the possibility of being separated. I could not stand you back then and wished for the day we would go our separate ways."

"Odd, isn't it?" Azita mused drily, "you also have grown much more tolerable over time."

"Well, that makes no sense." Deena registered surprise. "I was the good sister, just perfect from the start. Everyone agreed on that. You were the spoiled, lazy cow."

Azita laughed again. "When did you turn into such a jokester? Really, you were such a sourpuss as a teenager."

"Actually, I do know when it started, well, when I started to grow up." Deena paused a moment before continuing as if vetting her next thought. "It was the day you were pummeled by the Taliban morality police, that day woke me up. Sure, I felt much guilt for shaming you into going to the market. However, something else happened that awful day. I looked hard at myself and did not like what I saw. I was coasting, just getting by."

"I don't understand," Azita murmured, realizing their conversation had taken a serious turn.

"Think about it. Everyone said how beautiful I was, so I thought that I didn't need to try. I would be taken care of... by some man. Then, a funny thing happened. Increasingly, the image of a man taking care of me had faded from my mind. It no longer fit with my...feelings. The thought became rather repulsive. Nothing real had replaced it but that future of being the pampered wife was simply going away, not that many wives in our country are pampered. Then, father had come to me that day of your beating and talked about how special my beauty was. He was saying that was a good thing and that you were not so blessed."

"Wait…what?" Azita wondered if she should feel insulted.

"Just shush," Deena cut her off. "He was simply trying to make me feel better. It was his way of saying that each of us had a special gift but, at the same time, each gift contained its own burdens and responsibilities. Your life was not as easy as it had looked to me. I should not have been so jealous of you. There were so many obstacles in your life that I never considered. Of course, I had never considered such things. I thought you were just a pampered little brat who only thought of herself."

"You were not wrong," Azita inserted quickly. The path that wound its way through the peninsula was shaped by trees on both sides, occasionally offering a canopy overhead to provide shelter against the late spring sun. They had come upon a spot where an opening in the trees permitted a view of Lake Mendota. They looked over the waters, roughed up with a rather brisk breeze. In the distance, sailboats skipped over the surface as university student sailors honed their new skills. "We are so far from Kabul and home." Azita's private thought escaped her.

Deena didn't respond. She yet embraced her own dialogue. "That day, father helped me in a different way, perhaps in a way he had not intended. He helped me realize that physical beauty is as much a curse as a blessing. If I were not careful, I would use this…this accident of birth as a crutch to avoid doing anything with my life. And that was what I was doing."

"No…" Azita tried to protest.

"Yes, I was. Listen to me. I had felt sorry for myself all those years. It started with Majeeb, our sweet brother. He was a boy and, by definition, therefore special. His world was open to him, at least it seemed that way. Of course, by the time I was aware of him as a person, his goal was to fight the Taliban even when he could not. Do you realize how gentle and wise father was? Of course you do. Pamir never betrayed that he was disappointed in his eldest child, his only son. He must have realized early that Majeeb did not have any interest in medicine, nor talent for it. It did not matter. In my eyes, he was spoiled as the heir apparent to the family name. I thought that unfair. I knew I was much smarter than my brother, but I was to be the pretty one. I didn't know what to do. I also had no interest in medicine and following mother into teaching was just a dream during the Taliban years. It was as if I just existed, helping mother with the domestic chores and drifting further and further into a haze of depression. I played as if I embraced this vision of future domesticity and motherhood when the thought of being forever with a man loomed as a lifetime in hell. Did you never see my anguish?" She looked to her sister.

"No…I am so sorry. I was too young, too self-absorbed, too…" Azita wanted to embrace her sibling but decided Deena might whack her. "I thought you were confident of who you were while I despaired at my foolish wish to follow in father's footsteps. It was hopeless, but I could not shake it. I had become obsessed."

"Yes, of course," Deena said softly as if she had never lost her reverie. "When you were young, I thought that you were a godsend for me. You were not pretty in any classical sense. You were kind of fetching with those large eyes, but I thought that at least I would be the beautiful one and you my plain younger sister. That seemed important then, how odd. Then, one day, you turned out to be this brilliant little spoiled shit, the family prodigy."

"You are…"

"Shush, or I will beat you just like the Taliban did." Deena scowled. "You came along and then betrayed me by becoming Papa's favorite. At first, we all thought it cute the way you followed him around like a pet. This will not last, we said behind your back. Even Mama told me not to yell at you for skipping on your chores since this was merely a fad that would soon pass. But it never did. Worse, Papa began to take you seriously. That crushed me." Deena suddenly looked into her sister's eyes. "That really was such a crushing blow. Now, I felt like nothing. Majeeb was the crown prince and you would carry on father's work and I would be nothing. The fact that you becoming a doctor was impossible at the time escaped me. What I saw was Papa taking your dream seriously. Never, not for one moment, did I ever really understand your own anguish or doubts. You seemed so self-assured."

"I was not."

"Of course. Now that is clear to me. You had a passion…no, an obsession and no way to satisfy it. That is a true definition of hell. But that day, when Papa came to soothe me when I grieved that my selfishness almost got you killed, he awakened me in a way. He got me to come and talk to you without asking. Maybe that day woke me up, finally got me to be honest. I think…I think that it was then that I first appreciated what you were going through. We started talking after that. No, not just talking but sharing. You know what - inspiration replaced jealousy. I didn't just mope around with envy. I even convinced myself that you were not that smart, you just tried harder. One day, shortly after, I got up the courage to ask Mama if she would tutor me. She had done so when I was younger, but I never encouraged her to continue. Now, I asked her. I was so fearful she would say no, that I was not smart enough, not like her prize student, you. Do you know what happened?"

"She agreed of course."

"She said not a word. I saw the most wonderful expression in her eyes, and tears. I saw tears. She merely put aside her things and pulled out a book. I think she and I had a very difficult time that first day, reading the lesson through our tears."

"Funny," Azita responded when her sister seemed to pause in memory. "I was not even aware of the change at first."

"Of course not, you were still a selfish brat and, besides, you were following Papa around even more as you got older. That gave Mama and I plenty of time to be alone. She knew I wanted to do this quietly. I think she knew that to make this a big thing in the family might scare me off. I felt so insecure and she was so sensitive…I miss her."

Azita looked up through the trees to the crisp blue sky, as if the answer to her internal debate might be found there. "You remember that book that saved me?"

"Of course. The bullet that glanced off my skull struck it in your blouse. Talk about Allah's protection. You had just found it in mother's possessions. Am I remembering these things in the right way? Some memories from that time seem real, some I am not sure about."

"Yes," Azita said softly. "You are remembering perfectly."

Deena now looked very interested. "You were going to show it to me but never did. Given my memory problems back then, it slipped my mind."

"Just listen to me." Azita took a big breath. "That was not just any book. It was mother's private journal. Perhaps that is why I stuffed it into the front of my blouse, that I felt some guilt just taking it. Good that it was thick, in any case. It stopped the bullet headed for my heart, and I do have one by the way." But Azita saw that her preemptive strike was not necessary, her sister was staring intently into her eyes. "I think you are ready for Mother's journal though it takes some talent to get around a big bullet hole. Mother loved you so deeply. She saw your talent even if you did not. She knew you were destined to be an educator, like her. I was to be like Papa, the doctor."

"But she never said anything," Deena protested.

"Don't you see? She knew you had to make that decision on your own. She had been dropping hints, but you never seemed to respond. It had to be your choice. No one can give an obsession to another, it has to have been put inside them by God."

"Oh my God, I think I remember that. I was just too wrapped up I my own self-loathing to hear anything back then."

"She talks about the day you finally came to her as being one of the happiest in her life. She could never again be an educator, which she so loved, but she now could pass that on to her beloved daughter…you."

Rather than embrace, the two began walking again, engrossed in their private thoughts. Azita kept looking up through a break in the canopy of trees overhead, mostly to avoid acknowledging the tears that had run down her sister's cheeks. The sky seemed a brittle blue suggesting air that was dry and on the edge of bracing. She enjoyed the intermittent ripples of breeze on her skin. Still, perfect weather could not quite erase a heaviness that poked at the edges of her heart. "Sometimes, I wish we could go back to where we were, have a do-over as I have heard the kids here say. Of course, I would want my head to be filled with the things I now know and maybe some of the confidence I now feel, at least on occasion."

"You always looked confident," Deena noted.

"Hah," Azita laughed. "that is how little we knew one another back then. Think about it. We spent so much time together since, as youngish girls, we were rather prisoners in our homes and yet we hardly knew one another. I so wish to make up for lost time and yet, we are to be separated again."

This time Deena stopped walking and took her sister's hands. "Dear Azita, we will never be parted. No matter the physical distance between us, our hearts will beat as one. Besides, we also possess the wonder of today's communications devices. We will speak to one another always, share all the details and agonies of our lives. And we will do so even with more intensity than we do now. Why? Because we shall be aware of that very physical distance between us. When we were in England, separated by just dozens of kilometers, days went by without any contact between us. We were busy and somehow knew that there would always be tomorrow so connecting was not such an urgency. That will not happen now, that will never happen again. Now, we know something that shall never be forgotten."

"What is that?" Azita asked.

"Now we know, completely, just how precious each day of life is. That boy in our village did me a favor; too bad I cannot thank him."

"Some favor, putting a bullet into your head."

"No, no. How many people go through life never being in any danger of having it ripped away from them? Once you have experienced that, you never go back to taking things for granted. When I was laying in my bed after I realized I would not die and, of course, after I would finish yelling at you, I would think about things. There was little else to do. Silly, I suppose, but I made two vows. Now, don't you laugh."

"I won't…unless you say something really stupid, which I am sure you will."

Deena glared at her for a moment before accepting her sister's jest. "First, I would, no matter what, make my life count. And don't say that I already was doing that. What I vowed to myself was that I would not back away from danger. I will always be a target because I advocate and work on behalf of the education of our young girls. It would be easy to do that from a distance, from a place like this I suppose. But I vowed that, when necessary, I would go back, I would not let them intimidate me. I must read our mother's journal. If you are being honest, she did see me as her legacy. Now, I have no doubt at all. If I cannot live the life our mother, Madeena, prepared me for, I will have disappointed her. I will not do that. I cannot do that." With that Deena paused.

"Yes, I understand that pledge, entirely. And the other?"

"Oh, it is something we already touched upon. I vowed never to become complacent about the people I love. I will make sure they know how I feel, how much they mean to me, always. Karen knows, of course. But I cannot recall when I last told Kay or Amar or even Chris how much they mean to me. You assume people know but you should tell them."

"Someone is missing from your list." Azita looked a bit hurt.

"Who?" Deena looked perplexed.

"Me, you idiot."

"Oh." Deena looked thoughtful. "Let me see. I think you made the waiting list, but pretty close to the top in fact." Deena started to walk faster, keeping just out of striking distance of her sibling. "But listen, I think we have talked way too much about serious stuff. Let us rather talk about funny and absurd things."

"Like what?"

"As usual, your love life," Deena responded. "That always makes me laugh, but you know that." She giggled and ran ahead of her sister to where the peninsula came to an end. There was an arena-type facility built into an open area where picnics could easily be held. She found a place to sit while she waited for Azita to arrive.

When Azita arrived, she sat next to her sibling and said nothing. They both took in the serenity of their surroundings. An occasional boat added the breeze in disturbing the quiet surface of the waters. Deena became uneasy as Azita remained wordless. Finally, the younger sister spoke. "Did you ever learn to swim?"

"No." Deena answered uncertainly.

"Good." Azita looked at her mischievously. "But I will wait for these students now approaching to leave before I push you into the lake. There should be no witnesses."

Deena ignored her humorous threat. "Really, I do want to know about Ahmad and Ben. I know you still are in contact with both, which surprises me. Have you become a wanton woman?"

Azita looked away as if ashamed at what she was about to say. "Hardly, I have not had sex in a year. Perhaps I should think about becoming a nun."

"As if the church would take a Muslim nun." Then, Deena absorbed what her sister had just said. "Wait? You have never slept with Ahmad and he still has not dumped you?"

"Why is that surprising? Don't you think I am not worth the wait?" Azita asked cautiously.

"In truth, no. Alright, you are somewhat pretty now but any man that desires your body has to know that he will pay a big price." Deena betrayed no humor in her words. "What do the Westerners say? You're high maintenance."

"What do you mean?"

"Oh, dear Zita." Deena had picked up on the nickname Chris used. "You are willful, have no domestic skills, are absorbed by your profession, and have a terribly wicked wit. A man must endure much pain and suffering to put up with you. Ben was perfect. He was soft and followed you around like a puppy dog. He became trained. But Ahmad is so handsome and worldly. He must have many women wanting him. He is waiting for you to make up your mind. I cannot believe that, really."

"Hmmm." Azita looked out to the lake. "I wonder how long it will take them to find your body after I push you in." Then she sighed. "The thing is that I know you're right. I know it. So many times, my body cried out for him to take me, but my damn mind got in the way."

"What in Allah's name were you thinking?"

"Don't laugh, okay."

Deena looked sincere. "I won't…unless I can't help it."

Azita glared at her but continued. "Ben has not made this easy. He kept showing up in Oxford, hoping I would take him back. I thought about it, a lot. He is devoted to me and we have much in common. It surely would be relationship that is…comfortable. And yet, I cannot get around the reality that his parents, his family, will never accept me. Perhaps they have arrived at the point where they will not oppose a marriage, not that I am certain of that, but they cannot fully embrace me and who I am. I am spoiled by the love of my original family and by Chris and Amar and Kay. I only know that kind of acceptance. Still, it is hard."

"This is not my place, of course, but I am going to say something. You may be a great brain and are a science wizard, but you can be very extraordinarily dumb at times. If you had loved Ben you would have married him, nothing would have stood in your way. You are the girl that defied the Taliban, don't you see? You took him in as you would a stray dog. He is the man that would make a great colleague in your lab. But that does not make him the man with whom to share your life, bear your children. A husband is someone you wake up next to every day, every damn day." Deena struggled with where to go next, then decided. "Okay, here is the test. Did you orgasm when you made love to Ben?"

"Deena!" Azita exclaimed. "That's personal."

"Don't be a child - did you?"

"Well…it was nice."

"I thought not." Deena grabbed her sister by the shoulders. "I could have ended up in some arranged marriage to a man with whom I went through the motions. Now, I cannot even imagine that life. Never settle, do you hear me? Never. Go after Ahmad and throw yourself at him. Do you hear me? Rip off his clothes and violate him. I just hope it is not too late. And until then, I desperately hope you are gratifying yourself."

Deena braced for a response of shock from her sister, but Azita merely looked out over the waters that surrounded them. Without comment, she reached into a cloth bag that had been slung over her shoulder and pulled out a book. "Deena. I have been carrying this around with me, waiting for the right time to hand it over." She handed the journal to her sister who looked at the bullet hole in the binding. "You must work your way around the bullet hole but that is not hard. The message is clear enough, that cannot be obscured. Her lesson is all about love…you cannot miss that."

This time, Deena was the one to embrace her sister.

⤙ ⤚

The group now working with Chris settled on the deck of the Crawford's temporary Madison home overlooking Lake Mendota. An expanse of green lawn flowed down to the water's edge where a dock sat to permit one to sit and enjoy the sunsets. "Not bad, huh? I even have a boat which, of course, I don't know how to use. This being a lake though, I suppose I could not get too lost," Chris said.

"Let's not put that hypothesis to the test," Kat responded with a smile, enjoying any opportunity to tease her older sibling. "I want to thank you, Chris, for luring me away from the Windy City, even for a day or two. I believe I was the only one of the Crawford children not to be corrupted by spending time in Madtown as a wild youth, which I missed, the wild part that is. This place took on the aura of the mysterious Shangri-La for me. How come you never brought me here?"

Chris chuckled. "You can understand, Kat, can't you? You were an innocent child, the pure one. We didn't want you to be corrupted by this sinful place. That, and the fact that you were a bratty kid at the time."

Kat took charge, it had become her character. "Thanks for nothing. But to business. This will be the core team as I understand it. Let me see if I have this straight. Obviously, I know April and Josef quite well. I recently met Atle Bergstrom who Chris has brought with him from London. Atle has been working as a top executive with your international service organization and before that was with the Center for Global and Comparative History of Ideas in Oslo. Is that as impressive as it sounds?" She looked directly at the middle-aged man with nice features, brilliant blue eyes that conveyed considerable intelligence, and a slightly receding hairline of blondish, but not quite blond, hair.

"It was a place with great pretense to cognitive superiority and I did enjoy it a lot, very stimulating. In the end, though, I wanted something with more practical effects. Besides, I ran across Chris's writings and was impressed though I am a mere epigone of the master."

When Kat momentarily looked uncertain, Chris explained. "Epigone means a pale imitator of the real thing. You know those Norwegians, always showing off their literary creds." At this, Atle laughed heartily.

Kat smiled and turned to a woman whose pleasant face was framed with a cascade of brown, tightly curled hair. "But this young lady I know not at all. Tell me about yourself."

The young woman broke into a broad smile and then evidenced a slight accent suggesting a youth spent in the southern hill country when she spoke. "My name is Pamela Stuart. Originally, I was born and raised in West Virginia, in a rural part of the state. My parents passed when I was young, and I was raised by relatives. We struggled, in truth I experienced tough times. In any case, I did my undergraduate at Harvard and…"

Chris interrupted. "Tell Kat, all of us, how you made it to Harvard from rural West Virginia."

Pamela's smile broadened even more. "I guess I was reasonably smart but pretty isolated and quite naïve. I did not know much about the Ivy League until I saw this Reece Witherspoon movie, Legally Blond. If you remember, she was also a naïve girl who somehow landed at Harvard. It seemed like a cool place in the movie, so I gave it a shot. I barely knew where Boston was located."

"There is more, I believe," Chris prompted her.

"Not too much more. The admissions process at most Ivy schools depends upon so-called candidate advocates who are assigned a region or group of applicants. They select the ones from their pool they like and push them in the final decision process. A lot depends on how much they like you and how aggressively they push. In retrospect, I suspect I profited from the right demographics…poor, rural, and southern, that is if you consider West Virginia southern, which I do at least. I met my advocate once after I had arrived at school, she told me that my essay won the day for me."

"What did you compose that was so compelling?" Atle asked.

"I wrote about my upbringing and some of my struggles growing up, about losing my parents so young and the poverty and the hopelessness around me. I did leave out the part about the movie though. I lied and said Harvard was the aspiration that had driven me forward even as a child. It was that beacon on the hill that inspired me beyond my humble origins, though I did not go so far as to claim birth in a log cabin. I cannot reread that essay now without blushing. So disingenuous."

Kat looked at Chris. "What would you have written to get into Harvard? Perhaps you could have summoned some sympathy from the stories about the limo getting stuck in Chicago traffic while bringing you to your posh private school or about the suffering you experienced on those days when the caviar had not been flown in fresh from Russia."

"Bite me." Chris smiled.

"Poor thing," Kat continued. "had to settle for Princeton."

"And then I only got in because I could play basketball. I didn't exactly apply myself academically in my misspent youth, too many distractions like being a sex object. The girls just would not let me alone." Chris then smiled more broadly in case anyone might take him seriously. "As you all can see, my dear sister is deathly jealous of my scholarly and professional success. All she has done is earn more money than God. I will give credit where credit is due, though, her filthy lucre does greatly help us sojourners for truth and justice who labor to create a better world. We don't have to work for a living."

Kat made a face. "Oh, bring me the family barf bag ASAP. Are we the only set of siblings with a community barf bag?"

Chris laughed aloud. "Welcome to the Crawford sibling-rivalry road show. We appear nightly in the Crown Room of the Bellagio Hotel in Vegas. Now, if Kay were here, ably assisted by my adoring wife, I would be toast by know. You can well see why I have no problem staying humble." He paused long enough for the crowd to audibly groan, then continued. "Seriously, though, this is quite the international team…Norway, Poland, North Korea, and a southern state, the most backward place of all."

"Now that we have bonded," Kat interjected, "let me get back on track. Chris showed me the office set up he has put together. It seems nice, very close to the west end of the campus on Old University Road. It is perfectly situated in an innocuous looking office building, a fact of some importance. I have come to appreciate the need for remaining low key. It took me a while, but he convinced me that the analytics for our effort should run out of Madison, away from some prying eyes that would be way too interested in what we are doing. I don't think any of you would be in danger, but we are delving into matters that involve powerful people who do not like to lose. For example, recently, we uncovered that one Konstantin Nikolaev, a Russian billionaire oligarch, has been engaging in some suspicious behaviors in the

U.S. We are likely to push back against the agenda of these... gentlemen and they play rough, very rough. We delved into Konstantin's background and found that he is a confidante of Putin which is quite necessary to get rich and stay free and, most importantly, remain alive. He has some major investments in the gas and oil industries both in Russia and around the world. That is, he is in with the Koch brothers."

"How symmetrical," Chris added. "the patriarch of the Koch dynasty made millions doing some work for Stalin. Now, the current generation of Kochs are radical libertarians while the once Russian bear is run by a kleptocracy of billionaires who want a strong government to regulate things for their own ends."

"And the difference?" Atle asked.

"None, in the end, your average American libertarian only hates those regulations that benefit others and not him," Chris answered after considering the question. "The point is that the people who threaten our democracy and world stability, such as it is, were enemies. Now, they are joined together, not in any fraternal sense but in a compact based on mutual greed and lust for power. They will do whatever it takes to keep their hegemony and their fortunes. The members of this loose oligarchy are drawn from around the world. The common denominator is a dislike for anything resembling democratic protocols, an obsession for personal control, and an unreasoned hate for anything touching upon the public good. In their world view, power is money and money is power. They are fungible commodities. Yet, this shadowy group are not totally united, not like some secret illuminati. There are distinct styles and interests among them, at least as far as we can detect with imperfect information. They may, however, be inching toward some form of cohesive group based on interim common interests."

"What kind of cohesive group?" asked Pamela, "I am the newest member and feel behind the rest of you."

"Probably no further behind than I," added Chris. "But let me give it a try. If I get a failing grade, perhaps I will get fired, I hope, I hope." He took silence to suggest he was free to continue. "A generation ago, many of these guys, and most are men but not all, were enemies. They were separated by ideology. But the fall of the Soviet Union, and the gradual softening of China economically, suggested areas where dialogue and cooperation would be preferable to confrontation. As the shackles of the old regimes fell away, a few oligarchs emerged with the spoils, usually the same who had won under the previous communist governments. Culture is a funny thing, though. I see major differences between East and West. Russia bridges the European and Asian cultures but looks west. They are seeking a working alliance with Republicans in America and the rising fascist parties in Europe like Marine Le Pen's hard-right group in France, the National Front party. They see these groups as a strategy for breaking the hold of Western liberalism and globalism that kept Russia relatively isolated in the post-Soviet world. But ideology and culture always interfere with pure self-interest. For example, China is moving toward hegemony over renewable energy sources, looking toward the future. Russia and America are controlled by an elite wedded to old style energy concepts, fossil fuels and such. They have billions invested in those assets, what we term 'stranded assets', as most of you know. They will fight to the death anyone who threatens those resources, like the scientific community pointing to the reality of climate change. To date, some Americans and their Russian allies are working diligently to push this country to the right. Unbelievably, Donald Trump will be their hero."

"Shoot me first," Jules uttered as she and Beverly walked up onto the deck. "Sorry to be late. Getting out of Chicago is such a chore and I had to wait for the princess here to get ready, she waived toward Chris's sister-in-law.

"Don't blame me," Beverly protested. "I have to be careful. I am always paranoid about meeting with Chris or Kat, afraid that Charles Senior will find out."

As the two newcomers found seats and joined the group, Chris registered his surprise. "Wait, I thought visiting my young girls was a good excuse that Father had bought into?"

Beverly gave Chris that known female look that says, *are you a cretin?* "Not when I am traveling with Jules. He sees her on the news all the time and knows she is a pinko-leftist beyond redemption."

"Worse," Jules affirmed, "I am the wrong color to be a pinko, which makes him hate me even more. Hell, I am surprised he has not sued me for the silverware he thought Ricky and I stole when we visited you during our wild teen years." She looked directly at Chris.

"You did, didn't you?" Chris deadpanned.

"Steal the silverware? Hah. We may have been black and struggling financially, but I knew enough to walk off with the priceless art and jewelry, not the petty-ante stuff. Hell, the art work in the guest bathroom alone was worth more than I am now, and I am famous and rather well-off. Okay, who is new here?"

They went through the introduction ritual, got more drinks, and settled back to business. Jules asked what they had missed.

"Chris was just about to put the staff into a coma with one of his lectures," Kat joked, "but we should discuss the risks involved now that you are here. You might add something on this, I want everyone involved to have full information."

Jules and Beverly looked at one another but it was Beverly that spoke. "I sure hope you all can be trusted."

"They can," Kat responded.

"Okay, then. While you all know I am Chris's sister-in-law, you may not know that I have kept close relations with his father, a key figure in this shadowy group of right-wing conspirators. Charles Senior still views me as his meek and inoffensive daughter-in-law. He keeps me close, I think, because he likes to rub me in the noses of his children, whom he sees as traitors. Either that, or he sees me as his one conduit into what they are up to. The point is, I really don't know what goes on in his head, but I have access to him and his associates. I am like his substitute hostess since Chris's mother left her sociopath of a husband after a lifetime of abuse. Let us just say he is a despicable human being. All that you might have heard about him is true."

"Wow," Pamela murmured.

"Yes," Jules added, "Beverly is a hero in my book, very brave. I have been doing investigative reporting for some time now. You might well imagine that I have made enemies and been threatened. Let me tell you, the only man that truly frightens me is Charles Crawford Senior. His eyes are penetrating and utterly cold. I have looked into the eyes of several known sociopaths, like network brass. He has those eyes, but worse."

Kat picked up the conversation. "In my mind, Chris and I are likely the real targets of Father's wrath or that of his associates. The stakes are high and who knows what they are capable of. Of course, if he stumbles on to Bev's role, she would be high on his hit list. The rest of you are likely too small to get their attention but I want you to be fully apprised of the risks. If you wish to seek safer employment, I would fully understand. Now is a good time to make that decision. Or think about it for a few days and let me know."

She paused while the others looked at one another. April spoke up: "My family faced down the North Koreans. I am with you."

Joseph added: "And I the faced down the Polish communists."

"I have been a dedicated socialist all my life," Atle affirmed. "You know risks come with fighting for the things in which you believe."

Then Pamela chimed up: "Hell, I was a hillbilly who confronted the snobs at Harvard. That is more frightening than anything you guys faced."

"Yes," Chris exclaimed, "the bravest of them all, other than me who has had to put up with my evil sisters all of my tragic life."

"Now you can just bite me." Kat smiled, looking at him. "My God, we just have to come up with new material when we insult one another. Seriously, though, I want to thank you all. One final point before I hand this over to my brother: what is said among us, who attends our private meetings, and the nature of our work remains secret. You cannot talk about it with any outsider, not a soul. We have a cover story for you to tell others, it is in the material we will be handing out shortly. Basically, you are working for a small consulting company doing marketing research to sell feminine hygiene products."

"What?" Atle seemed a bit shocked.

"Just my sister's awful humor," Chris noted. "Unfortunately, it's all she picked up from me. In fact, though, you will be posing as marketing consultants doing research on a variety of household products. I think we even have some spiels you can use if anyone gets nosey."

Jules laughed softly. "Yes, Chris's sense of humor, which only makes himself laugh, he picked up originally from me." Jules and Chris looked at each other. The chemistry between them was not to be ignored.

"If I picked it up from you, no one would laugh at me, with me, whatever." Chris realized he had lost his joke and turned professional. "Seriously, we are the core group. In the packets I am about to distribute, Kat and I have developed a basic plan. All of you have been collecting information in one way or another for a year or more, except for Atle and Pamela who are new to the team. As you can imagine there is a greater sense of urgency now. The national elections are just months away. It will be Trump, heaven forbid, versus Clinton. The basics are well known to all. Both candidates have high negatives. The Republican base is highly energized but, of course, it is not enough to elect a loser like Donald even with the voter suppression and the other anti-democratic tactics of the GOP. Their agenda primarily serves the interests of the economic elite, so they must convince millions of ordinary folks to vote against their own self-interests. Right now, that seems unlikely except for the suspicious cyber-stuff going on."

"Okay," Atle said. "I am newest on the American scene, but I can say with certainty that Europe is utterly amazed that Trump got this far. No way he will be elected. In fact, my people see a rollback of existing Republican power coming."

Chris spoke as if he was introducing Atle for the first time. "I stole Atle from Karen, who runs the international service organization I founded. He comes from the rarified world of a Scandinavian country where people are educated and sane. America will be a rude awakening for him. When April and Josef get finished bringing you up to date, I am confident my favorite socialist here will be swimming desperately back across the Atlantic to Norway. As they will inform you, a good thirty-five percent of the population, maybe more, want an authoritarian leader. Add your random full-blown racists and nativists and greedy one-percenters or elite pretenders and you are well over forty percent. Let's go beyond all the known tools they will use to nudge the support for Trump even higher. It is the evidence of direct foreign meddling that worries us. Sure, you got the money coming in from Russia through front organizations like the NRA. And we know that Russian oligarchs have been bailing out Trump, that utter disaster of a business man, for years. Think about what has been going on in Russia. I recently read a paper by Alexander Buzgalin, a modern Marxist professor at Moscow State University. You probably have heard of him, Josef?"

"I have, in fact. A thoughtful man, if a bit left-wing."

Chris continued. "In any case, he stresses that Putin has about a seventy-percent approval rating in Russia, if not more. That level of favorability persists despite great economic inequality. Why? Because he brought stability to the chaos that reigned after the fall of communism and the rise of the robber barons. For some reason, people will put up with a lot of crap if someone comes along and tells them they will take care of things, put the house in order so to speak. In fact, that is what made the Taliban popular in Afghanistan, at least in the beginning. They eventually moved into the power vacuum and initially dampened the chaos that existed after the Russians were driven out. People wanted order and lost their freedom. This is a classic Faustian choice for sure, less chaos at the price of little personal control over things. Russians wanted the same thing after the wild days of Yeltsin. Americans, I mean working-class and much of middle-class America, are scared. They are struggling and still going under, but they cannot figure out whom to blame. Well, Trump is going to come along and tell them. It is those damn immigrants and effete liberals and selfish blacks on welfare. Get tough, clean up the neighborhood, lash out at those foreigners who don't play fair and all will be well again. We look at that buffoon and see a conman. A lot of typical Americans look at his pitch and see a savior. Hell, the religious right even buys into the absurd notion that he is a Christian." Chris paused to let that sink in. "What worries Kat and I, and I assume Bev and Jules, is the sophisticated cyber crap going on. It seems very sophisticated, highly targeted, and designed to foster division and hostility within the electorate. The liberal and left are vulnerable. Why? They think the election is theirs, that Trump is the weak card. These hackers and outside forces will come in and exploit that sense of self-satisfaction, that feeling that we have the luxury to debate which wing of the party best represents the country. In the meantime, the mainstream Democratic Party plays it safe. Vote for us because we are not bat-shit crazy. Totally logical but woefully insufficient."

"I remain skeptical." Atle tried holding his ground. "Even Americans are not that stupid."

"I appreciate that. But here is my take. The Republicans have already gone through their party purge. It took several decades, but the emergence of the well-funded Tea Party was the final nail in the coffin for the old guard. They may be a bunch of vile sons-of-bitches, but they are focused and dedicated on keeping power at all costs. The Dems are yet struggling with their identity. Are they a centrist party that can hold on to the middle class and wealthy donors or are they a party of the common man? Is a populist or a centrist message the key to a resurgence? They have not figured that out yet. With Hillary, as I mentioned, they are likely to run a campaign that is merely anti-Trump, based on the plausible, yet flawed, notion that no sane person would vote for this maniac. You would think it would work but I am not sure. It worked for Johnson in 1964, don't vote for that nutcase, Goldwater, because he will blow up the world. That pitch doesn't work anymore, Americans now like nutcases. Somehow, when Trump says something stupid and mean, he comes across as genuine and not programmed. Hillary is safe and well scripted and thus seems to be a phony politician. Around this table we know that running a government is hard work that requires great skill. Out in the heartland, that reality is lost. The same people who would not let an incompetent doctor treat an ingrown toenail would willingly turn our country over to a total clown. Besides, the right has spent a quarter-century demonizing the Clintons. All those racists out there are spitting mad that Obama had a scandal-free eight years in power. Can you just imagine how that violated their world view? This cyber campaign does not have to shift millions of voters, just thousands in a few key states. Josef and April know that better than I. They also know that mysterious Russian sites, using fake identities, are lasering in on specific populations in the given areas to rile up the right and sow discord among liberals and the left. Then there is the usual hacking and using outlets like WikiLeaks to foment suspicion of Hillary. Call me a pessimist but I am predicting a Trump victory right now."

There was a long silence, and then Kat spoke up. "When I lobbied my brother to join me, I wanted his big picture vision of things. He does see what others do not and not just when he is experiencing acid flashbacks from his high-school days spent in Madison. I hope that we can weather the storm in this coming election, find out what is going on sub-rosa, and then come up with a longer-range plan to take this country back. Then I would let my brother go back to his real life. Of course, if he is right about a Trump win, then…"

"Amar will never let him stay long, of that I am sure." It was Jules, who looked directly at her former lover. Chris met her eyes and quickly looked away.

Kat wanted to retake control of the conversation. "Well, we all have a sense of the stakes. Let us focus on what we will do over the coming months. And remember, we are not alone. Through me and Chris and Jules, we have connections to many others concerned about the future of both our country and the world. I want to start by making sure we know our respective roles and how we will work together over these coming critical months."

As the dialogue became work-related and specific, Chris kept looking over at Jules. He could not get her last comment out of his head.

⚜

That evening, they were all gathered in the lakeside house eating and socializing. Amar had returned from a day at the university hospital where she was beginning her medical duties. Azita and Deena had returned from their tour of the campus. The conversation had turned to socializing and bonding, everyone sharing bits of their lives.

At some point, Amar noticed that Azita was missing. Already, she knew where her adopted daughter was likely to be. She slipped out of the house unnoticed and made her way down the lawn to the boat dock. In the gathering darkness, she could see an outline seated on a bench.

"Still counting those stars up there?" Amar asked as she slid next to her.

Azita smiled weakly. "It is not Kashmir. Too many nearby lights. I might be able to count all these stars."

"No other night sky is like Kashmir where you are close to the top of the world, or even the Panjshir Valley for that matter." They sat in silence for a moment before Amar asked. "What drove you from the festivities up at the house?"

"I might ask the same, what drove you down here?" Azita retorted.

"Clever lass, responding to a question with a question. Another of my husband's tactics?"

Azita let out a small laugh. "I am finding that having such a smart mother is not a good thing. I could never fool Madeena either. It is such a curse to be burdened with such clever mothers." Azita realized that deflection would not work. "Okay, I escaped

to think about something Deena said earlier, two things really."
Then she stopped.

"Daughter." Amar swung about to look more directly at her.
"Surely you are not ending there?"

Another laugh. "I did not think that would work." Then, the
girl sighed. "She said something about not backing down in the
face of fear. I think that her getting shot has made her stronger,
possibly stronger and more committed than I. When we were
young, she was the silly and frivolous one and I was obsessed with
medicine and contributing something to the world. Now...I am
not sure. Oh, I remain committed to medicine but with the same
old question...how to contribute? Most of all, I cannot stand
the thought of her putting herself back in harm's way. She can
contribute from London, can she not? If she is killed, I ... I could
not stand that. She is all that remains of my blood."

Amar put her arm around her daughter and pulled her closer.
"That, my dear, is the very agony of love. We must let those most
precious to you go, so that they may be what was intended for
them. To do otherwise would be utterly cruel."

"You would let me go back into harm's way?"

"Yes. And die inside while doing it." Amar said the words but
doubted her conviction.

Azita looked hard at her mother but surprised her with
where she went next. "You don't want to be here, do you?"

Amar said nothing for many moments, merely watching the lights of a boat making its way home. "This is very nice and seductive but no, I don't believe I will be happy here. I am drawn back to a place where I can feel useful. They have plenty of excellent doctors here."

"What will you do if this - what shall I call it? - project goes on and on?"

Amar sighed. "Well, I don't have to decide that today, but I think about it a lot. I talk to Karen a lot. They have initiated a program in Syria with what are called the White Helmets. It is a multi-national force of volunteers trying to help those caught up in the devastating civil war there. Her sources tell her that it is a matter of time before Assad destroys the rebels, the slaughter could be terrible. It is horrendous already."

"And you feel you should be there?"

Amar nodded her head. "Of course. That is my life. But now, with Chris and the children…"

"You do love Chris, don't you?" From Azita's inflection, this came out more as an affirmation than a question.

"Desperately," Amar managed.

"Then you will work it out, the two of you. Your love will overcome everything else."

"My word," Amar said and chuckled, "this from the girl who dismissed all boys as smelly and obnoxious. The older I get, the more I have come around to your point of view. Oh, not that they are smelly or obnoxious, at least not all of them. But they can be a lot of trouble."

"That is so true." Azita exhaled.

"Hmmm, you mentioned Deena saying two things on which you have been dwelling. Boys must be the other. Ahmad?"

Azita nodded. "She told me to make love to him, to Ahmad. Maybe I shouldn't tell you that."

Amar kissed the top of her head. "I will share another agony of being a parent. You want to know everything about your child while trying to respect their privacy. I had guessed that nothing had happened and, quite frankly, I was rather shocked by that."

"Why?"

"Because you obviously love him." She said the words in such a matter-of-fact manner.

"I think I have been an idiot." Azita said the words so softly that Amar could barely recognize them. "I have kept him at arm's length because…"

"Why?" Amar pressed.

"I assumed I would fail him, that he could never accept me for who I am."

"Sometimes, my dear, we women are too clever by half. We think way too hard on things. I know what I am going to say next is not what a mother is supposed to say to her daughter. But here it is: if you get the chance, you tear that boy's clothes off and ravage his body."

Azita laughed aloud. "Some motherly advice. I cannot imagine Madeena telling me that."

"Well, kiddo," Amar said and smiled, "I was the best offer you were going to get as a substitute mother."

"I think you did okay, better than okay." Azita rested her head on Amar's shoulder.

The two women sat quietly looking up at the stars while listening to the water slap against the dock. Neither said another word for a long time. The Amar spoke. "Not as many stars, but still mesmerizing. You know, the closest cluster of stars is Alpha Centauri. And yet, it takes over four years for the light to reach us even traveling 186,000 miles per second. All we see up there is history. My brother also told me that one night as we shared the Kashmir heavens."

Azita looked away from the sky and toward her mother. "Do you know what is sad?"

"No."

"That you have been married to Chris for so long that your head is almost as filled with as much useless stuff as his is."

"Is that right?" Amar hugged her daughter a bit closer. "And I bet you haven't learned how to swim yet. Look how close the water is to us."

"Ah, wait, what I really meant to say is that you are so smart, and I love you very much and every word you utter is brilliant."

"Good girl," Amar said and smiled, "I am gratified to see that all that education has not been wasted."

The two enjoyed their solitude together. They could hear the conversation and laughter coming from the house behind them. This, however, was where they wanted to be.

CHAPTER 11

THE EMAILS

Karen Fisher sat back in her easy chair that had been provided as a matter of course by one of Kabul's finer hotels that catered to Westerners. It was situated in the embassy section of the city, not far from Wazir Akbar Khan Park where she and her colleagues had strolled while discussing their busy day of meetings. As dusk arrived, they decided to return to the hotel for dinner, lamenting the fact that they could not simply walk to the Hairy Hare for laughs and drinks. As they entered the lobby, Karen squinted at the faux luxury with distaste. She always bridled at staying in first-class accommodation. It went against her working-class roots. However, the safety of her staff was of paramount importance. Afghanistan was still at war, though at a rather low boiling point. Still, even in the big cities, bombs went off and anyone who looked like an infidel was considered a prime target. She never fully let her guard down.

At dinner, they unanimously complained that they should have found an authentic Afghan restaurant to dine in. The food was of a decent quality but more suited to bland, Western tastes. Why had northern Europeans and so many Americans settled for such uninspiring cuisine? Perhaps it was a manifestation of their tendency to seek out similarly bland lives where they entombed themselves in hermetically-sealed suburbs. Karen concluded that such a life was death by dripping compromise with anything real shunned as if it were the reprise of the bubonic plague.

As Karen propped her laptop on her thighs, she smiled. She remembered frequent debates with Chris when they had traveled in safe, European cities. She would argue that they did not have to waste money on the best hotels, they could easily stay at accommodation with a lower rating. Chris would give her his *are you nuts* look and make his usual joke about wanting the toilet to be inside his room. She would call him a snob and he would retort that she was still a peasant. Then they would register at a fine offering with which she was secretly pleased. *Oh my God,* she thought to herself, *I hate the fact that he is back in America. I will miss him terribly.*

She had completed some routine correspondence with her staff back in London. She leaned back a moment. She was both energized and taken aback by her newly attained position. She had been nominally in charge of the service organization for some time now but had never quite shaken the sense that she was the associate director on paper, acting director in reality. Yes, she was making the day-to-day decisions but always with the knowledge and comfort that Chris was nearby, down the road in Oxford. She could pop down and he always made time for her. They would wander over to the Hairy Hare where she could talk through whatever bothered her at the time. Better, she could trade insults with him. There was no better sport than that. She wondered if any other subordinate ever treated their superior as badly as she treated Chris. Then again, she considered the matter and concluded that everyone treated him badly. He rather enjoyed it.

In the early days, when they had traveled together, she sometimes let a nasty thought enter her mind after a few drinks in the evening. Perhaps she should give him a shot in the sack? Males held little interest for her, but she really did like him and had bedded some boys early on in life. He was such a hit with the ladies, her curiosity did cross over into the realm of considered interest to find out why. However, the man who reputedly would 'mount a coatrack' never made the slightest move on her, always treating her like a sister. In the end, she always realized that her affection for him was as the brother she had always wanted, unlike the one she had. She shook her head. Putting the moves on him would have been a disaster.

Once, her curiosity did get the better of her. After they were very comfortable with one another, she asked him if he had ever been tempted to make a pass, perhaps her body had influenced his decision to hire her. She had never considered herself very attractive, but he did make many jokes about her great body, comments that would have been challenged in a more up-tight professional environment. *No*, he responded, *that never crossed his mind*. When he intuited that Karen found this disappointing, he rushed to complete his thought. *She had a great rack, but he knew she was a lesbian from the beginning of the recruitment interview.* When Karen looked puzzled by this, he offered that *she had to be a lesbian since she was not drooling over his good looks and charm.* She could no longer recall what she threw at him in that moment, but it was something with some weight to it.

The truth was, however, that she sometimes was scared. She had hired more staff in London. They were good people who worked hard and seemed dedicated to the work and the mission. But they were new. She really had relied on the originals. Now, damn Chris had stolen Atle to take to America. To her relief, she found that finding quality staff was not difficult, the program had gained some interest in select circles. Moreover, Kay had remained as well as Carlotta, who now was one of the veterans. And, of course, she had her partner Deena who was now 100 percent again. Karen had insisted that Deena visit her sister in America. It would be a good test to see if her stamina and health had returned enough to withstand the trials of international travel. It had all been a ruse on her part. She could not stand the thought of her lover and partner returning to the country where she had been pushed to the very cusp of death by an assassin's bullet. Terror seized her heart at the very thought. She dreaded the thought of the day when she could not keep Deena away from her home and her obsession to advance the education of young Afghan girls. Of course, they had educational initiatives for girls in the Mideast and the Horn of Africa. And the Muslim population of London and England was growing exponentially. But Afghanistan was where Deena's heart lay. Karen understood that all too well. At some level, she understood one thing: her relationship with this woman would never last. It would break on two fronts: there was not enough desire to keep them together and Deena's lust for her roots could not be ignored forever.

Now, she stared at the screen. Should she email Deena or Chris first? She could not immediately decide so she sat there ambivalent. Her mind wandered to a strange occurrence that took place just before they left the UK. Ahmad Zubair showed up at her office. She knew the young man as the mysterious boy with whom Azita had become involved after her relationship with Benjamin had fallen on hard times. In truth, she could never figure out what was going on since Azita seemed conflicted and uncertain about the situation. Karen did not know the young man well but had recalled deciding that, if she were interested in boys, this would have been her choice, or someone like him. It was not his good looks and lean, athletic body. It was not even his easy charm and intelligence. No, there was something deeper in him, an innocence and naivete that proved irresistible. But what did she know about such matters?

When she agreed to meet him that day, he told her that Azita had mentioned in an email that Karen and her executive team would be visiting Afghanistan and other sites in the coming weeks. *Please let me become part of your party*, he argued forcefully. *I have lived in several Mideast countries and know the culture and several languages. I can be of great help. You don't have to pay me, and I can take care of my own expenses.* At first, she was most reluctant, but Kay convinced her to relent, arguing that the young man would be of great assistance in several ways. Not only did he have local knowledge and many contacts through his father, but his knowledge of Mideastern politics and economic circumstances was encyclopedic. Besides, she had wanted to get to know better the mystery man who was apparently causing such considerable anguish on the part of her adored niece. Karen relented and, of course, picked up his expenses. He was proving invaluable and such a quick learner. Karen quickly understood that his academic preparation in economics and international affairs could make him very useful if they expanded beyond traditional human services. Karen was already wondering how they might pull him into a permanent position with the organization. She would have to check with Deena on how the relationship between Ahmad and Azita was progressing, if it was at all.

She would start with Chris. Yes, better to get that one out of the way and then she could focus on her message to her partner. The latter one might need more thought. Yes, that sequence made sense.

TO: Chris Crawford

FROM: Karen Fisher

SUBJECT: How is the traitor doing?

Now, I am not saying you are on par with Guy Fawkes or that American rebellion guy, Benedict something or other, but I am still a bit pissed at you for running off to America, just to save the world. Is that any excuse? And then you went and kidnapped my top technical guy, Atle. But you know me, forgive and forget. I won't stay mad at you. After all, you hired me when I pretty much thought I was unemployable, just because I gave a snarky response to one of your questions. You do realize that I only gave that response since I had concluded you had dismissed me as a candidate? Hell, why not be honest when it was already over, but you felt the need to fill up an appropriate amount of time. So, let's say we are even though you still might check on packages from me with the bomb squad before trying to open them.

Who would have suspected in the beginning that I would be running the place? Who would have predicted that? I should not put what is coming in writing because I know it will come back to bite me in the ass. I sometimes wake up in the middle of the night in a panic. My personal demon is that I will fail you. I don't want to screw things up after you put so much trust in me. Let me confess something: I may seem together and tough, but I still have this working-class girl inside me, not feeling that I belong. It doesn't matter that I beat out the snobby public-school brats at university. As you always said, you never shake those early scripts.

Bottom line, I guess I am scared that you are not nearby. Modern communications are great but not the same as looking someone you trust in the eyes. Whether or not you were aware of this, I watched you very closely when we worked together, in between my insults. You really did smooth off the rough edges and managed to shape-up this energetic but rather clueless sad sack into something of substance. There is no way I can thank you enough.

Karen had not meant to go there and was shocked at the words on the screen. She almost deleted them but held back. *No,* she said inside her head. *He should know these things.* Suddenly, she realized the moisture on her cheeks. My God, she was crying.

Wow, enough of this maudlin crap. To business. Afghanistan is the same - bloody hot and fucked up. What was in the minds of that long-ago marauding horde that invaded from the north and decided this was the place to set up shop? Were they nuts? Of course, it might have been right after an ice age and the place was still habitable. But that was not the case when my British ancestors tried to conquer the place and had their tails handed to them. Bloody idiots.

But enough whining. The meetings today went well. Tomorrow should be very interesting. I am going to be visiting Bahiri and Ferhana Gupta, a husband and wife doctor team that serve women and try not to only heal their bodies but also nudge their female patients in the direction of greater self-respect and independence. You know, make them more like me. How great is that. By the way, I know exactly what you would say in response to that…

Eventually, we will make our way to back to the Panjshir site. I am sure I will be a wreck there, not so much for me as the memories of what happened to Deena. Still, Dr. Singleton, Archie that is, continues doing great work, along with his wife, Agnes. He obviously was taken with Azita when she was there last year and still talks about getting her back, maybe even after she completes her internship. When I told him that she would then do a residency, he scoffed. That is for students who have never worked around bodies, but she has been doing that since her early teens. The man has a point, she has been working around bodies since she was a kid. Still, I wonder what you and Amar think?

One other confession. It is a little odd to be travelling with Kay but without Deena or Amar or even you being in the party. Truth is, I still find your sister attractive. Don't get your whitey-tighties in a bunch since nothing will happen but I do reminisce about my fling with her back in the early days during these long evenings. In my opinion, she has the most sex appeal of all the Crawford kids. Wow, it must be getting time for my cold shower.

I will fill you in as we make our way around to the other sites. Syria really intrigues me. One thing: I hope you know that I do understand what you are doing and why it is important. Just miss you is all. You are such an easy target and I have such a hard time being nice.

Much love,

Karen

PS: Give all my best to Amar and Azita. For the life of me, I cannot understand how you lucked out with Amar...she seems so sensible.

After she hit send, Karen scowled. *Damn,* she thought, *why did I end with much love - way too sentimental.* It was accurate, however. In fact, she did love him as a brother. Then she began to regret her comments about his sister, Kay. She should not have been so revealing there. But hell, she was lonely right now, and very needy. She would never have acted on it, would she?

Three doors down, Carlotta Ciganda sat looking at her laptop. She had been trying to work up the courage to send a message to her colleague, Atle Bergstrom, who had recently left London for America with Chris. It should have been an easy message, so why was she finding it difficult to get going? After all, they had conversed nearly daily for over a year. Somehow, in her heart, she realized that deeper emotions might easily push her words from friendship to another, more dangerous place. After all, he had a partner, even if they were not married. This other woman was an artist of some ilk, an odd pairing she'd decided. She erased that running dialogue in her mind and started writing.

> *TO: Atle Bergstrom*
> *FROM: Carlotta Ciganda*
> *SUBJECT LINE: Missing you.*
> *Hi,*
> *We are in Kabul right now. After we visit the Panjshir site, we will visit other Mideast and Horn of Africa sites. I am looking forward to the Syria visit with anticipation and apprehension. It is a new place for us and the situation is yet unfolding. There are two great pleasures to this job...starting something new and realizing that an established*

site is working. I am not certain which is the more exhilarating.

You should have insisted on joining us on these trips. Even if you were seen as a central office type, I am sure you would have gotten so much out of the field trips. It would have made the work, the mission, more personal for you. I am convinced that those at the top of any organization must spend time with those who do the real work. Perhaps then, you would have not been so eager to move on to this new adventure in America.

What I will miss is not having you there when we return. I always enjoyed telling you the stuff not included in the reports, the gossip and the small stuff. That was like sharing a bit of myself with someone close enough to understand. But the communication was not just one way. I remember you sharing with me the things that interested you. I can still recall one evening at the Hairy Hare. You went on and on about quantum bits where each had the property of being in the on and off position at the same time. This would lead to another exponential explosion of computing power. You were astounded when I came back with the observation that it was a bit like the Heisenberg uncertainty principle where you could only determine a particle's position or speed but not both simultaneously. I thought at the time you were impressed that a Spanish gal could be so clever. You did think me clever, didn't you?

So, tell me. How is America? I realize you have not been there except for some visits but any first impressions?

The comely woman sat back in her chair. For a moment or two, she played with her long, black hair, twisting it rather compulsively in her fingers. Damn, here she was in her thirties and had focused almost entirely on her work. Her parents were convinced she was a lesbian though never talked about it. That certainly was not the case. Still, she had largely avoided men, desperately wishing to avoid the fate of her two sisters who were already burdened with children and unfaithful husbands. She thought their lives hell on earth. At the same time, a desperate loneliness stalked her, something she could not shake. At times, it crawled up inside her, turning her stomach into an agonizing knot.

Alright, I will get to my point. I am not interested in your impressions of America. I have visited there often enough to form my own impressions. You have my sympathy to be stuck among such people with so much ego and so little sophistication. Oh my, I have become such a snob. Don't tell Chris…

In truth, I am circling around what I want to say. I don't just miss our conversations, I miss you and will really miss you when I get home and you are not there at the office. Do you have any idea of how many times I was on the verge of propositioning you? You seemed to like me but never made a move and I was raised not to be so bold. I just assumed you saw me as a silly girl or not attractive enough. No matter, I always saw us as complementary, you the cerebral Scandinavian and me the passionate, Iberian lass. In my dreams I saw us somehow coming together, making love on the sands of the Costa del Sol, the sun warming our bodies even more than the fires of intense lovemaking.

Okay, I just realized how juvenile that sounds. Still I am glad I got it out and am not taking it back. We live lives dedicated to bigger things and that is good. I don't regret that for a moment. In doing so, however, we miss out on the human connection. You cannot tear yourself away from that. I cannot at least. Sometimes I think these longings are peculiar to my gender but so what? As the kids say today, it is what it is.

Sometimes, I look at Chris and Amar, or Kay and Jamie, or Karen and Deena. They are couples and love one another. Each has children, their own or adopted. But each couple is pulled in separate directions. No one says anything but, if you watch and listen closely enough, you can see these things. These are relationships where there is great love but also forces, obsessions really, pulling them apart. Look at Amar. Can she be happy as a wife and mother and doctor to the affluent or does she need to be back here or, better still, in one of our troubled sites?

Why did I even go there? I know. I look at these couples and see two possibilities or two examples for me. Sometimes, the lesson I draw is that it is better for me to focus on my work which I love and forget about conventional love. Other times, I see hope in the examples of my friends. If they can make their relationships work, then so can I…we? But then we don't know if they can make them work, do we?

I have made a big enough fool of myself. So, just a little more then. I love you.

xoxoxo

Carlotta looked at the screen. Her fingers went back and forth between the delete and the send buttons. *Oh shit, no guts, no glory* she uttered to herself, and then hit the send button.

Several rooms away, Kay sat back in an easy chair and looked out over Kabul at night. She wondered what plots and intrigues were taking place out there. Darkness in this tortured land was not a time of rest and renewal. It was the respite used for seeking out new ways to destroy one's enemies, real and imagined. What diabolical recesses of the human mind can become so distorted with hate that one finds pleasure and gratification only in the affliction of pain or suffering in others? Her melancholy mood brought her back to Chicago, the ER room where she had toiled for several years. Broken and wounded bodies nightly arrived, shot and maimed for such noble reasons as a suspicious look or a pair of Air Jordan shoes coveted by another. How had human life become so cheap and should she still care? Of course, she did. She knew she always would. Somehow, in her mind, she was balancing some celestial scale, offsetting the evil her father brought to the world with her small acts of goodness. Completing that balancing act, she grimly calculated, would take way more good works than she could summon.

This mood grabbed her from time to time, but she had always fought back. Reach out, she told herself. Connect with her world. Then, a cold thought struck her. Perhaps this was not the usual malaise brought on by too much violence and negativity out there in the real world. Perhaps this was a more personal affliction stemming from something closer to home. She had to write to Jamie, but what to say? Kay felt a chill even though the air conditioning did not cool down the temperature that much in her room. She went to the desk in her hotel room and flipped up the lid on her laptop.

FROM: Kay Crawford

TO: Jamie Whitehead

SUBJECT LINE: Miss you.

Hey love. I am sitting in my hotel thinking of you and the girls. Perhaps I am just lonely, but I am overcome with a bit of ennui this evening. My guess is that this is what I call the 'Capitol Syndrome'. This is an affliction that is self-diagnosed and named. I generally love the road trips but the necessary visits to the central government leave me cold. Here, you can feel the duplicity, the scheming, and the corruption. It is not universal, of course. There are plenty of good folk around. Still, there is enough obvious shit to drag you down.

It will start getting better tomorrow. I am looking forward to meeting the Guptas that Azita and Deena talked about. I think Karen might have plans to make them part of our team, we will see.

I will be honest here. I am looking at the screen wondering what to say next. I could churn out a few sentences and say good night but then I would toss and turn in bed. I love you Jamie, and the girls. Never doubt that for a moment. You have given me stability and an anchor on which to hold. You can never fully appreciate what that means to me.

And yet, there are days when I feel something is missing. Our life in England is too comfortable. Isn't that silly? Most females I know would kill to have a husband like you, a family like ours, and the money and material things we take for granted. But you know, and I know that there is more out there. We are pushed by broader and more fundamental obsessions – to make some difference in the world. Even my brother, whom I love dearly despite our squabbles, seems to have gotten it all together. On second thought, I doubt Chris will ever fully have life's riddles solved, no matter how bright he is.

Okay, what am I trying to say here? I need to find some way to remain involved, to find some way of contributing to a greater good but without sacrificing the wonderful things I have in my life. Is that way too selfish? I worry about that, about being the girl who grew up with the silver spoon and got everything she wanted. I desperately do not want to become some whiney bitch, the very kind of woman I find so offensive.

Jamie, am I making sense here? The thing is that, when I am out in the field, the real field, I am alive.

The people who come for my help are totally needy. Chris sometimes talks about being everything to some people. He is right. I hate to admit it but occasionally he gets something right. They have nowhere else to go. That very fact brings a rush to me. I mean something. I am needed. I cannot get that feeling at the NHS, it is just not the same. I know that if I don't attend to someone, another physician will. I am fungible. I am not everything to the people I serve.

The thing is that I don't know how to make this all happen. How do you feel about things? How do we balance the needs of the children against my aspirations, our aspirations? It is all such a jumble for me. Promise me one thing, that we will chat about this when I return. Okay?

Remember this…I love you dearly.

Kay continued to stare at the screen. She could not push away the sense that she had not been honest, not totally at least. There was so much more welling up inside. Damn, why was life so complicated? She did love Jamie, but it sometimes lacked intensity. Her life as a wife and mother often struck her as overly vanilla, lacking in passion and bite. True, Jamie was kind and smart and helpful and perfect in so many ways. Above all, he was the ultimate father. She thought about that for a moment. Without question, he was a better father than she was a mother.

She tried hard but often felt she was going through the motions. That phrase, *going through the motions*, circled inside her head.

While Kay ruminated about her state of mind, Karen sat in her room trying to sort out her own feelings. After finishing her message to Chris, Karen had spent time looking out the hotel room window at the flickering lights of the city. She had been here once or twice when she saw an explosion or two from a similar vantage point. On those occasions, she never felt endangered, it was like watching a show. But it always reminded her of the reality out there. Tonight, though, all was quiet. Then again, you never knew, that was the hell these people endured every day of their lives. Now she turned to a message for Deena, her partner. She felt a sharp need to connect with her.

> *TO: Deena Masoud*
>
> *FROM: Karen Fisher*
>
> *SUBJECT LINE: Note from Kabul*
>
> *Hi…I desperately hope this finds you well. We just finished a busy day in Kabul, will be seeing your friends who have their clinic in your old family home here tomorrow. I will let you know how that goes.*
>
> *As you might guess, this is the time when I miss you the most, the evenings. Back in London, this is when we would snuggle on cold winter evenings, sometimes before a fire. I love those moments. I yet cannot fathom what favorable whim of the Gods*

brought you into my world. I feel like the luckiest gal in the world somedays. I hope you feel the same.

I do miss the girls terribly. Sometimes I feel terrible foisting them on you and my now rather elderly parents, but I know in my heart they love taking care of them. To think, a lifetime of misunderstanding and tension has been erased by two cute Afghan orphans. Well, in truth, my siblings helped me out loads by generally screwing up their own lives. Thanks for small favors.

One part of this trip that does not bring me joy is the thought of returning north, near to the place where you were shot. That memory, of you being near death, is burned into my head. I think, in the end, you are braver than I. I know you talk about returning here someday. I understand, even if I cannot quite envision how we will make that work. But we will. I promise. I need you to remain part of my life.

More tomorrow…all my love,

Karen

Was that enough? Karen now wondered why the message was so brief and further worried that the sentiments were overwrought, perhaps lacking authenticity. Did she not have more to say? Was she afraid that continuing would somehow lead to places she was not prepared to explore? Yes, that was it. She knew at some level that words led to more words and superficial thoughts to deeper sentiments. Better to turn the tap off early than let everything run out for all to see. She sat there stewing, turning all sorts of thoughts and fears over in her mind.

Ahmad Zubair could not seem to get enough of the city. He knew it was dangerous, but he walked the streets even after dark. It was the embassy area, so security was better. Still, there was no place in the whole country where disaster might not strike, and he knew it. Yet, he wanted to bask in the warmth of an Afghan evening after the sun had escaped its daily duty. He stopped in a coffee shop and enjoyed some familiar sweets - a flakey concoction seeped in honey. It all was so familiar, even the conversations that swirled around him. It was like nothing had changed, he had never left. Then, a feeling swept over him. Finishing his treat, he started back to the hotel, first at a brisk walk and soon at a trot. Entering his room, he flipped open his laptop and went to his emails. His heart sunk momentarily when he saw nothing from her, but she was busy after all. He started typing with purpose.

> *TO: Azita Masoud*
> *FROM: Ahmad Zubair*
> *SUBJECT LINE: Will you marry me?*
> *Dearest Azita,*
> *I will get straight to the point. I have spent much time on this trip thinking about all the reasons you*

have kept pushing me away. Really, to any objective observer, your actions make little sense since I am such an obvious catch. In any case, this is what I have come up with.

First, I considered the fact that I am not good looking enough or sexy enough for you. However, I have looked in the mirror and I am satisfied that I am very handsome. As far as being sexy enough, how would you know? We have yet to make love. On that score, I could bring written testimonies to my skills. However, I fully believe that we should try things out in that department so that you have proof of my skills. In the end, despite the lack of direct evidence, I have dismissed that as a valid reason.

Of course, you might believe that I am not smart enough for you or, more likely, that I am not smart in the same disciplines in which you focus. This is true, the second part that is. I am more involved in economics and international development than in the hard sciences though my colleagues always considered economics a real science. But here is my real argument. You would get bored with any husband who is identical to you in interests and vocation. I will argue that some differences between partners helps sustain interest over time. Okay, that is my story and I am sticking with it. I admit that you may be smarter than I am overall, but we do not know that for sure. Pushing me away is proof that you are not as omniscient as you think. Besides, good luck in finding any boy as smart as you. I should say, good luck finding a boy who is as smart as you and who also is as sexy as me.

Of course, it might be that you love this boy Ben very deeply. I have given this matter great thought. He must have many fine qualities if he has reached your heart. Though I know many girls who make awful decisions about boys, I cannot believe that you would be foolish in this area. You are not a foolish girl, except when it comes to me. If such is the case, that your love for him is strong and unshakable, I have no other choice but to withdraw and suffer my fate.

Then I think it is not that but something else. You cannot love me because of something to do with our common culture. Here, I am less certain about what the issue might be. Are you trying to pull yourself away from me because I remind you of a religious culture that you are escaping, even though I am the most marginal of Muslims, not really one at all? Or could it be that you are searching for someone who has a firm grip on their roots, who embraces their traditions more fully? I know the torture of being plucked from one set of understandings about the world and placed in another.

I think, maybe, the problem lies here. I am guessing, but you are likely wondering about returning to Afghanistan one day and perhaps feel that it would be unfair to me if you did. Okay, we will put aside the fact that it would be fairer to me if you simply raised the issue and not assume my response. I know that women think about things in odd ways, indirectly and then get mad when the boy cannot see what is in their head. Abdul, my wise father, explained such to me. I might point out that I am here, in Kabul, and soon will be in Panjshir. I cannot quite explain my feelings tonight, but I feel that I am home. I walked the streets tonight. The sights and sounds all seemed so familiar, almost comforting despite all. I was home.

Dear Azita, I have never forgotten my roots, where I come from. I study the things I do, not to make money, but to someday perhaps help those struggling countries, like Afghanistan find a way forward. We are not so far apart. In different ways, we are striving for the same things.

Suddenly, the young man stood up and stared out of his window. How many times as a young man had he dreamed of escaping this place, going to some fabled, western land where the young could dream absent guilt? How many times had he prayed to Allah to whisk him away from under the thumb of a regime that suppressed the very feelings that made people human? Now, he looked out over the city with longing. Why, for God's sake? He read in his classes that migration decisions were a complex set of push and pull factors. Was he being pushed to possibly return by some emptiness he found in the West or was he pulled by some magical connection to this place? Suddenly, he focused on the lights of the embassies that dominated the near view. Which one was it? He tried to do a quick calculation. It was India, he decided, but was not sure. Then it hit him that he was merely procrastinating. With resolve, he sat back down. Time to say what needed to be said.

> *But all the arguments in the world pale against one inescapable fact…I love you. I have loved you since I was a pudgy boy annoying you and you were that young girl following your father around desperately trying to ignore me. Funny, I remember the first moments as if they were yesterday. My heart raced, my hands perspired, and my brain froze. You would understand it better as my limbic system*

overdosing me with dopamine. And yes, I looked this up a while ago just to impress you.

What is important is not those reactions from long ago. Even I, foolish boy that I was, thought they would fade. Funny thing, though, those feelings never have. They remain as strong now as they were then. Apparently, some attractions are primal and unavoidable. I guess we are not creatures of free will unless it is a freedom to pursue that which is dictated by something deep within us.

Well, enough avoiding the question which is – will you marry me? I have been walking about the streets of Kabul this evening thinking about you on the other side of the world. I can wait for as long as necessary. But I must know if I have any shot at all. All I need to know to quiet my beating heart is that we are committed to one another.

It helps even to say what is in my heart. Now I think I will be able to sleep tonight. Who am I kidding? I will spend most of the night thinking of you.

All my love, Ahmad.

He looked at what he had written, paused, and hit send. He watched a little icon whirl as the word 'sending' seemed to stay on his screen forever. Perhaps the Gods of cyberspace were rejecting his message. Then, another blip and the words 'message sent' appeared. He sighed deeply, wondering how the object of his desperate affections would receive his words on the other side of the world. Just what did lovers do before cyberspace, he wondered?

Kay was still restless and knew that sleep would elude her until she completed one more personal message. For some reason, her brother had been on her mind most of the day. She knew why. He would not be in England when she returned. It was easy to ignore him when he was nearby. But now? There was a sharp sound out there in the night. Had it been a bomb? But she saw no smoke nor heard no subsequent commotion. Her reverie had been broken though. There were words and sentiments that had been floating around inside her head all day, for several days. Perhaps it was time that she permitted them to escape.

TO: Chris Crawford

FROM: Kay Crawford

SUBJECT LINE: An apology?

Hi there,

Yes, it is really me. I know I don't get in touch as often as I should. Mea culpa, mea culpa, mea maxima culpa. I think that may be the last residue of mother's Catholicism, the term mea culpa. Not the term so much as the ever-present sense of guilt. The priests sure did a great job of making us feel guilty about everything. Hell, maybe that is why I am writing to you late at night, to assuage a little excess guilt.

Now that I have started, I am not sure where to go next. Okay, I do. It is just hard to express it. All these years, ever since we were little, I have never been very nice to you, and I don't mean our usual banter. I treated you like an outcast when you left for Oxford and, worse, when you never returned. I blamed you when you did the very things that I desperately wished to do myself but for which I lacked the courage. I came to hate you simply because I could not summon any personal conviction or sense of purpose. How pathetic is that? It was not difficult to poke fun at such an easy target. You never fought back. Oh, you had that dry wit but that was directed at everyone, at least everyone you liked. Perhaps that made me even angrier. You absorbed my anger without complaint. Do you have any idea how infuriating that was?

Then, when I finally was getting to know you again, you ran off in the other direction. Really, must we always have an ocean between us? It is true, I said nothing but went through a few more furious days thinking you had abandoned me again. What a silly sot I am. In truth, I never said what really was on my mind. Before Amar, I was terribly cruel to you about your love life. Why should I have cared? Of course, I know why since I am being honest. I was so confused about myself, and so lonely. Just a typical female, am I not. Wow, I hate that.

I know you cannot see me right now. But I am calming down. The thing is, I do miss you. I felt us coming together, through our children and spouses and similar interests. We were not exactly neighbors but close enough to get together often. I had grown to love that. It was like having my brother again, as when we whispered our first treasonous thoughts against Father. Then, suddenly, that warm feeling of being co-conspirators was gone again.

You will probably find this overly sentimental but, speaking of treasonous thoughts against the patriarch, I often go back to those nights when I snuck into your room and we hid under the blanket to talk about the things that Father was trying to shove down our throats. I was the good student and you the goof off, but you seemed to have this wealth of information on what was going on in the wider world, even back then. I guess it was your gift and I absorbed it all. Funny what I remember after all this time. I can still recall you going on about how people like Father had been fighting progress for so long. You mentioned this guy Merwin K. Hart and the National Economic Council. The DuPont's and Pews of the 1940s put up great money so that he could spout away at the socialist threat. He focused on all those immigrants that were allowed in after World War II and the havoc they would undoubtedly wreak on this country. I recall you saying that he would go after universities to convince administrators that it was their duty to stop the spread of pernicious ideas like those that had invaded Britain which, he was sure, would soon be as red as the Russians.

Why did that come back to me? Maybe it was his name…Merwin. I remember laughing when you mentioned it. But no, it is because you have gone off to fight the very same thing decades later. I know Kat is beside herself with worry, but I kept wondering why this is so important now. After all, the rich have been at this forever. You don't have to answer that one. I think I figured it out.

At that very moment, there was a knock on the door, so faint that she was not sure it was her door or another down the hall. She stared at the door with indecision before getting up and looking through the peephole. A female figure was walking away. She opened and called out, "Karen."

"Oh, you are still awake," Karen said, turning back. "I was restless, hoping you were still up."

"Yeah, come in. I am writing my brother an email." She walked back and sat down. "This will take just a few moments to finish up. It is a confessional, I am apologizing for being such a shit to him."

"Apologizing?" Karen cried. "Don't do that. He will expect the same from all of us."

Kay laughed. "I am glad you stopped by, I was getting way too serious inside. But I suppose I should finish this thought."

> *Here is the thing. I want you to know that I love you, that I have always loved you. Yes, you have faults, more than the stars in the sky as I once said. But you are also the kindest and most sensitive man I know with Jamie being a close second of course. So many people don't see that. They only hear the cutting wit and assume some lurking malevolence or, more likely, a lack of sincerity. I know you though, from a childhood where we learned evil and endured our individual tortures and from all those nights hiding and commiserating under the covers. That is when I first saw your character, your optimism, your love… even as a young boy.*
>
> *One thing, this momentary lapse of judgement does not mean I will treat you any differently in the*

future. Not at all and surely not in public. I cannot have people thinking that I have gone all soft and squishy now, can I? You and I will know, though, even as I skewer your sorry ass in our typical battle of insults, that underneath I love and respect you deeply.

Chris, I know why you are back home. It doesn't make your absence easier for me, but I do know and understand. I wish I shared your optimism that something can be done. Honestly, though, I don't. Perhaps that is what separates us. I focus on the things in front of me, the broken body I might be able to heal. You, my hopeless knight, will forever tilt at windmills that will remain beyond y our reach.

Enough of this. Karen arrived a few moments ago. She is leaning over my shoulder reading this, starting to gag I believe. Wait, now she is picking up a large lamp and seems poised to attack me. I doubt that she approves of my feelings. In the end, though, you cannot take out what God has put in. A wise brother told me that…too many times to count.

I love you.

K

Karen sighed. "Are you bloody bonkers? You do realize that it will now take me months to whip him back into shape. I thought our unwritten rule was to always, always treat Chris like shit. You must really be in a bad mood."

Kay rose and walked to the window. The lights yet blinked in the inky dark of a summer's night. She looked up trying to see some stars but only a handful were visible. Suddenly, she was terribly sad not to be in the Panjshir where the night sky would sparkle, and one might sense the Milky Way shift as Earth spun on its axis. Finally, she spoke: "Not so much sad, Karen. Maybe more confused and just a bit melancholy. Hell, do you think I would say such nice things to Chris if I were on my game?" Kay tried a weak smile even though she knew Karen could not see.

When Karen spoke, Kay realized that she was immediately behind her. "Yeah, if we were back in London, I would suggest that we head out to get blitzed. Not so easy here in Kabul." Suddenly, strong hands were massaging her shoulders.

Kay felt Karen's hand move up to massage her neck. In a soft voice she managed to speak. "I know what the problem is."

"And," Karen prompted as she moved a bit closer so that her full breasts lightly touched Kay's back.

"Shit," Kay uttered as a shock of desire swept through her. "The thing is…I just don't know where I belong. After all this time, I just don't know. How can that be? I was supposed to be the adult child. Damn it."

"Kay?" Karen then said no more, simply continuing her neck massage while gently rubbing her nipples across the other woman's back.

Out there, in the darkness, they could hear the wail of an ambulance. It struck Kay as a plaintiff wail, a call for help. Why did she feel so alone suddenly? Her confidence and strength were ebbing. She needed touch, comfort, the human connection that might only be sated by physical contact. Everything in her said no. And yet.

"We can't do this," Kay protested without conviction.

"We shouldn't," Karen whispered with even less force.

Without a further word, both women turned and walked to the bed.

CHAPTER 12

THE 2016 ELECTION LOOMS

Azita examined the sad face looking back at her from her computer screen.

"Hello Ben."

She was alarmed by the vision before her. His face was forlorn, his skin sallow. It was more than that, he appeared gaunt, with a haunting aura about him. He must have lost considerable weight, something she found troubling given his original slight frame. It was the eyes most of all, a bit sunken and dark. Perhaps it was the shadowing in the room where he was located. She hoped that was the case. She did not want to contemplate other possibilities. He had been pestering her for some time to chat on Skype. Typically, she employed her busy schedule as an excuse, not exactly a lie but not exactly the truth either.

"Hi," he responded.

They stared at one another in silence for a moment. "It is good to see you," she offered. "It has been some time." She tried to recall when they had last connected other than via email or texts but could not. She had struggled with this. Part of her wished to cut him off with finality. It was not that she no longer had feelings for him. She did, deep feelings. Not love, but something close. She still felt respect, admiration, even affection. Those emotions had been so new to her with any boy that she initially had confused them with something more profound. She now tried desperately to find some accommodation of mutual sentiments that would permit a continuation of their friendship. That had proved far more difficult that she first imagined. Asymmetrical affections are, by design, destined to inflict pain. This was no exception.

Still, she was grateful to him, for many things, even the physical lovemaking. That had always been lacking in some respects yet had suggested a dimension of the human experience that intrigued her. She found that untapped part of her life something that she wanted to embrace with this other young man, Ahmad, and yet was so reluctant to do so. Why was that? Was she afraid that she would respond to it fully, or not fully enough?

"Are you well?" She asked, thinking inside that she should be honest and ask why he looked like shit. That question formed at the back of her mouth, but she could not force it out.

"I am well enough, I guess…getting by. Well, to be honest, I have been distracted. My work has…stalled."

She knew he wanted her to ask by what. Desperately, she hoped that he had merely run into a technical or theoretical challenge. Perhaps he was just run down from excess work while trying to jump start his research. That was possible. She knew better, though. She knew what was holding him back and it broke her heart. She did not want to go there, so sought another route for the conversation. "Benjie, I hope you are not letting your work suffer. Science is hard, we all get discouraged. I know you can overcome any problem." She was listening to her own words and cringing inside. "You have so many gifts…please don't let me hear that you are not using them."

"I am gratified to hear that you care." His expression remained remote, lifeless. "Frankly, I am surprised."

"Yes, I care. Damn it, I care." She exploded and could see his body jump a bit on the screen. "I have never stopped caring about you and how you are doing. We have meant a lot to one another…"

"Past tense, I see." He intruded.

"Benjie, don't go there, please don't."

"Why not? I faced down my parents for you. That was not easy, but I did it." His demeanor changed, showing signs of animation. "I told them that I was going to marry you no matter what. I was willing to give you my all, to break with my family and my culture. And then you turned me away, just because of this Arab boy who just walked into your life."

Her temper flared but she held it in check. "Please don't go there. Don't you dare. Listen, I broke off our engagement when it was clear that your parents would never fully accept me. They might be courteous, but they could never embrace me as a daughter. How could we live together knowing I had driven a wedge between you and your world? You know that to be the case."

"No," he protested. "I don't. They were coming around, really. They were changing, I swear."

"Oh, dear Ben, please don't delude yourself. If they softened toward me, it was only because they began to see the marriage would never happen. They will always love me at a distance, only at a distance. And don't you see, there were…there are other things. Yes, we had this shared dream at one point, we would both be scientists. We would work together on medical research. That was a fine ambition, but I was always torn. I don't believe you ever saw it, but I was. Others kept telling me what a fine mind I had, how I was destined for the academy and a laboratory. When I protested about wanting to work with people, that was dismissed with the 'you can always have your private practice' trope. Sure, I could treat a bunch of spoiled academics in Oxford or Cambridge or some similar intellectual sanctuary. It hit me at one point, I was being swept along, permitting others to tell me what I should be, who I was. Even you were part of that."

"No…no, I never."

"Listen to me Benjie. You never said, 'Azita, you must be a scientist'. But we talked about the things we shared, a lot. We did not talk about the things we did not share, like this pull I feel to go back."

"Back where?" He sounded increasingly plaintiff.

"To my home."

"Don't be absurd, for Christ's sake. Why would you ever want to go back to that hell hole?" The words had simply escaped him. He could not take them back.

Azita looked at him hard. She tried to recall if she had ever heard him swear before. She could not. Then she tried to recall whether they had ever talked about her returning to Afghanistan. To her surprise, such a memory escaped her. Her response was measured, absent any anger. "Listen to me, I want you to move on with your life. You have a marvelous mind, focus on your work. Forget about me. I am not worth it. Think about all that you can contribute, please." Something in his expression made her stop. "Benjie, are you even listening to me, are you?"

"No," he said. "I have stopped listening."

"We can still be friends. I want…"

"Stop Azita, just stop. Don't you understand?"

"Understand what?" She thought she knew but had to ask.

"That I cannot continue without you."

"What does that mean?" Her voice was full of concern.

"Nothing. I just mean that you are the one with the fine mind, the exceptional mind really. I am…" Then he stopped. His expression was replete with pathos.

She opened her mouth to respond but the screen went blank. She sat their thinking of all the arguments she might make in return. Was he foolish enough to dismiss his own talents? What was wrong with him? She should call him back, force him to listen. She could push him back on track. She knew she could. But all she could do was look at the blank screen and feel the tears stream down her cheeks.

For the next few days, Azita tried to push her conversation with Ben out of her head, burying herself in the impossible workload pushed upon interns. She loved the work. It was primarily with children but, as is the case at this level of medical training, eclectic in the topics covered. They assume that the students have much book learning and virtually no hands-on experience. Her mentors continually were amazed at this prodigy who could work her way around the human body with such aplomb. What were they teaching her? In rounds, she often became a teacher to the other students, relating similar situations faced back home, sometimes without all the comforts of modern technology. In practicum situations, the others scrambled to be her partner. In some ways, she was bringing lessons learned the hard way back into the academy. Yet, she did it in such a way that she did not generate envy or hostility. She had not a hint of hubris, she merely wanted to share with the others. They understood that.

No matter the pace of the work, she could not escape the image of his face just before the screen went blank. He had looked devastated. But how could she make it better? Different dialogues coursed through her head but none of them were satisfactory. They all ended badly.

∽ ∾

Amar was waiting one day as Azita headed out for her walk home at the end of a long shift. It was a decent walk to their temporary home on the lake, but she loved the time to clear her head. "Why the ride?" Azita asked.

"Jump in, let's go over to Picnic Point." This was a favorite place of theirs to walk and talk when they had the chance. Somehow, Azita could sense this was not to be a casual stroll, nor chat.

"What is wrong?" Azita asked as they started out. When Amar did not reply, they took the short ride in silence. After parking at the entrance to the peninsula, they started down the now familiar path. The light of the day was beginning to fade, one could see a hint of the evening lights across the water. The dome of the state capitol was clearly visible, framed by an increasingly dark blue to purple background. A brisk breeze brushed up against the two walkers as they buttoned up their jackets against autumn's reminder of what was about to come. Yet, they were surrounded by the beauty of fall's coronation of color. The trees were already past their peak with a growing carpet of leaves cushioning their feet, occasionally crunching under their steps. They remained in silence for a while until her anxiety was about to burst. "Just tell me. What is wrong?"

Amar turned to her with an ashen face. "Sweetheart, this is not easy. Ben's parents tracked me down, through Karen. Apparently, they did not know how to reach you…"

"No…" Azita groaned. "He killed himself, didn't he? Please God, no."

"I'm sorry." Amar moved to hug her daughter but Azita kept backing up.

"I killed him. Oh my God, I killed him. I did."

"Azita, stop. You did not kill him, he did that to himself."

"No, no, no, you don't understand. I killed him just as if I had plunged a knife into his heart with my very hand."

"No, no my dear, apparently he had been planning this for some time. He stockpiled pills, so he had been planning this, probably for some time."

"He called, just the other day. He looked so desperate and I gave him so little. And then, and then I should have called back. I just knew it…I did. His look, at the end…his look was haunting. But I didn't. You know why?"

"Sweetheart, don't."

"Why not, I am nothing but a selfish bitch. I was busy. I couldn't be bothered. He had become an inconvenience. What kind of monster am I?" Azita kept backing up as Amar approached, tears flowing down her face.

"Don't you dare say that." Amar's voice teetered on anger.

"Why not? Goddamn it, it is true." With that, the girl turned and walked away quickly.

For a moment, Amar was taken aback by language she had not heard before. She sprang forward, grabbed her daughter by an arm and spun her around. "Stop it."

"No, let me go, I killed him."

Suddenly, Amar's hand swept up and across Azita's face. The smack was loud and seemed to echo across the hushed evening. The young woman staggered back, blinking. She had hardly heard a cross word from Amar in all these years, never mind experienced such an expression of anger. A couple waking nearby looked briefly and then moved on at a quicker pace, not wanting to become embroiled in a clearly domestic dispute. Azita's tears stopped as a red welt surfaced on her cheek. Amar spoke clearly and with conviction. "I am not going to let you do this. Do you hear me? Just stop it, damn it."

Azita stared at her mother with eyes that were fixed by surprise. Finally, she managed a response. "But I…I…" That was as far as she could get.

Amar caught her by the shoulders and shook her. "You listen to me, young lady. You have a decision to make here. Yes, this is a tragedy. Yes, we should all mourn his passing. Yes, in hindsight, we are all imperfect. All that is true. But I never, ever want to hear you take this burden on yourself. You did nothing wrong. His family never accepted you. That, my dear, is the fact, the source of all this tragedy. That was always the issue…from day one. What if you had run off with him? You would have had to rip him from his roots, his culture. For God's sake, how long would that have lasted? Do you understand what I am saying?"

Azita stood there, shivering in the chilled air. She knew that Amar was right and not quite right. "I'm cold."

It seemed like a non sequitur to Amar, whose anger dissipated as she looked upon the stricken girl in front of her. She wrapped up her daughter and pulled her tight. "Azita, you have to understand. There was nothing you could do for Ben. He was just a sweet boy, too sweet. He could not break with is family nor could he deal with losing you. I will be honest with you. I loathed involving myself in your relationship with Ben. Frankly, though, I was thrilled when it began to dissolve. I could see what lie ahead. Nothing but disaster. You would have married him out of pity, not love. His parents, his family, could never have embraced you despite any affection they might have had. The chasm was just too wide, just too wide." Amar stroked Azita's hair and kissed her head. "I talked with his parents when they reached me. In fact, we talked at some length. They blame themselves, not you. They realize what they had done to him, they had consciously driven a wedge between you two without saying it aloud. Now, they are shattered. They realize the cost of their narrowness. And then, when they realized the price to be paid for their prejudice, it was too late. They did nothing, could do nothing. They watched him decline and did nothing. In the moment, they were yet happy the relationship was over. Then they watched him die. Now, they would go back and do it differently."

"My God."

"His mother confessed to me," Amar's voice now caught, "that she and her husband fully understand that they killed their son, just as if they had put a gun to his head. They understand that they tried to separate him from who he was and what he wanted. Some people are more sensitive than others, they can't fight back. Ben couldn't. This was his way of dealing with the intolerable."

Azita took a big sigh. "All this…all this is just a tragedy. It all feels so unavoidable …so inevitable. Why are things so complicated?" Her tears slowed but had not stopped.

"Azita, I want you to remember one thing. Now, listen very carefully. In all our talks recently, I have become aware of one thing. Ben would have been asking you to walk away from whom and what you are. He might never have asked out right but every day, in so many ways, that is what he would have been asking, needing. And it would have torn you apart because you might have been too kind to say no. Sometimes, the supreme kindness is saying no. And you are so kind, saying no to this boy for whom you cared so much would have torn you apart. It did tear you apart, but after marriage the trauma would have destroyed you both. I could not bear to see that. And hear this. I do not know

Ahmad well enough to understand if he is the one for you. Still, he came along to shed a light on who you are inside. I sense that at least. We cannot bring Ben back. But I won't let this drag you down."

Azita sighed again. "It will take me some time."

"I know." Amar hugged her. "And I am sorry for hitting you."

"Why?" Azita asked, though knowing the answer.

"Not my finest moment."

"But it was." Azita whispered softly. "It was your finest hour as a mother."

"What?" Amar pulled away to look at her.

"It told me how much you love me." Azita tried a smile.

"You have no idea of how much I love you. You could not possibly know," Amar whispered. "Come, it is getting dark. Let's go home and have a good cry."

⤳ ⤶

"Mr. Crawford. Please go into Ms. Crawford's office, she wants to see you privately for a moment before the meeting starts.

Kat was staring out of her window at the panoramic view of Lake Michigan, seemingly lost in her own thoughts. "What's up?" he asked, more to announce his presence than ask a question.

She remained silent for a few moments, almost to the point where Chris was tempted to call out again. Then she spoke: "Remember when life was simpler, all you had to worry about was your bratty, younger sister pestering you to take her to the beach? It is not much but I loved walking along the lake shore watching all the joggers, if you were with me that is. Then I felt safe. Nothing would harm me if you were there. I must have been such a pain in the ass to you."

"Sentimentality," Chris affected shock, "what brought that on? And yes, you were by the way."

Kat whirled to face him. "Last night, Ricky and I worked late and got a bite to eat nearby. Usually we have food delivered but decided on some fresh air, as if that could be found in the city. It was only a couple of blocks back to the penthouse. I started crossing a side-street first, no traffic, and then a car appeared and swerved right at me. Good thing my husband has the reflexes of a professional athlete. He yanked me back just in time. The car roared away, never even slowed. It just seemed to appear out of nowhere, as if it were waiting for me, and then disappeared into the shadows just as quickly."

"You think it was deliberate?"

She gave him her best 'are you a total moron' look. "What do you think?" Her look was grim. "Of course, I cannot say for sure, but I caught a glimpse of a man, just before I was yanked back. There was something vaguely familiar…oh, I don't know. Perhaps paranoia is taking over."

"Well, it is not paranoia if someone really is out to get you. I've been tempted to do you in a couple of times myself."

She managed to smile. "My God, I believe you will have Satan himself laughing, you know, just before he pushes you into a pit of brimstone."

"Well, I think we both have our suspicions about what might be going on. It is almost impossible to believe but still."

Kat looked directly at her brother. "This is what I wanted to talk to you about before we joined the group. I don't want to be an alarmist, but I don't want to put others in jeopardy either. Usually, I make my own decisions but even I must admit, this is beyond me."

Now it was Chris's turn to walk to the window. He looked out over the city and the lake. "I do remember those times. And yes, you were a pain in the butt."

"You already made that point, you are repeating yourself, a sure sign of age or maybe premature dementia - probably paying the piper for your misspent youth."

"Just making sure you heard me." Then, he turned to look directly at her. "And look at what this obnoxious pain in the butt has become. I am so proud of you."

Kat smiled. "Unfortunately, undeserved flattery does not excuse how callously you treated me when I was a young, impressionable tot."

"Damn, disingenuous flattery used to work with all the girls, and what the hell do you mean I treated you with callous disregard. No way, I catered to your every whim and wish." He turned and took his sister by the shoulders. "Damn, not even I can joke my way through this one. There is not a doubt in my mind that we must at least treat this as real, and we must be fully transparent, totally honest with those in possible danger, no matter how remotely. We must tell our people that there are dangers involved in this work. Perhaps we are being a bit conspiratorial here, but we must act as if the threat is real, even if we lose good people."

"And that," dear brother, "is why I keep you around. Let's go."

The others were all seated around the large conference room table: April, Atle, Beverly, Jules, Pamela, Ricky, and a couple of staffers that were unknown to Chris. This time, there were no introductions, no bonding. The room was serious, businesslike, markedly tense.

Kat took command. "Everyone - heads up! We will get to the data briefing in a moment. First, we need to discuss a…security issue."

Jules looked puzzled. "Security issue, like a leak from one of us? I accuse Chris, probably spilled everything to a cute Russian spy."

Kat did not smile, which surprised Jules who suddenly paid attention. "Personal security," Kat went on, "it is not entirely clear, but Ricky and I think there was an attempt on my life last night."

There was silence, and several furtive glances toward Ricky who nodded in affirmation. "Looks like it. I saw it better than she did. As Kat stepped off a curb, this car came out of nowhere. I believe it may have been waiting for her. It sped up and looked like it aimed right for her. Then it sped off."

"I'm only here because Ricky has cat-like reflexes." She leaned forward over the table in her aggressive pose. "Now, let's get very serious for a moment." She realized her comment was spurious since everyone was totally serious. "We may be mistaken. It might have been just another drunk driver on the streets of Chicago. Maybe it was even a business rival, though we go after one another in the courts. On the other hand, it may have been someone who really does not like what we are up to. No need to get into a guessing game here but you are bright people, it is most likely someone with a grudge against me, Chris, or… Beverly. That would be personal, family." She paused to let that sink in. Then, in a more emphatic voice: "However, it could be that anyone working on this project is in danger. I cannot, in good conscience, put any of you in harm's way. So, please, please understand that I would fully understand, we all would, if you would prefer a safer role with me in another part of the organization or to leave altogether. I can easily find a place for any of you in Crawford Enterprises. You all have technical skills I can use to make more money. Questions, concerns?"

There was silence around the table. Each person looked at the others as if someone else would tell them how to respond. Finally, it was Atle who spoke up. "Shit, if I wanted to make money, I would have gone to work as a quant on Wall Street. Hell, this makes me feel a bit like James Bond."

April's face lit up with a beatific smile. "You forget, Ms. Crawford, I faced down Kim Jong-Un, my parents did at least."

"For me, this story just got a whole lot better." Jules smiled. "You cannot possibly think that I would walk away."

"Thank you, but please think about this hard. It might be nothing or everything. If you have any doubts, come to me, please." Then she turned toward Beverly. "I worry about you the most."

"Kat, I know what I want. I finally know. After all these years I am finally a part of this family. That means so much to me. Besides, I have a score to settle with that son-of-a-bitch."

"Okay, now to the briefing. Who is starting?"

Atle rose and walked to the screen. April worked the graphics. "As you know, we have focused more on the national election recently and not on the larger, longer-term issues. It was not that long ago that people were talking about a blue wave, about Hillary being a lock. Then, we saw troubling signs…huge Hillary negatives and troubling, unsettling trends in several swing states. Since we last met, we have enhanced the data we have available to us and drilled down into electoral sentiments with even more precision. We number crunchers want to thank Chris for smoothing our contacts with others doing similar work, especially those in non-academic places we don't normally interact with. The cross-fertilization of both data and analyses has been extremely helpful."

'That has always amazed me." Kat tried to feign shock. "People do seem to like him. Go on."

"Over the past several weeks, the danger signs have been there. There is tremendous working- class angst out there. It is no secret that wages have stagnated for a long time, life is precarious for wage earners, if they have jobs, and fears for the future are real and palpable. For so many, one accident or illness can push them over the fiscal abyss. That anger and fear is coalescing around a populist message based on xenophobia and racism. There is a kind of 'let's blow the thing up and see what happens since it cannot get worse' attitude."

"But it can," Kat insisted.

"Of course, it can. Anger and fear are mutating into a viral form of vitriol. The underlying groundswell of hate in this country astounds me. Pick the target *du jour* - blacks, Hispanics, Muslims, immigrants of all stripes, everyone except the elites who really are screwing them." Atle paused, he had drifted off script. "I thought you were supposed to be the melting pot. But let's look at the details…" Atle went on making specific points as April put state-specific slide after slide up on the screen. From time to time, someone made a specific comment but mostly they absorbed what was in front of them. He was just making a point about how educated white women and uneducated white males were close in the political preferences in the early 1990s, both tending slightly toward the GOP. Now, almost a generation later, educated white women had swung to the democrats while uneducated white men had drifted deeply into the Republican fold. They had become a firm base on which a demagogue might weave an evil spell.

Pamela Stuart interrupted at this point. "I have a bad feeling here. You people are looking at numbers, but I grew up among these poor whites you have been discussing. They would sacrifice almost everything to ensure that the 'others,' however defined, don't get public help. It is insane. I remember…"

Chris cut her off. "It's over."

Pamela stopped mid-thought while Atle tried to protest. "No, we have several more slides to go."

"Sorry, the election is over, not the presentation. I can feel it. Trump is going to win."

"Bullshit," Ricky offered, "that's just your usual Irish pessimism talking."

"I wish it were." The others realized that Chris was about to take over the session and visibly leaned forward. "Listen, the Republicans cannot win a straight-up national vote, even with all the crap they have thrown at Hillary for over a quarter-century.

The interests they serve, in truth, only represent a sliver of the total population. They must rely upon misdirection, division, and straight-out cheating. If they can get close enough through the first two, they can get over the top with the third. Most of you are too young. In Richard Nixon's day, though, he was known for his dirty tricks. They put out fake media bites about opponents like Muskie, they made up stories about prostitutes and top Democrats, they raised mounds of cash for use by operatives doing God knows what. The sad part about tricky Dick is that he didn't have to do it. He was winning in 72. McGovern was way too liberal for this country and Nixon was a lock, but paranoid. Nixon was, despite of his rhetoric, damn liberal. This year, they have a candidate and an agenda that, by all reasonable standards, should be crushed. Hell, Trump is just as conservative as Goldwater was in 64 but without any of that man's core principles. Today's Republican party serves the interests of a smaller slice of the population than back then and the Donald only cares about his megalomaniac delusions. However, what they have is a way, way more sophisticated dirty-tricks campaign under way, and it will put them over the top. Just listen to Trump, he is playing right out of Hitler's playbook of the early 30s: fanning fear and hate of the outsider, coming up with classic scapegoats, attacking anyone who opposes him. Remember that the Nazi tactics did not work well enough to put Hitler over the top at the ballot box, he topped out at 36 or 37 percent of the vote when their elections were still legit. But economic conditions continued to deteriorate, the Wall Street crash. That should have been just a major correction, but conventional conservative economic policies pushed it into a depression. America had been propping up the Weimar Republic through economic loans but called them in as the U.S. economy tanked. Angst turned to fear in Germany and Hindenburg felt he had no choice. Once Hitler was handed power legally, their experiment in democracy was finished. Is history repeating itself? Trump could squeak in, perhaps a tainted victory but legal on the surface. Once in, what next? This is not the old Republican party. This gang cares not one whit for democracy, they rather loath it."

"I am losing your point. Where are you going?" It was Beverly asking the question.

"Sorry, you know me and my historical parallels. I have this terrible habit of thinking out loud. All that the republicans, and I now mean the hard-right these days, need to do is get close, since winning outright is impossible. Then, they can crawl over the top through a modern version of dirty tricks and the electoral college to squeak in. We have known their 'dirty tricks' have been going on for some time. Forget about the incessant cries from the right-wing propaganda outlets like Fox or the foreign cash being dumped into the campaign by Russian sources, the real danger lies in the hidden and very sophisticated campaign being waged that targets the tiniest subgroups you can imagine. I've been talking to people around the country. They are also picking up weird signals about fake cyber accounts and suspicious server connections that traffic heavy in political crap. People's fears, left and right, are being inflamed and very successfully. Read up on Cambridge Analytica. They seem to be working just as hard at sowing discord among the liberal left as they are fanning angst among the conservative right. Look at how vicious the fighting has become among the Bernie-bots, the Stein-devotees, and the conventional Hillary supporters. Sure, the DNC fucked up, but party shenanigans are nothing new. Huge rifts are being driven amongst the left, that is not just happening, that is being aided and abetted by design, and from Russia with love, as it appears. Unfortunately, we cannot figure out the details and it is probably too late to respond in any case. I hate to say this but by election day they should be close enough in the swing states to go the last mile."

"Meaning?" Kat asked.

"They will be in a position to hack a few voting machines to push razor thin elections in their favor. However, they need to be close enough on election day so that it is not obvious. I believe they will, and Trump's coronation will be a *fait accompli*."

"But surely such a flawed election cannot be permitted to stand?" Beverly protested.

"Hah," Chris guffawed and then raised his hand as if to apologize. "Sorry. But look back at 2000, the evidence that Gore won Florida was overwhelming to no avail. The highest court in the land acted as common partisan hacks. Back in 1960, Nixon likely won Illinois and thus the election, but Richard Daley stuffed the Cook County ballot boxes and handed the election to Kennedy. It was common knowledge. Remarkably, Nixon decided that it would do the country harm to push the illegality of what happened in the courts. I have no idea what it would take to reverse a national election in this country, aside from an uprising and civil war."

Kat stood suddenly and began pacing. "You are telling us that the election is, for all practical purposes, over."

"Yes."

"Trump will win, that is your educated guess." Kat pushed him.

"I am ready to bet the farm on it." Chris looked at his sister without expression.

"What should we do then?" Ricky chimed in.

"Start moving on to a post-election strategy. The right has unlimited money, organization, a defined purpose, and now foreign allies in a country they once despised. But they also have worries. Really, can they continue to redistribute a country's wealth up to the very top of the distribution forever without at least some of the working stiffs realizing they are being hosed? Can they alter immigration laws to keep what they consider undesirables out, who increasingly will vote democratic and, more importantly, deport the millions already here so that a white majority can be preserved? If they can, who will do all those jobs poor whites no longer will do? Can they somehow reach millennials or- what do they call the kids today? Anyone know? - and turn them into conservative robots? If nothing else, these kids don't buy the social message of the right. What the economic elite needs to keep the evangelical nut cases in the fold - a hate driven social agenda - will drive the kids away. You cannot wish away that problem with sophisticated message targeting. What every group that aspires to dictatorial aspirations hates the most is a real democracy where everyone gets to vote. When the GOP has control of everything, the will make the last push to dismantle the last vestiges of the American experiment."

"No way." This exasperated comment seemed to come from several around the table.

"They will need just one more vote on the court. What if Anthony Kennedy resigns? He is the swing vote? If all else fails, you don't think that a madman like Trump could not gin up a national crisis? He could do that in a heartbeat, get some conflict going with Iran or North Korea, or some fake border issue. Never forget that Hitler dressed up some SS men in Polish army uniforms and created border 'provocations' to invade that hapless country. That is one story from my father I have not forgotten. Spill some American blood and people will accept a lot. Remember our concentration camps in World War II for

Japanese-Americans? Hell, we treated German prisoners of war better. Face it, as I have said before in different ways, this is their last best chance to advance their agenda on a permanent basis and America's Achilles heel - our embedded racial hatreds - is their path to ultimate triumph." Chris paused and turned to Beverly. "Oddly enough, you probably know my father better than anyone these days. What do you think he is capable of?"

Beverly leaned back and seemed to ponder her brother-in-law's question. "I have been thinking about this question a lot lately. Funny, he has become more animated lately, his mood has improved. He even has been more open with me, bringing me into his confidence as if I were really his daughter, and not just by marriage. I wondered why. Now, listening to you, Chris, I think I am figuring it out. He is winning, or he thinks he is winning. He was not a Trump fan, thinking him a fool. They all know that Trump is a moron. But he also believes that he is such an idiot that he can be used. I think it is as Chris says, his group, whatever they call themselves, had never thought this day possible, the day they could control everything. Now that they can taste it, they will stop at nothing." Beverly then turned to Kat. "He will stop at nothing…not even murder."

Chris stopped at the security desk and had an extended conversation with a guard. Then, he was told to sit and wait.

Several minutes later, a well-built man in a suit exited an elevator and walked directly toward him. "Come with me, Mr. Crawford."

As the man turned away to lead Chris back to the elevator, his suit jacket opened slightly to reveal a holster and large automatic handgun. Suddenly, Chris wished he had told someone where he was going, but this was an impetuous act, something that had sprung unbidden from the deeper recesses of his heart. He had felt this urge to confront Charles Crawford Senior.

The elevator slowly rose to the top of the building, opening to a foyer where another security person sat at a desk. Chris had expected efficient-looking secretaries, not refugees from the World Federation of Wrestling. What was going on here? He was sure that his father retained an active investment life on his own. He had probably screwed many investment partners and competitors. His felt need for such security was ominous indeed. Was it necessary or simply a manifestation of a crippling paranoia? He was ushered through a side door. After his mother had moved out, his father had sold the old place and moved into a new penthouse suite that, Chris reflected, probably better reflected his new world, whatever that was. Of course, it was conceivable that his father had relocated because the old place reminded him of his lost family connections. Chris dismissed that notion as absurd. That would imply that the man had a residue of human sensibilities when it was clear that he had none whatsoever.

The destination was a modest sized library. The walls were lined with bookcases filled with what appeared to be first editions of the classics. Chris almost laughed. Did his father bring in an interior decorator to fill in the décor of the library? Surely, the family patriarch had not read these works. On the other hand, Chris would have loved this place growing up. When not improving his athletic skills on the playing fields of Chicago, he loved old bookstores, not the chains, but the old ones where the musty smell was unmistakable. He loved touching what he assumed were old masterpieces. The feel of antiquity itself lent them an air of authority with which no glossy publication of recent vintage could possibly compete.

Sitting in an overstuffed chair adjacent to a large globe of the world sat the patriarch of the Crawford clan. With one glance, Chris was satisfied that not a single hair was out of place. His clothes were impeccably tailored and his blue eyes as intense and penetrating as ever. He managed a tiny, forced smile as he indicated a chair to his only surviving male heir. Chris focused on the hand that pointed to a vacant chair. Like the rest of the man, it was manicured to perfection. If his father had suffered from the dissolution of the family and breakup of his marriage, Chris could not see the effects. He had not paid attention during his one exchange with him a few months back. Now, Chris was focused on what the man looked like. What he saw was a man apparently comfortable with his world and his place in it.

"My, this is an unexpected pleasure. To what do I owe my good fortune?" Charles senior issued his unctuous smile.

"Simply a son visiting his father."

"I am most gratified that you still accord me that station in life." The elder man continued to smile.

"Well, one cannot easily undo biological reality."

"True, son, but I suspect you know that fatherhood is more than impregnating a woman." There was an emphasis on the word 'son'.

"That, Father, is a lesson from which we all might benefit."

"However, I doubt that you came by to exchange views on parenting. Let me add that I do hope your family is well up there in Madison."

"Very well, indeed. It is a lovely place and we are thriving. But you are right, that is not why I am here. I came by to congratulate you."

"On what, may I ask?"

Now Chris smiled. "Why, I am convinced your man is about to win the presidency."

"I believe such congratulations are decidedly premature. Not even Nate Silver is predicting a Republican win."

"Ah, yes, but the pundits and political seers are not looking deep enough, they are not seeing what is really going on."

The older man's eyes narrowed just a sliver. "And I am sure you are about to educate me on the, what shall we say, reality of things?"

"I don't have to, dear Father." Chris emphasized the final word. "You are the one in a position to educate me. But I suspect that hell shall freeze over before that happens."

"Remember this, son," he said and again emphasized the word 'son', "I gave you every opportunity to join me. I wanted you at my side. But you chose to run off and join your younger sister. In fact, I am a patient and forgiving man. I always hold out for the possibility of personal redemption, even among those who seem long lost. The story of the prodigal son was always one of my favorite biblical fables."

There was something in the way he said the word 'sister' that sent a chill down Chris's spine. The younger man recovered and continued. "Nevertheless, I spent enough time in athletic contests to know when the game is over, and I don't switch teams just because I am on the losing side. I could be wrong of course, but I suspect the world shall be shocked the day after the election. Am I wrong? Tell me I am wrong."

Charles smiled but said nothing for a while. "You are very intelligent. I am proud of that. You are wasting it, but I am too often surrounded by lesser men with no imaginations. Oh, these men are bright enough, the best of educations and training, and blessed with great wealth or at least aspiring to it, but often they lack something. Perhaps it is wisdom, or maybe something we have never defined. You, however, have it all and are throwing it away. Too bad we have free will, some employ it to their disadvantage. So sad, but we have been down that road before many times. In truth, I am not terribly certain that anyone will win come election day."

Chris was legitimately puzzled at this. "I am not sure I understand."

"Oh, Mr. Trump may well come out with a plurality of electoral college votes but look at that man. Have you listened to him, seen the people at his rallies? They are rabble, less than rabble. Mrs. Clinton was correct when she called them the deplorables." Then the elder man suddenly stopped as if he were on the cusp of revealing too much. After a pause, he apparently decided to finish his thought. "Of course, it is also true that the rabble is easy to manipulate."

"Unless they begin to believe an uncontrollable leader. We both know full well that Trump is so dumb that he doesn't know how dumb he is. He has only one style - bullying, insulting, and intimidating his way through life. And he has an unhealthy fascination with the Russian bear, clearly something is amiss there."

Charles Senior now widened his ever-present smile. "It is very likely that you know more than I do. You clearly have taken a strong interest in my...hobbies. But yes, he is so stupid that he cannot fathom his own limitations. That is sad and perhaps a challenge."

"Challenge? For whom? The country? The Democrats?"

"Country? Democrats? Don't be silly my son. When you walk the streets of Chicago, what do you see? You see unthinking robots going about their desperate and limited lives. They have no idea what is going on, what the big stakes are. They are like those rats in experimental mazes. They barely understand what is happening around them. They have their little routines. You control their maze, the available rewards, and you control them. You can shape behaviors simply by altering opportunities and incentives. They are barely conscious beings."

"And you are the grand experimenter, the man in the white coat behind the curtain?"

Charles Senior tilted his head back slightly, as if thinking. "I wish it were that simple. The truth is, a wild card like Trump can…upset the best of plans. He is so vile, he could tarnish the brand, get the rabble to think, to feel something beyond their own base needs. There is nothing so dangerous as rabble that think about their situation. Surely, son, you must look about you and recognize how superior you are? You really were meant to be with me, to lead."

"You know, Trump's greatest contribution to mankind might not be discrediting the hard right, as you fear, but uniting the other side of the spectrum. Alas, the center left is always squabbling about silly and inconsequential things like who is the purist on the left. They just might unite in their hate of this man." Chris looked as if he had just thought of this.

His father hesitated as if Chris had said something unexpected. His response was a non sequitur. "You know, all the babble you see on twenty-four-seven news and commentary is just a side show, Trump-mania, the evangelical nut cases, abortion, and immigration and nativism, and all the rest. Those are just the tools to be used for what really counts."

"Which is?" Chris asked though he could guess.

Charles Senior hesitated but he had to finish now. "Control. Mastery over all that counts. Do you think, really think, that the future should be entrusted to the unwashed hordes out there? Hell, most of them cannot control their own families, their pathetic little aspirations, let alone determine the fate of a country, or mankind. Don't be an idiot. What you think of as democracy is a free-for-all by a bunch of morons fighting for short-term gain, for scraps. There is no vision there, no purpose beyond the next election cycle. What we need are the few with exemplary intelligence, with vision, with a long-term perspective. We need those who can make hard decisions, not coddle or sustain miserable existences on the palaver that all life is noble or sacred. What hogwash!" He was warming to his topic now. "You surely have studied Schumpeter, the concept of creative destruction? You probably adore Darwin, he is scientific enough for you, with his principle of survival of the fittest. Progress, the future, the next transformation of mankind will not just happen. Darwin's devotee, Herbert Spencer, was right. It will be forged by the will of those capable of making it happen, those capable of seeing what needs to be done, and strong enough to make it happen. If we must destroy some, or many, wipe out old useless governmental forms, then we will. If even the seemingly mighty become inconvenient, even that moron Trump, he will be…neutralized. And if he becomes a distraction, he will be… removed. No one will stop us."

"Even those you love," Chris barely whispered, now beginning to wonder if his father had read some of the classics in this library.

Charles, the patriarch, looked at his son for a long time. "They will be among the first," he said in a clear voice. "But I don't want that. Above all, I don't want that, believe me." The elder man's face almost softened a bit. "I beg you, one last time. Join the correct side of history."

"Father, we have been down that road too many times. You don't seem to understand. I am on the right side."

His father grunted, it was an odd sound. "Yes, yes, a road oft-visited, I fear. Just remember that there really are only two types of people in the world, those that lead and…the rest." The patriarch's jaw was set, his eyes flashed with an animal intensity. "I can still remember the stories when I was little more than an infant. They were fresh recollections, and I was like a sponge. My Polish family, neighbors, and friends were crushed and brutalized simply because they had no power to resist. I was never, never going to let that happen to me. If anyone was going to be crushed, I would be on the right side of that equation. I still recall that, as a child, I vowed I would be the one to do the crushing." He seemed on the verge of saying more but controlled himself.

Chris stared at the elderly man across from him. It was almost impossible to believe they were connected by blood. They were so different in almost every respect. If his mother had not been such a virtuous Catholic, wedded to the principle that sex was justified only for the sake of procreation, Chris might have concluded that he and his twin sister Kristen were the bastard issues of an illicit tryst. He had long concluded that personal dispositions and attributes are at least partially hard-wired, a product of the genetic roll of the dice. Did he take everything from his mother and nothing from his father? That seemed unlikely, perhaps impossible. He must ask Kay about these matters one day. Of course, it just might be that he had some recessed beliefs and behaviors waiting to erupt at the correct moment. Perhaps his father would say a code word and suddenly all that had been repressed would come out. Then Chris realized that his mind had been wandering. What had his father just said? He decided to pick up where he had last paid attention.

"Sometimes, Father, you do amuse me. You call your interests, your vision, what…hobbies? What a quaint way to refer to it." Chris tried to smile.

"Well," Charles Senior mused, looking at his slender hands poised on his lap. "I strongly suspect you have another term for it. Otherwise, you and your sibling would not be spending so much time and effort looking into it."

"I have always taken an interest in you. Didn't you realize that?" Chris fought to maintain his calm. Yet, a chill swept through him. His adversary was way too crafty to reveal too much. Beverly was the only hope for inside information. Besides, that is not why he had come. Still, did this man know exactly what he and Kat were about? Was he merely guessing, or did he have inside information? For one moment, the notion that Beverly really was spying for her father-in-law occurred to him. But he quickly dismissed that, though he knew not why.

"Just remember this. Remember this. I will always want you at my side. I asked you to be at my side, many times. Your feckless brother was too weak. You were the one I needed. And you so bitterly disappointed me. You know that my associates and I are focused on things way beyond mere political power. That is merely a means to an end. Evolutionary direction will be dictated by the strong, those meant to lead. You are either a part of that vanguard or…not." There was something very ominous in the way he ended his sentence.

Chris stood up. "Enough of this. In truth, I stopped by to deliver one message. Listen to me and listen carefully. If any of my siblings or immediate family come to harm, in any remotely suspicious way, let us say an automobile accident, I will come after you. Do you understand? I will get you if it is the last thing I do, and your fucking palace guard won't be able to stop me. That is not a threat, it is a promise. No, even more than that. It is a solemn vow. Do you understand me?"

"Totally." The elder man smiled grimly. "But you remember this, son. We are engaged in a struggle where there are winners and losers. My associates will not be on the losing side, that I can guarantee you. And neither will I. On that, you have my word, my vow. Do you understand me?"

"At least we understand one another." Chris rose from his seat.

"One last thing, Christopher. You are not on the winning side. Never forget that."

Chris registered that he was no longer referred to as 'son.' Without comment, he turned and headed to the door through which he had entered the room. He did not see his father push a button, but a man appeared to escort him on his way out.

A half-hour later, Chris sat on a bench looking over Lake Michigan. He felt dissatisfied. Yes, he managed to say what he went there to say. But to what effect? His father appeared unmoved, implacable. Chris tried to recall the final moments. Had he flinched at all? Did the patriarch essentially say that anyone who got in his way was expendable? That was insane but, then again, he had entertained the notion that his own father might have tried to hurt his younger sister, either to scare her or worse. Had he really sworn to avenge any suspicious demise? Was he capable of that?

Suddenly, he felt himself go cold even though it was a warm fall day. The hard reality was that they were in a life-and-death struggle with the very man responsible for their birth. How could that be? How had things come to this? Then he realized, this was no provincial family drama. It was much larger than that. Suddenly, the sanctuary of Oxford seemed very inviting indeed, not even Madison was far enough from the madness he feared was consuming him. The academy was seductive precisely because it was irrelevant.

He became aware of a movement to his right. Jules effortlessly slid onto the bench next to him. "I got your text," she said.

"I thought that might be a long shot. Glad you were able to join me."

Jules gave him a quick kiss on the cheek. "Not grab a chance to spend some alone time with my 43rd favorite ex-lover? Perish that thought. And when he is not available, you will do. I simply told Rachel Maddow that the man of my dreams just texted and that I had to run."

"You are making that up."

"No, really. I was on the phone with her."

Chris smiled. "I believe the part about Rachel, it was your BS about me being the man of your dreams, or at least his stand-in."

"Oh that, Brad Pitt also texted me, but I blew him off."

"You are such a riot." Chris returned her affectionate kiss. "Shit, I would love to meet her."

"Rachel? Give it up, stud, she is a lesbian."

"Ha, ha, you of all people should know those days are past, my womanizing days that is. I am in love with her mind."

"Oh, I bet she hears that from all the guys." Then Jules turned serious. "Why did you summon me? Something is up I suspect."

Chris exhaled. "I just met with my father."

"Really?" Jules was surprised. "Why, for God's sake?"

"I could not get Kat's incident out of my head, just the possibility that Father initiated it or approved it or, at a minimum, accepted that it would happen if, in fact, it is something more than our overactive imaginations at work. God, that man is a monster, but I thought he had limits. I can never quite accept that my own father would…oh never mind. The whole thing was impulsive, stupid, but I am just the guy to do something totally moronic."

"Now Chris, don't beat yourself up."

"Yeah, I know, that is your job."

Jules tried to suppress the brief smile that crossed her lips. "So, what did you conclude based on your foolhardy, yet fearless journey into the heart of darkness? Was he involved in the attempt on Kat's life? Perhaps I should ask whether you left believing he had something to do with it?"

"Hell, I don't know but I will tell you one thing: he is cold. Have you ever been with someone who left you feeling like you have just been in the presence of evil itself?"

"Guess you have never been to a network management meeting?" Jules quickly inserted.

Chris didn't seem to hear her. "I mean, I am simply astounded that I am from his seed. Do I harbor something bad deep inside? I was thinking about that as I left. Maybe that is why I texted you. I wanted to ask if you see something bad in me, something I repress or suppress or whatever the term is. It hit me that maybe what everyone sees, what I see every morning, is a façade that hides my real self. But I could never hide it from you, not for all these years, could I? No, there would be no way."

"Shut up."

"What?" he stammered.

"Just shut the fuck up. You are blubbering like a total moron. You're not your father. I have met your father. I have spent time in your home, not lately of course. And I fell in love with you. Do you, for one moment, think I would love a fucking sociopath?" Her stare was penetrating.

"I … I guess not."

"Guess not? You guess not? You better do better than that or the joggers are going to see a black woman in her power suit beat the shit out of a wimpy white guy. Got that?"

"Yeah, sorry for being such a putz. I guess he still gets to me." Chris looked beaten.

"No shit, Sherlock. But I don't blame you. Not really. For the longest time I never got it when you would go on about how much you loved my folks. They were just my folks, you don't really understand when you are in the middle of growing up. But now, now that I have more perspective, I wish I had told them how much I loved them back then, been a better daughter. You were right. They were…special. Mother still is, but I never told dad how much…" Then her voice caught, and she stopped.

Chris looked at her, she was struggling. "What are you talking about, you were a perfect daughter."

"Not in my eyes but I suppose we are all a bit blind in that regard. But you, they always loved you and your love for them was so there. For a moment, in the beginning, I thought you were trying to score with me through them. But no, you really did love them and then won my heart as well. You enriched their lives. I almost let you ravage me out of appreciation."

"Thanks kiddo. You have no idea that hearing those words mean to me, not the part about ravaging you but the part about meaning so much to your folks." He took his finger and traced it along the outline of her face. "You are still a knockout. Now that you are available again, guys must be all over you."

She laughed out loud. "Don't I wish, but I have a theory to explain the apparent lack of interest of the male species in me."

"This should be good for a laugh."

She poked him in the arm. "Just listen. I am too successful. Guys are intimidated."

"Sure, let's go with that." His voice dripped with sarcasm.

"You are a shit," she said, still laughing. "And how is Amar? I cannot believe she hasn't dumped you yet. The woman truly is a saint."

Chris looked serious. "My sisters wonder the same thing. In truth, she is not the happiest of campers. I have torn her and Azita from their worlds. You know what, I feel like shit about that, but I don't know what to do."

"Oh Chris, she loves you, they both love you. You will figure out a way to make everything work. I don't know the answer, but you will find it…together."

"Yes…together," he responded. "By the way, you really are important to me. I know you will be there, whenever I need someone."

She started to smile, a witticism was on the tip of her tongue, but she knew this was not the time. "Of course. And I know you would be there for me." She paused, looking at him. "Sorry about my language but you piss…upset me with that talk about being your father. You are, without doubt, the finest man I know."

Chris again waited for a comeback. That was not to be, however. He took her hand. They sat silently together, looking out over the water. They need not fill in the silence. Over the years they found that the best of friends demand no sound from one another when they are communicating. Mere presence was enough.

CHAPTER 13

POST 2016 ELECTION: AFGHANISTAN

The head of Chris Crawford popped up on his twin sister's computer screen.

"You look better than I expected," Kay started.

"What, exactly, were you expecting?" He tried a smile.

"Oh, something like your lifeless body on a morgue slab with the toe tag prominently displayed. You know, famous philanthropist, is that what you are by the way? Never mind, I've been expecting to see a news flash. Famous philanthropist takes own life in despair after Trump's unexpected triumph." Kay tried her best smile.

"Not that I didn't try. I popped a bottle of pills, but Amar had replaced the real ones with sugar substitutes. Next, I shot myself with a gun, but she had replaced the bullets with blanks. I moved on to a knife, but you know how long that takes and I hate the sight of blood, especially my own. Besides, she put rubber joke alternatives where the real ones had been. My last attempt was hanging but the damn rope broke when I jumped off the chair. Gotta go on a diet one of these days. Besides, the results were no surprise to me."

Kay tried to look disappointed. "Of course not, I keep forgetting that you are all-knowing. But damn, I have got to talk to that woman, your long-suffering spouse that is. She is being way too nice to you. Could be she is suffering from Stockholm syndrome. You did tell her that she gets all the money if you croak? I hope she understands that."

"Never thought of that, good suggestion. Actually, I had told her that all my money was promised to the bimbos from my dissolute early life." When Kay did not come back with a quick retort, he continued. "Kidding, of course, but the thing is I have been predicting this for weeks. Still, even though I expected it, there was still shock. How could sixty-three million voters be so stupid? Why in heaven's name did I return to such a backward country?"

"To save it from itself, of course. I continue to believe it is a fool's errand, but you are just the fool for the job."

"You mean, as opposed to saving the world one poor person at a time? But I thank you for your touching sentiments."

"Touché, asshole. I so miss trading insults with you. It is what you do best, we do best."

"And you, my dear, are a worthy adversary. I go back and forth between you and Karen being the bigger asshole. And my daughter, Zita, is learning from the women around her. I am doomed, doomed."

"Oh dear," Kay exclaimed with faux alarm, "I will have to up my game. But wait, did you really predict this or is this more of your BS?"

"BS, from me? Perish the thought. No, we have been looking at the data very carefully. It was all there. I am shocked that Nate Silver didn't see this coming. Maybe he did at the end, I stopped watching. Perhaps he did but could not accept what the numbers were telling him. I knew if they got close enough, it would not take much in a few key states to push the right over the top in the electoral college."

"Hmm, I have my doubts here. No one else saw this coming, as far as I can see. I really didn't think you were such a bang-on prophet."

"Such little confidence from my own twin. Check with our younger sibling if you doubt me. I told her weeks ago. For me, though, it was more than the data. Okay, I know I have this Irish dark cloud that hangs over me. By the way, how did you escape that? Are we really twins? Maybe there was a mix up in the hospital."

"If there was, you are the mistake for sure." Kay chuckled.

"No question on that, I was born into a nice, sane family and somehow got lumped in with you. Surely, a tragedy of Greek proportions." Chris decided that the banter had run its course. "In any case, you know my fascination with history. Beyond the survey data and the evidence of foreign meddling, I saw things from the past coming back to life. Someday, go back and look at film from the early 1960s. Look at the white faces screaming at young black girls walking into a formerly all-white school. Then, look at the faces at a Trump rally, the same hate and vitriol. The looks of pure bile are unforgettable and, eerily enough, identical. But we got complacent after that initial response to desegregation, we thought the worst hate had dissipated or at least had been relegated to a few scattered nut cases. But it never did. There were a thousand groups like the Posse Comitatus up north and Aryan defense leagues out west and the KKK or its offshoots, in the south. They were all just waiting and preparing for the coming Armageddon. They have been there all this time, simply looking for an opportunity. The funny thing is that so many thought the election of Obama spelled the end of the far-right fantasy of an America dominated by the pure racial stock. If you recall, many pundits talked about the post-racial period of American politics being ushered in. Remember all those savants eager to usher in the post-racial society? I recall thinking at the time that those people were idiots, not pundits. With a few exceptions, they tended to look at the day's events or the most recent polls and make exaggerated claims. Obama's election threatened the hell out of all those that had been seething with fear and hate since federal troops forced the end of apartheid in America. For all those millions, it was now or never. They saw the end of white hegemony and they could not bear it and certainly would not accept it."

"Shit." Kay exhaled.

"What?"

"It is like being huddled under the blanket again as kids listening to you ramble on and on. Did I say ramble? I meant listening to you educate me with your pearls of wisdom."

"Good catch, kiddo." Chris decided to change the topic. "So, are you enjoying being back in the field, working with the unwashed? At least you are not there during the summer. I never got used to that."

"I do worry about global warming, what it will do to places like this. Problem is, the nighttime temps stay higher than they used to, which means people cannot recover from the day's heat. That wears you down, makes people without air conditioning more vulnerable. In any case, you never got used to it because you are soft and a wuss."

"No doubt, which is why I always prefer first-class accommodation. But you know what that asshole is going to do first, or maybe second, when he takes over next January? He is going to get the U.S. out of the Paris accords on climate change. Can you believe that? It is a race between that and torpedoing the Iran nuclear pact. Let's see, how do we want to end mankind? Should we go with nuclear conflict or global warming? Both make divine apocalyptic ends, so hard to decide. Doesn't matter though, at least he will be putting it to Obama. Trump is so petty he cannot stand the thought that Obama is more popular than he is. Did you catch the crap about his claim that he did not win a plurality because of voter fraud? Oh, oh, I have started again."

"I hate to say this, but you have. I believe you asked me how I was doing, still interested?" Kay was a little taken with the emotional turn of her twin who, she had to admit, tended to descend into a saturnine mood during heavier political discussions. "Predicted or not, Trump has gotten to you."

"Oops, sorry, yes, he has. I fully expected it and yet, the morning after I still could not believe it. However, really, I do want to hear about what you are up to, really."

"Good thing, since I have you on screen, the mute button is at the ready." Kay tried to look cross.

"Nope, you got my full attention, such as it is."

"Be still, my heart! In truth, though, I am a little excited. You remember Archie Singleton and his wife?"

"He runs the Panjshir site, correct?"

"Yes, you haven't lost touch, good."

"No way, you forget I have an eidetic memory."

"No you don't." Kay protested.

"Well, a damn good one. Anyways, I still do the rounds of the movers and shakers to raise money for your good works. To do that, I need to keep abreast of what is going on with the program." Then he smiled. "And I solemnly promise that I won't go back into political crap with you, enough moaning for one morning."

"Better not, asshole." Kay was smiling. "I have you right where I want you. One finger on the button that will turn your smiling mug into a blank screen. Ooh, we should always talk this way. This is such an advantage."

"I am at your command, then."

"As I was saying, Archie will be joining us in Kabul where we also will meet with Azita and Deena's new friends, the Guptas, and some government officials. Deena and I have been chatting. We have some ideas about how to expand the range of services, particularly around girls. We need cultural change, not just education and health. They are the starting blocks but so much more is needed. One thing is exposure to the outside world. Think about it. What if you had not met Ricky and Jules? Today, you might be just another rich parasite living off your trust fund in Monte Carlo."

"Ha, ha, but you do have something there. I really hate to admit that. Tell me more."

"As you have said forever, we need to take a comprehensive look. You got it off to a good start but now that things have stabilized, we can do more, particularly with technology. There are so many impediments to learning beyond encrusted cultural beliefs. These kids have eye problems and nutrition problems, and other things we don't often worry about in the West. Just getting corrective lenses to them is a start, along with simple corrective eye surgeries. Then, when we get beyond the basic stuff, I keep asking why we aren't doing more with distance communications. We could have medical experts on call back in London that we can bring on board for difficult cases, here. It is available, let's use it. And these girls need to see women who are successful in other fields. Through technology, we can bring these role models into the villages with a simple message: you can be anything you want."

"Sounds great. See, you did learn something from me."

"Don't push it buster, my finger is hovering above the button." She cracked. "I can fill you in more later after we finish up our discussions. I will want to give you some talking points for your money-grubbing sessions."

"Ah, how the mighty have fallen." He feigned a groan. "Once a revered visionary and leader of women and now a mere money-grubber."

"Hah, the only place you led women was to your bed. Visionary my ass."

Chris let out a distinct laugh. "Hey, my ass was the vision, never doubt that. Before I forget, tell me, how is Deena doing? We were surprised she did not accompany you on this trip. Wasn't it supposed to be a dry run? Azita will be all over me if I forget to ask."

"Good," Kay replied. Chris noticed a slight discomfort pass over his sister's face. "She is doing good. Someone had to stay behind and mind the shop."

"Wait." His antennae were up. "Are you holding something back?"

"No, she is doing great, physically. There are no side effects from the head trauma as far as I can see. I suppose we did worry that there might be psychological consequences coming here on her first site visit since the…incident. Of course, she was not happy to be left behind."

"I am sure of that."

"There is something else, but I am not prepared to talk about it. It has nothing to do with her work or health. Leave it at that, okay?" She gave Chris a stare that he knew so well. He dared pursue the topic at serious risk to his life and limb. Then she opened her mouth as if she had changed her mind and was about to share something more when there was a noise in the background. She glanced to the side with a relieved expression. "Oops, someone at the door. Work calls. Talk to you later. Love you."

"Love you back." Then the screen was black. He was left to ponder the strange ending to the conversation. Suddenly, Chris became very disquieted inside. He desperately wanted back to where his life had been, sharing secrets and ideas under the blanket with his twin sister. They were so close then. But events and people had proved merciless over time. As he grew, he uncovered a priceless insight. Virtually nothing is as it seems at first glance. He tried to think for a moment about a time when he was at peace, in a very quiet place. Perhaps it was in a field somewhere in the English countryside, on a sunny day without a breath of any breeze anywhere. There were such days when nothing was moving, the tall whispery grasses about him were silent and the leaves adorning the nearby trees were serene. The whole world appeared still and stationary. The universe was at complete rest. Or had it been? Inside, he knew that not to be correct.

In truth, though, everything moved, as it always had. He realized that the planet on which he stood was orbiting daily on its axis. That same planet, mother earth, was circling the rather insignificant star at the center of our solar system at a rate of 30 kilometers per second. That insignificant star, our sun, located in a remote part of the Milky Way Galaxy, was moving around some distant black hole at 250km/s. And the galaxy, one of countless others, was speeding through a wider universe at 600km/s. In fact, he mused to himself, it is moving even faster than we had previously thought. It hit him, in just the few moments it took to have these thoughts, he had traveled some 3000 kilometers. Nothing, it appeared, was as it seemed. All was illusion, the slight-of-hand of a mischievous deity. He tried to remember when he first embraced that epiphany. Was it at Oxford, Princeton, even earlier? He could not recall the moment, but he was confident that he was young at the time.

As he stared at the blank screen, he mused on the nature of his world. The certainties of the world he saw as reality were subject to relational constructs, perspectives, and ways of looking at things. When he was a student taking a psychology course, many years ago, he recalled spending a fair amount of time examining perceptual conundrums. Is line A bigger or smaller than line B when the ends of the lines are framed by two convex as opposed to concave horizontal-laying V shapes? Even when told the two lines were the same length his brain would tell him something quite different. Is the man in a room taller or shorter than the table in the depiction of a room you are asked to observe? The answer was obvious until he realized that his sense of perspective had been tricked and the rear of the specially constructed enclosure, where the table was located, was much smaller than where the man was standing.

Common sense observation was not everything. His mind floated to the Dali Museum in St. Petersburg, Florida some days. There was a portrait of a famous person. Up close, what he saw were details of very tiny portraits and had no clue as to the iconic leader in front of him. As he backed away, the outline of President Lincoln emerged. From the other side of the room, the visage of the sixteenth president was unmistakable, the obscuring details from the close-up look now gone. Another famous piece of art was a collection of furniture from the side. He walked around and changed his perspective and, once again, there was a portrait of Lincoln. The world was always playing with him. What he saw depended on where he stood and how he looked at things. He suddenly had an urge for certainty and answers, things he had not enjoyed since he began thinking for himself.

Karen, Kay, and Carlotta swept into what the Gupta's used as their area clinic and what had been Pamir Masoud's medical facility so many years ago. Archie Singleton and his wife Agnes were sitting with Ferhana and Bahiri. These four had spent the previous day discussing possibilities long into the night. In the space of a single day, they appeared to have bonded.

"I see you have gotten a head start," Karen offered as they all sat around a large table. "I am glad you had a chance to get to know one another."

"We are already like fast friends," Bahiri enthused. "I am thinking that we have much in common even though we are from different cultures and parts of the world. And we have many ideas on which we agree."

"Well mate," Archie added, "we do have one thing in common. England ran our respective countries for a while, but we managed to kick her out. No offense, Karen."

"None taken, it was all before my time in any case." Then, a big smile spread across her face. "Besides, your version is all bollocks. We walked away, too much bloody trouble taking care of you blokes."

At this, Kay laughed aloud. "When Karen goes into her Brit vernacular, it is time to get the meeting under way. She tries so hard to be like regular folk and fails so miserably. In any case, no need to relive the independence movements since we Americans were the first to kick them in their rears." Karen opened her mouth to protest but Kay quickly moved on. "So, tell me, what are you cooking up?"

Archie and Bahiri looked at one another, waiting for the other to start. Ferhana broke the awkward silence. "While the men play at being polite, I will start. Besides, these are mostly ideas that Agnes and I have been kicking around." When Bahiri opened his mouth, apparently to dispute her claim to authorship of what they were about to say, she silenced him with one look. Karen was very impressed. Satisfied that the men were in their place, Ferhana continued. "We are not talking about anything totally new, of course. What concerns us is that we do a wonderful job of healing bodies, or at least a pretty good job. We don't, however, treat the whole person. This is something that Professor Crawford…"

"You mean my brother?" Kay smiled.

"Yes." Ferhana looked uncertain.

Kay suppressed a witticism that might require too much explanation in the moment. "Sorry, you are right. It is just that I call him something else. Please continue."

Bahiri spoke up excitedly. "This is something your brother has talked about so many times in his books and papers. We are thinking that we physicians must go beyond merely healing the body. We focus on the children because they are the future. But there is so much more to be done than merely binding-up their wounds and preventing illness through basic public health education and inoculations. We need to work with families early, so much is hopeless by the time children walk through our doors. And physical health, as we know, is only part of the total picture. Sound bodies only make sense if they are kept whole for some greater purpose."

"And that purpose is?"

"Part of it is just the education thing you already do, building schools and teaching girls basic skills. But one thing we see here, and Archie and Agnes see in the north, it is how narrow the world is for so many of these children. They only know what they see about them, their own culture and way of looking at things. I recall listening to my dear parents talk about the India of their youth. In many parts of the country, there were at least three realities. Sure, there were always some who were educated and could speak and read English. For them, and my family was among them, they understood and appreciated the wider world including the diversity of cultures and perspectives out there. Then there were the kids of the less affluent but who were not mired in suffocating poverty. These children would have had some schooling, but it would have been rather rudimentary. They might have known a few words of English but spoke Hindi or Marathi or whatever major language was spoken in their area. The final group were the many kids who were destitute, whose parents scraped by on a few rupees per day. Often, these children could only communicate in a local dialect and had no concept of a world beyond their direct experience. You could look around you in a rural Indian town and see kids existing in three separate worlds, if we had paid attention. For some, it was a small and cramped place that existed only in what they could see and hear through the limiting lens of a local dialect. For others, it was a broader world that might encompass their country and a smattering of larger understandings since they could read in Hindi or another major language of India. For the lucky few, there was a big world out there since they could read and speak English. Many would not take advantage of the opportunities before them, but many would. The thing, the fortunate ones had the opportunity, the chance. I can remember so clearly playing with the child of the family servants, when I was a child myself. In certain moments, I had this insight, understanding if you will. It was so painful that it still hurts today. My playmate would never get to see the wider world, never be able to dream big. My playmate would be married off at a young age, have many children, look old and haggard by the time she was thirty, and work herself into an early grave. I bristled at the unfairness of it."

"So, you want to bring the world to these poor children somehow?" It was Carlotta.

Archie spoke up. "Exactly. It may sound foolish, but we think we can take the first steps. They come to us seeking help with their pain and disease and desperation and, when we are fortunate enough, we solve those issues. With many, we develop a relationship over time. They come to trust us. They send their girls, some of them do, to our schools. But there is so much more we could do with that relationship."

"Like what?" Carlotta seemed quite interested.

"Think about this. There are an increasing number of videos and distance learning opportunities that Western kids have easy access to. With computers and the web, we can bring the world to these kids. Of course, we would need to carefully select the material, translate it into the local vernacular, and find ways to discuss the ideas and lessons, make them relevant to their world. But I am convinced we can do it. We need to heal bodies, prepare minds, and offer a wider perspective on the world. And not just for the children. The here is so much we can bring to the parents about family planning and raising children and nutrition. The possibilities are endless."

"Yes, Atle and I have talked about using distance learning more. I wish the hell he had not run off to America." Carlotta seemed on the verge of continuing but then had second thoughts.

Kay leaned over to her. "Don't forget he has a significant other." Then, in a louder voice. "Yes, I am still in touch with my sister-in-law, who also has been dragged off to America. She and I have been talking about using modern communications technology in this work. Sure, I know that most of the work our doctors do in the field is elementary, but we are expected to be all things to all people. How many times did I get a situation where I was way out of my depth and I thought I had seen it all in the ER in Chicago, the hell hole of all hell holes? Wouldn't it be great to be able to touch base with experts back in London or the Mayo Clinic for a diagnosis or treatment options? Sure, you don't have to worry about being sued in Kabul but still, it would be nice not to be flying blind all the time. I guess I am saying that just because we are working in desperately poor conditions, we don't have to settle for primitive technologies and dated knowledge."

"Oh yes," Bahiri chimed back in. "I am so supportive of these ideas. Many times, Ferhana and I have talked at night about some case that we were losing because we could not figure out what was wrong or what to do about it. We would do our best to find people and answers, but we were so inefficient. If we had a list of resources or one place to go which could direct us…that would be so fine."

Carlotta then quickly added. "And just think. We can use the same technologies for multiple purposes, keeping our field personnel up to date and bringing the world to the next generation in those parts of the world that risk being left behind."

"Brilliant," Karen chimed in with a slight touch of a scowl on her face. "now all we have to do is make this a reality with Chris and Amar and Ricky and Atle gone, and Deena…" Karen stopped there but looked at Kay with an expression that others noted but could not interpret.

Kay quickly looked away but recovered almost instantaneously, though a hint of a blush remained on her face. She spoke quickly. "There is no doubt that this is a lot of work and that Karen feels short-staffed right now because, frankly, she is. One thing is clear to me, this is more than buying a few computers. It is how we use them that counts. But we can get more staff and my brother can raise more money. Hell, now that he has failed to stem the fascist tide in America, he will have time on his hands."

Carlotta's face brightened. "Is there a chance of getting them back to London? Yes, this is a much bigger project than it seems, to do it right. We should pilot it here, on a small scale. Then we can spread it to other sits in the Mideast and Africa. You can be our on-site traveling experts, a lighthouse site." She looked at the Guptas and the Singletons before turning back to Kay. "You have been in touch with your brother. Has he given up on his fool's errand in America now that they have elected Trump? My friends in Spain cannot believe that, they call Trump America's Franco, you know, our former dictator and our embarrassment before the world."

Kay did not respond immediately. She seemed to be considering her response. To her surprise, everyone waited with patience. "I fear that any hope for a speedy return of the prodigal brother may be in vain. He anticipated Trump's triumph and is preparing for a longer contest."

"Amar cannot be pleased," Karen said, hopefully.

"No, she is not. However, she is resigned to this year and, unfortunately, she is in Madison and not Chicago. That can be a seductive place. On the other hand, her uneasiness has more to do with work. She is restless being just another doc to the affluent and entitled. It does not satisfy her."

"These are difficult decisions for professional couples," Archie said thoughtfully. "Agnes and I have been very fortunate. We have always wanted the same thing. From what I know, the same is true of the Guptas."

"Very much so," Ferhana affirmed with conviction. "Maybe we have so little conflict because we shared so much at the beginning. I don't know." She seemed to be thinking of a distant memory. "I recall chatting with my husband when we first met in school, talking about our backgrounds. I don't know why but

I told him a story that I heard as a young girl. It was about a local prince, from the time before we became a united country, a time when the families of local rulers had power and wealth. This local ruler had been sent to be educated in England and had many Western friends who would visit. One young British visitor stayed with him one night and was mysteriously found dead the next morning. After that, no visitor could spend the night in this palace, all swore the palace was haunted by the spirit of this dead man. Even the Westerners swore to this, swore that they had seen or heard the dead man's spirit, and all believed it."

"Did you?" Carlotta asked.

"Well, when young I did. The point is, though, that Bahiri had a similar story from where he was raised. The more we talked, the more we realized how much we shared, even the stories that scared us as children. And we decided that we had a shared vision - to eradicate those beliefs that held people back. Your culture provides many things. It also can hold you back. Our common stories helped us bond, as if we were one bound together."

"You are very fortunate," Kay said wistfully, glancing once again in Karen's direction. "We have such complicated lives these days. We try to balance so many different...obsessions. Sometimes, the effort becomes exhausting."

"But it can be done," said Agnes in her sweet voice. Those who met Archie's spouse always had difficulty deciding why she seemed so wholesome and trustworthy. Was it her graying hair and almost premature grandmotherly look or the sweet lilt in her voice? Perhaps it might be the translucent, green eyes. In any case, people trusted her implicitly, and listened as if she was parting with considerable wisdom. "If people love one another, they find a way, they always find a way. Certainly, Archie and I have for all these years. It did not start well, my mother never wanted me to marry him. My family was Catholic, and he was Protestant. That was important to them in those days, seems silly now. We ran off, had nothing at the time. But I worked hard, and Archie studied hard, and we made it. My mother refused to speak to me for ten years. One day, she came and cried. She thought I could not or would not forgive her. Silly woman, I never stopped loving her. Whatever mountains appear before you, they can be surmounted. Just never stop loving." She looked at her husband with great fondness.

After what seemed like a long time, Kay spoke. "You know, I remember something that happened when I was a college student. One summer, a girlfriend and I went on a trip. We wanted to see some of the country before we got too serious about our careers. We didn't have much of an itinerary, just followed our instincts while looking for things outside our normal lives. You know. We were just crazy kids, looking for a little bit of adventure and maybe a better understanding of our world. Anyways, we met these girls from an Indian reservation somewhere in the mid-west." She paused as if she were trying to recapture the memory.

"They were from a place called Cherry something…yes, Cherry Creek, in South Dakota. We met in some country bar and somehow just started talking. Eventually, they took us there, to show us their world. I had never seen such a bleak place. It seemed like one of those barren landscapes where nothing could grow. The Cheyenne River flowed through that God-forsaken place stuck in the middle of nowhere." Kay paused as if retrieving the remainder of her story. "It was ungodly hot, and we wanted some relief. I walked into the river and the Indian girls laughed. When I emerged from the water, I was caked with silt that was being swept along. Well, that means nothing I suppose. But these girls wanted to hear about our world. I never talked about my wealth and status, but my girlfriend and I did chat a lot about college. They seemed fascinated, so I guess we tried to let them know what college life was like. They had not known anyone who had gone beyond high school. At the end of the visit, and this I remember the most, one of them said she was going to go to college. It wasn't said casually. She was adamant. She was going." Kay smiled. "Of course, I never believed her. How could she go from where she was to college? But what stayed with me is that meeting us changed her aspirations. College had never entered her head before. What if she had been exposed to it earlier or had some support? Some kids, even in America, just never have a chance, never. We can do just a little to bring opportunity to those who never had a chance. Only a few will take advantage but only a few would make it all worthwhile."

"Okay," Karen said firmly. "Let's talk more about how we can make this happen."

That evening, Karen, Kay, and Carlotta sat around in Karen's hotel room. "I must be a favored guest in this fine hotel now," Karen said. "They upgraded me to a suite. That always makes me feel a bit guilty. You know, someone fighting want and desperation staying first class. I didn't even ask. They just assigned me this top floor suite."

"Hmmm," Carlotta murmured with a smile. "I see you didn't turn them down."

"Hah, don't get cheeky, lass. Your next assignment will be doing an inventory of the office paper clips. But I have a remedy to deal with my guilt." She went over, opened a drawer, and pulled out a bottle of top-shelf scotch. "Now, this won't be as refreshing as the warm Guinness at the Hairy Hare, but we will make do."

Kay laughed. "You didn't get this at the local liquor store. Did you sneak it past customs?"

"Do I look daft? Don't answer that. No, I have friends over at the British Embassy."

"I know why you got the suite," Kay chimed in as if she just made a great discovery. "My first guess was that they wanted to keep you as far away from the decent people as possible, but now I have a different theory."

"Pray tell," Karen said, "enlighten us."

"Simple," Kay enthused. "You have that to-the-manor-born look. You know, as if you belong to the aristocracy or on some PBS mini-series. It's written all over you."

"Bollocks. Scotch for Carlotta and me, local polluted water for you."

After the drinks were poured, they clinked glasses as Karen pronounced, "To saving the world."

Kay was still smiling. "Friends at the embassy. Really? You know, Chris told me you had friends. I never would have believed it."

"And you, my dear, will be helping Carlotta with the paper clips. Why is it that every Crawford thinks of themselves as a stand-up comic? Must be the Irish part of you all. By the way, did I ever tell you the story about why your brother hired me?" Karen looked at Kay.

"I don't recall. I suspect it wasn't because you slept with him though, and I hate to admit this now, I did assume that at the time."

"Hah, hah. But I did worry that another candidate might have. I saw this girl leaving as I was waiting for the interview, short skirt and legs that never quit. She had that snobbish upper crust look of the entitled, probably a graduate of an elite, public school. I should have smacked her, or maybe I should have given her my number. She was hot. Anyways, at that moment I desperately wished I had worn a tighter blouse, to show off my assets such as they were."

"Would not have helped. My brother surely was a pig in those days, but he never let it cloud his professional judgment. Well, that is not quite true. He was deathly afraid of entanglements. If he slept with women he worked closely with, it would be harder to dump them when he got bored. He was always looking for an escape route."

"Hmm, I never thought about that. Now that you mention it, he seldom asked me to pimp for him to meet women, but he always tried to get my help in dumping them. *Oh, sorry Alice or Olivia or Gretchen, Mr. Crawford has left town for the month...to Borneo where he cannot be reached.* Why did I do that for him? Oh, for the raises it got me I suppose." Karen smiled to herself. "Anyways, back to my hiring story. I could tell it was not going well at first. I was considering just ripping my blouse off when he asked one of those hypotheticals to which you know there is probably not a correct answer. It was something like what I would do if I saw him making a big mistake in a meeting."

"I know what I would do." Kay guffawed.

"Great minds run in the same gutter, I guess. I am not sure of my exact words, but my response involved politely taking him outside the room and ripping his balls off. This look came over his face and I was just sure he was about to have me chucked out on my rear. In fact, I was just about to get up, apologize for wasting his time, and just leave. Instead, he kind of leaned forward and peppered me with more questions. Not sure why, but I relaxed and started answering them honestly and stopped trying to figure out some textbook correct response. It kept going and I lost track of time. Sometime later, he shocked the shit out of me by calling and asking me back. At the end of that talk, he offered me the job. I was bloggers. Much later, he confirmed that he had dismissed me until that response. Imagine, one flip remark was the difference between my life now and being the barmaid at the Hairy Hare."

"Oh, come on, you really think you could have gotten hired at the Hairy Hare?" Carlotta said as she and Kay roared with delight and poured more drinks.

"You know, if Chris figured out that you preferred women that would have helped you."

"How?" Karen seemed genuinely puzzled.

"Even a horny numb nut like my twin would realize that the temptation to bed his assistant, at the time, would be a burden, and he did not like inconveniences."

As Karen pondered that theory, Carlotta leaned back, clearly feeling the early effects of the scotch. "You know, those stories about opening up worlds for kids from that reservation reminded me of my youth."

"What?" Karen could not resist. "You really were raised on an American Indian reservation? Okay, I see a bit of Native American in you. Holy shit, though. All this time I had been convinced that you were a pampered brat from the Costa del Sol."

"Hilarious," she retorted. "True, I was a pampered brat but let me explain. It would have been easy to stay where I was as a girl, lounging on the beach in my bikini, or less than that. I could have snagged some guy with money and just continued lounging. But we had a lot of kids coming through from northern Europe, Scandinavia and such. I started talking with them about new stuff, ideas and struggles and issues that had never entered my head before. Hard to believe but I was a flighty girl back then, mostly interested in teasing boys."

"Not surprising to me." Karen chuckled. "What about you, Kay, surprised?"

"She hasn't changed a bit, still chasing poor Atle, teasing the hell out of him."

"Oh, bite me. See, I have picked up your vernacular, I think that phrase has become the office motto. I never even knew that phrase until I met you two, now I use it all the time. We all do. I think it has become the program's motto, but I digress." Carlotta scowled, taking another big sip of scotch while grimacing. "Couldn't you have friends at the Spanish Embassy and get some good wine from Spain? Anyways, to continue after I was once again rudely interrupted, these tourist-types changed my world. Well, they were not exactly tourists in the sense that they had big cars and money. A lot of them were students escaping the cold for a while or artists and kids searching for themselves and their futures. Sometimes, we would talk on the beach until almost dawn since many could not afford a room. We drank good Spanish wine, or at least what we could afford. My mind kept exploding with new thoughts. At school, I switched from thinking about becoming an architect, the next Gaudi you know, to the study of revolution. But even I figured out that there was not such a big market for majors in revolution so drifted toward social work and nursing. That felt comfortable and here I am, saving the world with you two."

"Thank God for horny, young male tourists trying to score with the local beauties on the Costa del Sol." Karen raised her glass. "They brought you to us."

"Wait," Carlotta sputtered, she was not used to scotch and was feeling very relaxed already. "You guys are the last ones to be making fun of my sex life." Suddenly, the room became silent. Carlotta let out a breath along with the word "shit". When no one spoke, she started to stand. "Maybe I should go? I am not used to this scotch and you two…"

"No, don't," Kay snapped while looking into her glass. "At least I need to know. Is it obvious? Karen and I, that is, are we obvious?"

Carlotta looked as if she would rather be anywhere else. "Well, I watch people. It is something I do well. I mean, I knew you two had been an item at some point and then I wondered why Deena was not with us. After all, she is fine now. So, maybe my antenna was up. But hey, it is none of my business. I am in no position to question anyone else's romantic choices. Here I am lusting after a guy who is in a relationship. I don't judge." She took another sip while deciding what to say next. "Okay, I noticed small things. I doubt others would though." Then she stopped, not sure where to go next.

Kay rose and walked to the window. She stared out over a city with twinkling lights. "Quiet out there tonight. I don't think I have heard any sound of violence, not a single emergency vehicle. Isn't it funny? Silence can be louder than noise. When you expect to hear something and don't, that can be the most deafening. Why is that, I wonder? Maybe that is what first attracted me to Kabul. It reminded me of Chicago in a way. Way too much violence. Funny, from here we go to Syria and Yemen, way more violence there now but this country will always have a special place in my heart. Here is where I changed."

Karen leaned back in her overstuffed chair, looking up at the ceiling. She fixed on a spot up there, a blemish. Had it moved, was it some insect? *Bugs should not be permitted in a luxury suite,* she said only to herself. "Deena really wanted to come. I tried to argue with her that she needed more time to heal.

That was bullshit and she knew it. So, I went with the story that Afghanistan might raise too many issues for her, psychologically. Wait for a field trip where it wasn't on the itinerary, I argued. She scoffed at that. The girls, I said, my mom cannot take care of the girls this time, she needs a knee replaced. Hell, her knee is bad, that is true. But no surgery is scheduled, my mother could have looked after the girls. But Deena bought that story and it was a lie. That one will catch up to me."

Carlotta rose again. "Listen, I probably should go."

"Please," Kay spoke abruptly. "Stay, please. It is so good to have someone who knows. Isn't that weird? Here we are in this clandestine affair and it is such a fucking relief that someone knows. What is with that?"

"I know. It is easier to talk about things with another, things that you cannot express to your lover." Karen added softly, as if suggesting the thought to herself.

Carlotta looked at Karen with a perplexed expression but sat back down. "I…okay, I'll sit." She looked back and forth between Karen and Kay but neither of them uttered a word at first.

Kay was back looking out of the window. "When I was young, when Chris was out playing ball, I often was home, studying or staring out the window. I loved watching the lake during the day and the city lights at night. You could watch the stream of headlights below as darkness fell, it would mesmerize me. The other girls got into boys, endless discussions about them. I tried to seem interested, but it all seemed so tedious to me. I preferred chemistry and biology or even listening to Chris talk politics. The worst was listening to some of the girls at school talk about Chris, what they would like to do with him if only he would pay attention to them. I know that eighty percent of my popularity was based on my gal pals getting invites to our palatial suite on the off-chance that Chris would be there. Oh God, it was awful. I was too much of a nerd to get friends on my own."

"Really, you were not popular?" Carlotta seemed genuinely surprised.

"Oh, I had been too isolated early on. I was a hermit while Chris was the one that explored the world. By my teens, I was a bookworm and awkward. As I said, a total nerd. Everything I learned about people and the world was through him. Some teacher, huh?" She looked wistfully at the city out of the window. "Maybe that is why I became an ER doctor. You don't have to talk to people, just sop up the blood and gore."

"I never thought I would feel sorry for any rich kids. You Crawfords, though, did have it rough." Karen stayed away from any hint of sarcasm. "I'm serious about that."

Kay merely chuckled. "Nice try Karen. I know I sound pathetic. But when you are that age, and have never experienced anything else, your world is the world. Your passions have never been felt by anyone else, at least that is how you see it. Your pain is unique. That is the irony of it all. I was not feeling much of anything. I could not stand the girls at school, they were so spoiled and vapid. I tried a bit to get involved with boys, it was expected. So, I went out with a few of them, dates arranged for me mostly. These guys would paw at me and my skin would crawl, they were pigs. Eventually, I gave in, out of weariness and maybe a bit of curiosity. But the sex left me cold. So, I stopped. I loved it when Chris brought Ricky and Jules around. I fell in love with her I think, but she clearly preferred my brother. That seemed weird at the time. Maybe it still does. I wonder if she ever figured that out?" Then she stopped as if trying to answer her own question.

After some moments, Carlotta spoke in a low, uncertain voice. "I feel this is not my place and that I will say the wrong thing but…"

"Go ahead."

Carlotta heaved a big sigh. "Oh, I thought no one was listening to me." She took another quick sip and looked at Kay. "Do you love Jamie at all?"

At this, Kay turned from the window and returned to her seat, splashing down onto the cushion with conviction. "Do I love the nicest, sweetest man I have ever met? Other than Chris and he does not count. Yes, dearly. The question is whether I am *in* love with him."

Karen had seemed fixated on the ceiling but now turned to the others. "What is wrong with us? I mean, really. Carlotta, you are a sexy Mediterranean lass who is now long-in-the tooth and without any serious boyfriends that I can recall. When is the last time you got laid? Don't answer that. Kay is married to Dr. Wonderful, with two beautiful kids, and comes back to me. Really, what can be more stupid than that? Wait, don't answer that one either. I got it. How about a gal from a working-class family who achieves far more in life than she could ever imagine, mostly by luck, and then finds the most beautiful partner she ever imagined finding that all my lesbian gal pals would drool over, and she is still not satisfied. What the fuck is wrong with me? Definitely don't answer that one."

Kay cracked a grim smile. "Karen, my dear, you had more than luck going for you in life. Luck just got you in the door. You did the rest on your own. Regarding all that is wrong with you, though, I don't believe we have enough scotch to cover that one."

"Not to worry, I got more."

Carlotta suddenly jumped up and went to the bottle. She poured another drink. "I may be incapacitated tomorrow but I suddenly need this." She took a big sip. "God almighty, that is awful. I think it is scarring my insides. But anyways, you know what we are? - adolescents. We have never grown up. Sure, we are educated and sophisticated, even Karen can fake that…"

"Hey," Karen protested.

"That's a compliment." Carlotta shot back. "But we never did the one thing that all kids must do. Really, you have only one task back then and we fucked it up."

"What the hell are you talking about?"

Carlotta sighed. "As kids, all you have to do is figure out what you want when you grow up. That's it. And we messed that up. When I sat with those kids on the beach and my mind seemed to be expanding with new ideas and possibilities, I thought that a total blessing. Our universities are into rote learning, not places to think like many in America and even some British schools. So, I reveled in my new intellectual journey. It was a blessing and it also was a total curse. Possibilities make choices that much more difficult. Now, here we are sitting around a hotel in Kabul, getting blasted, still trying to figure things out that should have been resolved decades ago. How sad is that?"

"Do you know what is really sad?" Kay asked no one in particular.

"No," Karen answered, "but I will bet my last euro that you are about to tell us."

"We are out of scotch." She waived an empty bottle in the air.

"No, no, no. I told you I have more. However, I am in charge and we do have to work tomorrow so everyone to bed. Besides, I don't want to go back to the embassy too soon for refills, they will think I am a lush."

They looked at one another for several moments and then suddenly began to laugh. Once started, they could not stop. The giggling went on for some time.

Carlotta weaved to her computer and pulled up her email account.

TO: Atle Bergstrom

FROM: Carlotta Ciganda

RE: Ultimatum.

Dear sir, I must first say that I am quite drunk.

Nevertheless, I am giving you an ultimatum. You must decide what you want in life by the first of the year.

Love always…Carlotta

PS: In case you are confused, the answer is that you want me.

Kay sat down in her room.

TO: Jamie

FROM: Kay

RE: Pictures

Please take some pictures of you and the girls and send them.

Karen sat after the others had left. She tried to decide if she should call Kay and ask her to come back. In the end she did not. She also flipped her computer open.

TO. Deena

FROM: Karen

RE: A secret.

Dear Deena,

There is something I have been meaning to tell you. This is hard…

Then she stopped, she could no longer see the screen through the tears cascading down her face. She quietly buried her face in her hands.

CHAPTER 14

PRE-CHRISTMAS: LONDON 2016

Karen had found a Victorian townhouse to rent for the months of December and January, which the Crawford clan and associates could use during their visits. At one point or another, Chris, Amar, Azita, Kat and Ricky, Chris's mother Mary, along with Atle and Carlotta and other staff, were expected to stop in to celebrate the holiday season. Beverly decided not to join the others, concerned that doing so might jeopardize the illusion that she had not joined the family cabal that had broken with the family patriarch. Ricky and Jules would also remain in Chicago to be with their mother, who was not well.

With some work, Chris's place in Oxford might have handled part of the crowd but it was being used by a visiting American academic family and therefore was unavailable. Besides, London was better at Christmas time, more people and lights and festivities. It seemed dark all the time but that merely added to the cheer inside the houses and pubs and restaurants that now seemed in continuous revelry. It was also cold and bracing, but then again, Madison could be freezing and often miserable. The rental was pricy and would be unused for much of the period, but Chris did not hesitate for a moment.

The location was great, and the place was large enough to accommodate the expected crowds for some planned events that involved key staff from his London-based service organization and a few university colleagues. Besides, some of the stateside people might have needed a place to stay. People would be coming and going as schedules permitted but they would find room for all that wanted to share in the season's good cheer. Hell, for the younger staff, they could throw sleeping bags on the floor. This was to be a break from the troubles in the world and a break it would be. Chris was even considering leasing the place long-term as a possible accommodation where the unmarried staff might live. London was burdened with high housing costs and this might prove a seductive recruiting perk.

Chris had flown over before the rest to work with Karen, Deena, Carlotta, and the other top staff. His early arrival also gave him a chance to catch up with his Oxford colleagues and to prepare for the arrival of all the others. As the rest began to arrive in London and settle in, he decided to get a tree and do the traditional things, though he could not quite figure out why. As he propped it up in the corner, Amar looked at him with a bemused expression.

"A tree, really?"

"Yeah, why?"

"And how many practicing Christians will be with us while we're here?" Amar's eyes took on a dubious look.

"Ah, there is Karen," he tried.

Amar guffawed. "Karen? Give me a break."

"Ah, there is what's-his-name from Oxford? He said he would stop by. He is a believer, I think."

"Now I see," Amar grinned broadly. "Your good friend what's-his-name. That convinces me."

Chris stared at the tree for a moment or two. "Aha, mother. Mother is still a believer. That reminds me, we should find her a Catholic church to attend."

"Okay, I give you your mother, but let me find the church, not you."

"Why?"

"Because," Amar chuckled. "If you entered a church, you would probably burst into flames."

"Hah, says the woman who shamelessly threw herself at me the first night we met."

"And who has never stopped regretting that deplorable lack of judgement ever since," she said as she pulled him toward her and kissed him. "Damn, you are sexy even if you are an idiot."

"Sure, that is what all the girls say."

"That you are an idiot? That I can believe."

He kissed her back. "My, you are on your game today. As punishment, you must help me decorate."

"What? Me? I've never done that. Wait for your family."

"Nah, we can surprise them. Besides, you are my family." He grinned. "Hmmm, now that I think on it, we have the place to ourselves. Mom and the girls are with Kay, Azita is with Deena, I can remind you just how sexy I am. Why don't we screw each other's brains out in front of the fireplace?" He had his endearing crooked grin plastered over his face. "On second thought, let's do the tree first. I am running out to the car to get ornaments and lights from the…boot. Might as well convert to Brit talk while back here."

As he quickly moved to the door, she called out: "I am still not admitting in public that I agreed voluntarily to marry you. I am sticking to my shotgun wedding story. What in God's name was I thinking?" She smiled to herself, she was on her game this morning. When she heard no retort from him, she picked up her cell phone.

Minutes later, as he sat unpacking and organizing the lights and baubles with a big smile on his face, Amar sighed. "By the way, Ahmad will be spending a lot of time here, another non-Christian."

"Not to worry, I will get everyone smashed on spiked eggnog, he will believe in anything after a few belts of my famous Christmas libation."

"Tell me, when did Father Christmas take possession of you?"

"You know, this amazes me more than you. I seem like the guy who loves people and can easily work a crowd but inside it is not easy for me. I am very private."

"I know." Amar remained serious, "but tell me how you see yourself."

Chris considered a response as he began putting ornaments on the tree. Then, he started. "Well, it strikes me that there are two kinds of people in the world. Some get charged up being around people even if they start out at a low-energy level. Others deplete their energy level in the very act of being social. I am the latter. I need to work myself up to being around others. Not you and the kids, of course, but people who count."

"What? Did you just hear yourself?" Before he could respond, however, she changed directions. "Never mind, as usual your mouth was engaged before your brain. However, speaking of Ahmad, which we were a bit ago before your tangent, I had an interesting chat with our eldest daughter. After Benjamin, she has been reluctant to…how shall I put it? - consummate any relationship."

"What? They haven't had sex yet?"

"Why are you surprised? Think of her culture. It is not easy for a Muslim girl and her experiences with Benji were…not so good. A lot of guilt at least."

"What did you tell her?"

"I told her that the next time they were alone, she should rip his clothes off and ravage his body."

For some reason, Amar's graphic words, coming out with her lyrical Indian-British fused lilt, struck Chris as funny and he chortled aloud. "I never should have let you have the sex talk with her, I am the expert."

"And if we ever have a male child, I will let you corrupt him. But Azita needs another woman, and someone from a similar culture. I strongly suspect your witty advice, which you probably got from Playboy magazine, would not be quite right. This had to be my responsibility."

"Yeah, I can see that." He was serious now and stopped fooling with the trinkets. "So, what is the story?"

"Well," Amar responded, "I fear she has picked up way too much of your wit, as have I. You really do corrupt women."

"It is my life's obsession."

"Right, in any case, she laughed at my advice and told me I was a very poor representative of the Indian culture. Then, she asked if my mother told me to go for it with some guy. We both laughed at that one."

"What did you say in the end?"

Amar stared at the tree leaning against the wall. "Oh, I told her that we both had been raised wrong, that sex was neither good nor bad, not in itself. It is what we do with it, the meaning that we assign to it that is important. If she really comes to believe that this boy is the one that she wants to be with, she should join with him physically, not to trap him or buy his affection since that will not work. She should join with him to deepen her feelings and express what is inside her in this more intimate way. She nodded at my wise counsel, so I think she understood."

Chris leaned over and kissed Amar again lightly. "I am glad you had that discussion with her and not me since I have no idea about what you just said."

"Yes, I am sure Azita and I have the same feeling on that score. Anyways, I wanted you to know just in case Ahmad spends a night…with her or, more likely, she with him. I seriously doubt she would flaunt their physical relationship, should they ever have one."

Chris absorbed that thought quickly, rather taken that he had paused for a moment over that possibility. He really did not want to think about his daughter having sex. "Got it. On another matter," he returned to his light banter, "while you are evil and doomed to a tragic karmic fate, at least I know why you seduced me on that first night. You wanted to share your deep sense of love for me in an intimate way."

"What?" Amar responded with incredulity. "Keep deluding yourself. I was just damn horny, and Kay told me that you would mount a coat rack. And then you turned me down at first. Not a good start I might say."

"But a helluva finish, as they say." He started kissing along her neck and she shivered. "I still recall how you orgasmed that night."

"This is a great idea," she cooed softly, "but I called people to help with the tree. Sorry. And to set the story straight about that orgasm, I faked it."

"Your loss on the sex today, but how about a rain check?"

"Rain check for sure." She smiled back.

"Hey, wait! You faked what? No, you didn't."

He was going to press his case, but the doorbell rang. It was not long before the large townhouse began to fill with people. Food appeared and drinks. There was the expected banter about the tree. Chris listened to the sarcasm and criticism for a while before rising to his own defense. "Alright everyone, listen up. I am still the titular head of the ISO and the day-to-day main guy on whatever we are doing in the States. So, you all work for me. One more word about the tree and you are all out on your ear. But I understand that Britain yet has a generous dole, so you should be okay." He looked about the room with what he hoped was a menacing glare.

Amar laughed first. "Well, I am his wife and that puts me in charge of him. So, here is my dictate. The tree is stupid but, in the interests of universal love and to recognize my husband's inner child, let us decorate the damn thing."

A cheer went up. Atle was there, without his significant other. Carlotta was ecstatic, her eyes were bright, her look radiant. Karen and Kay showed up together, but not Jamie. April and Josef from the stateside staff also took advantage of Chris's offer to visit London and take some time off. There were also a few of the London staff arriving, and even several from Oxford. Somehow the word spread, and a spontaneous party was developing. Chris managed to grab a couple of the London staff and send them out for more food and drink.

Karen and Kay found their way to Chris and Amar who were handing out ornaments. "Atle, you are a technical guy." He yelled across the room. "Deal with these damn lights, will you?" Then he turned to those near him and said in a lower tone. "I better keep him occupied or Carlotta will jump his bones in front of everyone. If anyone is going to make a fool of himself this blessed season, it will be me - a known apostate and moral derelict."

"And you are just the guy to do it," Karen joked before moving on to a topic that dominated her thinking these days. "So, with that clown in the White House, probably no need for you to stay in the States after this spring. It is over, right?"

Karen was looking at Chris, but it was Amar who broke the ensuing silence as Chris looked at the ornament in his hand and then at the tree. "I was rather wondering the same thing."

Chris still said nothing, putting the ornament on one branch, looking at it critically, before moving it to another. Amar reached over to take the bauble out of his hands.

Chris suddenly asked a question. "Have you ever heard of Sophie Scholl?" When the others looked confused, he continued. "She and her brother were students when Hitler was at the height of his powers in the early 1940s. There was little resistance to the Nazis in Germany by this time. They, however, decided to take a stand. They created the White Rose movement, a form of resistance to Hitlerism and what it stood for. They flooded the streets with pamphlets trying to wake up the people to what had happened to them, what was happening to them. She, and others in that small band, tried to tell them that they had slowly sacrificed their souls to a godless machine bent on nothing more that nihilistic destruction. Few heard the message at a time when Hitler marched toward control of all Europe. But they never stopped."

"What happened to her, them?" Amar asked.

Chris did not answer. Rather, it was Kay, in a low, rather hard voice. "What would you expect? The Gestapo eventually caught her, and some of the others. She was tortured and killed, in 1943 I believe."

"They should be doing documentaries about her on the History Channel and not the freaking Nazis." Chris sounded bitter.

As Amar was about to speak, Chris's phone rang. He looked relieved, as if making a deft escape. He glanced at the number and his eyes brightened. "Oops, need to take this one, everyone keep working," he said as he found a quieter location. "Jules, merry Christmas. Wish you were here, as they say."

"Wish I was as well. Sounds like a party there."

"Yeah, we are putting up a tree, if you can believe it. My idea even." Chris could not quite understand why he was embarrassed by that.

"Good for you. And you convinced Kat to join you without Ricky. He and I will be with mom. She is alone now and failing. It will likely be our last time as a family, her final Christmas with us. All rather bittersweet though she never has a down word."

"Please give her my best." Chris realized that his voice caught with emotion. "She is an amazing woman and has meant so much to me."

"I will, she always said that you were the white boy she never had."

"I…" Then he realized he could not say more without breaking up.

Jules knew and switched gears. "Listen, I will make this quick, let you get back to the party. I am making headway on some of this Russian stuff. Kat should be arriving there soon, but I didn't have time to brief her before she left. Things are breaking fast. It is still under wraps, but Obama will accuse Russia of interfering in the U.S. elections before the end of the year. He will expel a bunch of Russians, low-level embassy personnel and private citizens."

"Whew." Chris exhaled and then asked. "Does this affect the election outcome?"

"Oh, no, not in the least. The fact that the Russians did it is not evidence of collusion, other than the fact that Trump publicly invited Putin to get Hillary's emails and publish them. If he had done so in a clandestine fashion and got caught, that might be treason. I suppose he could now claim he was joking but there has got to be more there, and I am beginning to see what I can uncover."

"I always knew you were devious," Chris said.

"You were damn lucky to escape my clutches, kiddo. Now listen. I am getting inside info on several Russian players, Oleg Deripiska, Emin Agalapov, Viktor Vekselberg, and Eugeny Prigozhin."

Never heard of these guys."

"You are not supposed to. They are Putin confidants and, more importantly, they have connections to the Trump team, people like Cohen, Manafort and the family - Kushner and Donald Junior. The web is complicated, some even involving WikiLeaks, and some of the connections are indirect but there was a steady stream of communications between guys like this and the Trump inner team to manipulate the election. That, you cannot do. That violates a lot of U.S. laws."

"Jules, if you were here, I would kiss you.

"Hey buddy, for stuff like this I expect a lot more than a kiss. But never mind. I sometimes forget that you are off limits. Damn, I am going to have to get laid one of these days. In any case, there is a long way to go, but still, you can sense the knots unravelling just a bit. It's not all good stuff, though." Her voice betrayed a hint of concern.

"What do you mean?" he asked.

"Well, nothing that I can put my finger on. Maybe I am just getting paranoid, but I sometimes worry that I am being followed, shadowed. I see a guy more than once, who seems to be where I am too often for coincidence, and I get paranoid. If you see them in the lobby at work, that is one thing. But then the coffee shop and the gym and jogging. It is not always obvious, so I am never certain."

"Shit." That was all that Chris could get out. "Damn, I feel so helpless here. What about Beverly? Has she noticed anything?"

"Well, she has mentioned becoming more nervous of late. She senses changes in your father, and she wonders if he has become more suspicious of her. He is, by instinct, susceptible to paranoia, as I guess we all are. Of course, in my instance it is justified. Well, maybe we are all getting hyper-sensitive. We are not cloak-and-dagger types. We know nothing about covert operations and shit like that."

"Oh, I wish I had convinced her to come with us. But she argued that would really raise Father's suspicions. Look after her the best you can, and yourself." He could not quite figure out where to go next. "Do you carry a gun?"

"Yes. I can't stand the things, but I broke down and got one. Even without all this political espionage crap, this is Chicago. As you always say, more dangerous than Kabul. Well, gotta go."

"Wait…" Then he stopped, unsure of what to say. "Love you, kiddo."

"Love you more." She laughed as the connection was lost.

Chris stood there for several minutes, lost in thought,

"Where are we going?" Deena complained to her sister. "It is cold, and I don't even recognize these streets."

"It is Christmas, look at the shop windows and the lights and the happy faces."

Deena looked about as they shuffled along the slippery sidewalk. Snowflakes fluttered through the brisk air, beginning to accumulate at long last. "What I see are a bunch of frantic people rushing about because they have too much to do and not enough time in which to do it. I think these Western holidays are designed to inflict the maximum unhappiness on the celebrants."

"Ah, the problem with you, my sister, is that you have no romance in your soul."

"I have romance," she uttered too harshly. "It is the others in my life who don't."

Azita stopped and Deena followed her lead after a couple more steps. "All this is more than usual grumpiness, isn't it?"

"Not now. You have this surprise for me. Later, perhaps."

Azita stared at her. "I am not moving until you tell me." Neither moved. "We will freeze to death here, together. People will think it very romantic. Two sisters, like a suicide pact."

Deena shifted her feet for a few moments until she realized that her sister would not be moved. Her face quivered a bit as she spoke. "Oh, dear sister, I think Karen does not care for me anymore. We don't connect like we did. It is different."

"Are you sure?"

"No, of course I am not sure. I know as much about love and life as your average twelve-year-old Brit girl…maybe no more than an eight-year-old."

Azita held her sister. The rushing crowd made a path around them, their pain remained private amidst the chaos about them. "Maybe I can cancel this, we can find a place to talk."

"Tell me this surprise first." The tears still flowed down her cheeks. "Please tell me."

"We are on the way to meet Ahmad, and his father, Abdul. Remember Abdul, from my father's clinic in Kabul?"

"Yes," Deena brightened. "No, we must go and meet them. That is exactly what I need. I must connect to…something familiar. Yes, let us go."

Azita was about to ask if her sister was sure that was what she wanted but Deena quickly grabbed her hand and pulled her in the direction they had been heading. They crossed the street and moved another block before stopping at a small Afghan restaurant. The two girls peered inside.

"There is Ahmad, in that booth back there. That must be Abdul with him, it has been so many years."

"It is, I am sure of it. I was older when we last saw him, just before heading north out of Kabul."

Moments later, Ahmad jumped up to greet them as they approached the table. His body hung in indecision before he held out his hand in a formal way. "So good to see you, after so long." He glanced at Deena but kept his eyes on Azita. When Abdul rose from his eat, Azita hesitated a moment but then hugged the father and then his son.

After the reintroductions and some small talk, Abdul took the initiative. "You girls are now such women. I remember you both so well. Deena was the quiet one, always by the side of your lovely mother. And you, Azita, were always following along after your dear father. Oh, how much I miss him. I recall the day we sat with the Taliban official to secure the documents that enabled you to escape Kabul. I was ecstatic to learn you successfully made it to what I thought was safety and then…so tragic." He did not need to finish. "Well, perhaps Allah will join all of us together again in paradise someday. And now, my Ahmad tells me, that you are both such successes."

"Allah has been kind to us. But we want to express our condolences for the loss of your wife and to thank you for all you did to help us escape the Taliban. I only wish our parents were here to thank you themselves. They loved you so."

"Ach, those wicked people, the Taliban. They pervert the wisdom of the Prophet so. I am too old, but you, your generation, must go back and save our people. They do not deserve all the pain and suffering they have endured. The killing, it goes on and on. Someone must put a stop to it. The Americans I fear are abandoning us. They had 100,000 troops at one point and now it is like 10,000. The old fanatics now grow stronger."

Ahmad looked at his father fondly. "Oh, Papa, I think that if we are to survive, we must do it ourselves and not rely upon the Americans."

"Such a wise boy, is he not girls?" The question was rhetorical. Abdul beamed at his son.

Ahmad chuckled. "You see all those grey hairs on my poor father's head? I am sure I put many of them there myself. He worried so much that he had raised such a useless son, a boy who liked to party and hang around with Western girls."

Abdul smiled. "I have thought on occasion that children are God's way of punishing us for our sins. But I never stopped loving you and look at you know. I am so proud. He is a such a good- looking young man, is he not girls?"

"Without question," Deena said quickly.

"Oh, he has possibilities," Azita said with a wry smile.

Abdul laughed. "Yes, my son, you have told me she has a wicked wit. You will have to be careful of this one. That I can see."

Azita continued to smile. "Sir, I still recall you and my father talking at the end of the day in his clinic. I did not always understand what was being said but I knew that my father appreciated your experience and wisdom. He looked up to you, admired you very much. I know we will remain close to you, that you will always feel a part of our family." Abdul started to speak but Azita continued. "I…I usually am a cautious scientist, letting the evidence lead me to any conclusion. But sometimes, just sometimes, something is simply self-evident. Sir, you have raised a wonderful son and should be very proud of him."

"Oh, I am, young lady, I am."

"Yes, he must be extremely good since I…I intend to marry him and the two of us shall return to our country. You are right sir, someone must save our homeland."

Abdul gulped. Deena's jaw dropped open. Abdul simply smiled.

ひ ~

Kay found Chris still standing with his phone in his hand. "Let's go," she said, grabbing him by the arm.

"What, where?"

"Pick up our sister. She is arriving in her corporate jet. She tried to talk me out of coming to get her, but I insisted."

"Why?" Chris was puzzled. "This seems like a bother."

"Shush, I want to get you alone in any case." Kay took a deep breath.

They said nothing to each other as they made their way to her car. Chris had a pretty good idea what was on his sibling's mind, but he decided to let her take the lead. They were well on their way before his curiosity betrayed him. "Okay, you have me alone."

"Sorry, I was lost in my thoughts. The thing is, I have been thinking about stuff…where I am, the future, that kind of stuff." She stopped.

"Go ahead Kay, just spit it out."

"I think you probably have guessed. I am not happy with… things." She hesitated again. Chris was about to push her along when it flew out of her. "Oh shit, I have taken up with Karen again." The pace of her words now picked up speed. "The thing is that Jamie is wonderful, sweet and smart and a great father. I like him desperately, and the girls, but that is not me. I was not meant to be a wife and mother. I thought, maybe, but…" She hit her horn and sped around the car in front as Chris looked intently at her. "Isn't that the biggest thing in life, to figure out what you are supposed to be in life? Doesn't everyone figure that out by college? I am middle aged and still struggling. What is wrong with me?"

Chris looked at the road ahead. He wanted to quip that they did not have time to review all her shortcomings but knew this was not the time. In fact, no response came easily to him. His strong points were humor and policy, after that he felt helpless. He was afraid to look at his sister in case she was crying. She would not want that, for him to see her weak. It was Sunday. The traffic was light, but it was never totally absent on London streets and dusk was rapidly approaching. He was tempted to ask Kay if he should drive but held back. Instead, he searched for words that would not sound utterly moronic. "That is what we are all doing…Azita, Deena, Karen, Jules, even Amar and I."

"You and Amar are not in trouble, I can't believe that."

"No, she is the best thing that has happened to me. But we are struggling to find a place in life that works for us as a couple. That is our curse, not just for Amar and me, but all of us. Only Kat and Ricky seem solid, know what they are doing, and Ricky tried several things before getting it right. Here is the thing, I think. We are too talented. We have choices. To make matters worse, we all partnered with people who also are smart, independent, and have choices. That really complicates things. I should have married one of the bimbos."

"No shit," Kay uttered with some bite, "not the bimbo part but the smart partner stuff. And stop calling them bimbos, you sexist. I can call them bimbos, but you can't."

"Right," Chris said apologetically. "Listen, I am saying things that we all know, have all covered a million times in our own minds, you know those internal dialogues we have late at night. Still, let me have my say."

"Go ahead," she whispered.

"Remember the old aphorism of most people living lives of quiet desperation, or some such nonsense? We are meant to feel sorry for them, but they are not the people suffering. Sure, they may struggle to pay bills and yearn for the greener pastures just beyond their reach, but I sense they are not totally unhappy. Oops, sorry about the double negative. They probably cannot envision anything much beyond their own experience. I am arrogant enough to look down upon them on occasion. What an idiot. I cannot imagine many of them caught up on great existential questions about meaning and purpose and destiny. People like us are given great gifts and, with that, awesome responsibilities." Now, his words spilled a bit quicker as he realized what he wanted to say. "Don't you think I would not like to slink back to Oxford, bury myself in academia with a few books to be written and some occasional do-good philanthropic work? What a life, with the biggest impediments to happiness being terrifically inane faculty meetings. I have what most would give their right arm for, an unbelievable spouse and children, wonderful career, money, and a great circle of friends. And yet…yet…"

"You are being asked to do more and your own conscience will not permit you to walk away." Kay finished his thoughts as he struggled.

"Yeah, something like that. But this conversation is not about me. Kay, you are not being kind to Jamie. Staying with him out of guilt or a sense of responsibility or sheer stubbornness will not work in the long run. The one thing that catches me up is the girls. They will grow up and realize that something is wrong if you stay together for them. I now know just how insightful kids can be, they are like sponges, seeing everything even when you are not looking. They will figure stuff out and internalize all the disappointments and sadness and basic things that are missing. Just be honest with him, as Karen must be with Deena. I like the guy. I didn't really understand it when you suddenly married him, but I did like him. He is a great catch and deserves someone who can give him her all."

"Thank you." Her voice caught. "That helps. You know, I look back and wonder what I was thinking at that time as well. Was I denying my feelings toward women, was I jealous that you found a perfect partner, was I looking for a way, more like an excuse, to return to civilization? I had spent so many years in the ER, at the edges of the civilized world, surrounded by blood and carnage. I was not sure I wanted to spend the remainder of my life doing that except…"

"You would be wracked with guilt if you walked away, and maybe a bit empty."

Kay glanced quickly at him. "Damn, you are not as dumb as you look." For the first time that day, she permitted a slim smile to escape. "I am getting it now, finally. Going into trauma surgery, first in a public hospital and then in the Third World. I knew that would piss off father. He first tried to push me toward business. When that failed, he wanted me to use my medical training to make money, push expensive pharmaceuticals on to sick people who were desperately searching for the holy grail to save their lives. He was willing to provide that hope but only for some unconscionable price, knowing that many would die because they did not have enough money. For the life of him, he could not comprehend that some people went into medicine to help others. That was beyond his world. I so wanted to stuff that very thought down his throat. So much of it was about pissing him off, what a way to make a career choice."

"But you were so good at it. You did a lot of good," Chris argued.

"You're right, and I get that," she quickly said. "I was good… am good, damn good. And I have no real regrets for how I used my gifts. It is just time to figure out where I want to be, where I want to go." Again, she paused, and Chris wondered if she was waiting for him to comment. But he glanced at her and decided not. She confirmed his conclusion by continuing. "Want to hear something funny? Know why I married Jamie, the real reason, I think? Don't answer that, it was rhetorical. He reminded me of you."

"What?" Chris uttered incredulously.

"Oh, I know, you two are night and day in many ways. But I saw some similarities. He had a dry sense of humor, was kind, and wanted to do good. Of course, unlike you he had standards. No way he would mount a coat rack. But he was close enough in some ways. Without realizing it, I wanted someone who was like you. And no, I never, ever had an incestuous thought."

Chris went to his default position - humor. "Makes sense, I am every woman's dream."

She laughed out loud, and he felt better.

It was quite a walk back to the house where everyone was putting the finishing touches on the tree but Azita and Deena decided to walk. The temperature kept dropping and a light snow, which had stopped for a while, once again was falling. Daylight had faded into the gray of another brief mid-winter's day about to expire. The girls had never quite accustomed themselves to the short tenure of daylight this far north. It was like being cheated. Still, they buttoned their coats up and quickly moved along the streets, rather enjoying the frantic movements of holiday celebrants about them and the lights emanating from stores and restaurants. Each waited for the other to begin.

"I think you have lost your mind," Deena finally blurted out.

"You are just changing the topic. You tell me your relationship may be over and nothing more. I am not the crazy one here."

"No, no…don't deflect from the issue at hand. What kind of Muslim girl are you, proposing to a boy you hardly know, and in front of his father? I have no words."

"Abdul was pleased, so there," Azita responded. "And you always have words, too many in fact."

"That does not excuse your behavior. I was mortified."

"You are lecturing me? You are mortified?" Azita sounded wounded. "You sleep with women, women! That is not exactly good behavior for a proper Muslim girl." Deena stopped walking. "Oh my God, I am so sorry. I didn't mean…" Azita did not know what to say next.

Deena's face turned cold. "Really? Perhaps this is what you have felt all this time, that your sister is a pervert, an affront to Allah to be kept secret from polite company? I notice you didn't mention my preferences to Abdul. Have you ever bothered to tell Ahmad?"

"What? No," Azita sputtered. "But neither did you. It is not my place."

"That is just your convenient excuse. Finally, I know what you really think of me." With that, Deena whirled and started down the street at a fast pace. Where she should have turned at the corner, she kept on straight.

Azita looked after her, paralyzed by surprise. Eventually, the reality of the situation caught up to her and she started running after her sister, not stopping or looking about when she reached the corner. As she crossed the street, a taxi, traveling too fast in hope of making an impending stop light swerved to avoid striking her. The car almost missed her but not quite. The girl felt a hard blow to her rear and sprawled forward onto the pavement, rising quickly to stumble forward before collapsing to the ground a second time. A woman screamed, and the taxi screeched to a halt. The stricken girl struggled to her feet again and tried moving toward her sister. The driver called after her but Azita kept stumbling toward Deena who now stood looking back to her with an expression that hung somewhere between anger and anguish. A man approached Azita to offer his help, reaching to take her arm. She pulled away, shouting: "I am fine. I am fine." Clearly, that was not the case as she continued to stumble forward.

"What are you doing?" That was all Deena could think to say.

"You…you are going the wrong way. I…I thought you might like to know." Azita wavered as the pain in her backside came into full focus as she sank back to the sidewalk.

Deena wiped the tears from her eyes and seemed on the verge of words when the cabbie pulled up. The driver, a man wearing a turban, jumped out. "Miss, are you alright? Can I take you to the hospital?"

It was Deena who finally responded. "I think just take us home if you will, there are several doctors there." She looked hard at Azita who merely nodded.

"Oh Pagwan! Yes, please enter my taxi. It is getting dark and you came out of nowhere."

"My fault, sir. Please do not blame yourself," Azita said through some pain. "But a ride would be appreciated.

"Yes, yes," the driver said as he and the passerby helped her to the vehicle. She visibly winced getting into his vehicle. Getting the address from Deena, they headed off at breakneck speed.

Azita knew the man to be a Sikh. She momentarily thought of mentioning that her adoptive mother was also Sikh but that seemed like too much trouble and not terribly relevant.

"You did that just to make me feel bad for you. It won't work, you know." Deena whimpered.

"Bollocks," Azita whispered to her sister, wondering why British slang slipped from her mouth. "Next time I will get myself killed."

"Good," Deena said with more conviction. "And don't expect me to mourn you."

"No problem, you won't be invited to my send off."

The driver looked back at them in the rear-view mirror, clearly confused. "She is my evil sister," Deena said as an explanation. Then she realized that explained nothing though the man nodded as if it explained everything. Perhaps it did. Turning slightly toward her sister, she put her arm around her and pulled her close. "My fault. I am just angry that you are happy, and that I am miserable."

"It was terrible timing on my part, to spring this proposal thing. Don't mention it when we get home." Azita let out a small groan.

Deena ignored it. "I will keep it a secret that you are a selfish idiot who only considers her own happiness."

"You are very kind," Azita said and tried to smile but that did not last. "Oow, my backside is really beginning to hurt. And I have these scrapes on my arms."

Deena realized the pain was real. She took off her scarf and wrapped up one arm that had tiny rivulets of blood dripping down. She then pulled her sister even closer, kissing her forehead. "Idiot."

Upon arriving, Jamie carried Azita inside where Amar joined him as they both fussed over her until they were convinced that all she had suffered were severe bruises and deep contusions. Nothing was broken but the pain would linger.

❧ ❧

"Kat. Over here," Kay called and ran to embrace her younger sister. "I am so glad you are here."

"Good to see you, boss." Chris gave her his crooked smile and swept her off the ground in a big bear hug.

"Yikes!" she squealed in surprise and delight. "Good to see you guys…I think. Before I forget, Ricky sends his regards but with his mom's health, well, you know. And, I brought a surprise." Turning slightly, she pointed back to the elderly woman who trailed a bit behind.

"Mother!" Kay and Chris yelled simultaneously as if rehearsed. "The rumors were true. You are here. So glad you could join us," Chris finished. The twins gave their mother a warm embrace.

"We can head right to your car," Kat said as if giving directions. "I arranged for transport for the staff that came with me on the plane, they will handle all the luggage and presents. That is one benefit of being filthy rich, you don't worry about the details of life. Of course, there are bigger things to worry about but not today."

Chris took his mother's arm and started off as she filled him in on the goings on in Chicago. Kay and Kat, he noticed, talked all the way to the car. He was a bit taken aback. They had never seemed close as children. If anything, Kat and Kay had always been happy in their own worlds though Kat did make herself a nuisance to Chris on occasion Mostly, though, Kat spent much more time by herself, almost invisible to the others. Kay and

Chris at one point speculated that she might be developmentally disabled but then concluded she was pathologically shy. Now, Chris knew better. His youngest sibling was watching and absorbing the world about her. She probably had been somewhat intimidated by her family's notoriety and social standing as well as the obvious talents of her older twin siblings. But her mind was incisive, cutting sharp, and her curiosity was not easily quenched.

There were those other times, though. Kat would follow Chris around like a puppy scuttling after the master, often being underfoot when he was with his friends or circling another female prospect. He tolerated that, partly out of pity and partly because it did not happen that often. Where had that girl gone? She and Kay were chatting away as if they had been bosom buddies all their lives. Chris noticed another thing: Kay had put their conversation about Jamie and Karen behind her. It was as if nothing of note was happening in her personal life. How easily she compartmentalized her emotions. He had not met that many women capable of that.

As Kay's car made its way toward the M1, Kat suddenly switched from small talk with Kay to serious topics with Chris. "Well Chris, I got a good briefing from Jules and Bev before leaving, which is why I suggested to Kay that she drag you along when she insisted on picking me up. No need to bring everyone down during the holidays."

"Good thought," inserted Kay. "They are doing up the Christmas tree right now."

"Christmas tree?" Kat guffawed. "Turn the car around right now, I am heading back to civilization."

"Nonsense, this will be just like when we were young kids, singing carols around the tree, roasting chestnuts over the open fire…"

"Are you delusional?" Kay bellowed. "You are remembering Ricky's family, they celebrated the holiday. Father lectured us on why Scrooge was right, and that Christmas was humbug. He read to us, all right, from Adam Smith, Ayn Rand, and Milton Friedman."

"Oh yeah." Chris mused.

"I would like a tree," Mary offered. "We always had one when I was a child."

"Mother is right, tradition is tradition. And enough squabbling you two. Funny, though, I don't remember the early celebrations. Maybe I wasn't old enough to know what was going on." Kat then decided to shift away from uncomfortable personal memories. "Listen Chris, when all this seasonal nonsense is over there is a lot to do."

"Actually, I was thinking of some Alpine skiing."

"You don't ski," Kat responded, missing his meaning.

"I can take it up." This time, his sarcasm was unmistakable.

"Hah, hah, now listen nimrod." She assumed her serious tone. "Father is kicking into high gear now that the asshole is in the White House, or soon will be. He used to consort mostly with his fellow deep pockets of the hard-right, you know that gang all too well. Now, he is meeting with the front-line operatives. What do you think that means?"

Chris breathed heavily, reluctantly turning his mind to her query. "He has decided to move beyond funding the movement to taking a hands-on role in running it. At a minimum, he wants to shape the agenda."

"As I always say, you are not a Rhodes scholar for nothing," Kat offered.

"I always thought you said I was just another pretty face."

"Really? Why would I ever say that? That was probably Kay. Now shush. Beverly has been feeding me the identities of his recent visitors. It is like a who's who of the crazy right, except they are in power now."

"Whom are we talking about?" Chris was now involved in the conversation.

"From memory, we have Alex Azar. He was one of Kenneth Starr's counsels during the Clinton impeachment fiasco and rumored for a cabinet position. He is the guy who boosted the price of insulin way up as head of a big pharma firm, becoming yet another Republican serial killer. There is Mark Paoletta, an advisor to Pence. And we have Barbara Comstock, now GOP house member and all-around right-wing crazy. Oh, I shouldn't forget Kellyanne Conway and Ted Olson, who was Chief Solicitor under Bush and a hard-right zealot if there ever was one. You might recall that his wife died on 9-11 on the flight that ploughed into the field in Pennsylvania. Then we have the media mavens including Laura Ingraham, Ann Coulter, Tucker Carlson, and Matt Drudge. Oh, and Hannity, can't forget that wacko. They have all circled through his private lair in recent weeks, either singly or in small groups. The most frequent visitors have been Bannon and Miller, modern-day replicas of the Know-Nothings. If Hitler has risen from the grave, he has taken the human form of Miller."

"What are the Know-Nothings? "Kay asked. "Chris must have skipped that lesson in his tutorials for me or perhaps I just fell asleep. I often doze off to the drone of his voice. Oddly enough, he never noticed."

Chris just smiled. "You just can't reach some students, sigh. I recall that they were formally known as the American Party but became known as the 'Know Nothings' since they were very secretive. They were a nativist party who were very popular before the civil war, the 'America for white protestants' gang of that era. They had a huge following, briefly replacing the Whigs as the second most powerful political party as that group was disintegrating. At one point, they had 8 governorships and got at least 20 percent of the popular vote for President in 1856. In the end, the new Republican Party replaced the Whigs. I am certain I lectured you on them at length when I tried to educate you."

"Sorry," Kay said and chuckled. "you certainly know by now that I seldom listened to your ramblings."

Chris gave her a light tap on the shoulder and moved on. "Hmm, I wonder if Father tried to hit on Ingraham and Coulter? Oops, sorry mother."

"Doesn't bother me, son."

"Good! I bet he tried, though screwing Coulter would be like doing it with a coat rack and who should know better than me?"

"You had sex with Coulter?" Kay was incredulous.

"Hell no, I have standards, I never did anything uglier than a coat rack."

"Now I am getting uneasy," Mary added.

"Focus, you moron, focus," Kat yelled from the back seat.

"Yes, of course, sorry." Chris went back into serious mode. "You know, my last conversation with him, if you can call it that, fits. He has gone beyond merely tilting the economic rules in favor of the uber-wealthy like himself. He has been thinking hard about what to do with his vast treasure. I don't have all the details but, with the Republicans in power, he can see the next steps in the master plan. First, they jettison what remains of democracy in America, establish a totalitarian regime with his version of philosopher kings in charge. They might need a constitutional convention for that if they need legal cover. Then, they will reach out to like- minded leaders around the world. Part of the plan would involve disrupting the global alliances that have maintained order since World War Two, like NATO, the G-20, and the World Bank. Finally, and this is where it gets mystical and vague, they will orchestrate the next evolutionary step for mankind with the elite, the only people worth saving, in charge. Oh, and by the way, I chatted with Jules a short time ago. She has learned that Obama will expel a bunch of Russians given their apparent interference in the election. Those ex-commies are a crafty lot."

Kat whistled. "So, it must be deeper than we thought. Do they have the goods on the Republicans?"

"She didn't know."

"Wait," Kat said quickly, "when did you have this conversation with Father?"

"After you were nearly run down on the streets of Chicago. It was a spur-of-the-moment thing, I merely wanted to make sure he understood that I would come after him if he harmed anyone that I loved."

"And you never told me." Kat was incredulous.

"Well, I told Jules."

"Okay, never mind." Kat wanted to let it go but needed to get one more thought out. "Thanks for having my back. It was a stupid and futile gesture, but I appreciate your effort."

"Futile?" Chris responded with incredulity. "You are still with us, no?"

"True, but back to business. His agenda now puts the other thing I wanted to share in perspective. This intelligence comes from your new…confidant, Jules." Her tone dipped into sarcasm at the end.

"Not new, and I apologize for not mentioning my visit to the patriarch," Chris protested weakly. "That was my bad."

Kat was determined to go on. "He is also in contact with right-wingers from Europe. Some have visited him, he has visited others. It is like a football program but with a line-up of neo-Nazis."

"For example?" he asked.

"Alright, here is a partial list, again from memory. There is Victor Orban from Hungary, Matteo Salvini from Italy, Kaczynski from Poland and Strache from Austria. Let's see. Oh yeah, there is Jussi Halla-aho from Finland, Jimmie Akesson from Sweden, and the always popular Alexander Gauland from Germany - and Le Pen from France, of course. I will get you a complete list."

"I have never heard of these guys," Kay protested.

"I have, or most of them," Chris said grimly. "They are anti-immigration, Europe is for white European purists trying to fan the flames of extreme nationalism. They fit into the Bannon-Miller fold very well, Trump would love them if they ever seized power. Apparently, Father would love them as well. Undoubtedly, our family patriarch is supporting a like-minded revolution of the right in Europe or at least a breakup of the EU when they can pick off the more vulnerable countries. That would play well into Trump and Putin's short-term agenda and Father's longer-term vision." Chris stopped. He was obviously thinking on something. "Shit," he suddenly exclaimed. "I thought he was mostly dolling his money and fantasizing about unachievable dreams. But he is actively pursuing them. He is taking a more hands-on approach to this revolution of theirs."

"Bingo," Kat said. "By the way, how did Father react when you threatened him?"

"He gave me his most sinister grin. The bastard was still trying to recruit me. Why doesn't he get it? Isn't it obvious I hate his guts? Bottom line he did a non-denial, denial. But I could not tell if he would do such a thing or merely wanted me to believe he was capable of it."

Kat looked pensive. "Chris, you may have the most to worry about. Losing you to the other side is something he cannot accept. He must know it is hopeless, doesn't he? Yet, he keeps trying to lure you back - a sign of emerging insanity, perhaps? You know, trying the same hopeless gesture over and over. He really doesn't like to lose. Still, I worry a lot about Beverly, Jules, and even myself. And yet, I really think he will come after you, if he ever snaps that is."

"Ah, I'm a big boy. Besides, I can still run fast, have not gone totally over to flabby middle age."

"Don't joke, not about this." There was an intensity in Kat's voice that silenced Chris. "I never thought it would come to this when I enticed you over to the States. So sorry. Maybe we should rethink things?"

Chris reached deep for some positive note. "Well, maybe we are just getting too paranoid. Your near hit-and-run may have been just a drunk. We will see."

"Yes," Kay whispered uncertainly. "We will see."

Deena slipped into the bedroom where her sister was recovering. She sat quietly on the edge of the bed, simply looking at Azita's chest as it rose and receded with each breath. For an instant, she panicked at the thought that her respiration would suddenly stop, and her sibling would be gone forever. She knew that would not happen, but the fear remained in her.

"What are you doing here?" Azita murmured drowsily as her sister tried to rise from the edge of the bed just as quietly as she had arrived.

"Well, I slipped away from the others to see if you were resting well," Deena replied.

"Hah, fat chance of that when you wake me just as I am dozing off."

Deena grunted. "Good, then you know how I felt when you tortured me when I was recovering."

"But I knew what I was doing. You…you are just a teacher."

Deena winced. "Don't you mean just a lesbian teacher?"

"Oooh," Azita cried out.

"Where does it hurt." Deena was suddenly concerned.

"In my heart, you idiot. Why did you remind me about how awful I was, even if I didn't mean it? I am so sorry, my sister. I am such a selfish girl, not as selfish as you, but still…I keep thinking I am beyond that but no. You have every right to hate me."

Deena said nothing for a minute. "Turn."

"What?" Azita was confused. "Just turn. I am putting some salve on your contusions."

It took some doing but she finally got her sister turned and disrobed enough to see the black and blue down her backside. "Aach," she exclaimed. "If Ahmad could see this, he would cast you aside." Deena gasped at the discoloration. "This is hideous looking, worse than earlier I think."

"You have a terrible bedside manner," Azita said as her sister began to rub a soothing salve over the discolored area. "And Ahmad would not care about such irrelevant things. He loves me for my soul."

"No boy loves a girl for her soul" Deena now laughed aloud. "I cannot believe this, my sister the romantic. And why, for Allah's sake, did you propose in that restaurant? I never did get an answer." When Azita still said nothing, Deena hit her on her bruised rump.

"Ow! That hurt."

"Good. Now answer me," Deena insisted.

"Okay, but mercy! Even with the pills, it is still sore there." Azita tried to look back at her sister but the effort proved too difficult. "The truth, I have no idea why I did it. Okay, that is not true. I have a rationale, but I cannot believe I did it in the moment. You see…this is not easy. Let me start again. Mother, Amar that is, once told me I would know when the right man came along. There would be a connection, an electric feeling that was unique and unforgettable."

"Wait," Deena protested, "have you even touched this boy, kissed him? How could you have this feeling?"

"Once, for a few brief moments, we embraced. We kissed. It was enough. I knew, or thought I knew, in that very moment. Then, at the restaurant, the sight of him, the quick embrace, it all came back again. It was as if my mind and body froze. And then, when Abdul said that our generation must save our country, those words just came out of my mouth. It made sense in that moment."

Deena finished applying the salve and adjusted her sister's nightgown. "It is now official. You are a crazy woman. But we will find you a nice asylum." Then she leaned over and kissed

Azita's forehead. "I am so sorry for my anger earlier, so very sorry. I am confused. Perhaps we all are."

"I am also confused, about a lot of things," Azita murmured. "Here, alone in this room, I had a chance to think. Maybe, somewhere deep inside I am not such an advanced thinker as I wish to be. You just don't throw out all your old culture, your old ways." She grimaced as she moved onto her side. "Funny, I would sometimes imagine us both married, with our own children, and we would picnic on the Oxford green with our husbands, who would be perfect of course, though mine would be considerably more perfect than yours. Silly, but there you have it."

"Of course, that is silly. I would have gotten the perfect husband. After all, I am the family beauty." Deena brushed back some of Azita's hair that had fallen over her face. "But you have turned into quite a beauty yourself. When you smiled at Ahmad in the restaurant earlier…well."

"Well what?" Azita said groggily, the pills kicking in.

"Nothing, dear sister. But let us never forget, as you keep reminding me, you cannot take out what God has put in you."

Azita opened her eyes as if trying to understand those last words, then closed them again. "I love you Deena, never forget that. Please, never forget. You are my life."

"You get some sleep," Deena said as she took a couple of steps toward the door. "The part about returning to Afghanistan.

What about that?" Then Deena kicked herself, her sister was too far gone to respond.

The girl lying on her good side did respond though, with obvious effort. "I think so. There is much to consider, however. It seemed the right thing to say in the moment. I thought…" There, her words drifted to an end.

Deena looked back at the woman turning in a futile effort to find comfort from her severe bruises. "Sister, one thing. I don't want us to be separated, ever again. I am certain I will return home. I will break off my relationship with Karen. I will do it. And then…" She wasn't sure if Azita still heard her, the sedatives and pain medication had taken hold. Still, she thought she heard an assent, an agreement. Had she? It was impossible to tell.

Deena merely smiled. "I love you, dear sister." Then she went out the door.

CHAPTER 15

CHRISTMAS DAY

Chris sat pensively on the end of a comfy sofa. Stretched out next to him with her head resting on his thigh was Azita. She, of course, was impatient with her recovery. Each morning was agony as she stretched her body out from the night's rest and remained so until she fought her way through some exercises and the morning meds completely kicked in. Despite her training, she somehow believed the pain was part of the healing process, the more she felt during these morning tortures, the better it was for her. She would ambulate around the apartment with great determination for a while before dropping into some comfortable place with a semi-audible expletive. To make matters worse, Deena would bustle about her to attend to her needs while Azita griped at her attentions. Chris thought the sibling drama hilarious. Today, Azita tried to read but then dozed off while Chris pondered how long he could last without urinating.

For the first time in days, the place was mostly empty. Gifts had been exchanged in the morning and the debris from the gift giving was still largely evident. Amar and the girls had adjourned to Jamie and Kay's place where more gift exchanges would take place and additional celebrations would occur, this time with medical and personal friends. Chris had begged off. He wanted time to think. It was his default position, solitude and the absence of others. That was odd, he realized. He had come to terms with the dichotomy between his public and private selves. Every so often, quite often in fact, he needed his private space to regenerate his internal batteries.

Besides Azita, only Deena remained, ostensibly to care for her sister. That was nonsense, Chris concluded. He could take care of his daughter but chose to avoid alternative explanations for her sisterly attentions. Tension between Deena and Karen was now evident. That would soon work itself out, he thought, and hoped that the fallout would not be severe. In fact, just underneath the seasonal cheer, unrest seemed to bubble about him. Karen and Jamie remained the same in public, but he could read between the lines, now that he knew the truth. Even the Masoud sisters squabbled a bit more than usual. It is mostly the classic seasonal disorder, he concluded. It contributes to the worsening of all family discord. All this good cheer makes people cranky. He had said that for years, assuming the mantle of Mr. Scrooge. People dismissed his negative attitude but, damn it, he was serious… sort of. Better for people to avoid trying to generate too much good cheer, that was bound to end in disappointment.

He gently stroked Azita's hair, as he often did on the picnics the family enjoyed during summers at Oxford. On those occasions, she would pretend to be annoyed but he knew that she enjoyed his gentle touch. His mind turned to what would happen at the end of her internship. She already had the technical skills to practice in parts of the world desperate for her talents. She seemed to be drifting toward returning to Afghanistan. That seemed like a noble gesture when it was far off. Now that the real possibility loomed, it frightened the daylights out of him. How could he let her go back? The war continued. It was less intense in some ways, but the Taliban had been emboldened by America's diminished presence. People still died daily, and the Taliban held sway over a considerable part of the country. He could not shake the hollowness he felt that day when he heard Deena had been shot while visiting the original Masoud village.

He shook his head. He did not have to deal with that today, but he would have to push along his plan to steer her in a different direction, a place where her brilliance might shine. That was her gift, her talent, dammit. Alright, that might be his wish and not hers, but he was permitted an ounce of selfishness, was he not? Or had he used up all his earlier in life? No matter, he would do his best to keep her in England, even the States would do, without seeming obvious about it. He had to. The thought of losing her had become unbearable.

And what was this thing with Ahmad? He was supposed to be there for Christmas eve, but she put him off until she was feeling a bit better. He might be there later, when everyone returned. Something was up. Amar had warned him not to be surprised by anything at this point, but she hardly knew this boy.

Chris knew him not at all. Was he good enough for his pride and joy? Of course not, no boy was good enough. Karen vouched for him but what did she know, she was on the wrong team? Chris sat in his spot ruminating about raising girls. What would he do when his biological daughters hit puberty? He often joked about locking them up and out of harm's way, knowing what he was like as a horny teenager. Everyone laughed but now he thought seriously about the possibility. Perhaps he could get away with chastity belts. They weren't against the law, were they?

Then he chuckled inside, which he then realized had come out as a sound. He looked but Deena was in the kitchen, she had not seen him talking to himself. But really, a chastity belt was not so ridiculous. Hell, all boys wanted was sexual gratification, something of little interest to girls. Why did females even put up with lecherous juveniles? Why had they put up with him? He now shuddered at the thought of what he had been. These were considerations he seldom permitted to linger long in his mind when he had been a young man on the prowl. He tried to recollect his behavior during those years. Had he been a predator? No, not really. In truth, he had been passive, not seeking conquests and often turning them down. Opportunities came his way, due to wealth, position, and athletic reputation. When they did, he always calculated the price associated with sexual gratification, and there was always a price. Girls that he thought would be too clingy or obviously manipulative or not witty and clever enough to interest him were avoided. The more he thought on the matter, he had been far, far from the lothario others believed him to be. He had dabbled enough to justify his reputation but always circled back to Jules, always Jules.

He dared not move at the risk of waking Azita, whose hair he continued to gently stroke. Unable to reach a book or his laptop, he merely sat there permitting his mind to wander freely. It drifted back to the election. He found anger rising inside. He probably could have held off the pleas of his younger sister to abandon his now comfortable life and get involved if only the stupid Democrats had not blown it. Okay, he thought, he was angrier at the American people than the politicians. Voters were, on balance, dumber than the water buffalo he came across in some of the rural areas his programs served. Those beasts lumbered down dusty roads and reacted to a passing bus several seconds after it passed them by. The route to their brains apparently was a laborious one. Yup, just like Republican voters. How could they support such an obvious conman and habitual liar? How could working-class voters, riven with angst about diminishing economic opportunities and rising debt, turn to a man whose whole life had been dedicating to stiffing his creditors and fleecing others? Just how stupid were they?

Chris felt the flush of rage and frustration rise inside, feelings he hated and which he typically tried to repress by cauterizing his emotional self with a sharp wit. But there was no one to joke with there, just himself. Defeated, he let the anger sit there. Part of the problem, he knew, was the orchestrated and systemic campaign on the right, something they had been at since the 1970s. Most people fought out the political battles in front of them. But the hard-right, people like his father, were in this for the long haul. They had strategic initiatives designed to erode democratic principles and shape the political dialogue through the body politic, the courts, the universities, and the media, and the very creation of ideas and philosophical arguments. He had waxed eloquent on that broad campaign to create a permanent ruling class of the elite many times, daily it seemed in the past months. His liberal donors and supporters would nod their heads in agreement, but did they understand? Sometimes, he felt so isolated and alone. Kat understood, as did Ricky.

He also felt totally inept for the task he had assumed. He was not a politician. He hated that game. No, he was more of a social entrepreneur or policy wonk or, heaven forbid, an intellectual. Someone else should have been taking those guys on. His real weakness, much like that of so many on the liberal left, was that he believed in fairness and reason. He still believed that principles, like objectivity, accuracy, and real elections mattered. He believed that process mattered, that fidelity to the rule of law must be upheld no matter what. How naïve. The other side entered the ring without such onerous impediments. Winning was everything, no matter how it was achieved. Reason, evidence, truth, process, and fairness were concepts for losers, the weak, and they were not about to lose. It was a final struggle, and everything was at stake. They could feel that permanent control was in their grasp, nothing would stand in their way now.

Could his father have been right? Why not be on the winning side for once? That would have made life easier. But no, that as not tempting in the least! He simply was not like them. In the end, he was not his father. He never could be, never. He would rather be correct and kind and thus a loser than powerful and successful and therefore a winner. Sometimes, Amar would take him to a remote place where they could look at the night sky. She would tell him about the stars and things about the cosmos that astounded him - no longer an easy task - things she apparently learned from her brother. He loved those moments, as did Azita. They uplifted him, gave him a sense of peace and connectedness with things beyond himself that was both soothing and inspiring. Now, he was mired in the raw sewage that was the struggle for power and leverage. He was grubbing for money, not necessarily to help the dispossessed directly, but to fight an apocalyptic battle against a grim and implacable foe. Worst of all, he had put his family in jeopardy, at least he feared that he had. How had all this come to pass?

He looked down at Azita once again. How had she wormed her way so deep into his heart? Did she have some potion that she placed secretly into his drink? After all, she did know all that sciency stuff. No need to get into wild conspiracy thoughts, the answer was certain: large brown eyes that reflected the kindest and purest soul imaginable. Was it for the Azitas of the world that he fought this battle? He was about to ponder this thought further when the doorbell rang. Azita stirred and grumbled. Deena emerged from the kitchen and signaled that she would get it.

A moment later, he heard her surprised tone. "Ahmad, what are you doing here?"

After some confused and awkward conversation among the four of them, Azita and Ahmad wandered off to converse alone. Chris looked after them wondering if he should intervene in any way. Intervene? He caught himself, she was a grown adult. Rather, he asked Deena to join him. She had brought out something to eat which they ate in silence as Chris looked at the debris of wrapping paper and scattered gifts that always accompanied yuletide festivities. He enjoyed the memories of the morning for a few moments before turning to the topic he had turned over in his mind several times since his trip with Kay to pick up Kat.

"Deena, I want to ask you something. It is somewhat delicate so…"

"Yes, Karen and I will split soon," she said the words with little emotion.

"Wow, I was wondering how to even ask."

Deena looked at him with her large, open eyes. "I assumed that Kay might talk with you about her and Karen. I have wanted to talk with her, not to complain but to tell her I understand. She is agonizing over this and does not know how to approach me."

"Wow," Chris uttered. "I am not sure I understand. You seem very calm about this. Am I wrong? Are you torn up somewhere I cannot see?" He looked at her searchingly.

She continued to eat for a moment. Then she stopped, looking directly at him. "It is complicated. A Muslim woman is raised to believe there is only one pairing in life. One love, one God, one truth. It is all rather simple and, I suppose, symmetrical. Then, of course, they tell us nothing about the ultimate human connection, about the one emotional love that is supposed to complete you. How do you know when you have it, when it is right? Perhaps if something had been arranged for me but I doubt that even my sainted parents would have arranged a woman for me." She forced a smile at what she considered a witty remark.

"You know, Deena," he said looking at her with admiration, "you don't need to explain anything to me. It is not my place."

"Please, Chris, don't apologize. I want to talk about this. It is…I do not have many people to talk to here. There is Azita, but I feel I am a burden on her. Sometimes I envy that she has Amar. I miss a mother in my life, another close female. Even among friends and coworkers, I am separated by something, my preference for women or culture or gender or something. Somehow, you are okay. I don't believe you will judge me."

"Really…me? I am okay?"

"Of course, you are the one that would - what does everyone say? - mount a coat rack. How could you judge others?"

"Oh my God." Chris winced.

"No, no, that is a good thing, at least in this case. You will not think poorly of me, no matter what I say. I can just talk, and you will just listen, without much judgment." She paused and looked at him. Satisfied at some level, she continued. "You must understand what was happening when I met Karen. By this time, I realized that my sensual feelings were not…typical. I was not like other women. Of course, there was no one in my own culture with whom to talk. Yes, some women caused me to pause, I wondered about them. In the end, the taboo was too strong. I doubt you can have any idea."

Chris was going to disagree but realized that would be stupid. "Probably not," he merely said.

"My parents had died. Azita found a new family in you and Amar. I was a young adult but alone. My extended family, aunts and uncles, were rural and not like my own parents. They were much more traditional and conservative. I was uncertain and frightened." She paused as if seeing herself back in those times. "And then Karen started paying attention to me. I knew what she was, of course. To me, she was a person of authority and she was paying attention to me. It seemed a miracle at the time. She was…an answer."

"Deena, I need to ask something."

"Anything."

"Did you ever love her?"

The beautiful girl thought hard about his question. "Perhaps as much as my sister loved Benjamin, perhaps like that."

"I'm sorry, I should not have interrupted you."

Deena raised a fist to him in mock anger. "I have one rule for you sir. Do not apologize. My poor sister knows my wrath, but you don't." Then she smiled at him.

"Ah, yes, I have learned one thing over my long and adventurous life. Always agree with the woman. How do you think I survived this long?"

"Yes, a mystery for sure. But to answer your question, I liked her a lot. She opened so many things for me: my sexuality, my education, my exposure to Western thought, so much. For a while I thought this was love and all I might expect. Then, small things began to happen. We didn't talk as often, laugh as often. There were no big issues, and perhaps that was a problem. We went through our days without disputes or passion. It was comfortable. You know, I probably could have gone on forever like that. It was fine. But Karen needed more, I doubt that I was…passionate enough. Then Kay returned to the picture to provide that. Funny, I recall Karen saying that her initial fling with your sister had been a mistake, that Kay was no lesbian. I guess she is."

"Well, we all have had problems figuring out Kay."

"Yes, I suppose so, she is a complicated woman. Then, however, my sister made me think hard about things, nothing she did intentionally but more by example. How to explain this? She had this strange new relationship with Ahmad. I looked and saw a transformation in her. That...inspired me." She paused with a smile. "You do realize that they are alone in her bedroom, right now."

Chris started. "Really?"

Deena laughed. "You would make a terrible Muslim father."

"I am not worried. She could barely get off this couch, what trouble could they get into?"

Deena laughed aloud. "You underestimate her. I watched her fall for this boy almost without knowing him, and then loving him desperately from afar. Then, she told me what Amar said about falling in love with you. She knew, from the first moment, when she touched you. Azita knew, from the moment she embraced this boy, that he was the one. I never had that connection with Karen, with anyone. Perhaps it is a boy-girl thing. I suspect I knew it would not last with Karen after that. Time to accept the inevitable."

"Wow, I hardly know you Deena. You are a remarkable young woman. If you don't mind, I have another question for you."

"Please."

"How to put this?" Chris struggled for the right words. "What about the girls you adopted and brought back?"

"That is the biggest issue for me." She sighed, a hint of pain in her eyes. "At the least, I am comforted by the fact that their life here is infinitely better than it would have been. I will not walk away from them, totally. Karen loves them, as do her parents, and Kay…" She stopped.

"Kay has told me, I know."

"The girls will be loved, I have no doubt about that. But this is not without issues, I hope they never come to hate me. Still," she said quickly as if to escape an unpleasant topic, "I will feel more freedom to shape the life I want. I love what I can do in London, on a large scale, about educating girls but I need to stay connected to those girls out there who have little hope. I need to walk among their villages, sit in their classrooms, watch their faces as they learn new things. The wonder in their eyes is brilliant. Nothing matches those magical moments. The thing is… I have not worked this out yet, but I want to go between these two worlds. That may be selfish of me and I don't think that the life I see before me would be fair to any partner. I suspect I will go through life alone but that does not bother me."

"Really? Do you believe…"

"Yes, I know you are thinking I am responding emotionally. Perhaps I am." Deena was clearly struggling to find the right words. "People look at me and think I have an easy life. I know the world finds me attractive and thus assumes I have no challenges. But they are wrong of course. Inside, everything churns all the time. Why can I not be an ordinary female, grab some man and grow fat eating sweets while he supports me? Why do I feel so different?"

"Because you are better than most others. You do know we are alike in some respects."

"What, you are a secret homosexual?"

Oh, no," he said quickly, "not that. I mean that we are alike in being driven. You don't think I have not kicked my rear more than once for not taking the easy road? I could have led a life of debauched leisure luxuriating on the Costa del Sol as a hedonist, my biggest worries being which five-star restaurant to dine in that night and which gorgeous woman to pursue that day. Could never have done that, just could not. You know, people struggle for all kinds of reasons. Some face awful circumstances in life, some simply do not have the wherewithal to reach their simplest dreams, still others are just dedicated to hating their life no matter what. But some, the most unfortunate of all, are doomed to struggle precisely because they have both talent and opportunities and, most of all, a sense of purpose. They are perhaps the most damned of all. You, and your sister, see a world in pain and therefore must do something about it. That is your curse, your private and personal demon."

"Why a curse?" Deena asked.

"Because then you cannot grow fat eating sweets while leading a conventional life. Nothing is easy, and these are things we bring on ourselves. Everyone in my circle is like that, some more than others. We are all driven, obsessed by these larger purposes. You know, Amar has often taken me out to look at the night sky and the stars. She tells me all these wonderful facts about the immensity of the universe, probably in the hope that I will be brought to earth by my insignificance in this vast, strange universe."

"Does that work?"

"Never, some of us are hopeless, beyond any hope of being cured. You and Azita are among those so afflicted I fear." Then, he smiled. "I want to confess something to you. When I first stumbled upon you and Azita, I did not see the promise in you. My bad. I yet regret not formally adopting you, but we thought of you as a legal adult even then. I should have looked into it."

"Please don't apologize." Deena looked uncomfortable.

"Keep one thing in mind. You will do great things, my dear, great things. Of that I am now sure. And what I label a curse, that is something none of us should regret nor reject. As you struggle with things, never forget that you have Amar and I. Adoption or no, we think of you as a daughter. I mean that."

"Thank you." she managed to get out.

"But damn it," Chris said in a lighter vice, "we do agonize a lot, that is for darn sure."

She laughed in a self-conscious way. "I know you say that to all the girls, that they are destined for great things. Still, I cannot for the life of me believe it worked. Still, I hope you are right, I hope I have…" Then she trailed off before shifting into a stronger voice. "However, if I were you, I would not be concerned with my fate. I would be more worried about what your daughter is doing to that poor boy in her bedroom."

"Oh God, should I do something?" he asked as if the situation had just occurred to him.

"Aha," Deena exclaimed with some glee, "some father you are. And no, leave them alone. To get to the bedroom, you would have to get past me first. Amar and Kay have trained me where to hit you." She waived a clenched fist in his direction.

"Okay, I give. You probably know best. By the way, just what is the deal with Zita and Ahmad?"

Deena hesitated. "Well…that night of the accident, we met with Ahmad and his father, Abdul, at a restaurant. To my shock, Azita came right out and said…"

Chris looked perplexed. "Said what?"

"That she intended to marry Ahmad and they would return to help save their homeland."

Now Chris looked stricken, to Deena's dismay. "Perhaps I should have stayed silent, do you not like Ahmad?"

"Not that, I hardly know the boy. It is her intention to return home that saddens me."

Deena smiled at him. "A wise man told me that you cannot take out what God has put in."

"Yeah, I know that guy," Chris replied and smiled grimly. "He is a total idiot. One last thing, Deena. That thing about walking between cultures, between worlds. I have been thinking about that a lot, an awful lot."

She looked at him, waiting for him to explain. But it was clear he would not.

The young man and woman sat on her bed. Azita bravely fought to conceal the discomfort that never left her when she moved in the slightest.

"Azita, being with you here is hard for me, which is not the only thing that is hard." The young man said with a distinctly forlorn look on his face.

"Aha," she laughed, "you are bored with me already." Then his pun reached her. "Oh, you are such a naughty boy."

"Not so naughty I think." He joked while breaking into a sardonic smile. "I wish…I wish. Alas, Allah is toying with me. He has brought me close to you, but I have never touched…we have never. I should not go there, the thoughts in my head are not those of a good Muslim boy."

"As if you would know what a good Muslim boy is." She leaned over, wincing with pain at the effort, and kissed him on the cheek before pulling back quickly. "Not now, here. I want to, desperately, you must know that. But I want privacy and a body not wracked with pain and looking so terrible."

"Can I look?"

"Look at what? You have seen women before, many if the rumors spread by you are to be believed." She expressed mild bemusement.

"Not that, silly. I want to see your bruises, maybe I can kiss them and make it all better."

Azita scoffed. "That is just about the worst pass any boy has ever made on me."

"I bet there have been many…passes that is." He looked uncertain. "Wow, I am jealous."

"Good." But then she struggled up and partially disrobed so that he might look at her backside. "Happy?"

"Not really, your backside does look awful," he replied as he bent over and kissed near the center of the still-obscene discoloring. The he realized he may have been too honest and tried to recover. "But it looks not so bad, really, even this turns me on."

"Pervert." She pulled away from him but was laughing. "What am I to do with you?"

"That, I believe, has been decided."

"Oh my God." Dismay came over her face.

"Wait, you have not changed your mind, have you?"

"Oh no, I want you more than ever. That kiss did work miracles. Well, at least it did not make things worse. No, I just remembered. I blurted everything out in front of your father. What was I thinking? What must he think of me?"

"Aha," Ahmad smiled, "you are a brazen girl. I thought for sure I would have to call a cardiac specialist to restart his heart, and mine."

"Oh, I am so ashamed. My sister was so angry with me. That is why I am here, like this. We fought after leaving the restaurant and I ran after her, not looking for the traffic."

The young man shifted closer to her kissed her lightly on the lips. "It really was not bad at all. Good thing he knew your family and, oddly enough, loves you. Bad taste in women runs in the male half of my family, it must be a genetic weakness. In truth, my father is delighted with the thought of us as a couple, though he keeps warning me I will have my hands full with you."

Azita kissed him back and then lay her head on his shoulder. "He is right, you should pay attention to his wisdom. I will not be easy."

"I know," he said without hesitation. "He told me later that night, that when he brought me around to your father's clinic, he had dreams of an arranged marriage between us."

Azita broke into an astonished laugh. "No way!"

"It is true, I swear by Allah. But I don't think your father was enthusiastic. I must not have looked like a catch back then. And Pamir was wise enough to know that no one would tell you whom to marry. You were willful even then."

"Dear Ahmad, I still am, that same willful girl. That has not changed. You do realize that, don't you?"

"Yes…I…" He did not get to continue.

"Don't just agree. I am serious. Think about what you would be getting. I would be no typical Muslim wife. I don't even know how to cook. I am a terrible bargain."

Ahmad smiled gently. "Don't you think I have considered everything? I know what I would be getting."

"One more thing," she pushed on, "I may want to go back home…to help. That is not some idle sentiment. I am yet struggling with that but…are you sure about me, Ahmad, really sure?"

"Azita, I have never been more certain of anything in my life." Ahmad kissed her head. "We will work everything out, as long as we are together. Of that I have no doubt. It is not that I am a believer in miracles, or divine inspiration. Still, I am certain of us. This was meant to be. Remember, in the green at Oxford when I finally worked up the courage to approach you?"

"Of course, you were fortunate I did not have any pepper spray with me."

"Well, you hugged me, very briefly, when you finally realized who I was. I had fantasized about you for years, but in some idealized way. You were a mere abstraction. That touch, so innocent, sent a shock though me. I knew in that moment this was meant to be."

The young woman looked at him and then sighed deeply. "It is now official, I am hopelessly in love with you. It is good that my body will not work right now, or your virtue surely would be lost." She strained to lean forward and kissed him deeply on the lips. "May Allah have mercy on my soul. Unfortunately, I doubt Allah can save you since I fear you are totally lost."

People started to arrive from their various Christmas Day destinations. Chris looked carefully at Atle and Carlotta and saw evidence that long-simmering lust had been sated. Perhaps he should have a policy about sex among co-workers? Then he laughed at himself - like that would work. Besides, Atle worked for him but Carlotta worked for Karen. Technically speaking, they probably would not be breaking any workplace rules, if such had existed. Kat and Kay returned in a bubbly mood with even more packages. *Where in God's name can you shop on Christmas Day, isn't that illegal?* he thought to himself. Josef had arrived with his wife. Chris would have to introduce himself to her. Then he noticed April Song, and Pamela Stuart, and a few others from the Madison-based staff. Chris gave them time in London as a seasonal bonus. They were good, damned good. Besides, he would find a way to make Kat pay the bill. He noticed April would glance in his direction and smile. Was Kat right, did she have a crush on him? Wasn't he old enough to be her father? Then he noticed Karen, Amar, and his mother standing by the tree, talking away as if they had all been lifelong friends. Occasionally, the three would look toward him, share some words, and break into laughter. Finally, he turned to Deena who eagerly watched the display of merriment before her.

"Do me a favor. Go and get your sister, or at least break up whatever disgusting things they are doing. Her absence will be missed momentarily and Amar for sure will seek her out. I don't want her walking in on them mid…you know what."

Deena burst into a short laugh. "You are such a child. You can say sex or coitus."

"Say it? I don't even want to think it."

Deena arose. Before heading off to Azita's bedroom, she quickly took Chris's hand. "Thank you."

"For what?" He was perplexed.

"For this chat," Deena replied. "We never have talked like this. I can see why my sister adores you."

Chris broke into his crooked smile. "I bet you also say that to all the guys, oops, guess you wouldn't. Besides, she adores me since I am, guess what, adorable."

Deena rolled her eyes and quickly made her way through the crowd as his mother walked over and took her spot next to him. "Christopher, I am so glad you talked me into coming over here. I am sure Beverly would have been great company for me, and your childhood friends also offered me company, the Jacksons." Then she hesitated. "Can I admit something shameful? I was very uncomfortable around them when you were young."

"Why?" Chris asked while knowing the answer.

"Son, they were not…our kind."

"Did you think they would steal the silverware? Father did."

"Now, be kind to an old woman."

"Sorry." And he was, kicking himself for his uncontrollable wit.

"But I am afraid you are right. I was afraid of them, I think. It seems silly now, but I had so little experience in the world."

"Mother, you have no need to apologize."

"Yes, I do," she insisted. "I now realize how much you learned from that family, and how much I failed as a mother."

"Please…"

"No, let an old woman talk. Even when I first heard that you married a girl from India, suddenly I was flummoxed, and a bit discombobulated. I knew nothing about that place except that it was crowded and…colorful. But she is wonderful. Every time I talk with her, I come away realizing that it was she who married down in class."

"Mother, was that a joke?"

His mother smiled. "I wish it were. But when I think of all those girls you brought around when young. Oh, some of them gave me nightmares, some struck me as lacking in class."

Chris was tempted to say that was the point in selecting such girls but decided to be straight. "Yes, those were not my finest hours."

"I so feared you would turn out to be like your father. But you, all of you in fact, turned out totally different. I thank God every day for that, every single day."

"Now it is your turn to listen to me. I have thought long and hard about why we all turned out so different, just the opposite of Father. I suppose each of us, Kat and Kay and me, has a different story to tell but there is one common denominator."

"What are you talking about?"

"You, you are the common denominator. Whatever was inside you, no matter what you were thinking, you were always kind to everyone, no matter their culture or color or class."

"But that is just being a good Christian," she protested.

Chris wanted to comment that those professing to be Christian often were the most clueless about Christ's teachings but let it pass. "You were kind, mother, you always had empathy for others no matter how uncomfortable you might have been. You could not deny your own culture and upbringing but something inside helped you rise above it. At your core, you were kind and curious. In fact, I am totally convinced that all of us children inherited your traits. I believe you bequeathed to us what defines each of us. We all are not only very intelligent, Father is at least that, but also imaginative, inquisitive, and have large hearts. Those traits we did not get from Father, but from you. I want to thank you, mother, deeply. I know my sisters feel the same."

"Christopher..." She wanted to say more but tears were forming in her eyes and she looked away. "I still wonder where you got that awful sense of humor of yours, certainly not from your father or me." Suddenly, she arose. "Oh, there is Azita. I must see how she is doing." With that, his mother walked across the room while wiping her eyes away.

At that moment, Chris's cell phone rang. He glanced at the number and answered right away. "Ricky," he said. "Merry Christmas."

"Same to you, buddy. We are at mother's house. For some totally unfathomable reason, she wants to talk to you. Before I hand the phone over, how is my lovely spouse?"

"She is great, but one thing confuses me."

"What?" There was a hint of concern in Ricky's voice.

"She keeps bringing strange men back with her and claims they are distant cousins. But I know all the cousins, there aren't that many..."

"You are a flaming asshole, know that - great, mother is now yelling at me for being nasty to you. I think she prefers you to me. Then again, she doesn't know you like we do. Here she is."

"Christopher? Are you there?"

"Of course, mother Jackson. Merry Christmas."

"And to you. But I must apologize for my son. I did raise him better, you know. I always told him that he should be more like you, follow your example." There was a noise in the background, it was Ricky protesting. "But I suppose he didn't turn out too bad."

"Mother Jackson, you raised three great children, you should be very proud."

"Three, but there are only Richard and Julianna."

"Are you forgetting me? You helped raise me."

"Oh, posh. I cannot take credit for that. I did little…"

"Listen to me," Chris said, sounding deadly serious. "Listen to me carefully. I did inherit some good qualities from my mother, in fact I just thanked her for those. But as I grew into my teens, she was less…available. She was dealing with her own struggles. Did you ever wonder why I spent so much time at your home?"

"You were friends with my children?" She phrased it more as a question.

"That was part of it. The bigger part was what I was getting from you, and your husband. I learned what being part of a family was in your home, what love was all about, what decency meant.

I cannot thank you enough. There are no words to express the love I have for you and what you gave me."

Chris waited but there was noise on the other end but nothing he could make out. The first clear voice he heard was Jules. "Thanks a lot. Now you have my mother in tears."

"And Merry Christmas to you." He laughed.

"This from the Grinch himself. But I do thank you, whatever you said to mother has made her holiday season." Then in a lower voice. "I fear there is not much time left."

"I am stopping by to see her when I get stateside."

"Good, she will need another good cry by then. I think she has recovered though, she just yelled at me, once again, for not marrying you."

"Really, she wanted you to get stuck with me?" Chris said. "All this time I thought she liked you. By the way, I also made my mother cry a few minutes ago, good tears that is. But I fear she may finally be losing her mental sharpness."

"Really?"

"Yes, she went on about how much she came to like you and Ricky."

"Why, in God's name, why do I still serve you up softballs to knock out of the park, after all these years?" The tone of her voice altered a bit signaling a new topic. "Beverly stopped by a while ago, just to drop off some presents, then she wanted to get back to your Father, keep up pretenses. Chris, she seems stressed to me. She is worried about people following her. She is beginning to feel that your father's paranoia, or his suspicions, are on the rise. My advice - pull her out of that situation. I don't care what she is doing for you." She listened for a response before adding, "Are you still there?"

"Oh, sorry, yes. Just thinking. And what about you?"

"Me? I know I am being followed. He has also been having people talk to those who know me, probably to dig up dirt when we go public with what he is doing. My stories on him have been soft so far, but enough to concern him. Fortunately, I was such a saint in my past, just this ill-advised relationship with his son."

"Hah, hah. But seriously, be careful. Maybe you ought to stick to uncovering your everyday government corruption and sex scandals? There is plenty of both in Chicago. I worry about you, you know that."

"I know, but I am a big girl now. I can take care of myself. Just focus on Beverly, okay?"

"Got it, and hey, still love you kiddo."

"Me too, but now I have to go and cheer up mother and listen once again to all that BS about you being the best thing in my life. Okay, wish everyone the best for me." The call ended.

Chris slowly got up and made his way to the tree. He was headed toward Kat and Kay, who were still in deep conversation, but was turning over Jules's warning about Beverly in his mind. He paused by the tree as if to adjust some ornaments.

Most of the stateside staff had now gathered and were heatedly discussing politics. *How odd, yet predictable*, he said under his breath. Here they were amidst a seasonal celebration and they instinctively reverted to the substance of the professional lives. If it were just the females, perhaps they would be talking about their relationships and why the men in their lives were such pigs. If it were just the guys, he was sure the conversation would turn to sports and sex, or their lack of success in that latter arena. But the mixed group found common ground in a safe topic, their animosity toward the political drift in the States, which inevitably infected the world.

He now heard Pamela going on about the results she had found in her deeper analysis of political attitudes and behaviors among the American public. "Here is the thing. Americans are not as right-wing as the election results suggest. The problem is that between gerrymandering and the electoral college thing, a minority view prevails. Democrats have most of the votes cast, but Republicans control everything. Somehow, about 40 percent of the votes gets translated into a minority party holding on to power."

Chris walked over, and she stopped. "No, don't stop, please go on."

Now she seemed less sure of herself. "Well, I have been looking at the attributes of this great political divide we see. The Republican base is less educated, less affluent, and much more rural than the Democratic base. I estimate that each Democratic adult voter contributes $23,000 more dollars to the GDP on average. Why, you might ask? Well, they live in more dynamic parts of the country, the coasts, areas that still invest in education and the public good. Am I wrong?" She looked toward Chris for feedback.

When he did not immediately respond, Atle spoke up. "I have no doubt your analysis is correct, but we still have a conundrum. I have been looking at overall population sentiments, at least when it comes to political leanings. I find a slight population preference leaning toward the conservative side of things."

"How so?" Pamela asked.

"Well, these are all round numbers, but here is the big picture. About a quarter of the population don't give a shit and probably would have trouble identifying who is president, and certainly who is the VP. Of the remainder some forty-percent are passive liberals or conservatives, half lean one way and half the other. These are not the activists but, all things being equal, do have a measurable preference, rather a default choice if you will. Now we get closer to the true believers. My view of the data suggests about one-quarter constitute the liberal or progressive base. However, one-third fall into conservative or hard-right base with six to eight percent falling into the category of full-fledged Nazis with guns at their side and hate in their hearts. So, if I were to label this country, I would say it leans to the right, not as you described."

"But…" Pamela seemed to be thinking through her comeback.

April cut her off. "What do you think, Professor Crawford?"

"First, I think you should call me Chris, as I have mentioned many times before. Second, how many of you have read my book, *Confessions of an Accidental Scholar*?" He looked at the group as Atle and April raised their hands. "Well, I see that I should have made it a job requirement. No matter, in it I talk about the conundrums and complexities of making sense of policy questions at great length, it is a great sleep aid. No matter, when data exists in abundance, confusion and conflicting interpretations are inevitable. Guess I better make it a reading assignment." Then he broke into a big smile. "Finally, and this is my big point, why the hell are you talking about work stuff here? Relax, have some fun. And besides reading my book, which I am sure you all will do now, immerse yourself in some history. One example for now, look at the system of rotten boroughs in England in the first half of the 1800s. As the industrial revolution was taking off, the old landed interests fought hard to maintain their power. It turns out that many parliamentary seats were in rural areas with few voters. They existed by virtue of tradition and entitlement rather than any sense of democracy. The populace had moved to the cities but these largely inherited seats in rural places kept England's government from supporting legislation for a changing society. They voted repeatedly for policies that kept commodity prices inflated as the urban classes struggled to buy bread. They needed a revolution, not a violent one, but one that brought their democratic protocols up to date. That is the power of Pamela's analysis, the future of America has shifted to the coasts and big urban centers but the red states, largely poorer, less educated, and rural, are hanging on for dear life. They want to preserve a world that is past and doesn't even represent their own self-interests. The thing is, data is great but incomplete. Data, at best, describes but does not explain. You need a plausible narrative to give numbers authenticity, meaning, and power. Okay, now have some fun, damn it."

As Chris walked toward his two sisters, he heard Carlotta ask Atle. "Did you really read his book, or did you just say you did to impress him?"

"Nothing wrong with sucking up to the boss, Carlotta," Pamela interjected.

That was the last of the exchange Chris could hear. Now he approached Kat and Kay, who had heard his parting advice to the staff. Kat smiled. "Excellent advice for a change."

"My God," Chris responded to her, "they were talking work. When I was their age, I would have been plying some vixen with spiked eggnog in anticipation of exchanging some real season's cheer."

"Still the pig, I see, no wonder you loved those Porky movies," Kay offered. "I must see Amar about resuming the daily beatings."

"And what was with all those packages I saw you bring in?" Chris fought to regain the high ground. "More crap to exchange."

Kay hit her brother on the arm. "Nothing for you, Mr. Scrooge, so don't bitch. More stuff for the staff. Besides, I wanted to help out the British economy."

"I would say you are trying to keep it afloat all by yourself." Then Chris turned serious. "Listen. I just chatted with Jules, and mother Jackson who sends her best."

"I have got to visit her when I get back to the states," Kay offered in a wistful way.

"Don't wait too long," Chris said as he reached out to touch Kay's arm. Then Chris looked at Kat. "Listen, Jules had a warning. Father may well be spying on us. Jules is convinced that he is digging up dirt to use on her, but I guess I am the only skeleton in her closet."

"I am sure of it, that he is keeping tabs on us and not that you are the only skeleton in her closet, not that she has had a boring life…oh, never mind." Kat responded but obviously deep in thought. "By the way, it would be very embarrassing for her to be linked to you." Her witticism fell flat, no one was in the mood.

"No, it is worse than Father just spying on us." Chris realized he had not issued his warning clearly enough. "Jules thinks Bev might be in danger, that he has figured things out. Kat, have you forgotten your near-death experience in that so-called traffic accident?"

Kat considered his words. "No, but nothing has happened since. Maybe I was just imagining things."

"And maybe not. I want to pull her out of the cold."

"My God," Kay expelled. "Just listen to yourselves. You two are sounding like your players in a cold-war spy movie."

Kat and Chris turned on her as Kay fell silent, and she understood they were deadly serious. Kat spoke to break the momentary uncomfortableness. "Yes, whatever she can provide us about his doings is not worth putting her in harm's way. The thing is, we really do not know how evil that man is. We detest his politics and his ambitions, but he is our blood. Sometimes, in the middle of the night, when I cannot sleep, I fear the worst, that he would come after us all if pushed. Then, in the cold reality of day, I think that is just nuts. Most days, I don't know what to believe. But we cannot take any chances with Beverly, of that I am sure."

Suddenly Chris looked to the other side of the room. There was his mother with Amar and his two young daughters. Seated next to that group, enjoying the antics of the toddlers, sat Azita, Ahmad, and Deena. "Look over there. That is my family now. It was not that many years ago that I had only myself. I could take chances or go after dreams without thought or care. But now…"

"My fault," Kay interjected, "if I had not run off to Afghanistan to join Amar, you never would have come to drag me away and you probably still would be that carefree bachelor."

His head spun back to focus on his twin sister. "You are apologizing? Are you kidding? I owe you large. But it does complicate life. I now care so much about others, not like a do-gooder but in a far more intimate way." He stopped to organize the thoughts rushing through his head. "Listen, Amar feels lost in America, she wants to work more closely with ISO. Azita, I fear, is really thinking about spurning a research career in medicine and running back home with that new boy of hers."

"Really?" his two sisters said simultaneously.

"Yes, damnit. They spent time alone in her bedroom earlier, I did not know what to do."

"Oh, the horror." Kat said as the two sisters laughed.

"Okay, that was stupid. Seriously, though, Deena is convinced she will go back, as will Deena, since she and Karen are drifting apart." Chris kicked himself for letting that slip but quickly went on. "Frankly, I have been beside myself about this. Used to be that I only worried about what I would do when I grew up."

"And that was an easy problem since we all knew you never would." Kat said not so much in jest but with real concern. "Dear brother, you are a royal pain-in-the-ass, but I love you. I think even Kay loves you and we all now think of her as the sensible, rational member of the family. The thing is you are not alone.

Whatever comes up, whatever we must confront, we will do it together." Kat reached out to grab one of Chris's hands and one of Kay's. "It is no longer like the old days, when we let Father kill Chuck by driving him into a life he hated. We must each bear that sin for the remainder of our lives, but we are a family now, not intentionally separated by oceans or past hurts or hidden secrets or distorted views of one another. We are the Crawford kids and nothing, absolutely nothing, is ever going to separate us again." With that, Kat first hugged Kay and then Chris. Her gaze paused on her brother. "Who knows, maybe I will even start being nice to you."

"No, don't ever do that." Chris protested.

"What?" Kay protested, "Show affection in public?"

"Not so much that, but don't start being nice to me, that would really throw me off my game." Each of them smiled but knew somewhere that some threshold of familial bonding had been crossed. "Listen, I have been thinking about a day trip to Oxford, just the family. Mother can take care of the little girls, she will have plenty of help. But we must take Deena and Azita and what's his name? - Ahmad."

"He is family?" Kay inquired.

"Yes, I believe he is now. In any case, this place is like a zoo and Oxford is quiet this week. No problem getting a table at the Hairy Hare. I want us to talk things out a bit. Besides, I have been thinking, no wise cracks on that, and been touching base with people at the university. This engine never stops." He tapped one finger to the side of his head just above the ear.

"Oh my God, it sounds like you have a plan," Kat said with mock concern.

"I do, long in the works. Problem is, I have no freaking idea if it is any good."

CHAPTER 16

POST-CHRISTMAS: DAYTRIP TO OXFORD

Several days after Christmas, the Crawford clan wandered among the various colleges that made up Oxford University. It was a day after Kat had returned from a quick business trip to the continent. The weather was cool but not exceptionally cold for late December. It was not difficult to walk about that ancient town. What made the day special was a crisp, blue sky interrupted only by occasional layers of thin, high clouds. Chris acted as visitor guide, mostly for Kat and Deena's benefit, though even the others in his small audience who thought themselves familiar with the institution found themselves listening. He obviously loved the place, the history and the traditions, having absorbed more local knowledge than most natives. He often mused that, if he had to do it all over, he would have become a historian. He loved to immerse himself in the past of wherever he as. Perhaps that was why he preferred Europe to the States, it had more history as well as the architectural detritus of past eras. He could feel the people and events of former times yet vibrating through the cold stones, the spires that pierced the sky, and the stained glass that afforded some color to otherwise austere edifices. His life would have been much simpler had he pursued history as a vocation. Everything would have focused on the crusty past and not the momentous struggles of the present day.

During the morning they wandered through the buildings where Azita had done her studies, then the college where Ahmad was completing his. Most were rather quiet, but each ran into an old acquaintance or two and greetings were exchanged. They also stopped to show Kat and Deena some of Oxford's finest architectural wonders. Oddly enough, even those who had lived in Oxford looked upon those structures with the enthusiastic eyes of tourists visiting for the first time. *Funny,* Chris thought inside, *you can pass a site a hundred times and never really see it. Bring someone else and you notice it for the first time.*

After stopping for hot drinks to refresh themselves, Chris looked at his watch. "Okay, time to be off. I want you to meet some colleagues of mine. They have some ideas they want to share."

"Really?" Azita mildly protested. "I was thinking of tracking down some friends."

"Nope," Chris responded a bit too quickly and emphatically, "this is a must-do engagement for all of us. This time, I am speaking as your father…and uncle I suppose." He looked from Azita to Deena.

Azita first looked at Deena, who shrugged, and then back at her father with a puzzled expression. She was confused by the mystery of it all. Why was this being sprung on her and Deena like this? About twenty minutes later they were being ushered into an ornate conference room. An attractive woman was seated at one end of the table. Perhaps in her mid-30s, she had the dark hair and light brownish skin that suggested she might be of Mideastern origin. As she rose, Chris walked directly to her, shaking her hand. "Good to see you again. It has been too long."

"I agree," she responded, dropping his hand and giving him a brief hug. "Many of us were not happy to see you run off to America."

"True, I never did explain, did I?" He gave the tiniest of shrugs but continued quickly before she could respond. "Duty called, which I will explain more fully one of these days. But first, I want to introduce you to…"

At that moment, a side door opened. A tall, angular man of distinguished bearing entered. He held himself with the easy grace one associated with the upper British classes, quickly surveying the scene and satisfying some internal calculation that all was in order. "Ah Christopher, the prodigal son returns. Good to see you. You look none the worse for wear for having spent far too much time in the former colonies. And Amar, how lovely to see you again. Now, the fact that he took you away from us is the sin for which we have never forgiven your husband."

"Neither have I," Amar said with a genuine smile.

"Listen everyone," Chris said as he looked to his group as they stood about not sure what to do. "I want to introduce my favorite Oxford Don, Sir Charles Howard, and this lovely woman is a rising star at this fine institution, Dr. Shahed Al-Hussein." Chris then went about introducing his entourage before they sat down around the table. More *bon mots* were exchanged between Chris and the Don while tea and biscuits were served.

Suddenly, Sir Howard cleared his throat. "I suspect we should get started. Let me say a bit about my past, not necessarily because I am an irredeemable egotist, which many of my colleagues believe to be true, but because I believe it is somewhat germane to why we are here." He rose and walked to several pictures on the wall. "See these fine gentlemen. These are my male ancestors, all Oxford dons, though if you go back far enough, you will find a Cambridge don or two but that was before photography had become popular. Besides, such traitors would never be permitted to grace these walls. My great-grandfather here fought in the war to end all wars, was gassed at Ypres. He never fully recovered but it did not slow him up though he sadly passed too early in life. My father here could have had a safe post during World War II in the war office but volunteered for active flight duty in the RAF. Had a marvelous record and survived two crashes, escaping only with a distinct limp that, again, never slowed him up. Go further back, and you will find a Howard who served under Wellington at Waterloo. You are asking yourself, why is this doddering fool boring us with his family history?"

"I was," Chris quipped.

"Shush," Amar chided him.

Sir Howard laughed heartedly. "That is precisely why we miss him, that American irreverence. The point is that these men made real sacrifices for a better world. Their examples of duty and loyalty to something beyond themselves have always stayed with me. On the other hand, I have been fortunate enough never to have been asked for any special commitment. I have spent my life cloistered in this fine place as so many of my lineage before me. Then, when my best years as an active scholar were behind me, they kicked me up into the higher levels of university administration where I could do little harm."

"Or where you might apply your leadership qualities and vision to greater effect," Chris interjected.

"Watch out for this one," The elder man cackled. "He is way too charming."

"I found out that too late," Amar added.

"Yes, my dear, you did." Sir Howard chuckled again before turning serious. "You know, if you go north from here, about an hour or so, you can visit the Howard estate, one of the great houses open to tourists. What made my family somewhat special, in my eyes at least, is that my predecessors remained true to that in which they believed. Many, though not all, stayed within the church of Rome when such an act was viewed as treason. They hid priests and attended the Latin mass when discovery might have led them to the block where they would have met whatever awaited them on the other side." Then he looked directly at Azita and Deena. "Do you get my point?"

The two girls looked at one another before Azita spoke in a hesitating voice. "I suspect you are telling us to be true to what we believe."

Sir Howard smiled. "Dr. Masoud, you will not recall me, but I was on the dais when you gave your Profile in Courage talk a number of years ago. In fact, I pushed your candidacy for the award and was most distressed when you ran off to the colonies to do an internship after medical school here. I almost called on you personally to persuade you to remain with us but was informed that such a gesture would do no good. Now, however, I think it is time for me to make a different pitch."

"To bring me back to Oxford, Sir Howard? Oh, I don't think…"

The elderly man raised a hand. "I will exercise a prerogative of age and position to suggest that you listen before saying no. May I be permitted that?"

"I am so sorry, Sir, that was very rude of me." Azita looked mortified.

'That is quite alright. By the way, please call me Charles. And may I call you Azita…and Deena?" Deena's head snapped up in surprise. They both nodded affirmatively. "Excellent. Let me start by affirming that I love this institution. I have been very happy here. Yet, I am fully aware of its limitations. We are too cloistered, too removed from the real world. We need more connections to the world outside our college greens, not just in Britain, but in the wider world. While Britannia has enjoyed a remarkable run across the globe, at least for a small island, it also has inflicted pain and mischief in many areas. Alas, our history in Afghanistan, and the Middle East writ large, is not exemplary to say the least. We acted with such unwarranted hubris. I yet recoil at the thought that our foreign office simply drew lines on a map after World War I that became national boundaries. There was no notion of caring about indigenous religious and ethnic affinities. Only the interests of the West mattered. Our sin was to divide people into artificial enclaves with no concept of respecting the deep enmities that existed among them. It was a recipe for disaster and disaster ensued, as anyone with a bit of intelligence and compassion might have foretold. Perhaps there was no perfect solution to the tensions that existed, but we did not even try. Dr. Al-Hussein, that is Shahed, and I have talked about this at some length and I will, much to your relief I would say, turn this over to her in a moment. Of course, we cannot make amends for all our past sins. But we can start. Thus, what Shahed will describe now addresses some of my deeper - how shall I put it? - irritations. This initiative will break down the walls that separate the academy from the world, at least a bit, and perhaps expiate some of our past sins. That is a long-winded way of expressing my support for what Shahed will now explain."

She looked about the table for a moment as if calculating where to begin. "Chris and Amar know me but let me say a few words about my past for the rest of you, especially Deena and Azita. Much like the Masoud sisters, I was raised as a Muslim, a Sunni Muslim, in Jordon. With respect to our early years, that is where our life experiences depart. You two were raised by the most twisted version of Islam imaginable, that oppressive set of beliefs imposed by the Taliban. I was more fortunate, having been raised in a cosmopolitan family that expected all their children, including the daughters, to succeed. From my last name, you might be wondering whether I am related to the Jordanian royal family. I will confess. Yes, but it is a rather distant connection."

"Not as distant as she suggests," Sir Howard interjected, "but all her achievement have been earned on her own."

Shahed smiled. "Charles and I have different interpretations of a close connection. In any case, my path was easy. I could always wear Western attire, immerse myself in your culture and music and films, study what and where I wanted, and even date whom I wished, though some discretion was demanded on that last matter." At that point, she glanced at Deena who instinctively looked away. "Thus, I was free to study at a better public school in England, then try Harvard to get a taste of the States, before finishing up my graduate studies here."

Chris could not resist. "If I had known her then, I would have steered her toward a decent American college - Princeton."

"Frankly, I am shocked that they let Princeton remain in the Ivy League," she responded as Chris raised his hands in mock surrender. "My point is this. Though born a Muslim girl in the Middle-East, I was never held back. I had every opportunity denied to so many girls whose potential is thwarted and destroyed. It sickens me that we yet have honor killings and genital mutilations and forced marriages of girls barely reaching puberty to men they do not know. Fanaticism in the name of religion, whether practiced by Muslims or Christians, is the very definition of sin to my mind. We all should execrate such practices. They are an abomination to everything we hold precious and a waste of human potential."

"On that," Deena spoke up, "we can surely agree. But why have you brought us here?"

Shahed sighed subtly as she transitioned to the topic at hand. "Sir Howard, myself, and I believe your father here, at least to the extent that I know him, are all motivated by a sense of guilt. We have had all the advantages while others labor under cultural limitations, if not outright oppression. I am not naive, we cannot raise everyone up. There are real differences in talent, disposition, and motivation among people. These differences are real. But we can do better in elevating many of the future generation so that they, in turn, can contribute to their own communities and cultures." Then Shahed leaned forward. "Listen carefully to me. Chris has told me about the schools you have started back home, the first was in the Panjshir valley I believe, and Amar has filled me in about the pilot programs you wish to start in Afghanistan with Drs. Gupta and Singleton. These are exactly the kinds of initiatives we have in mind to launch our program, but in ways that can use the power of the university to maximize their impact."

"What program?" Azita looked confused and a bit wary.

"Yes, I am not being direct. You young women can only do so much by yourself, even with the assistance of your father's organization. Here, at Oxford, with Sir Howard's strong support, we want to launch a new center of study and innovation dedicated to reaching the young women of the Middle-East, Muslim girls of all persuasions for whom the future is bleak indeed. Momentous change starts with great ideas and universities are the incubator of great ideas. I am convinced that an academic setting is perfect for what we have in mind. In this institutional setting, we can document what young girls are facing, spread that knowledge to the world, devise new strategies and tactics for reaching them, and recruit the best and brightest to advance their educations and help us with this endeavor. You have talked about the power of technology among yourselves, which is our advantage. It will be like a crusade though from the Muslim side and devoted to doing good."

"I still do not understand. Why are you telling us this?" It was Deena who asked.

"Oh," Shahed seemed somewhat surprised, "so you can help us run this program of course, be my right-hand women so to speak. We three Muslim women will launch this concept. I believe Deena has a master's level academic degree, but I think we can find a way to have her finish off her terminal studies. It helps to have a terminal degree in such a classist world as this, especially if you are to teach courses here. The academy is so stuffy about credentials, no offense sir Howard."

"None taken," he responded.

"Of course, we will work closely with your father's operation, well I guess it is Karen Fisher's now, but I will always associate it with Chris. That always helps in the academy, that one of their own created something. We, members of the academy, are a closed-minded lot. Again, no offense, Charles."

He now laughed. "None taken, I totally agree with you."

"Think of it this way," Shahed was now enthused. "What do you call it, Chris, the ISO?" He nodded. "That will be the operations arm of our initiative while the university-based center will be the incubator of new ideas and the developer of the next generation of talent to carry on the work. One part of this initiative would be to bring the best and brightest of young

Muslim women to study at our best universities, become leaders for the next generation like you are becoming. You two, Deena and Azita, are perfect for launching what we have in mind. You lived the very life we want to bring to other girls. You know it better than anyone else, both the challenges and the possibilities. Moreover, you are smart, brave, and share the values we need. Both of you are perfect for what we have in mind."

"This is rather overwhelming," Azita mumbled.

"I fear your father did not say anything in advance."

"No," Chris admitted, "I am a terrible dad, but I was afraid they would not come. I will explain later."

Azita looked at Chris, her look of confusion dissipating somewhat. "One question, from where are the resources for this center coming?"

Shahed looked to Sir Howard who answered the query. "The Mary Kelly Foundation. Chris's mother has created a very generous endowment to support this venture, with additional support having been pledged from her children. There were surprisingly few conditions attached to this gift other than to provide a name. It shall be known as the Pamir and Madeena Masoud Center for the Advancement of Muslim Women."

"Mary Kelly?" Amar was confused.

Chris leaned toward his wife. "Mother's maiden name, she is jettisoning her married name, I don't blame her. I am thinking of doing the same." Then he smiled. "How does Christopher Singh sound to you?"

Deena fought to control her voice. "This is such an honor to our parents, I am…we are…" She could not quite finish the sentence. "Still, I must ask one thing. I have never considered myself a brain. I am not sure I would fit in here. Are you only asking me because of the money?"

Shahed stood, so suddenly that Deena fell back a bit in her chair. "I will say this once. Wanting you, both of you, has nothing to do with the money, nothing. And do not sell yourself short, young lady." She looked directly at Deena, "I have checked you out, both of you. I have talked with your professors and those who know you, including associates in Afghanistan. I want you, your talents and your experience and your vision. Is that understood?" Then she returned to her seat, a little chagrined at her outburst.

"Yes," Azita was the one to respond, "understood. I have many questions but one big one."

"Please," Shahed prompted her, now in a soft voice.

"I have struggled with working in my homeland, of going home. In fact, Ahmad and I have talked about returning. This would make it more difficult, I think."

Azita braced for another strong reaction but Shahed smiled and spoke in measured tones. "Ah, yes, I do want to talk with Mr. Zubair. But listen, why don't the four of us meet by ourselves for a while, perhaps a half an hour or so? I suspect we can be more open among ourselves. The others can do what they wish while we go over details."

Chris, Amar, and Kat settled in comfortable chairs in Sir Howard's luxurious office. Kay lingered to admire his ornate personal desk made of deep mahogany. "Ah," Sir Charles offered without prompting, "everyone admires the desk and the paintings, which go back to King Charles before he lost his head. The paintings go back to Charles, not the desk. That was a gift from the Duke of Marlborough around the period of the Napoleonic Wars. I suspect it was a bribe to accept one of his less-than-ambitious offspring and give him an undeserved satisfactory at the end of his term. Alas, we are now into the meritocracy thing these days. Today, the bribes must be considerable and in cold cash to support the university."

Kat spoke first. "How long has this been in the works? I don't know much about how universities operate but I do realize that they move with glacial slowness. I often complain about how long it takes to make changes in the business world but let's face it, we move at the speed of light while you…" Her thought ended when she noticed her brother grimace at her directness.

"Molasses," Sir Charles laughed heartily.

Kat blushed. "Please forgive my directness."

"Give it not a second thought. This is precisely why we love Americans and so much appreciate your brother's willingness to remain part of our academic family. We Brits, the upper crust that tend to inhabit the academy that is, are way too indirect. It is not as bad as it used to be yet still can be found among old codgers like myself even to this very day."

Chris smiled. "I typically do not let my younger sibling join me in polite company, she is a constant embarrassment. It is okay for her to insult her business colleagues but…"

Sir Charles raised a hand. "No, she raises a good point. It has been a while since Christopher came to me with this concept. Obviously, the endowment from the matriarch's trust jump started the process and permitted me to circumvent some of the usual turf and budget wars. We were expanding the pie and not redistributing existing spoils among the restless crew. You have no idea how protective academics are of their individual fiefdoms."

"Yes, I think I can. That is where our two worlds probably overlap," Kat added.

Sir Charles nodded approvingly in her direction. "Yes, I suspect we are talking about universal human traits, are we not? I must note that the resources helped but it was more than that. Personally, my own national sense of guilt, of which I spoke earlier, was important but larger factors were in play. Islam is the fastest growing religion in England. It is now a major cultural force in this land. This institution cannot remain an isolated island dedicated to beliefs and principles long past. We must acknowledge the diversity in our land, embrace it, weave it into our identity and national fabric."

"Would you mind taking that lesson to our president-elect?" Chris threw out.

"I could try, but I fear the man is uneducable." Sir Charles chuckled. "Permit me to continue. Another key building block was bringing Shahed on board. She is key, totally respected within the university, tireless, devoted, and with wide connections among the Muslim community. She appears to throw herself into her work, never married, no children. Rather the exception in her world, no? In any case, among the more financially successful adherents to Islam here, she has already garnered significant pledges of economic and community support. Many of these people want to recast Islam in a more positive light, they are appalled that their religion has been hijacked by fanatics and extremists that impose an ideology they despise and reject. They also cannot accept that so many young women are relegated to hopeless, servile lives. Yes, the response has been amazing. We will have the ability to expand rapidly." Then he paused as if to change directions. He looked directly at Chris. "I am still puzzled by one thing: why not bring your daughters on board from the beginning? Why spring this on them so late in the game?"

"Ah, yes." Chris looked down at his hands. "By the way, only Azita is my legal daughter by virtue of adoption, but you are correct it turns out. I now think of both as my daughters." Amar reached over and squeezed his hand as he concluded. "I have been afraid at how they might react, I wanted the proposal to be set first."

"Afraid? I am not sure I understand."

"You see, Charles, I first came to you when Azita decided to return to Afghanistan with others from my international service organization, rather than do medical research with Professor Aronson. I knew, or at least suspected, that the tug of her culture, her sense of obligation, was winning the battle for her soul. Later, it became apparent that Deena was leaning the same way. This is selfish of me, I know, but the thought of them returning for good scared the crap out of me. That is what their father did, went back after finishing his medical studies at this very university, and he and his wife were butchered one morning. Then Deena was almost assassinated on a visit. I could not push those thoughts out of my head. I cannot keep them out of harm's way, not totally. I guess I am negotiating the best deal I can get."

Sir Charles leaned forward. "You do realize, my boy, that this initiative will not keep them totally safe, they will spend time back in harm's way, not as much, but it cannot be avoided."

Chris sighed. "Yes, but I will feel more connected to their lives. I wish I could say that I am doing this for altruistic reasons. Yes, that is a big part of it, but I also want to remain part of their lives, to be able to protect them as much as I can. Is that wrong?" He looked first at Amar and then swung toward Kay.

"No," his twin sister whispered, "it is not wrong at all."

"Well, I have gotten my just punishment for leading a rather dissolute life for so many years. I guess there is such a thing as karma. I now find that I love those two girls totally and that is the greatest feeling possible - and the worst."

Amar leaned over to her husband and whispered, "I love you."

He seemed not to hear her words. Instead, he regained control of himself. "Did I answer your question about why I kept this from the girls - young women - I mean? Let me try again. I was deathly afraid of their reaction, more Azita's than Deena's. You must understand Charles, Azita - both really - are headstrong. From what I know, they got this from their mother, an educated and headstrong woman herself. If they thought this was merely a plot to keep them from going back home permanently, they would have rebelled. I would be challenging their independence, their right to seek a path in life that is theirs. I could not separate them from their identity and their culture, not by some all-too-transparent wiles. They would reject that, and I am not clever enough to fool them. I had to come up with an offer they could embrace with their hearts, which meant it had to have advanced to the point where it was real and something they could not easily reject. Hell, I was on pins and needles in that room, expecting Azita to jump up and leave. I still don't know if she will accept this, nor Deena, with absolute certainty. But I grow more hopeful the longer that conversation in the other room continues."

Suddenly Kat stood up and walked to the office window. She looked out over the ancient buildings and, being high enough, could catch a glimpse of the countryside beyond. "Yes, I can see how this place can capture one's heart. I thought Madison might be good competition but…" Then she turned back to the group as all looked at her. "Chris, Amar. I have been selfish. I wanted my brother near me as I took on Father. But, in truth, Chris can help me from here. It was just my residual insecurity. I never let it show but I looked up to this lug. We are all tugging at him, but he now has a real family, real people to love. You must return here next year, Chris. Bring Amar back where she belongs. Be nearer to Kay, your daughters, your real work. We will work something out. Hey, we are the Crawford kids - we are nothing if not resourceful." Her voice caught at the end.

Chris stood and walked over to her, embracing her. "You be careful," Kat murmured to him, "people will think we actually like each other."

He laughed as he released her. "That would be a tragedy." Then he turned to the group. "Listen, I am hungry. I hear the Hairy Hare calling. Let me pop my head in and, if they are still going strong, let them know where we are headed."

He slipped through the door but returned momentarily. "They are huddled about a laptop, no idea what is going on, but they seem to be very engrossed in whatever it is." Chris beamed.

"They promised to join us in a bit. In the meantime, to the Hairy Hare."

"The Hairy Hare, really?" Sir Howard appeared astonished. "I know of a much more authentic establishment."

Chris cut him off. "Tradition, Charles, surely you understand tradition."

⤮

"The Hairy Hare is not quite the same with Karen missing," Chris noted as they sat at a table big enough to accommodate the whole crowd when Azita, Deena, and Ahmad arrived to join them. "I wish there were not this tension between Karen and Deena."

"Why is that? Not the tension, I get that, but why is the Hairy Hare not the same? Unfortunately, it never changes," Amar offered.

Kay cast a suspicious eye in her brother's direction and said, "I bet I know. You cannot make your usual tasteless jokes about Karen's rack and compare it to the barmaid's."

"Tasteless, perhaps, but she would be disappointed if I didn't make them."

Kay stuck her tongue out at her brother but decided not to continue that discussion. "Here is my thought. The fact that they are still talking is a good sign. Dear brother, I hate to admit this, but you are a clever sot."

"Methinks that is the best compliment I am likely to get from my sister who has always been bitterly jealous of my many skills and accomplishments."

The rest of the table looked at him for a moment before breaking out in laughter. Amar then turned serious. "Kat, what you said at the end. I am grateful but now I feel guilty."

"Yikes," Kat uttered loudly enough for nearby customers to turn in her direction. She continued in a lower register. "What is with the goddamn guilt today? It seems infectious. I am convinced that this is what separates you people from ninety percent of the sharks I deal with every day. You people care, for Christ's sake. You are capable of empathy. You cry at sad events and disasters. Most of the wealthy have no souls whatsoever. They are an abysmal lot of blatant narcissists and stone-cold sociopaths, but that is my burden. Amar, I am fine with my decision on this though I am not sure I could have kept Chris with me even if I tried. But here is the thing, and I have thought hard about this. His presence is not essential. I still need his mind and his connections and his persuasive powers. But he can operate out of Oxford or London or wherever. That is the blessing of modern communications. Come back here when Azita finishes her internship. By that time, we will have a plan."

"Another plan? The Soviets had nothing on us," Chris quipped with a broad smile as Kat threw a pretzel in his direction.

Amar rolled her eyes. "It is amazing they still let us in this place, the way you children keep throwing things at each other." With that the three Crawford siblings each threw a pretzel at Amar who squealed as she ducked to avoid the missiles.

"Seriously," Kat said. "You have to understand I was the kid sister, the quiet one who had almost zero self-confidence at first. Maybe I still suffer from just a little bit of insecurity, nice to have my big brother around to protect me and all that crap. But I am past that now, mostly, I think. I am a big girl. Besides, I have Ricky and a crack security team. The big test is when I must confront Father mano-a-mano. Hmm, that doesn't quite work, does it? If I can go head-to-head with him and not wet myself, then I know I am there."

"I don't know. You are a better man that any of the guys I know." Chris laughed and instinctively ducked, but no one threw anything. "Seriously, I do have a plan, well, a concept at least. Tell me, what political thinker said the following: *What good fortune for governments that men do not think.*"

"Ah, Socrates," tried Kay tentatively.

"Machiavelli," asserted Kat confidently.

"No," said Amar, "sounds like Winston Churchill to me."

"Should have done your homework. Adolf Hitler. Another one, easier. *'Can we build a wall high enough around this country to keep out the cheaper races?'*"

"Trump, of course," Kat offered absent hesitation.

"Give the lady a parting gift, Don Pardo. No, it was a man named Madison Grant, an early advocate of eugenics. My point is that he, along with Charles Davenport and Henry Goddard, along other devotees of eugenics, sold a simple idea to the American public about a century ago. Their big idea was that certain races were deficient and, by their very presence, polluted the pure American stock. Sound familiar? They had no rigorous empirical evidence, merely supposition and anecdotal examples. *Look at those Irish and Slavic immigrants,* they proselytized, *they are uneducated, diseased, given to drunkenness and sloth, and very likely to be of a criminal nature.* The eugenicists stressed that these deficiencies were not a choice. No! It was inborn and could not be cured. It was in their biological makeup and the only sensible policy was to keep the riff-raff out of the country and away from the pure American stock. They wrote numerous books and tracts and lectured relentlessly. Their impact went well beyond our borders. Hitler, in writing *Mein Kampf,* borrowed heavily from their writings. After 1880, a million immigrants a year poured into the country, some 75,000 through Ellis Island in most months. Starting in 1921, the eugenicists had put such fear into the country and its politicians, that the flow of newcomers was slowed to a trickle and remained so for over four decades. Their unsupportable idea became the national consensus."

"I sense a point is about to me made," Kat said hopefully.

"Of course. Most political types fight in conventional ways. They battle about candidates and short-term agendas and raising money and oppositional research to prove the other guy or gal is Satan. All well and good, that stuff needs to be done. Where the hard-right has dominated in recent decades is in the battle for the conceptual and normative underpinnings of the political discourse. Where are the default positions? Government is bad. Free markets are perfect. All benefit from unfettered capitalism. The mainstream media, and science, cannot be trusted. Diversity is a danger to America. We are constantly under some immediate threat by an ism - pick one. The poor are morally bankrupt and therefore responsible for their own situation. Guns really save lives despite our American carnage - a national embarrassment. The life of the embryo is sacred but, once born, if you have a pre-existing condition and cannot afford health care, tough shit. The list goes on." He took a breath as he decided where to go next. "Listen to this for a moment. You have heard me, and Kay, wax eloquently on how sad the American healthcare system is, the costliest in the world, by far. At the same time, it bankrupts tens of thousands of families each year, killed some 40,000 per year before Obamacare, and delivers generally sucky health outcomes on average. Yet, your average American will rail against Obamacare and socialized medicine while saying nonsensical things like 'get government out of our healthcare and expand Medicare instead'. I am speechless when I hear people talk."

"You can't fix stupid," Kay argued.

"No, not entirely. But we can take a page out of the far right's playbook. We need to win the war of ideas. There will be a lot of people doing the usual political stuff, getting out the vote. We need to focus on the power of ideas. Just think about the arsenal of weapons the right employs to shape the political dialogue: the Cato and Heritage Institutes, Citizens for a Sound Economy and the Club for Growth and the Americans for Prosperity and Freedom Works and the State Policy Network. Oh, and don't forget the Competitive Enterprise Institute or the Tax Foundation, the Reason Forum, the leadership Institute, the Federalist Society, and ALEC. Oh, how did I forget the Manhattan, Hoover, and Bradley Institutes, along with a growing number of media outlets to spread their propaganda? Has Murdoch bought up all the outlets yet?"

Kat looked at him for several moments without saying a word. "Hmm," she finally said. "I did wonder about what hook I could use to rope my sympathetic business colleagues into a more formal partnership. I have some meetings already set up to talk about the coming Trump debacle with money people like Tom Steyer, George Soros, Susan Sandler, and Gara LaMarche, to name a few. I wish we could flip more of the next generation of the elite. Listen, write something up for me, okay? In fact, join me."

"I will. But listen, the work our staff is doing will be very useful no matter which direction we go. They are drilling down into the deeper segments of the American political mind, who believes what and where are they. We can play the same game the Russians apparently are playing, targeted messages and misinformation. For us, we will not target misinformation, but real, evidence-backed information tailored in a way that people might listen."

"Oh look," Amar cried out as Kat was about to respond. "The prodigal children have decided to join us."

Azita, Deena, and Ahmad found seats as everyone looked at them. For several seconds, there was awkward silence.

"Well?" Amar could wait no longer.

The three newcomers looked at one another. Then Azita spoke up. "We turned the offer down. Shahed is a phony, we saw right through her. Connection to the Jordanian royal family my foot."

Deena then supported her sister. "And that Sir Charles whatever, where did you find him? Is he a paid actor?"

Ahmad just nodded his approval but added nothing.

"What!" Chris sputtered. "You did what...?" Then he lapsed into silence, not knowing what to say next.

Azita turned to her two companions. "Ahmad, Deena, look carefully. You are witnessing a miracle. After all these years, I have rendered him speechless." Then she broke into a broad smile, followed by the other two.

Chris continued to register uncertainty for another moment before his face relaxed into a grin. "Hoisted by my own daughter. Remember, young lady, I can still put you across my knee."

"And I keep reminding you, old man, you would have to catch me first. Besides, now I have a strong, young man to protect me."

"Do not worry, sir, I will help you catch her," Ahmad said tentatively as if feeling his way into the conversation.

"Ahmad!" Azita exclaimed in a light voice. "You traitor."

"Welcome to the family," Chris boomed. "Finally, a male ally." Then he looked at Amar and Azita to see if he had gone too far but neither registered disapproval, so he relaxed. "I think this young man realizes that he needs my permission to take on the burden of managing the new family jokester here." Chris pointed toward Azita. "He does have to ask me, doesn't he?"

"Now you are getting into deep water, my reckless husband," Amar chided him.

"I suspect I will," Ahmad said so lightly that not everyone around the table were quite sure of what he had said. He reached out to take Azita's hand.

"This was all Azita's idea, to play a joke on you." Deena jumped in to divert everyone.

"*Et tu*, my sister. Can I trust no one?" Azita protested and laughed nervously as Ahmad withdrew his hand.

"So," Kat now joined in, "what did you discuss after we left?"

"Much," Deena enthused. "I finally can see what I want to do now, and a reason to finish my education. Mother…I mean Madeena, would be so proud of me." Deena looked at her sister.

"We even discussed a role for me," Ahmad added with enthusiasm. "Okay, perhaps I will be a token male but the possibilities here are endless. I…I…I want to thank you, sir." He looked directly at Chris.

"Sir? You mean me? Charles Howard is to a royal lineage born, no royal blood in our family tree, that is for sure."

"I think there you are wrong, Father," Azita added softly. "From your mother, Mary…I think there is something royal in her line. She has, as I understand it, put up much of the initial endowment for this work. Why should she care? I don't understand."

"Oh," Chris responded immediately. "it is not hard to fathom. She loves you, and Deena. You can hardly imagine the depths of that love."

"But why?" It was Deena.

"Hmm, look at it this way. She had loved her first-born, Chuck, with a special passion. He was most like her, both kind and artistic with a passion for beauty and art. He was taken from her and then she was stuck, she thought, with a son who was a borderline pervert."

"Borderline?" Kay smiled.

"And not a word about any coat racks." Chris looked crossly at his twin sister. "In any case, I was a disappointment to her. Then, I came back from Afghanistan with a wife and a young girl who was to be my child. That shook her at first but soon she saw a totally different son. Sure, part of the transformation was due to marrying well but much was due to this child...you my dear. You probably are not aware of this, but my mother took an extraordinary interest in what you were doing, all your accomplishments. And she read about your culture and homeland. She wanted to know as much as she could about you and your world. With time, she got to know Deena a bit. Her fondness just grew."

"She was always kind, but I did not...was not..." Azita's voice caught.

"That's okay, kiddo, she does not want to be fussed over. Oddly enough, I think she has some of herself, or at least her family, in your story, at least I think so. You need to remember, while her generation of Irish-Americans were extremely wealthy, they came from typically poor immigrant stock. She remembers the stories of the struggles told by her great-grandfather when he first came here, the prejudice and the hate they faced. The Irish have long memories. But she also remembers something else. She had been a prisoner of her Catholic culture. She wanted to continue in school after college. But a BA from a Catholic girl's school was enough, her traditional father insisted. She would marry my father since he had impressed mother's dad with his drive and promise. I don't think she ever got over that feeling of being trapped, and incomplete. It weighed on her all her life."

"So now she sees us as trying to free Muslim girls from being trapped by their own culture," Deena proffered.

"Bingo. She never said as much but I think that is it."

Azita had been sitting there with that look which reflected hard thought. "I want you to know one thing, Father. Initially, in that room, I was not happy with you. In fact, I was rather upset at first. I kept thinking…why was this being sprung on us like this? Why hadn't you confided in us, trusted us…me?"

"I think you know," Chris responded softly, "though I hope you forgive me."

Azita smiled at him. "Well, I am yet considering putting you over my knee and giving you a good spanking."

"I would pay to see that," Kay interjected to laughter from around the table.

Azita smiled and then continued. "I do understand. I would have fought you. I would have thought it merely some half-brained excuse to keep me safe, the same impulse that brought you to our medical site in 2001 to rescue your sister from her own choices. I would have fought you out of stubbornness and you knew that." She tilted her head slightly as if seeking a lost thought. "This struggle with my culture, my future, what to do, has overwhelmed me at times. I think…I think it goes back to guilt. Funny, that is a theme we cannot seem to escape today. For me, the guilt is rather simple - I am alive while my sweet parents are not. In some real way, they died for me, for Deena, for Majeeb, for our selfish dreams. I have all these opportunities and so many girls back home have no hope at all." She suddenly let out a half-sob. "Sorry, but I cannot always handle this enormous weight inside me, that I am not good enough, have not done enough."

Chris's phone rang. With an annoyed look that he had not shut it off, he glanced at the number. His expression changed. He answered. "What's up? What? I cannot understand. Wait, I am moving to a better location." Then, to the table, he said. "I need to take this. Be right back." Then, he quickly headed out the door.

Amar looked vaguely annoyed at her husband before turning back to her daughter. "Listen sweetheart, you know I am not a religious person in any traditional sense. Still, I believe that some people are given these great gifts. When God, or whatever, bestows such things on you, the sin is not to use them the best way possible and to the best advantage. You must know that Chris and I are not omniscient nor are we saints. Perhaps we are even a tiny bit selfish in all this. But your father has worked very hard to make sure you can remain totally connected to your culture, your home and yet use those gifts that you have, that Deena has.

That is what Pamir and Madeena would have wanted. I have no doubt about that."

"I know." A tear escaped Azita's left eye.

"Good. Believe me, Chris and I plotted about how to steer you into a medical research career, and only that. We talked about that a lot, how to keep you from going back. In the end, we realized that would have been cruel…cruel to you. We would have been ripping you from what makes you whom you are. We would…" Suddenly, she stopped, looking up at Chris as he returned to the table. He was ashen, as he slumped into the chair, his gaze seemed unfocused.

"What's wrong?" Kay asked.

"That was Jules. I could barely understand her at first. She was crying, it was so hard to understand her." He said that as if it were important information and then stopped, realizing that it was not important at all.

"What? Goddamn it." It was Kat this time.

"Someone in her newsroom just told her, someone who knew her connection to me. Beverly, the police found her dead on the sidewalk below her penthouse suite. They believe it is suicide. That is their first theory except…"

"Except what?" Kay managed to get out through her tears. "What?"

"The body was a bit too far from the building. She could have been pushed."

"Damn him!" Kat exploded.

"Who?" Amar asked, fighting back her own emotions.

"Our fucking father. That son-of-a-bitch killed her." Chris got the words out through clenched teeth. "This is our fault, we should have gotten her out sooner. He found out what she was doing and killed her."

"No," Amar protested innocently, "surely, you do not believe that."

"You don't really know him." Then, Kay agreed with her sister. "That son-of-a-bitch killed her."

CHAPTER 17

THE WINDY CITY

Chris looked out over Lake Michigan from Kat's luxury suite. Funny, he thought, she had never moved to a mansion north of the city. Neither had Beverly. They both had remained city girls, connected by choice to a violent and unforgiving urban landscape. Yet, this time, death was not likely at the hands of some purveyor of random mayhem and unconscionable evil. No, this time the source of his pain was likely to be found closer to home and had been very intentional.

His agony was that he could not be certain. The police insisted that there was no obvious evidence of foul play, no forced entry to her place, no marks on the body, no signs of a struggle anywhere on the premises. Only the distance of the body from the building caused them to wonder and that was not enough. Perhaps the deceased had thrust herself off the balcony. They kept asking whether she was depressed, suicidal. After all, her husband had killed himself. Perhaps his self-inflicted ending had caught up to her.

No, Chris argued with them, she did not take her own life. She was happier than she had ever been, her life now had purpose. What kind of purpose, they asked? There he stumbled. How do you tell crusty homicide officers that this upper-crust woman was spying on the political doings of her father-in-law? His words sounded silly, perhaps delusional. Besides, it was not the kind of information one wanted to see in the newspapers. She had been sharing secrets with him and Kat Crawford, now head of Crawford Inc. His sister, with the help of her two siblings, had ousted the patriarch from control of his business empire. But the whole affair was more complicated than that. The children were on opposite sides of an ideological conflagration. They were fighting a battle for the soul of the country.

They listened to him politely as he went through an alternative scenario. She would have let in her father-in-law, no questions asked. He would have been accompanied by his security men, efficient at violence. That would have raised no suspicion in her since he had become very conscious for his safety, he was a controversial figure with many enemies. His security guys were always around. A little chloroform, just enough to render her momentarily helpless. Then her body could have been tossed over the balcony to the sidewalk some twenty floors below.

He could see the detectives lose interest. They were used to the usual story lines: jealous partner, greedy relative, a disappointed lover. In their book, it was always vengeance, greed, or sex. They kept going back to those themes. Did she have any enemies, any boyfriends or lovers? Was she into drugs, did she drink excessively? Who would get her money? He could not convince them that Charles Senior was a threat to her since she as often seen as his companion at public events around town. Chris wanted to scream after a while. In the end, he pleaded with them to look at the building's security tapes. Eventually, they did. *There were unexplained gaps,* they told him. *Wasn't that suspicious?* Chris argued. *Perhaps,* they responded, *but shit happens.* In the end, the police stopped returning his calls. They had too many undeniable murders to investigate. This was, after all, Chicago.

The sky over the lake was showing the first hint of dawn. In the summer, often a clear sky emerged as a distinct feature of the landscape above the water. At this time of year, mid-Winter, clouds often greeted the dawn. This added texture to the morning's palette of changing colors. Purples, and blues, and grays and off-whites emerged and evolved slowly, hiding the sun that motivated this cacophony of hues in the first instance. Even as a boy, he would stare out, waiting for indistinct shapes to take form and meaning. Yes, there is the horizon. Oh, yes, I can now see what kind of clouds are out there. He even considered becoming a meteorologist at one point, an aspiration that did not last more than a couple of weeks.

"Couldn't sleep?"

He jumped and turned to find Amar behind him.

"No, but there is no need for you to lose sleep, just to keep me company."

His wife ignored his suggestion, walking up behind him to run her fingers through his longish, dark hair. "I am beginning to notice grey up here, have you noticed?"

"Of course, I count them each morning. I keep a log," he deadpanned. "Are you thinking of dumping me for a newer model?"

"The thought has crossed my mind," she responded without missing a beat, "but the time and effort to train a new one would be exhausting. You are safe for the moment." She then walked around his chair and slipped on to his lap, cuddling up against his neck.

"Can I share something with you, something very sensitive?"

"Of course, anything," she murmured, wiggling her body to get even closer.

"You promise you won't get mad."

"I promise," she affirmed. "Please, share anything."

"Okay," he said and let out a big sigh. "Here it is. I think...I believe you have put on a few pounds."

She paused, digesting his words and then bellowed: "You shit."

As she struggled to get up, he pulled her back. "Sorry, I needed that. You know, humor is my final refuge."

She relaxed in his arms again. "Yeah, I know. Mother never prepared me for that part of marriage. Good woman that she is, she did warn me about enduring the sexual demands but not the daily jokes."

"You have any regrets?"

"What? You mean about marrying you?" She continued before he could answer. "No, no regrets, but you are lucky I must say."

How so?" he asked.

"The men in my early life were terrible losers, worse than you if you can believe that? They set the bar real low."

"Perhaps, but your life would have been easier."

"Really? How?" Amar was curious.

"Look how complicated things are now…you could have married some normal guy, had an uncomplicated life."

Amar pulled away from him and looked at him with incredulity. "Tell me you are kidding, please."

"No, I'm serious." No hint of humor crossed his expression.

Her face softened. "I think I get it, the hurt. But listen carefully. Just remember where we met, what I was doing, treating the casualties in a war zone that might have collapsed at any moment. I never wanted easy. I could have joined my brother in Canada if I wanted easy. In fact, life with you is easy, comparatively speaking."

"There it is," Chris said. "you see life with me as too easy, even though I have dumped you in this cesspool of political drama, national selfishness, and a family free-for-all that would make one helluva mini-series."

"What in God's name are you babbling about?" she asked.

"America. Haven't you noticed? We now live among a people so selfish and provincial that they routinely elect sociopaths dedicated to personal gain at the sacrifice of any form of public good, idiots who would drag us away from the world community when those international bonds are so necessary. I…"

"Shush," she said and put her hand over his mouth, "not another speech. Just listen for once." She looked at him crossly. Satisfied he would be quiet, she continued. "You are right about the States, this is not a nice place, shockingly backward politically. But that is not the important thing and, besides, Madison is more than tolerable, it is lovely."

"So, you agree?" Chris interrupted.

"Shush, do I have to whack you upside the head?" Her expression grew more severe. "I committed to you, not a place or a job or your money. And do you know why?"

"The sex?"

With that she slapped him across the face, not hard but it surprised him, and he yelped. Before he could complain she continued. "Hah, don't flatter yourself." Then her eyes widened just a bit. "When we met, I had so much and, at the same time, nothing. I was incomplete. From everything I heard, you were the last man on earth to fill that void, the very last man.

Then, the surprise. I saw though the constant jokes, the feigned indifference, that herculean effort to always display some distant cool. In truth, you were not that hard to figure out. You were just about the most passionate and caring man I had ever met, maybe next to my father and one of my brothers. Okay, you are third." Now she smiled. "Look at what I have now. I have a family, my own family. I have this amazing adoptive daughter who is on the cusp of doing great things and two children whom I can watch grow. I only hope they are half as good and kind as their father. And I have the greatest gift of all - love." She saw his eyes water and knew that would embarrass him. "And one of these days I will introduce you to my true love. You two will get along just great."

With that, Chris guffawed and pulled her back to where her head was nestled into his neck. "When did you get so witty? Damn, it is amazing how similar we are. We both seem so accomplished and successful on the outside, so damaged on the inside. I owe…"

Suddenly, there was a noise behind them. Kat cleared her throat loudly and then proclaimed. "Oh my God, I gave you two your own room. No need to go at it in front of the whole world. Just don't make me hose the two of you down." Kat sat down across from them. "Do you need more time by yourselves?"

"No," Chris deadpanned. "Besides, you should watch. Undoubtedly, you might learn something."

"Pervert," Kat smiled.

"Me?" Chris protested. "You're the voyeur."

Amar stood and found a seat. "Stop it you two. I am a good Indian girl."

"That ship has sailed," Chris murmured very softly. Then in a much louder voice: "Yes you are, dear wife. Kat, did we wake you up?"

"No, no, I am always up at this time, usually much earlier, the busy executive you know. This morning, though, I wanted to give you two time alone, but I did hear a couple of noises out here that sounded interesting. Ricky typically sleeps later than I. That gives me time to collect my thoughts before the day's battles."

"I am curious about one thing," Amar said. "Why is this memorial service, or whatever it is, at your father's place since he is under suspicion?"

Kat grimaced. "Good question. Thing is, we were in England when it happened. He just took charge. My guess is that he wants to play the grieving father-in-law for public consumption. He is the consummate actor. That, and he wants to rub our faces in it. I can just see his smarmy, fake look of concern and grief now. I have been preparing myself for it."

Chris stood and walked to the window looking east. The sky was illuminated now, the mysteries of what the day would bring revealed at last. It would be another cold and gray January day, like so many others. He stared for a few moments before speaking, more to himself than to the others. "Want to know something?" It was a rhetorical question. "When I was a young kid, I looked up to him. I rather worshiped him. He seemed so tall and invincible and all knowing. I can still remember one day saying to him that I wanted to be just like him when I grew up, just like him." Chris's voice trailed off.

"And what did he say?" Amar asked.

"That it would not be easy but if any one of his children could do it, it would be me. I remember that Kay and Chuck were there. They heard this, and I felt awkward about that, yet also proud. How could I have felt that? I should have seen the cruelty right there, he didn't need to say that in front of them. It took me too long to figure stuff out. You know, Kat, I cannot quite figure out if he was okay early on and turned vicious, or was he always that way?"

"Ha!" Kat expelled the sound. "Don't ask me. I am the baby of the family. By the time I was aware of stuff, he was already a first-class asshole. I just hid behind you and Kay, not so much Chuck. Funny, I just realized that. I hid behind you two, I must have realized at some level that Chuck was too weak."

Chris continued to stare out of the window, lost in thought. "Not weak, Kat, not weak. He was too good. There is a difference."

"Hmm," Kat murmured softly. "Then what does that make us?"

Chris, Amar, Kat, Ricky, and Mary Kelly, no longer Mary Crawford, arrived at the ground level of the building where the primary residence of Charles Senior was located. Mary had never divorced her husband, her Catholicism would not permit it, but she now took pride in shedding his name. At the bank of elevators toward the rear, they noticed a sign saying: 'Memorial Service for Mrs. Beverly Crawford.' Three prim women in identical business suits stood guard. As they approached, one stepped forward. "You are here for the service. I believe you are family."

"Yes," Chris replied.

The woman registered a form of recognition, she must have studied pictures beforehand, and then beckoned them to follow. They entered and were whisked to one of the top floors that could only be accessed with a key. The service was not in the living quarters of the patriarch but in a substantial space that was used for larger meetings and corporate functions. Chris looked about and concluded that it was now used for meetings of his new right-wing colleagues where they plotted their vision of world domination. Chris kicked himself for not bringing a bugging device of some sort before realizing that he had no clue as to how to conceal such a thing. Suddenly, he felt way out of his depth.

Several of Beverly's closer friends and acquaintances were already present. They immediately were drawn to the new arrivals. Condolences were exchanged, and small talk ensued. The patriarch of the Crawford clan remained standing aloof and alone near the casket. A large display of pictures had been erected, with images from her life. Chris found Beverly's brother, the only member of her family with whom she had shared any bond. They exchanged greetings and commiserated. The two of them looked over the pictures and admired the extravagant flourish of flowers that dominated the room. Amar made her way to Chris just as Beverly's brother saw another of her extended family arrive and made his way to greet them.

"I am surprised about the casket. I thought she was to be cremated?" She whispered.

"She will be eventually, but Kat and I convinced a judge to prohibit any cremation until the authorities are convinced there was no homicide. There is still some possibility of detecting an exotic drug beyond the alcohol that was found."

"I did not think that Beverly drank to any excess." Amar was puzzled.

"She didn't, another curious fact, but inconclusive. It is the season of excess, the police said, or maybe she was depressed to be alone during the yuletide festivities. Everything is frustratingly ambiguous." Chris kept eying his father who busied himself with other attendees.

"Are any of you going to even greet him?" Amar whispered.

Chris pulled her to a corner of the room. "My mother, for sure, won't get within twenty feet of him. She loathes the man. I just hope you never come to feel that way about me."

"Sorry," Amar said and tried to smile, "too late. But I can fake being cordial to you in public."

Chris smiled back, his first evidence of relaxation since they had arrived. "And I appreciate the pretense of affection. You are a good woman, well trained. But listen, we will just endure this until after the priest does his thing, then I am out of here. I cannot stand being this close to him."

Amar saw the tension in his jaw and neck. This was not her husband, the proximity to his father was taking a toll on him. She looked at him, trying to determine how to make him relax. She was quick enough to go one-on-one with him in the battle of wits but realized she did not have his inherent sense of humor. That was a Celtic gift, she had concluded and long ago decided not to compete with him on that field of battle. But now, here, she wished for some touch of lightness to bring him back. She settled for linking her arm in his. It seemed to have an effect, he smiled at her.

Then his phone rang. He glanced at the number and answered, deliberately walking a few feet away from his spouse. Amar was, as usual, annoyed at this. *Why couldn't he turn the damn thing off?* she thought to herself.

There was a brief heated discussion during which Amar could make out snatches of his side of the conversation. She could not quite determine if the expletives she made out were being directed at the caller or some third-party, most likely his father. She soon figured it out. He poked at the screen of his phone three times before successfully ending the call and then stared across the room at the man who had brought him into the world. 'That son of a bitch." It was not clear whether Charles Senior had heard what his son said, he remained impassive, erect, superior, watching his son with an ingratiating smile on his face.

Panic swept over Amar as she got out the word: "No!" She grabbed at Chris's arm, but he pulled away from her grasp, so she yelled to Ricky and Kat, who also noted Chris's movements. "Stop him," she pleaded.

At that moment, Chris reached his father whose smile was tempered with concern. "You son-on-a bitch."

"What is wrong, my son? You looked vexed." His father still managed to say calmly.

"Why did you have your people stop Jules in the lobby?"

"Oh yes, her." Charles Senior looked vaguely annoyed. "She has been rather unkind to me, in her professional capacity as a so-called journalist."

"Excuse me? She has been unkind? It is impossible to be too unkind to a piece-of-shit like you." Chris felt a hand on his arm and turned to see Kat pleading with him with her eyes. "No sis, let go! I'm okay."

"Yes, Julianna has been reporting some rather fanciful and, to be utterly truthful, fabricated stories about what I am up to these days. I am considering a libel suit."

"You cannot sue a journalist for reporting the truth, your lawyers should have told you that."

"The truth?" The older man said mockingly. "Why in God's name would you think she is reporting the truth?

"You know why. You know damn well why. That is why we are here." Chris spit out the words.

Chris felt another tug on his arm, this one with more force. It was Ricky. "Come on, man, time to leave. Let's go." His encouragement was to no avail.

Chris was unmoved and continued to stare at his father whom, for the first time, hesitated as if uncertain how to respond. When he did, it was in his same unctuous tone. "Frankly, my son, if I were to guess, I would suggest that you believe her side because she still whores for you in bed." As Charles Senior finished his words, he glanced in the direction of Amar who had joined the others to pull Chris away.

There was the briefest moment when all was suspended. Then Kat uttered one word, "Shit", as Chris leapt toward his father. He grabbed the man by the throat and lifted him up against the wall. Total, black fury swept through him. He cared not for the consequences, he could have squeezed the life out of that man right there. Strong arms pulled him away, but he refused to release the man. Screams filled the room. Then Ricky, and Beverly's brother, managed to pry Chris from his prey and fling him back several feet. All Chris focused on was that face, now finally red with anger or was it triumph, yet leering at him. As people relaxed just a fraction, Chris sprang forward once again. He made it halfway to his destination when a fist directed at his face suddenly appeared before him, followed by a searing pain in his nose and then blackness.

Kay and Ricky helped Chris to the elevator as blood spilled on to the floor and shocked attendees who gave them a wide berth. Kat turned back to her father. "We know you killed her, and we won't forget…we will never forget."

The patriarch was already regaining his composure. He never lost his smile even as the elevator doors closed. When they reached the lobby, Jules was still there, arguing with the women denying her entrance. "Oh, my God, what happened?"

"This idiot tried to defend your honor," Ricky said flatly. "It didn't go well."

◖ ◗

Back in Kat's penthouse suite, Chris looked around at the four women staring back at him - his two siblings, his spouse, and his former lover. Their expressions ranged from bemusement to concern. "What are you staring at?" he said to break the silence.

He was surprised to find his voice so thick and odd-sounding. His head still hurt but the sharpest pain had subsided quite a bit; a headache lingered.

"You look like shit," Jules said matter-of-factly.

"Well, your goddamn brother sucker-punched me, again. Why is he always doing that?"

"Because, you imbecile, you were trying to get back to Father, to kill him." Kay wore a weary expression.

Chris's unfocused gaze shifted from Jules to his younger sister, looking as if that fact had just dawned on him. "Are you implying that would be a bad thing?"

"No," Kat continued, "most days I would have cheered you on. But not in front of so many witnesses. Besides, one of our father's goons had pulled a gun. Had you gotten past Ricky he probably would have shot you. You owe Ricky. My husband probably saved your life."

"Did my first husband, embarrassment that he is, imply this has happened before? Does Ricky break his nose very often?" Amar asked.

"Just the one other time, as far as I know." Kay looked on with a bemused look. "It was when they first met. Some squabble during a high school basketball camp. That is how they became friends. Men! They bond in the most unusual ways."

"Well, he always sucker-punches me. One of these days, I am going to break his nose. Then we will see how he likes it."

"Hah," Kat squealed. "I would pay for that fight, wouldn't you, girls? I wouldn't pay much, it would be over in about 10 seconds. But look at it this way, the last time your nose never quite straightened out though it did give you a kind of rugged, sexy look. It made you look like a bad-boy, and girls like that look. But your days as a sexual predator are past, so maybe this time he straightened it back out. That would be nice. Alas, though, we won't know if your beak is now straight until they take all that stuff off and the swelling goes down."

"Does it look bad?" Chris asked, concerned.

Amar looked at him sympathetically. "Well, I still love you, but I am glad the girls are not here to see it."

"Where is he by the way, where is Ricky? Hiding from me?"

"Cowering from you, I am sure," Kat responded. "No, don't be silly. He took our mother home and then was going to stop by the office, check on world markets."

Amar stood and took his hands to help him up. "Okay, my favorite pugilist, time to put you to bed."

He groaned a bit as he got up, the pain medication and a sedative were kicking in, so it was more of a low moan. "Sounds good but I am not sure I am up for sex tonight." Then, he broke into a smile which quickly turned to a grimace - it still hurt.

By the time Amar returned a few minutes later, Kat had brought out a bottle of Chivas Regal scotch and four glasses.

"There is a bar over there with many offerings, but I am drinking this. You are welcome to join me. In fact, I hope you do."

Amar took a deep breath. "I am not experienced at this but tonight I will."

"Good for you, sister," Jules proffered as the drinks were poured and a first toast made. "To our grumpy patient." Glasses clinked.

"Yuck," Amar grunted. "That is awful, why do you drink it?"

Kay laughed. "Get some more into you, then you will understand." Another toast was made, this time to the evils of sobriety. That quickly evolved into a hearty agreement that all men were ridiculous and a discussion on why women put up with them.

"Tell me," Jules said, "did Chris really fly off just because of me, because his father would not let me in?"

"Mostly," Kay said too quickly.

Jules looked from one woman to the other, but all remained silent. Then it was Amar who spoke up. "I will say it. His father goaded him. He first said that you were libeling him, printing false stories. When Chris came to your defense, he implied it was only because you and Chris were…" Suddenly, Amar did not know how to finish her thought.

Kat sounded exasperated. "Oh, then I'll say it. He told Chris that he was defending you because the two of you were still screwing around. The bastard knew that would trigger him. My brother is a sweet guy, but he is part Irish and there is a temper there. You have to look hard, but it is there."

Jules looked pensive for a moment and then turned to Amar. "I want you to know…you must understand…"

"Jules, please, no need to say anything." Amar's voice was low, gentle.

"No, there is." The ebony woman sighed deeply. "We never talked about the past. I have always wondered if you…what you…thought about me…and Chris."

"I know that he loves you," Amar said simply.

"No…well, yes…but it is more difficult. Let's see if I can make sense of this. I turned him down, more than once. I think it never occurred to me that he would find love. I just figured he would always be there for me, you know, when I finally was ready. Then, the SOB went and found it, true love, with you. It was all so sudden. For some time, I admit I was not happy. I… even resented you though I tried not to let it show. But I could see that you made him…better, a content and complete man. I doubt I could have done that."

"Jules, there is no…"

But Jules continued. "Okay, maybe I could have but in the end it doesn't matter. After a long time, I discovered something about myself, about Chris and I or it is more accurate to say me and Chris. No matter, truth is…I do love him, I have always loved him, and I always will. At the heart of it, though, he is another brother to me though, I must tell you, I have never had carnal thoughts about Ricky like I had for Chris." Jules then laughed, and the others followed. "But there is this gap, more like a chasm, that exists between like and respect and admiration and all those positive feelings we can have about another human, between those things and being in love, pure love. Over time, I watched how he looked at you, acted around you. And I got it, why I turned him down. I understood for the first time. We would have been best friends, had a nice marriage. But we would not have been in love with one another. Thank you."

"What?" Amar was confused.

"For being in his life. Besides, he obviously needs to be married to a doctor." Jules chuckled again, as did the others. "And let me assert this even if it doesn't need to be said. We have not touched one another since he met you, not that I wasn't tempted at first. But no, we have not. Of course, now it is easy to ignore him since he is such damaged goods." Jules raised her glass. "Really, he now looks like shit."

"Thank you," Amar said to Jules as she took another tiny sip of scotch. "I have to go slow with this stuff. I think I am beginning to understand why you drink it. I am feeling - what is the word? Mellow, is that it? - So, I want to give this question a shot."

"Well," Kay offered, "either mellow or shitfaced. Time will tell."

"I am going with mellow," Amar insisted. "But now to the question I have for Kat, one I have kept inside for a long time."

"I deny it," Kat pronounced.

"Deny what?" Amar asked, "I haven't asked it yet."

"Oh, I have never slept with my brother, never even thought about it."

"Good to know, Kat. But that is not it. What has crept around my head from time to time is this: I have always felt Kay's love, something I treasure. She is a sister to me, a real sister. But I have always wondered if you, Kat, resented me a bit. I have worried about that. Have you resented me? I mean, things like my resisting coming to America. I have been a bloody bother, haven't I? You had Chris to yourself and now I stand in the way. I keep thinking about that."

There was a long silence as Kat stared toward the ceiling. "It's complicated."

"We got all night," Jules added. "There are times I have thought something similar, that you might not be comfortable when Chris and I were…well, Chris and me."

"Okay," Kat sighed. "Now you just made it more complicated. I never should have brought the scotch out." Then she sighed even deeper. "My feelings have nothing to do with you - either of you. The thing is I am the baby of the family. I felt lost and overlooked. I didn't count, partly because I was a girl, partly because I was always being compared to the twins who seemed invincible, at least to my young eyes. Chuck didn't count. He was old enough that I never connected with him in the same way. I mean, he was always so kind to me, so concerned about me. I loved him to death and never have gotten over the suicide. I never will. But I never thought I could lean on him, he was like a piece of fragile pottery, too much stress and he might break into a thousand pieces." She took another sip of scotch. "Oh, I suppose I am just like some typical girl, but I wanted my older brother to notice me, pay attention. I'm talking about Chris. He seemed like the strong one, the one who knew what he wanted. And I wanted him to be my father, because the real one was a total piece of shit. I was just the next piece of meat he could use up and spit out"

Amar gasped. "Oh, sorry," she quickly apologized.

"No problem. I so wanted to go to Chris, beg him to help. But I couldn't. It wasn't until recently that I realized Kay had gone through the same thing. A family of terrible secrets, no?" She laughed derisively. "In the end, I am not sure what that explains or excuses. Perhaps nothing. Suddenly, I was an adult or getting close. Chris was gone oversees, Kay had escaped in her own way. It was Chuck and me. That is when I threw myself into the business side of things. Never told Father, he would have dismissed me as some joke. But I was desperate to help Chuck, he was so sweet. "She looked around as if coming out of a trance. "Sorry, got lost there. You are probably wondering what the fuck I am talking about. Bottom line, I took on this enormous challenge of avenging Chuck, taking the company away from Father. I must have looked the part because the rest of the family followed me or, perhaps, they just hated that SOB so much they would have followed Satan. Problem was, I may have looked tough on the outside, but I didn't feel that on the inside. There, I was still this scared little girl."

"You fooled me," Kay said. "You should have come to me earlier, I would have been there for you - who am I kidding? Probably not! That would have meant coming out of hiding myself."

"Through all this, emotionally at least, I yet saw Chris as a lifeline. He was my big brother, the knight in shining armor who could make things right when I failed. To repeat, I was nowhere near as confident in myself as I pretended to be. So, when I saw him get close to a woman, any woman, I saw them as a threat. First, there was Jules and then this wife he suddenly brought home with him. I tried not to let it show but yeah, I was jealous. I knew you two were the best thing for him, surely better than the parade of gals that came through early in his life. It was just hard for me to let go, emotionally. So, when it became clear that Father had moved on to his political obsession, I wanted to take that SOB on again. You can guess, I wanted Chris next to me for that."

"But he didn't have to be here physically to help," Kay gently protested.

"Of course not. This was all about emotional support, just having him nearby. You just never get over the childhood scripts. Every time I am about to confront Father, I grow weak in the knees. I keep saying, he is just a man, an evil man, but he is not God. Sometimes that works, sometimes not. But you know what really worries me? Rhetorical question. I look at myself some mornings and say, I am just like him?"

"You mean Father? No way," Kay protested.

"I wish I could feel as confident as you. Increasingly, I feel this core of steel within me. I am going to beat that son-of-a-bitch."

"Well," Amar said softly, "at least you were not wary of me because I was foreign."

"Or me because I was black," Jules added.

At that, Kat looked at one woman and then the other before breaking into a hearty laugh. "Oh my God, is that what you thought?" The laughter spread.

Then, Kat got up and walked to the window, looking out into the brittle dark that had settled over the city. "I'm not that scared girl anymore. It was selfish of me to drag Chris over here. I realize that now. I wasn't quite ready to let go, I suppose. I still needed to lean on him, I thought, but that was so silly. Chris has no killer instinct. He is his mother's son, more like Chuck, a big heart, but unlike his older brother possesses an incisive mind." Then she turned back to the others. "But I am ready now. I am as strong as Father, just not as evil. I can go toe-to-toe with him. He can bait my brother but not me. In fact, I am convinced that baiting Chris today was his plan all along. He had his goon ready to gun him down. Ricky saved him, I am sure of it. Still, I doubt killing Chris was the point. No, he wanted the world to see how much Chris hated him. He will use that in the future. I am not sure how, but he will."

"No," Amar protested weakly, "do you really think he would have permitted the murder of his own flesh and blood, right there, in front of me and the family. I just can't believe it. No one is that evil."

Kay laughed derisively. "That is only because you don't know him Amar. You are from the civilized world, from a normal family."

Amar arose and joined Kat at the window. "Dear sister-in-law, I never understood what this was all about, I thought it merely a political difference. But I am seeing now. If you need…"

"Stop!" Kat interrupted abruptly. "No, you and the family should return to England when Azita finishes in Madison. Do not fear, I will continue to use my brother, but more on his terms and in ways that play to his strengths. That is the secret, right? You cannot tear people from what they are inside. That was Father's tragic mistake with my older brother. But if you tap into what makes them unique, well…Besides, what we are up against is not just here. Father is working with right-wing zealots in Europe and the Russians. This is big."

"What about me?" Kay asked, also arising and joining the growing group at the window. "Do you need me here? I would stay."

Kat smiled. "No, dear sister. You are a healer. You mend broken bodies and are damn good at it. And there are many of those out there, broken bodies. You have a gift, use it. The thing is, I sense, is that you also have an organized mind. Yes, in that way you are like me, almost like Father - directed and purposeful, not like Chris and certainly not like Chuck. You, my dear, go back and run that organization that Chris started. It is growing way beyond what Chris ever imagined, Karen and the management staff will need help. Don't forget, it will expand further with that mission to reclaim Muslim girls that Deena is already working on with Doctor Al-Hussein and that Azita will join next summer. It will overwhelm Karen."

"But you will be alone," Kay protested.

"No, she won't." Jules stood. "I am with her, she knows that, and so is her husband, my sweet brother whose purpose in life, it appears, is breaking Chris's nose." She laughed briefly at her small joke.

When Jules arrived at the group, Kat wrapped her arms around her. "The Jackson kids, what would I do without them?

But I so worry about you, your safety. You are alone now. At least I have Ricky and we know how good he is with his fists."

"Well, don't forget," Jules said and smiled, "he only beats up Chris and we know that boy can't fight worth a dime." At that joke, they now all laughed.

Kay looked out at the twinkling lights of early evening. "What a goddamn family. We all ran away, Chris to Oxford, Chuck to the other side, and me first to an ER hospital and then, when that was not far enough, to Afghanistan. All but one ran, the baby and the one we thought so little about. And she turned out to be the glue that brought us together. Ladies, get your drinks. Another toast!" They all retrieved their glasses. "To us, joined in sisterhood and in common cause, each pursuing our own individual obsession in our own ways. And yet, joined as one in all the ways that count." Glasses were raised amidst a small cheer.

Amar looked at the other three women. "I need to say this. For the first time, really for the first time, I feel connected to all of you, not just Kay. Either that, or you have gotten me… shitfaced."

They all laughed.

CHAPTER 18

SUMMER OF 2017

It was a fine early summer day in Madison. The sultry, mid-summer humidity had yet to arrive while the bitter winter chills were now a mere memory. The spring semester was over and, while a university never slept, this was a brief period of relative quiet. Chris always thought it a shame that serene institutions were despoiled on an annual basis by permitting noisy, bothersome students to return. This is ideal, he thought.

While the others trailed behind, he and Ahmad had carried out food to the end of Picnic Point, the lovely peninsula that jutted out into Lake Mendota. It was aptly named, a perfect spot for a family picnic. Everyone had migrated to Madison to celebrate Azita's completion of her internship, in which she functioned more like an adjunct faculty member than a student. Still, she often remarked how much she had learned. Teaching was a great way to learn, she now often told others. She could see why Chris enjoyed the classroom.

"Sir," Ahmad said nervously as they finished unloading the food, "may I have a word?"

"Of course, by carrying the heaviest stuff, you have earned that right."

"Thank you. Well, I wanted to ask...that is, if you are amenable...how should I put it?"

"Stop!" Chris said, working hard to suppress a smile. "Are you about to ask me for permission to marry Azita?"

"Ah, yes sir, if it is not too much trouble?"

"Trouble?" Chris was about to go on when he saw Azita, Deena, and Amar come into view. In a low voice, he murmured to the uneasy young man standing in front of him: "Okay, just play along with me, okay?"

This was not what Ahmad was expecting but he nodded. "Alright."

In a loud voice. "You want my permission to marry my daughter? Really? I don't think so, young man." Then, turning to the three women, looking directly at his daughter, he continued. "No way am I permitting you to marry this man."

The three women looked at him. Deena blinked, Amar looked on warily, while Azita merely smiled. "Ahmad, punch him in the nose. Everyone does it." Then she laughed.

"Damn," Chris complained, "there was a time when that would have worked. I trained you too well." Then Chris threw his arm around Ahmad's shoulder. "Son, you have more than my blessing, if such is possible. But mind you, she is a handful. What you need is my sympathy."

"Oh, I know sir."

"What am I going to do with you?" Amar said as she arrived at Chris's side. Then she hugged Ahmad. Hmm, I wonder if it is too late to teach my daughter some domestic skills?"

"Wouldn't someone have to teach you some first?" Chris shot out.

"Azita is right, Ahmad, punch him in the nose, the last punch did not quite straighten it out as we had hoped."

Ricky, Kat, Jules, and many of the staff Chris had been supervising then came into view, along with a few of Azita's new friends whom she had helped through their internship. This would be a celebration of another milestone in Azita's career and a commemoration of the family's return to Oxford. Good cheer and sadness would be mingled. Chris noted that Carlotta had come over for the event mostly, he observed to himself, to be with Atle, who now was free from other entanglements and who would be returning to England to work under Chris. *Yes, that was meant to be,* Chris said to himself. He went around chatting with Pamela, April, Josef, and the others with whom he had been working. Oddly enough, Pamela, the only native-born American, would be the only other stateside staff member besides Atle to cross the pond to work directly for Chris. The others would move to Chicago, though it was understood that Chris would provide a great deal of the intellectual input for their work. April had wanted to relocate but Kat was wary of her infatuation with Chris and decided to keep her close and out of emotional harm's way.

After Chris had chatted with each of them, he sought out Kat. "I am going to miss them, at least the ones staying here. If they only knew that each of them is smarter than me."

"Your secret is safe with me." Kat smiled. "It is amazing how much a little BS can cover."

"Hey," he said, "be honest, is my nose now straight, after this last break? It is, isn't it?"

"Oh, my dear brother, so vain. But do not worry, Amar still loves you. We cannot figure that out, a mystery for sure, but she still does."

"Tell me one thing," Chris said and smirked, "when did you turn from this shy, demure young girl into a total asshole?"

"Hah, when I started to pay attention to Father. And speaking of him, listen, our work continues. I know you understand that."

"Yes boss."

Kat would miss his sassy smile but continued. "You will spend more time on Russia and Europe, it is all part of their big plan. You do know that the Mercer family is funding a large part of the Brexit move? They hate the European Union which is a counter power center to their own designs. And you will have to pay attention to Igor Korobov, he is the Russian top dog directing the work of the old KGB guys in Section A in the First Chief Directorate, which is all part of the Russian Federation's Internet

Research Agency. We now know that during the election, this so-called consulting company was using thousands of English-speaking agents, first in St. Petersburg and then in Moscow. They reached 150 million citizens with their meta-narratives and misinformation. And Americans are so stupid that some believed Hillary and Podesta were trafficking children for sex out of a D.C. pizza parlor. Free election, my ass."

"Hey, Kat, we have been over this stuff. They won't have a free hand in the future. But today we're going to enjoy ourselves. Look about you, a beautiful setting and my daughter is now officially engaged. At least I believe she is. Then again, what the hell do I know?"

"Not much." Kat looked to locate Azita. "I am going to get to the truth about this engagement and then congratulate her. Just remember, I will miss you, you know."

"That is what all the girls say," he shouted to her as she made her way to his daughter.

"I could not help but overhear her. She is tough as nails, and so obsessed with what is going on. She thinks she gets that from Father." Kay came up to him and handed him a drink.

"She is not like Father, she has a conscicnce," Chris responded.

"Despite all that bravado, she needs you, she does," Kay said.

"And whom do you need?" He asked, looking at her tenderly. "We haven't really talked since Chicago."

"TBD, as they say, to be determined. I am solo now, though staying with Jamie for the kids' sake. I never did deserve him. And I have worked out a role with Shahed and Karen to liaison between the two efforts on medical matters, but in a way that will keep me in the field a lot. That will keep your daughter in England more."

"You are a saint, but you look after your own ass. I don't want to lose you, now that I have found you again." He hugged her. However, this also sounds like a perfect way to run away from things." Chris said too quickly to cover up a mixture of affection and concern. "Sorry, uncalled for."

"Perfectly called for," Kay responded coolly "but not today. Glad you are coming back." She kissed him on the cheek and wandered off to look across the water toward the city skyline and the state capitol.

Chris thought of going after her but was distracted as Azita and Deena approached. "That did not take long, everyone knows now," Azita said.

"Knows what? That you were drummed out of the medical profession?" Chris deadpanned.

"Hah, hah, that I am engaged," Azita said.

"You say that as if that is a bad thing."

"Well, my last attempt at this engagement thing did not turn out well." She looked uncertain.

"This one will, my dear, this one will. I guarantee it."

At his words, Azita smiled. Then she and Deena started rapidly talking about Oxford, telling him about the project, Ahmad's role, and all the things Deena and Doctor Shahed Al-Hussein had been working on over the previous few months. It was obvious that Azita had lost all her reservations about this new initiative. More importantly, she had fully forgiven him for his deviousness. He pretended to listen as he looked into her earnest eyes. Had he ever been that excited? Perhaps the time when his basket at the buzzer propelled Princeton into the Sweet Sixteen of the NCAA basketball tournament where their championship dreams would quickly end. But no, that was merely a game. Then it gripped him that his plan was not foolproof. Azita and Deena would be, on paper, stationed in Oxford but, by necessity, had to spend a lot of time in the Mideast doing things that would upset the fanatics of the region. Kay might keep her away from danger somewhat but not completely. He knew that he and Amar would die a thousand deaths every moment they were there. How had he lost his heart to these two young women?

His reverie was disrupted as people finally gathered in a big circle to eat and celebrate. People chatted away happily, individual conversations broken occasionally by a group joke. Ricky promised to break Chris's nose later that afternoon in a final attempt to straighten it out. Karen Fisher stated that she was petitioning parliament to label Chris an undesirable alien and keep him out of the U.K. His twin sister announced very seriously that she wanted to break the news that her brother was not returning to England but moving to D.C. to take a cabinet position in the Trump administration. Jules piled on that one by assuring all that Chris wasn't smart enough for that crowd, which brought even more laughter.

This went on for a while until Amar got everyone's attention. She reviewed for the crowd a few of Azita's accomplishments while at the university children's hospital. Then she paused and grew quite serious. "Of course, we all know she is very talented. I had the joy of discovering that when she was eleven or twelve years old. But permit me to share the opinion of another, someone who cannot be with us today." With that, Amar reached in to her bag and pulled out a worn book, a journal, that oddly enough looked as if it had been pierced by a bullet.

"Oh," Deena gasped. Azita cast her eyes down but said nothing.

"This is a journal, written by Madeena Masoud, Azita and Deena's mother. Azita found it when she and her sister visited their father's village. It was providence, I suppose, that she slipped it into her blouse. Moments later, they were attacked by a would-be assassin. A bullet heading for her heart was stopped by this…expression of a mother's love. Azita shared it with me and I have read it many times. Forgive me girls but I must share one passage, if I may?"

Deena nodded and Azita managed to say "Yes".

This is the final entry, written the night their parents were assassinated. It is toward the end of the journal, so the bullet never reached it, did not deface it. She opened to the page she had marked:

We are gathered once more in my dear husband's old village where he was raised. It is a sad visit, to honor our son, Majeeb, who died fighting the Taliban. He was a simple boy, but with a huge heart. Though I grieve terribly, part of me is at peace. Majeeb died in the right way, if that is possible, fighting for what he believed in, for what was necessary. I am so fortunate to yet have my two daughters. Now I can smile but they were such a bother growing up always fighting with one another. Deena seemed so lacking in ambition, she drove me to distraction. I thought her destined for an ordinary life at best, which I suppose would be fine, but I expected so much more. On the other hand, Azita seemed destined for crushing disappointment. She worshipped her father, following him around like a puppy dog. I thought her such a foolish and aimless girl, chasing a ridiculous dream, until I realized that she was blessed with a unique talent. I looked at them earlier this evening, both were in their books, ever improving themselves. It occurs to me, not for the first time, that Pamir and I are so blessed. He has a daughter who will carry on for him, a healer of bodies. And I have a daughter who will carry on for me, a shaper of girl's intellects. Now, for the first time, I believe they will be what they can be. It will happen. My heart may burst. Can any mother ever feel more happiness? Well, time to put this journal down and join my husband in sleep. He is snoring already.

Amar closed the book and wiped the tears away from her cheeks. She was not the only one who needed to do so.

Chris looked about him on this idyllic summer day, as people absorbed the written words of a loving mother. The waters that surrounded them were blue, not in themselves, but reflecting the pristine sky that protectively hovered above. Even that hue from the color spectrum was merely a byproduct of the sun's rays fighting through the layer surrounding Earth that gave life a chance to survive and thrive by deflecting that which would snuff it out. It is all remarkable, he thought. The intricacies of the divine thought that made this miracle of life possible in such a remote spot in a galaxy that itself was lost in a myriad of similar celestial miracles, some two-trillion of them. *Two trillion,* he silently repeated to himself. The universe never ceased to amaze him, humble him. At the same time, somewhere beyond the edge of his view, conflict and hate and greed despoiled this miracle. Everything in him screamed to ignore what was out there, forget it existed, to hold dearly onto this moment, this joy, this beauty, this peace.

He knew, though, that such could not be. This was a moment out of time, of necessity ephemeral. What lay ahead could not be discerned clearly. The future was opaque and lost in the mists of chance and choice. A heaviness descended on him for a moment, but he brushed it away. There was a price to pay for one's pursuit of an obsession. In that moment, he embraced one other truth. Despite all the apparent costs, some paths in life were not to be avoided, some fates not to be denied. Somewhere, it had been written thus.

ABOUT THE AUTHOR:

Tom Corbett is emeritus senior scientist and an affiliate of the Institute for Research on Poverty at the University of Wisconsin–Madison, where he served as associate and acting director for a decade before his retirement. He received a doctorate in social welfare from the University of Wisconsin and taught various social policy courses there for many years. During his long academic and policy career, he consulted with government at the local, state, and national levels including a stint in Washington, D.C. where he helped develop President Clinton's welfare reform legislation. He has written dozens of articles and reports on poverty, social policy, and human services issues and given hundreds of talks across the nation on these topics. His most recent co-authored books are *Evidence-Based Policymaking* (2010, with Karen Bogenschneider), *The Other Side of the World* (2011, with Mary Jo Clark, Michael Simonds, and Haywood Turrentine), and *Return to the Other Side of the World* (2013, with Mary Jo Clark, Michael Simonds, Katherine Sohn, and Haywood Turrentine). His recent sole-authored works include *Tenuous Tendrils* and *Palpable Passions*, both published in 2017. In 2018, he reworked and republished three earlier works in what is called the Confessions Trilogy: *Confessions of a Clueless Rebel, Confessions of a Wayward Academic, and Confessions of an Accidental Scholar.* The author resides in Madison, Wisconsin.